SCAREWAY TO HEAVEN: MURDER AT THE FILLMORE EAST

SCAREWAY TO HEAVEN
MURDER AT THE FILLMORE EAST

PATRICIA MORRISON

Lizard Queen Press

This book is a work of fiction. Although certain real locations, events and public figures are mentioned, all names, characters, places and events described herein are the product of the author's imagination or are used fictitiously. Any resemblance to actual events, places or persons (living or dead) is purely coincidental.

On the Web:
www.facebook.com/patriciakmorrison

"Walking With Tigers" and "Steel Roses" are by the author and are © 2007, 2013 for Lizard Queen Music

Jacket art and design by Andrew Przybyszewski
Interior book design by the author
Production by Lorrieann Russell and Jesse V. Coffey

AUTHOR'S NOTE AND ACKNOWLEDGMENTS

Although the full and correct name of impresario Bill Graham's legendary New York musical establishment was indeed the Fillmore East, we New Yorkers who went there every weekend, as part of our job, or even just once in a while, as part of our lives, generally referred to it as the Fillmore, *tout court*, at least on second and subsequent reference.

Graham's original Fillmore Auditorium in San Francisco was later relocated and renamed as the Fillmore West (the new site was the former Carousel Ballroom). Once *our* Fillmore opened, in March 1968, that was the only one that mattered to us, so we left the differentiation to the other coast. Because that's just how we rocked. And where we rocked.

Thanks to friends of many decades: Thomas Courtenay-Clack, for his recording-studio expertise, and for allowing me to put him into Rennie's world; and Lenny Kaye, for expertise both rock-critic and rock-star. And Bebe Buell, for general presence.

Thanks to the Usual Suspects, my eagle-eyed betas who

are really alphas: Donna L. Brown, Jesse V. Coffey, Susan Harwood Kaczmarczik, Carole McNall, Michael Rosenthal, Lorrieann Russell.

And belated thanks to Pat Costello, Jane Friedman and Pat Luce, for all the tickets and backstage passes; Bill Thompson and Kip Cohen likewise; Kim Yarbrough, for keeping the peace and being from the 'hood; to all the artists I saw play at the Fillmore East, great and lesser alike; and of course to Bill Graham, Wolfgang himself, for giving us three years of the best and most amazing venue ever.

WALKING WITH TIGERS

You never can tell
when real danger is near
When life seems the safest
that's when you should fear

Out here in the jungle
It's quiet and dark
But this is no stroll
through some paradise park
Bright eyes in the underbrush
Track every move
Paws pad beside us
Claws in the groove

I'm walking with tigers
I'm walking on coals
I've got you at my shoulder
For saving my soul

When tigers are hunting
You don't hear a sound
No twig to snap warning
No tread on the ground
Their stripes blend invisibly
Camouflage coat
Their minds are as sharp
as their fangs in your throat

We're walking with tigers
We're taking the air
We're out for survival
It just isn't fair

[bridge]

Tigers know where you are going
Tigers know where you have been
Tigers use their animal cunning
That is why they always win
They're in it for the triumph
They're out just for the thrill
They're roaming and they're hungry
And you might be their next kill

Don't think you can run
once they're hot on your track
If you keep right on walking
and never look back
they maybe might spare you
and let you pass by
But it's no guarantee
and a gamble to try

Go walking with tigers
you're flirting with fate

If you think to outsmart them
you're already too late
We're all tigers sometimes
Stripes, fangs and claws
If you think that you aren't
You're clutching at straws

So let's walk with tigers
Might even be fun
Just keep your eyes open
And for God's sake don't run

~Turk Wayland

For the kids, who are indeed alright:

Patricia Susan Kaczmarczik
Emma Rose Przybyszewski
Dalton Bruce Abbott
Tyler Quinlan Abbott
Catherine Elizabeth Kennely-Margolies
Shannon Rose Kennely
Jonathan Taylor Kennely
Stephanie Anne Kennely

PROLOGUE

New York City, December 1969

In the lightly falling snow, the Art Deco-styled theater marquee looms bright as an ocean liner seen through fog. Beneath its shelter and around the Second Avenue corner into East Sixth Street, masses of young people, in Navy peacoats and Army-surplus jackets and long Victorian cloaks and vintage furs and embroidered sheepskin Afghan coats, mill and shuffle in the bitter cold like steerage passengers on the Titanic, all steaming breath and stamping feet, waiting for the doors to open for the night's final show.

The place has had several lives: first it was a Yiddish theater, then it became the Village Theater, and now it is the Fillmore East, best and hippest rock venue on the Eastern Seaboard; some would say best in the world.

The heavy bronze doors, sculptural and polished, finally swing open, and the crowd begins to file inside, hooting and laughing, handing their tickets to the heads in green jerseys who stand smiling to collect them; clouds of pot smoke hang in the air. Just past the ticket-takers there is a bright mirrored lobby, and past that, the auditorium itself. Much of its original ornateness, now a trifle shabby, has been faithfully maintained: everywhere marble and plush and velvet, a huge central crystal chandelier, a heavy crimson curtain, gilt and fancy molding on the fronts of the mezzanine and balcony and boxes.

From the lobby, a sweeping staircase with polished brass banisters leads up to a fancy second-floor foyer, now the refreshment area, behind the mezzanine level. Two small stage boxes, gilded and curtained, flank the fancy proscenium arch: lighting paraphernalia in one, sound equipment in the other. The box on the right-hand side has a dual purpose: it serves as a VIP hideaway for visiting notables, rock and otherwise, to watch the show in private, concealed from the audience by a semicircle of velvet curtain.

A utilitarian flight of stairs leads up from backstage to two floors of even more utilitarian dressing rooms — the kind of dreary décor that would not be out of place in a politburo meeting hall in a drab city in Bulgaria. The most impressive thing about the dressing rooms is the people who use them: rock royalty, various ranks of lower rock peerage, and those who aspire to serve, or ascend to, either or both.

Down on the stage, the blue-lit work area is narrow, but it runs the full width of the house, with turntables to hold the heavy and bulky band equipment, tiers for the light show built like rabbit cages against the back wall, and tall loading doors that open right onto Sixth Street.

Bill Graham, owner, promoter and master of ceremonies, scuttles around like Groucho Marx on speed, swearing at people, hugging people, running down people who don't leap aside fast enough. He is of average height, wiry, dark-haired, attractively rumpled. He wears two wristwatches, one showing West Coast time, the other set to Eastern; he claims it saves endless mental arithmetic, sparing him from always adding or subtracting three hours. Ever since he began dividing his time between two coasts and two Fillmores, West and East, he has worn the twin timepieces.

Blond, bespectacled Kip Cohen walks by on his way to the tiny cluttered office just off the lobby, smiling serenely; Graham's second in command, the managing director for the venue, he looks like a scholar of troubadour poetry in the original Provençal, not a power in the rockerverse. Large and imposing Kim Yarborough, chief of security, watches as the excited crowd streams past, and confers with his house-t-shirted lieutenants.

After twenty minutes of scurry and scrum, the lights dim, the curtain goes up, the crowd settles down. Bill comes out onstage to greet the audience and announce the lineup, then introduces the opening act, who nervously troop out to grab their axes. Then the first real note of music rings out, beginning the continuous buzzing build all the way through to the headliner. Showtime!

Outside at two in the morning; both shows are over and the neighborhood has settled down for the night. Second Avenue is strangely quiet in the snow that has been falling heavily since before midnight. The streetlamps are fat fuzzy spheres of yellow light, fleets of snowflakes driving silently past. There is not a single vehicle moving on the avenue: no headlights as far as the eye can see, just the jewelled Christmasy flicker of traffic signals and the blowing snow like diamond dust in the road.

On the narrow, uneven sidewalks around Sixth Street, no one has lingered outside in the cold. The musicians have long since split for parties and hotel rooms and bars and beds, their own or someone else's; the fans have dispersed, happy, sated and stoned; the Fillmore stage and cleanup and front office crews are still busy inside wrapping up the night's business.

Some of the audience and performers alike have hit one of the nearby all-night Ukrainian restaurants; they can be seen through the steamed-up plate-glass windows, tucking into big bowls of soup, borscht or mushroom barley or chicken noodle, plates of pierogis, burgers, omelets and home fries. Two blocks up on the corner of St. Mark's Place, people are hanging around Gem Spa, drinking egg creams or coffee, eating pretzels, unwilling or unable to go home, or just waiting for the next interesting thing to come along.

A few blocks south, on East Second Street, erratic wavering footprints lead in from the avenue, marring the smooth whiteness. Sudden noise and laughter as three stoned people stagger up to the gates of the old cemetery, a surprisingly large expanse of trees and shrubs, the ornate tombs now mantled by snow. They consult briefly, then heave themselves clumsily up and over the high wrought-iron fence and gates: two young men, and a young woman whom they both pull up after them, one hauling on each arm. They are all still laughing as they run and stumble through the quiet graveyard, coming to rest at last in the lee of one of the largest and most dramatic monuments, their backs set against the cold, cold stone.

After a while, it grows quiet. One figure leaves; another enters, and leaves again shortly after. Then everything is very, very quiet.

CHAPTER ONE

Three weeks earlier

GOD, SHE LOVED New York. It was so nice being back. L.A. had been, well, L.A., there had certainly been moments; and San Francisco had of course been wonderful. But this was home, this was her home: clever, vital, grimy, sublimely uncaring of anything beyond its rivers.

"I never actually lived in New York before," Turk observed, mirroring his mate's thought as the pair of them so often did, and Rennie glanced up at him as they walked. "Just stayed for a month or so at a time on several occasions, at assorted rock dive hotels like the Albert and the Henry Hudson, back when we were getting started and playing clubs in the West Village or uptown. It's a real city, like London. All the little villages running together. I love the energy, too. Like Rome must have been, back in the day."

"Oh, we're better than Rome. We're the mightiest city that ever was. And I think you know what a very lucky boy you are to be living here."

Turk Wayland and Rennie Stride were heading down East Tenth Street from the Second Avenue Deli, half a block to their brownstone across from St. Mark's Church, laden down with shopping bags full of containers of soup and barbecued chicken and grilled hot dogs and potato salad and corned-beef sandwiches in wodges so massive that you had to unhinge your jaw like a python to take a bite. Recent snow lay in streaky patches on the ground: it was much, much colder than usual for mid-November. For the tiny distance they had to cover, they were dressed very warmly, and they were walking fast even for New Yorkers.

Back in February, when they had first become engaged, they had decided to keep their Hollywood Hills house but move their base of operations to Manhattan. It was three thousand miles closer to England, for one thing, and Turk, sadly and recently elevated to marquess status, now had new family obligations in his native land for which New York would be a lot more convenient. After seven years, he was weary of his band Lionheart's endless touring, and he wanted to go off the road for a year while he figured out the group's next direction and worked on the music to take them there. After that, he intended that he and Rennie should live like grownups: six months a year in New York, split the rest of their time between L.A. and England, schedule subject to change without notice. So Rennie had gone up to San Francisco, closed down her flat in the Haight, arranged to have everything shipped east and come ahead on her own to find a place for them.

She was a New York girl born and bred, and she was absolutely thrilled to be moving back home again after four years in West Coast exile. She'd been born in Park Slope and had grown up there and in Kew Gardens and Riverdale; after graduating from Cornell she had attended journalism school at Columbia, and she'd never imagined living anywhere but Manhattan for the rest of her life. The only borough she hadn't lived in was Staten Island, because, you know, *why*? Then she'd met and eloped with young corporate lawyer Stephen Lacing, and he'd made her drop out of grad school and dragged her out west to his hometown by the Golden Gate. It hadn't taken long for her to cut herself loose, though: she'd walked out on him and his super-wealthy society family after less than a year of unhappy wedlock—"lock" being the operative syllable— and once she'd gotten into the San Francisco rock scene she so badly wanted to be part of, she'd stayed on.

Then she'd moved to L.A., where she and Turk had crossed their fated paths, and they'd fallen madly in love, and she'd been living with him in his Nichols Canyon house ever since. Still, she'd never thought of herself as anything but a New Yorker. And she damn well knew her way around her island. But she dutifully checked out all possible neighborhoods when Turk had said go look for a house we can buy, just so she could tell him with a clear conscience that she had done so when they ended up living where she had planned on them living all along.

It had been great fun imperiously ruling out vast tracts of Manhattan real estate. Upper West Side: too uptown. Upper East Side: too uptight. West Village: possible, but only with care—Near West Village, smug; Far West Village, thugs. Gramercy Park: gorgeous houses, but however much Turk and Rennie might protest that they were quiet and well-behaved—which they really were, just a girl from the boroughs and a boy from an English castle or two, or six—

the gas-lit Gramercians would never cotton to a notorious rock and roll couple in their midst. Especially not with that superstar thing of Turk's possibly attracting fannish hordes; not to mention that pesky murder trip Rennie had going. Oh well, their loss. The Gramercians', not Turk's and Rennie's.

There was a new area called SoHo, *So*uth of *Ho*uston: huge loft spaces in former factories now coming available for regular people to live in, but it was like opening up the frontier — you had to walk miles to forage for food and the only laundry option was to go down to the river and smack it on a couple of stones. And despite her Columbia grad-school interlude, in an enormous apartment with three fellow-journo roommates, across the street from the cathedral of St. John the Divine, anything above the top latitudes of Central Park, East Side or West, was strictly Here Be Dragons territory.

Which left the East Village. Not as pretty as its western counterpart, but cool and historic and edgy, the perfect neighborhood: part young hippie and artist and student incomers, part elderly Ukrainians who'd supplanted Germans who'd supplanted Irish, part old Yiddish New York. All of which resulted in pleasingly ethnic restaurants and craft shops and boutiques and old theaters and clubs and, yes, food stores and laundries, all up and down the avenues and the side streets and over to Tompkins Square Park — much east of that few people ventured, as it was still a little too hardcore. But in 1969, from Third Avenue to Avenue A, Houston to Fourteenth Street, was really the hippest possible place for a hip rock and roll couple to hiply live.

But what could they live in? They had a lot of desires, needs and requirements, especially Turk, so it wouldn't be easy to find somewhere suitable and they'd have to extensively, and expensively, buy and renovate it when they did—renting was right out. She'd inspected brownstones on St. Mark's Place and the tree-lined blocks facing the park, a mini-Plaza-Hotel-styled building on the corner of Third Avenue and Seventh Street, even deconsecrated churches and synagogues and a small terra-cotta office building on Astor Place.

Then she'd seen this: the prow house, as she immediately dubbed it, sitting like the front end of a ship right on the acute angle made by Tenth and Stuyvesant Streets as they converged in front of the eighteenth-century St. Mark's Church-in-the-Bouwerie. It was a beautiful old Victorian brownstone, with bay windows on the point like a ship's bridge, at the end of a terraced double row of equally beautiful houses. Prettiest house on the prettiest block in the whole East Village. She fell in love on the spot, and so did Turk, who when he came east to check it out was instantly reminded of Hampstead, of Edinburgh's New Town.

They bought the whole building, which cost a lot less than you'd think and was a lot smaller than it looked. Then Turk decided it wasn't going to be big enough, and bought the two adjoining buildings as well, one on Stuyvesant and the other on Tenth—you can do that when you're one of the most famous rock stars in the world and your father is the second-richest duke in England, so there was not even a suggestion of anything as suburbanly mundane as a mortgage, or a budget, when it came to their new home.

Which made Rennie acutely uncomfortable. In all her previous relationships, she had always insisted on chipping in her fair share — though the guys as a rule never let her, and never understood why she insisted. But it meant a lot to her to be able to do so, and Turk, to his everlasting credit, understood perfectly. But this was too big and too serious: someone's pride would have to be sacrificed not only to the relationship but to the real-estate deal as well. She had known from the first that it would have to be hers: she had worked her way to being okay with it, and Turk had kissed her and blessed her for it.

At any rate, in a mere six months, at staggering expense and with consummate taste, and adding in colossal bribes to relocate former tenants, the three smallish brownstones had been reconfigured into one largish V-shaped mansion: hangout space and a music room for Turk on the top story, newly skylighted and roof-gardened; a writing den for Rennie behind the fourth-floor bay window; and their duplex bedroom-sitting room behind the second- and third-floor ones. Eight guest rooms — well, you need that many when your friends are always coming to town and your band is always wanting to crash; besides, a few would be required for nursery duty down the road.

Plus living room, dining room, morning room, breakfast room, two parlors and a library; big slate-floored eat-in kitchen on the windowed basement level; a wine *cave*, a guitar vault and a recording studio in the acres of cellars. Add a house office, a private flat for Hudson Link, their newly hired live-in assistant, and Daniel, her artist-handyman husband, a bunch of bathrooms, a tiny yard surrounding the street frontage and an equally tiny sliver of garden out back, and that was it. A nice home for them and an absolutely brilliant investment for the Duchy of Locksley.

Friends had suggested that there might be problems with importunate fans if they didn't dwell in a giant doormanned uptown fortress, but Rennie wasn't worried. This was her native heath, and she knew her people: New Yorkers wouldn't cross the street for the Second Coming, bless their pointed little hearts, and it was considered incredibly uncool to annoy famous neighbors in their actual lives, like at the newsstand or the dry cleaners or the butcher's. Besides, in even a hip, arty building like, say, the Dakota or the San Remo, they would never have the space, freedom or configuration they required. Not to mention the personal recording studio.

Even if fans figured out who was living in the prow house, it wouldn't really matter. Oh, they might get a few Lionheart diehards hanging around for autographs, but Turk wasn't a Beatle, he didn't attract that ridiculous obsessional level of attention—and they'd take precautions against anything more serious, having learned their stalker lessons in L.A., the hard way. Apart from that, no true New Yorker ever even *looked* at any other New Yorker, and that was the way New Yorkers liked it.

The house was set well back from the sidewalk like all the others on the block, behind the wrought-iron-fenced garden area and a code-locked gate; they'd put in an alarm system, cameras and one-way glass, and once they added some more shrubbery and maybe a bit of casbah-style grillework, they'd be fine. This was the way they wanted to live, not shut up in some pretentious Park Avenue pile infested with Social-Register Republicans. Besides, Bob and Sara Dylan had recently moved themselves and their tots into a townhouse over on Macdougal Street, living there pretty much the way Turk and Rennie would be living here, and they hadn't had any problems. Well, except for that wack job who kept "researching" their garbage.

Mental note to self: put bear traps in trashcans...

Speaking of bears, they had the dog now, an enormous, aristocratic, mahogany sable collie of ursine proportions— Macduff the Thane of Gondor, as they had frivolously named him when they rescued him from the ASPCA. But he was by no means as frivolous as they were, being as dignified and smart and cuddly and devoted as the best of his hyper-protective breed, beautifully behaved but always on the alert for trouble—to him, everybody was a possibly dangerous predator threatening his little flock.

And they'd left Turk's black Porsche and Rennie's burgundy Corvette back in L.A.: those wheels were too identifiable, and also too tempting to car thieves. Cars in Manhattan were a hassle anyway: you couldn't drive around on a daily basis without making yourself nuts. If they wanted to get away for weekends, they'd rent. Otherwise, they'd take subways and buses and taxis and limos and choppers and private jets like everybody else.

Turk had gotten into it immediately, the anonymity and ease. Realizing that he could go out on the street and no one would bug him except for a very occasional "Yo Wayland!", he'd quickly developed a routine of a morning walk with the dog to Tompkins Square Park and breakfast at one of the funky little Polish or Ukrainian coffee shops—Veselka on Second Avenue, Leshko's and Odessa over on A—where he would run into local artists or fellow musicians or Allan Ginsberg over the eggs and home fries.

As for location, location, location, it couldn't have been better for their needs and purposes: the Fillmore East a few short blocks south, hip little boutiques all over the place, the second-hand paradise of Fourth Avenue's Bookshop Row a brief stroll to the west, friends both old and new living in the neighborhood. It was perfect—East Tenth was a quiet, old-fashioned block lined with oaks, maples and flowering pear trees, with the sound of Westminster chimes from the bell tower of St. Mark's across the street. You wouldn't ordinarily think to find rock figures living in such staid surroundings; but both Turk and Rennie were far from ordinary rock figures.

"Doesn't he get hassled by fans all the time, walking around down there?" Prax McKenna, Rennie's best friend and a superstar herself, once asked. "He is, as you know, fairly recognizable."

Rennie had shaken her head. "Nope. First off, anyone tries to mess with him on the street, the dog rips their throat out. Plus he's this tall, strong guy, and he's been trained by your own adorably lethal boyfriend in unarmed combat—he could take anybody's head off with one deadly whack, no problem. But it's really *not* a problem. Below Fourteenth and east of Third every cat looks like a rock star. Long hair, beard, boots—he blends right in. He turns off the Turkitude, I've watched him do it, it's amazing, like flipping a switch—

he just decides he's going to be anonymous and so he is. He loves it. He even takes the subway."

"Oh, he's such a stud! And nobody ever recognizes him?"

"Couple of times, but only in context. Once outside the Fillmore when we went to see the Dead; one time when he went up to Manny's Music to buy another damn guitar, how many freakin' axes do you people *need*, and someone rumbled him while he was test-driving the possibles, which after all you'd expect someone would. Anyone else just thinks they're really, really stoned and it can't possibly be Turk Wayland sitting next to them at the movies eating popcorn. Besides, this is New York: don't look, don't ask, don't tell, don't care. It's not just a good idea, it's the *law*!"

Turk was home just now after the Miami gig, for a week's r&r: Lionheart was taking a well-deserved break from the killer tour schedule that had had them more or less continuously on the road since Woodstock, back in August. Now they were resting up, gathering their strength before the last few East Coast dates and the big huge grand finale at Madison Square Garden the first Saturday in December. While the other guys had promptly fled Miami for the Bahamas and tropical beachy goodness, Turk had caught the first plane up to New York to join Rennie for *his* idea of a break, helping her put the final touches on the new place before their first houseguests started arriving. And she was glad and grateful, both for his presence and his assistance. But sometimes she looked at him and sighed and wondered why the hell they couldn't be on a beach in the Bahamas themselves.

CHAPTER TWO

"**R**ENNIE LACING II," said the first of that name, with immense satisfaction. She tickled her goddaughter and namesake as the infant grabbed for the senior Rennie's long hair, swinging temptingly within reach of the chubby hands. "Well, Charlotte Rennie Lacing, as I should say. She's adorable, oh yes she is, yesyesyes she is, who's a clever pretty girl then, but I don't know —"

"Listen, if my brother can be Stephen IV, surely my daughter can be Rennie II," said her brother-in-law. "And what an inspiration her namesake godmother auntie will be to her."

"Uh-huuuuh… Even so, I think she'd better stay Carly," suggested Rennie, kissing the chuckling baby's head and handing her back to her father. Much to Macduff the collie's lively interest: how thoughtful of them, they got me a new lamb to look after! "At least around her granny. Or Grandmotherdear, also as I should say."

The deli grub Rennie and Turk had toted home earlier that day had been scarfed up at a family lunch. Rennie's handsome gay brother-in-law Eric Lacing and Eric's beautiful lesbian wife Petra and their gorgeous two-year-old daughter were in town on a visit — Carly's elder brother, Thomas, a bold and unconfinable toddler, had been left at home with his nanny and two sets of doting grandparents. Now that Eric's Wall Street Lacing family business was completed, the three of them were staying with Rennie and Turk for a few nights before returning to the Coast.

Turk had left right after lunch, some record company thing in midtown to do with Lionheart's upcoming Garden gig; but he'd be home for supper. It was only the third time Petra and Turk had been in each other's company—they'd met backstage at the Cow Palace when Lionheart had played there, and all four of them had had dinner once in San Francisco. Rennie had been nervous, wanting them to like each other. But it had been fine. Eric and Turk were of course old friends; they'd hit it off like gangbusters from their first meeting, and both of them were looking forward to spending some time together. After that, the Lacings would go back to San Francisco and on to Hawaii after Thanksgiving, meeting up with their real spouses, Trey and Davina, happily and conveniently also married to each other and with a year-old son.

It was so hip it made you laugh, but on the other hand it was so sad it made you want to cry: four-cornered marriage, the only way a gay couple and a lesbian couple could manage to live publicly and socially prominently, with safety and access to their partners, and have kids like everybody else. They were incredibly lucky that it had worked out so brilliantly for them, and if people ever wondered about all the time Mr. and Mrs. Eric Lacing and Mr. and Mrs. Thomas Copeland III seemed to spend together, they kept their wonderings to themselves, or just thought how fortunate the couples were to have found such good close friends.

"So, a society husband *and* a rock star boyfriend—what a

lucky little girl are *you*?" Eric teased. "Yes, and what a piggy one, selfishly hogging two beautiful men all for your selfish self when far more deserving lasses go without even one."

He and Rennie were down in the kitchen, Eric minding Carly and Rennie fixing supper, while Petra had gone upstairs for a liedown. The meal was going to be no great culinary shakes, just roast beef and freshly made tomato salad and herbed rice from a box, and that fabulous five-inch-high chocolate silk cream pie from Ratner's next door to the Fillmore East. Rennie was far from being the accomplished cook that Turk was, and had no intention of challenging his kitchen supremacy: when it was her turn at the stove they either ate out, ordered in or dined on one of the seven things she *could* cook, like roasts or steak or her killer spaghetti and meatballs, or else idiot-proof fare like hot dogs or burgers.

Rennie laughed, but her eyes had refocused unseeing on the curtain of ivy outside the ground-level kitchen windows.

"I never did share well with the other kids… As you say, it's been fun, but the times they are a-changin'." She ran some romaine under the cold-water tap in the old stone sink and started tearing it apart. "Anyway, I haven't hogged Stephen since I fled from Hell House three years back, as you very well know…in fact, I'm not sure that I ever hogged him at all, married or not. But you heard it here first: I'm officially ceding possession to Ling. The annulment is done. It's just a question of signing the papers. Stephen hasn't told you?"

"Well, yes, he did. But now *you* tell!" he commanded, arranging Carly in the hippie-craftsman-built highchair Rennie had bought expressly for the visit. "Which, I gather, is more than you've done for Turk yet. What are you up to?"

"You don't miss a thing, do you, snookums... Well, Turk and I will be together two years in January, and if you recall, he did officially propose matrimony back in February, ring and all, when we were in England, and I did officially say yes."

"So you told me back then. I was beginning to think he'd have to issue a nuptial ultimatum that you finally make an honest man of him. Or were you, *are* you, just afraid he'll run away screaming like a little girl now that it's all legitimate and settled and you are lawfully available? Or are you afraid that *you* are going to run away screaming like a little girl? Which one scares you more?" asked Eric shrewdly.

When Rennie made no answer: "Okay, let's just see here: he's brilliant, talented, gorgeous, famous, rich, titled, adores you, sex off the Richter scale, you told me so yourself, wants to marry you and give you brilliant gorgeous talented titled babies, he told me so himself. Well, obviously the unspeakable brute is unappealing in all respects, let alone as husband material. Darling one, he's *perfect*. You do love him, don't you?"

She cast the romaine into the salad spinner. "I love him so much I can't see straight. But I fucked up so badly with Stephen. I wasn't in love with him when I married him, or even after, and I hurt him really a lot, and I'm so afraid I'll do the same thing with Turk. Which would be miles worse, *because* I love him, and that would kill me stone cold dead. It was bad enough when we broke up last year and both suffered through three horrible torture months of apartness.

All I want is to be his love slave forever. Maybe trying for more is pushing it. Maybe I'm not meant to be married. Maybe I just can't *be* with someone like that."

"Sunbeam, you've been living with the man full-time monogamously for almost two flippin' years! You're here with him, you're in L.A. with him, you're on the road with him. You've even bunked with him—and, presumably, bonked with him—in the assorted ancestral castles of his forebears. By all reports, including yours and his, you've been *be*-ing with him blissfully and successfully, which sure sounds like married to me. It's not like it was with Stephen at *all*. Well, I say successfully, except for that one little hiccup breakup. But that all worked out fine—plus the world got a *great* album out of it. So what's the problem? He gave you a ring, as you just now mentioned, yes, yes, that very same ring right there, and from what I hear, your mothers have been wedding-planning ever since. Just how darn much more official can you get?"

"Quite a lot, actually," said Rennie vaguely, running a thumb over the big honking heart-shaped ruby on her left hand. "We couldn't be officially engaged before I was officially annulled. Little technicality there. And in the circles his family moves in, it's rather more than a technicality. Needs official announcing in posh publications, at the very least. Formal photograph of me in major gown and jewels, with Turk standing tall and lordly and possessive beside me, in Country Life, Times of London, sort of thing. So not because of me, oh no, because of *him*."

"Oh, I *see*, then it's less about love slave Rennie Stride, handmaiden of rock and roll, and more about Rennie

Tarrant, daughter-in-law to a duke. Not to mention
Ravenna, Marchioness of Raxton—and in the fullness of
time, Ravenna, Her Grace the Duchess of Locksley."

"Well, aren't *you* just too clever to live! Remembering all
his titles like that. 'Ravenna Raxton'! Sounds like a D-cup
C-list B-movie starlet. Yeesh."

Eric was quite right, though: that was indeed the
sticking place. When they first fell in love and moved in
together in L.A., in January of the previous year—in pretty
near as much time as it takes to say it—Turk hadn't told
Rennie of his secret identity and ancient noble heritage,
not right off the bat, for a number of what had seemed to
him very good reasons. Which had proved, of course, to
be a spectacularly bad mistake in judgment, and, also of
course, she'd found out about it in just about the worst
way possible—not from him his own self, the thirty-fourth
Earl of Saltire, but from the cops and the newspapers, in
the process of his arrest for the murder of one of her best
friends, his ex-girlfriend the singer Tansy Belladonna. Her
wrath and hurt had been epic, and she'd almost walked out
on him.

But they'd gotten through it, largely because Turk—not to
mention the Earl of Saltire—had been determined that they
should. Still, it had niggled away in the background, like a
little black cloud; and just over a year ago it had exploded
all over again, precipitating a ferocious public quarrel, an
even more ferocious private one, and a spectacular breakup.
After three bitterly unhappy months apart, not to mention
five huge and gloriously beautiful apologies in the form
of top-ten hit songs, and a number-one one in particular,

that took up the whole B-side of the then-current Lionheart album—nothing like having a global forum in which to say Honey I'm so sorry, I was a total dickhead, please take me back, only saying it much more artistically of course and for the whole world to hear and wonder at and, yes, envy— after all that, they had reunited in London and been joyfully inseparable ever since. He'd given her the ring, and they'd both gotten discreet tattoos; and if ink from celebrity-hippie tattooist Lyle Tuttle and a ring that had originally been a parting gift from King Edward VII to Turk's great-great-grandmother didn't say total commitment, she didn't know what did.

"Be that as it may and D-cups aside, apart from your lovely own," said Eric presently, "why on earth are you letting it bring you down? You told me you'd worked it all out between you, both sets of parents are thrilled; why are you getting cold feet again? This is getting so old, really, and you're a very silly girl to worry about any of it at all. Who cares if his godmother *is* the Queen of England? Suck it up, buttercup! He loves you, you love him, stop messing around. We're all dying to attend your stately and splendid wedding in the presence of Godmum Liz. Tiaras and everything. So just send out the invites already."

"It's not as simple as that."

"Uh, yeah, Rennie, it *is*? All that peerage pressure, it's years away, decades even. Whatever you do once you're married, it'll be her ladyship who does it, so it'll be fine with your husband's countrymen—that's just how they are. Turk will never give up his music, so eventually the peers of the realm are gonna *have* to deal with a rock and roll duke in the House of Lords; I say start breaking them in now. Come on, sweetie! Make 'em tug those forelocks like they mean it! They *love* all that feudalistic class crapola. The English are like horses—once you show them who's holding the reins and the whip, everybody has a nice canter."

"Even the horse?"

"Especially the horse."

"Did you know your father settled a ton of money on me as part of the annulment agreement?" Rennie asked, in an apparent change of subject. "Not alimony. A buyout. Or a startup. Possibly a reward. Or a bounty. Whether I remarry or not, it's mine. I don't know why the General would do that at this juncture, considering how I wouldn't take a penny of filthy Lacing lucre when I was living in your midst at Hell House, or even when I moved out to starve hippishly in the Haight."

"Yeah, he told us he was going to do it, and both Stephen and I heartily approve, so you just damn well better accept it or the annulment is off and then where will you and Turk be? My father always says you remind him of Princess Charlie," added Eric, grinning. "Oh, he knows you can take care of yourself, but he wanted to make sure that you were okay no matter what and didn't have to feel like Cinderella amongst Turk's fancypants relations. You're in the will too, by the way, majorly. My mother is fit to be tied. I love it."

Rennie was still back with Princess Charlie. "The General thinks I'm a *whore*? Because I'm living with Turk and still married to Stephen…"

"No, no, oh dear God no! Not at all! He thinks you've got the same damn-the-torpedoes attitude as Charlie did.

He likes that; he told you, remember, at the birthday ball? He likes *you* — he arranged the settlement and the bequests because everyone preferred annulment to divorce and he was pleased you suggested it and aren't making a fuss, like good old clever Anne of Cleves, and because he didn't want you to have to worry about money or work at things you don't want to do, the way the Princess had to."

"So I *am* just another Lacing whore. Only after the fact."

"Nooooo," said Eric, rolling his eyes, "it's just to make sure you have something besides the fruits of your own efforts, considerable though they are, to bring to the next marital table. Especially since it will be noble in nature."

"Oh. Well. That's different. I guess."

"Yes, it is. No strings. No obligation."

"Good. Because I don't like feeling, you know, obligated."

Rennie recalled the conversation very well. It had been after she and Stephen separated and she'd moved out, and she'd arrived at Hall Place — a.k.a. Hell House, the Lacing family mansion — late for mandatory attendance at a formal ball in honor of her father-in-law, the Lacing patriarch and CEO. Stephen had been coldly harsh, as he had never been with her before — she'd totally deserved it — and she'd fled the ballroom in tears to one of the nearby drawing rooms, where, unbeknownst to her, the General, as Stephen's father was known to his family and friends, had also taken shelter. There they'd had the first, and pretty much only, substantive and mutually understanding interchange of their lives, during which he'd pointed out to her the portrait of the family foundress and ancestress, hanging in pride of place over the marble mantelpiece.

Affectionately known to the family as Princess Charlie—
her very upscale stable had been equally affectionately
known to nineteenth-century San Franciscans as Charlotte's
Harlots—the enterprising Charlotte Louise Vidler had been
an intelligent, pretty, auburn-haired seventeen-year-old
teacher come west with the Gold Rush. Finding teaching
not so much to her liking, and needing to make money to
send to her family back in Buffalo, she'd become a discreet
and successful prostitute with an upscale clientele, and
then, still in her mid-twenties, a rich, famous and even more
successful and discreet brothelkeeper with an even more
upscale clientele.

After her scandalous marriage to the first Stephen Lacing,
a poor but brilliant lawyer of good lineage, Charlie had
carried the family into a wealthy and powerful future on
her curvaceous, creamy-skinned back. Well, at least not by
personally *lying* on her back. Well, at least not *anymore*. Well,
at least only once or twice, with magnates who admired the
voluptuousness and intellectual challenge she traded for
their concessions, the shrewd diplomacy she displayed in
negotiating—both parties always considered they'd gotten
the better of the deal, the mark of a perfect arrangement—
and the equally perfect tact and class she employed at all
times. She never told her husband about her few highly
personal business liaisons, and he never asked. Indeed, her
adoring Stephen had been burstingly proud of her, for her
dash and her beauty and her smarts, and together they had
ascended the twin pinnacles of San Francisco business and
society, ruthlessly and charmingly reshaping both to their
liking by the astuteness of Stephen and the sheer natural

force of Charlotte.

Rennie deeply admired Princess Charlie, not least because the founding hooker completely embarrassed Stephen's society-dragon mother, Marjorie, but mostly because once she was in a position to make it so, Charlie had done as she damn well pleased. She had gotten her own way and did whatever she wanted and had made people do things the way she wanted them done, and Rennie was all for that.

"Interesting that you and Petra named your beautiful daughter for two Lacing whores, though."

Eric flung his head back and cast up his eyes imploringly to heaven, but he was laughing. "Oh, give it a *rest*, will you! Okay then, think of the settlement as hazard pay for having been my mother's daughter-in-law for the past four years. A reward for valor in combat. Like a Purple Heart or a Bronze Star. You can get behind *that*, surely."

"And then of course there's my whole death and murder trip," said Rennie, abruptly moving on from money and whoredom.

Eric gently took the knife away from her before the salad tomatoes became purée. "What about it? It's not your fault."

"Maybe not, but still. Let's just see: four people dead in San Francisco, one seriously injured, me kidnapped and almost killed. Three dead in Monterey, one a suicide, again me and the hostage/almost killed thing. Three more in San Francisco on two separate occasions, two and one. *Five* in L.A., big score there, almost counting Turk and me amongst their number, twice, and oh yeah I did actually get personally shot, also twice. Another dead in Los Angeles.

Three dead in London, again on two different occasions. Two dead at Woodstock, and Turk was poisoned. One dead at Big Pink, two visitors almost winged, and a local was seriously wounded. None in Manhattan yet, but we all know it's only a matter of time. That's twenty-two. Twenty-two dead people in four years. Quite a body count. Even Prax says I'm the Grim Reaper's groupie."

Opening the oven door, Eric checked on the roast, closed the door again. "Honeybun, you're a reporter. Horrible stuff happens, and you're around when it does. And then you report on it. It's not you, it's the scene and the job. I've told you this before, don't make me tell you again! If you were a war correspondent, would you be assuming blame for the body counts coming out of Da Nang? No. You'd just be writing about it. Same here. Get over it."

Rennie managed a smile. "I should have married *you*, not Stephen."

"No, no, you like sleeping with men much too much. And so, of course, do I. This way we get to be family forever, us and Turk and Ling and everybody."

"I *so* love Trey," said Rennie, not at all irrelevantly. "And Petra, and Davina... Stephen and Ling want to get married, you know, before the baby's born," she added. "Once he and I decided on annulment rather than divorce — the wedding was just that little justice-of-the-peace elopement to Maryland, super-easy to nullify — we pushed it through. But it's been sitting there for a couple of months now, waiting for us to sign off on it. And why? Because we're lazy. Why do you think it took us three years to get around to it in the first place?"

"But now?"

"Well, Turk's grandfather dying a few weeks back kind of upped the ante, you know. Richard's the Marquess now, not the Earl anymore—the immediate, and only, direct heir. He's also just turned twenty-seven, and there have been all kinds of totally unsubtle hints that he needs to get the succession on the road. Which means we need the decks cleared for the wedding. So it's time to put the old Jane Hancock where it belongs! That's why I'm going back to San Francisco with you, just till Thursday, while Turk's finishing up with the tour. Stephen and I can take care of everything, and wish each other happy trails and bon voyage and best of luck in your new location. I can thank the General for the grubstake, do a few chores in the city and come home a lawfully unwedded woman. A never-married woman, actually, having being annulled into marital oblivion. So technically I will never have been a Lacing at all. Oooh, existential!"

"Well, all right then!" said Eric, laughing. "It will be lovely to fly out with you—a doting auntie to amuse the tot while her parents take long, well-deserved snoozes. And then, when you come back, you'll tell Turk you're Lord God Almighty free at last."

When she didn't answer at once: "Ravenna—"

"I know! I know. And I will. When it's time."

Eric studied her for a long moment. "You do realize, and I mean this in the nicest possible way, that to all of us you will *always* be a Lacing? Though perhaps not to my mother. But then, to her you never really were, were you…"

"No," agreed Rennie, with considerable satisfaction.

"No, I never really was."

They were saved further discussion by the appearance of Petra, refreshed from her nap, and, a little while later, Turk himself, back from his publicity meeting and behaving like a perfect member of this oddly assorted extended family, greeting Eric with real warmth, kissing Petra, cooing satisfactorily over young Charlotte Rennie, who'd been sleeping at lunch and hence unavailable for fussing over.

Petra indulgently watched him field the baby like a pro. "Where'd you learn your infant technique, Turk? You'd make a great nanny. Need a day job?"

Turk laughed, and so did Carly, who was waving her arms, grabbily fascinated by Uncle Turk's beard.

"I love kids. I'd like half a dozen, if my wife will indulge me. I never had any sibs around when I was growing up in assorted castles—my half-sisters didn't live with us, only visited for hols and summer vacs—but I do have thirty-odd first and second and once- or twice-removed cousins on both sides. Not to mention a bunch of nieces and nephews thoughtfully provided by my three oldest older sisters. I was the chief family baby-minder for quite a while growing up. Believe me, I learned fast."

"And of course all the anklebiters amongst your kin think you're totally groovy?" asked Eric, with a meaningful glance at Rennie, who had rolled her eyes at Turk's mention of the six kids and the wifely indulgence.

"I'm proud to say that quite a few of them appreciate my line of work. Though I think the little perishers do it more to annoy their disapproving parents than anything else. Still, it's great fun to bring them backstage when we're on tour at home, it rumpuses up everything. Here, best take her now, Petra, she'll have my beard out in a minute, and I need it for the show."

"Not to mention for your consort," said Rennie primly. "Can't have too much friction… I know, I know, not in front of the child! Now, you boys set the table, and Petra and I will start dishing up."

Over the roast beef and Yorkshire pudding, Turk's contribution to the meal, Rennie informed him she'd be on the road herself, flying back to San Francisco with her soon-to-be ex-laws, and he nodded amiably and didn't ask any questions.

Rennie watched him as he talked easily to Petra and Eric. God, not only was he a guitar hero for the ages, and really intelligent, graduated from Oxford with honors, and beautiful beyond belief — tall, blond, well-built, madly fuckable — but he was an absolute paragon of graciousness and affability and tact. Eric was right: he was perfect, and she was a stupid ungrateful cow and totally unworthy and she didn't deserve him. Except that he *wasn't* perfect, of course. Far from it. But even that was perfect, that he wasn't…

"I'm sorry we won't be around to see Lionheart play the Garden, Turk," said Petra. "It was so exciting at the San Francisco show."

"Except for that part where you collapsed onstage and they had to carry you off like Hamlet," added Eric. "Wait, what am I saying, that part was *incredibly* exciting. Especially since, unlike Hamlet, you weren't dead. And I loved how everybody thought it was part of the show. Added even more to the legend when they found out it wasn't."

"Hey! He had the damn flu and he'd been dosing himself with some vile British nostrum that turned out to be full of speed—*and* he came back out ten minutes later to finish the set, before I carted him off to the nearest emergency room," said Rennie indignantly, while her guests laughed at her instant defensiveness and praised Turk's trouperism.

"There I was, stretched out on the floor in the wings, being annoyingly revived from happy unconsciousness by solicitous roadies," said Turk, laughing too. "And Rennie just waded in and flung them aside and got me up on my feet again, and back out onstage with the band—whatever your methods, sweetheart, they certainly did the trick."

"Smelling salts and shiatsu. Still, don't be doing that any more, okay? I don't want to have to whisk you away in an ambulance yet again. Not my idea of a good time."

She found she didn't want to even think about it too much, how panicked she'd been to see him fall, what her instant terrified thought had been; and Turk chivalrously forbore to remind her how often he'd been in ambulances taking *her* to emergency rooms ever since they'd met. Sometimes he'd been in the ER on his own behalf as well, of course—both of them out like a light from the diabolical application of carbon monoxide, or shot at in his Malibu beach place, when Rennie was actually shot, twice, him being beaten up at Airplane House and Hyde Park and poisoned on the opening night of Woodstock. He had long since resigned himself to the life-or-death component that seemed to be inexplicably, and inextricably, welded into their relationship; bizarre and tiresome, yeah, but it was part of who they were and what they did, and if the choice was living together like that or living a less fraught life apart, well, there really *wasn't* any choice. They'd tried it the other way, and they'd both been utterly miserable.

"But *everybody* we like is playing New York for the holidays," lamented Petra. She loved rock as much as Rennie did, and she and Davina and Trey were thrilled, proud and more than a little awed to have Turk Wayland as de facto in-law—Eric's brother's almost-ex-wife's almost-husband. They'd all been a bit shy and fannish with him at first, until he'd gently but firmly made it clear that that sort of thing wasn't on, especially not from family.

"I'm sorry, Eric," she continued plaintively, "I know Hawaii will be great, but we have to miss it all here— Lionheart and Prax and the Stones and the Airplane and Sledger Cairns…"

"It always gets jammed up like that the last two months of the year," agreed Turk, offering a small spoonful of chocolate cream pie to an enthusiastic Carly. "With the holidays coming up, everyone wants to play a big gig to push whatever album they happen to have current. Since 'Cities of the Plain' tanked, we've only the greatest-hits one; Centaur rush-released it just to have *some* product to capitalize on once the tour began to heat up, and to have in stores for December. I made them tack on three previously unreleased bonus cuts, just so the fans wouldn't feel completely ripped off… Anyway, for us the Garden show's a huge deal; if it goes well enough, it'll be the foundation of our first live LP. But why don't you guys simply stay on for it? We have plenty of room here, not to mention live-in sitters for the kiddiewink, and we'd love to have you."

"Would that we could," said Eric with genuine regret. "But the Lacings have put in a prior Thanksgiving claim, and the prospect of escape to Kauai afterward with Trey and Davina and the tinies is the only thing that's making it bearable... Still, you probably don't want to be working *too* close to the end of the year?"

Turk nodded. "Quite right. Everybody also wants to get the hell out of town for the holidays. Though Jimi's playing the Fillmore East New Year's Eve with his new band—I'd really like to hear them, since I missed them at Woodstock, so maybe we'll drop in if we're around."

"If?"

"We were thinking of spending a couple of weeks in the Dolomites, before Lionheart has to go into the studio in January," said Rennie. "Or Banff, or Yellowstone, or the Pyrenees. Someplace snowy and mountainy and romantic where neither of us has been before—just hole up with no guitars and no typewriters and no goddamn rock and roll. Nothing but a big old bed and deep new snow and really good food and wine and skiing and a nice soft comfy bed and drugs and crackling fireplaces and horse-drawn sleigh rides under fur rugs and lots and lots of time in bed did I mention bed?"

Petra sighed. "Sounds perfect."

Three mornings later, Turk was up before dawn and getting ready to hit the road, bound for the airport and Lionheart's last four out-of-town dates. He had an early plane to catch for Atlanta, where the rest of the band would meet him, straight from their Bahamas stay. Now, having showered himself awake, and put his clothes on in his dressing room, he returned to the curtained bed where Rennie still lay as he had left her. Pulling back the rumpled sheets, he bent over and kissed her comprehensively, working his way from south to mouth.

She put her arms around his neck and shivered and held on tight. "I miss you already...safe, safe trip. Safe, safe there. And safe, safe home."

"It's the last mile. Well, last thousand miles. I'll be back on Thursday. And so will you. Safe there and back yourself." He kissed her again; her arms did not loosen. "You'd better get up soon too; I know it's a Lacing plane and they won't leave without you, but you shouldn't keep the pilots waiting. Eric and Petra and the baby are already awake; I heard them down the hall. Say hello to Stephen for me when you see him."

She sat up in a flurry of bedclothes and tousled hair. "Eric *told* you?"

"Told me what?"

"Oh — nothing."

The weather report had spoken of an early deep freeze and an approaching snowstorm that by the end of the week would reach the Eastern Seaboard and stretch from Georgia to Maine. They were both hoping to get out of town and back again before it hit; but just in case, Turk had put on his warmest, heaviest coat — thigh-length dappled-cocoa shearling. Rennie had never admitted to him that she sometimes slept under it when he was away, for the sense and scent of him, the weight of it on her like his own weight, the feel of his nearness. But now he'd grabbed his only luggage, a small beat-up Gladstone bag he'd owned since his Eton days and the funky tooled-leather duffel he'd bought at Woodstock, and stood by the bedroom door. His stage clothes and equipment had been shipped on from the last gig, and he was already onstage in Atlanta in his head.

"Yes? I just got the vibe that you would be seeing Stephen while you're out there. Was I wrong?"

Rennie lay back down again. "No. No, you're not wrong at all. And I *will* tell him. He'll be glad to hear."

CHAPTER THREE

O N THURSDAY AFTERNOON, RENNIE was sitting on the bed with the phone to her ear and the fur bedspread clutched around her inside out when she heard the front door slam, followed by the Thane of Gondor's delighted bark of greeting and boots on the stairs.

She had arrived home from San Francisco on the red-eye that morning, her copy of the annulment papers stashed in her luggage, along with lavish and lovely parting gifts from Stephen, who had been happy and sad and relieved to finally reach the formal dissolution of their wedlock. So had she, oddly enough: it had been a terrible marriage, a huge personal mistake, but it had always been a fine friendship and it always would be, and lots of people couldn't say even that much. There were also more lavish gifts for her and Turk from Ling, the future, indeed the imminent, Mrs. Stephen Lacing, with whom Rennie got along like crazy, and, like a diplomat exchanging offerings of state, she'd conveyed presents of equal magnificence for Ling and Stephen from Turk and herself. So all that was done with at last.

"Whoops, gotta go," she said into the phone. "The portable form of my noble lord has just returned home to the castle. Listen, after I admire his travelin' self — and, more to the point, find out what he brought me — I will call you back and we will talk about *every*thing. You know what I mean…yes…that's right, I do, m'hm. You'll be at the show, of course. And we'll be at yours. Late show tomorrow. No, no, shan't forget."

Appearing in the bedroom door, the collie frisking ecstatically beside him — Pack Leader is back! — Turk smiled to see Rennie, who smiled back and nodded at what she was hearing over the phone at the same time.

"Yes. No. Sure. Him too. Yes indeed."

"Hi, Prax!" Turk called out, then crossed to the dressing room and slung his bags inside.

"She says hi," Rennie conveyed, hanging up. "I'm too cold to get up, you have snow in your beard, how did you know it was Prax, she just got in from L.A. herself, I'm to kiss you for her, for me too, I love you, I missed you, what did you bring me?"

Turk sat on the edge of the bed and took off his coat and boots; she opened the bedspread to include him in, brushing away the melting snow.

"It's always Prax on the phone. And I say that in no bad way. Macduff, get down. Well, I heard you mention that we're going to her gig, bit of a tip-off. I love you too. I missed you too. What makes you think I brought you anything? I'll have that kiss now, madam, if you don't mind… And a couple more while you're at it… Duff, *down!* It's a blizzard outside now. Literally. The cab radio said it was twenty degrees and falling, and the wind makes it feel like a thousand below. The snow is so thick you can hardly see; we almost hit the U.N. building, coming downtown on the Drive. At least I think it was the U.N. building; it could have been anything. A wall, a trashcan, Stonehenge. Did you have a good flight?"

"Oh yeah, it was fine. I slept the whole way. No snow when we landed. But the airports are all shut down now, I just heard it on the news; you and Praxie were lucky to get in. Yours okay?"

"After I dropped a Mandrax it was. Good job I did; we circled La Guardia for a bloody hour while they plowed out the runways—I'd have been a basket case if I'd been straight. We were the last flight out of Boston. They had to de-ice us three times." After a while: "I love this bedspread with you in it...Christ, it's *freezing* in here, it's almost as cold as it is outside. No wonder you're wrapped up in this, though you'd probably be warmer if you had something on besides earrings. Where's the bloody heat? Isn't Hudson or Galina or Daniel supposed to take care of these things? What the hell do we have an assistant and a housekeeper and a handyman for?"

"Easy there, lord and master... I gave Galina the week off because we were both out of town, and Hudson just left with Daniel for a long weekend in the Berkshires, again because we were both out of town. The furnace shut down because it ran out of oil, and before she split Hudson called the oil company to come over and fill it up. Which they did. The heat's coming up now, I just turned it on. We're warm enough like this, though, aren't we, I see the heat's not the only thing turned on and coming up... And yes, Mr. Happy Pants, we are indeed going to see Prax at the Fillmore East." Rennie turned her head to him. "Problem? You guys are off till the Garden show, and Evenor's coming to see you, so it's only fair you return the favor."

Turk grinned at her choice of pronoun, which never failed to amuse him. All the other Lionheart ladies used the first-person plural when speaking of the band: did you like us at the Forum, have you heard our new single, we're number one with a bullet in next week's trades. But even though as the leader's mate Rennie had more right than any other band consort to the collective and inclusive "we", she scrupulously said "you" every time.

At first he'd been a little hurt, thinking she was doing some none too subtle distancing trip or critic thing. When he'd finally called her on it, though, she had muttered with astonishing deference about how she wasn't the one up there onstage and she had no right to say "we" and she didn't want to bogart something that wasn't hers. It was more than that, though: it was wanting to make honorably sure, even in conversation between them—or maybe especially in conversation between them—that credit went where credit was due. Because it wasn't "us" the fans came for. It was him.

He shifted her more comfortably in his arms and kissed her hair. "No problem at all. I love Evenor. I just like to know these things up front."

"You're not freaked out about the Garden show, are you?"

"Not about that, no."

"God, do I have to drag it out of you with a mule team? *And? So?* Atlanta, D.C., Philly, Boston? How did the new opening act work out? How did the new songs go over?"

"Don't you read the reviews, woman?"

"I want to hear *your* reviews."

"It won't color your professional judgment?"

"You already know what my professional judgment is. Prezackly the same as yours. We've been talking about it for months."

Turk rubbed a hand across tired eyes and was silent. He did know, that was the problem. And the problem went by the name of Niles Clay, Lionheart's incredible lead vocalist. When he'd asked Niles to join the band, five years ago this past summer, it had been a miracle marriage for both of them. Here was Niles, this skinny, poorly educated, working-class kid from South Shields, way up in the English northlands, who could do with his voice what Turk, the Eton-and-Oxford-schooled, Royal Academy of Music-trained heir of a duke, could do with his guitar. Rock and roll had made them comrades and superstars and very rich men, and that was as it should be. But it hadn't made them real equals and it hadn't made them true friends.

Before the advent of Niles Clay, Lionheart had already been a major group, adored by its fans and well received artistically, what with Turk being spoken of as a guitar innovator in the same breath as Hendrix and Clapton, and bass player Shane Sheehan right up there with Jack Casady and Phil Lesh, and drummer Jay-Jay Olvera, rhythm guitarist Mick Rouse and Rardi Lombardi, their violin and keyboards guy, all being staggeringly creative all over the place. It had taken Niles, though, to put them over the commercial top.

And that was where the canker g-nawed. Recently, encouraged by his hangers-on and, not least, by his wife, featherweight and feather-brained ex-model the lovely half-Persian Keitha Shiraz, Niles had started to believe his own hype, to the point of thinking he could be bigger without Lionheart than he was with them. But people in the business who really knew what was what had told him bluntly that without Turk's blazing guitar to play off, Niles would be just another British blueser, that the two of them together were greater than the sum of their parts, that he'd never find another guitarist to so complement his voice, that Turk and Lionheart would get along fine without him but the reverse was almost certainly not true. And it wasn't just record company people telling him this but other musicians—people with names like Sonnet and Sakerhawk and Lennon and Hendrix. People who knew how things went. People who should have been listened to.

Instead, Niles had chosen to heed those who stroked his ego and stoked his resentment of Turk, whom he perceived as diverting all the attention that should have been coming the way of Clay. After all, Niles *was* the lead singer: by all the rules of rock and roll, he should have been the band's star and god and sex symbol, and in any other band he would have been. But this band had Turk Wayland standing over there on the audience's right, and it had not gone unnoticed by Niles—and everybody but Turk himself—that more people were watching that side of the stage than were watching the middle.

The hot molten center of the issue was that Niles had for all the years of his presence in Lionheart refused to sign what was called a key-man clause: a legal restriction to the effect that personnel couldn't leave their employment for a specified period of time, like the duration of a tour or an album's recording time, because that would affect the overall success of the band, at least for the moment. Usually the clause worked the other way: if there was a personal manager or an executive at a label, say, without whom the group or artist would not wish to stay signed, the band could negotiate a key-man clause to keep the exec around. It was unusual for it to be employed within a band itself, but Turk's grandfather's solicitors had wanted to make sure that everything was nice and orderly for the young man who was both the corporate head of Lionheart and the ducal heir — their future employer in either guise. So Rardi, Shane and Jay-Jay, as original members, had all been offered such partnership clauses with Turk, and they had all been happy to sign, knowing that Turk considered them key and wanted to protect them as well as himself.

But Niles had always refused, preferring to stay on a year-by-year, tour-by-tour, album-by-album contract footing, even knowing that it nettled Turk that he remained apart from the agreement — or perhaps *because* it nettled him. It had been a matter of some contention within the band, especially since Turk had recently offered a key-man clause to Mick Rouse as well, who had joined along with Niles on the departure of fourth original member Fids Porter, and who had for a while felt rather insecure. Mick had been thrilled to bits to be promoted from contract status, and had signed right up.

It wasn't just that, though. Both Turk and Niles, and all the other members of Lionheart, for that matter, were products of their upbringing, unavoidably, and in Britain that meant issues of, well, class. Caste. Rank. Social status. Only Jay-Jay Olvera, the drummer, whose native heath was Texas, was immune to the caste tensions, and even he had been at Oxford with Turk and Rardi, so technically he counted as ruling class right along with them. The social friction wasn't usually an issue; generally it just kind of brooded along below the surface of group unity, like a low-grade fever. It didn't affect the friendships, or the success, or the art — it couldn't, not and still allow Lionheart to do what it did so superlatively and superbly.

For the most part, none of them were even consciously aware of it. Except, of course, when they were — when Niles *made* them aware, dragging out his mean little working-class inverse snobbery and insecurity and shoving it all up everybody's nose. It was, on the face of it, utterly ridiculous: as a superstar and a member of Lionheart, Niles was rich and famous and successful beyond dreams. Artists were no class in particular anyway, even in England, and artists of Lionheart's caliber counted as upper and were welcome guests at just about any dinner table in the land. But no matter how anyone sliced it, Niles wasn't playing in Turk's personal social league and never could, and he bitterly resented it.

On this tour, it had finally broken out like measles, all the envy and venom and spite, and Turk had only made it worse by patiently rising above it and treating Niles with greater considerateness than ever, which in turn had just fed the flames even more. Niles' attitude had soon begun to affect his performances, and the critics had pounced on it, to Lionheart's chagrin and futile denial. And that wasn't even factoring in Niles' jealous hostility to Rennie, which had begun almost two years ago in L.A., in the aftermath of Tansy Belladonna's murder, when Rennie and Turk had first met and fallen in love, and which had blown up at Woodstock like a burst appendix.

Rennie gave him a minute, then dug an elbow into his ribs. "Ground Control to Major Turk..."

"I'm here, I'm here," he said, sounding beat, and not wanting to get into it now, with her; he'd come home for comforting and coddling—the shelter of her loving arms and the welcome of her loving thighs—and by God he was going to get it. "It wasn't as bad as it has been, the past six weeks or so, once things started to pick up, but it's still not pleasant having to deal with him and his attitude. I've talked to the other lads, but we don't know quite what to do about it. If he wants to go, he's gone."

"And if?"

He shrugged. "We get a new lead singer to replace him. Or I could go back to singing lead. I did it for the first couple of years before Niles came along, and I could do it again, even though I don't want to. Or Shane thought he might try lead vocals himself, he's got the same range as Niles. And he'd be fine."

"He'd just not be as good or as forceful or as genius."

"No."

Rennie wrapped herself around him and snuggled as close as she could get, unfastening his pants for better access to his heat-rising self. "I love your singing, I wouldn't be even a tiny bit sorry to see you as lead singer again...you were fabulous at Woodstock, when Niles was too drugged out to stand, let alone show up and sing. Well, you know Clapton and Winwood are available, now that Blind Faith's gone bust. Oh, right, no, Eric's playing with Delaney and Bonnie these days, which I absolutely do *not* understand, so he's off the market. But Stevie does keyboards and guitar, and he can sing, too."

"His voice wouldn't work for our material. And very sorry to disappoint your hopes, but I don't really see myself making a comeback as a lead singer, at least not for the long haul. As for Eric, in case you haven't noticed, he's a lead guitarist, and a pretty okay one. We already *have* a lead guitarist."

"Also a pretty okay one. Ouch, don't pinch me there! Or if you do, you'd better mean business… Simplest solution, it would seem, then, is just to find yourself another lead singer and replace Niles."

"They're not exactly thick on the ground. And all the ones I'd want already have jobs. Unless you think Prax would care to jump ship from Evenor?"

Rennie pushed the bedspread open a little; the room had warmed up considerably, but she pulled the fur blanket close around them again anyway and plastered her bareness against him. It excited her in some obscure erotic way, to be stark naked in his arms while he was fully clothed, and she knew he liked the sensation just as much.

"I think—"she began, and he turned to her expectantly. "Praxie? No. Her voice wouldn't work for you either, and no offense, but you guys don't have a chick vibe going. At least not like *that* you don't. And I say this as a critic and a Lionheart fan, not as someone who doesn't want her old man and her best friend in the same band because it would drive her directly up the wall. Okay, maybe I say it a *little* like that. Because it would. But if I were to offer a genuine professional opinion—which I don't do lightly in a personal situation—I'd say that you're averse to singing lead again because you're afraid it'll affect your guitar work. Onstage, I mean. Studio doesn't matter, that's what sixteen tracks are for. But yes, I think *you* think that if you sing lead and play lead at the same time you can't give either one your full attention and complete excellence."

"I hate critics." But he was smiling as he ran his hands down her back. "And amateur shrinks. But I do think that. Not that I'm fishing for compliments. Not that you in any capacity would give me any I hadn't earned. But singing lead and playing lead at the same time is a lot harder than people imagine."

"I know it is. Especially for you, because your style of lead guitar functions more like a vocal. You use the axe as a voice, your voice, so you *don't* have to sing. And no. I mean no, I know you're not fishing. I think that you've gotten to the same place Jimi has, where you can do both. If you want to. Besides, one doesn't really sing lead and play lead at the same time, does one—it's more like sing, play, sing, play. And you're not the same guitarist who was trying to do it five years ago."

"Still me. Although you're quite right about that guitar as voice thing. But I don't want you or anyone else cutting me any artistic slack."

"No fear! Now what did you *bring* me?"

CHAPTER FOUR

"**T**OO DAMN MUCH MUSIC in this town this time of year," Rennie was mock-complaining the next day. She ticked off on her fingers. "You at the Fillmore East tonight and tomorrow night. Next week, which is Thanksgiving, the Stones at the Garden and the Airplane at the Fillmore. Not forgetting Bill's Thanksgiving dinner Thursday afternoon. Then our good friend Sledger Cairns at the Fillmore the *next* weekend, and Lionheart at the Garden to close out the tour that same Saturday night. It's rock amazingness. No wonder Petra and Eric wanted to stay for it all."

Prax McKenna, the "you" who was playing the Fillmore East that night and the next, had arrived the day before from Los Angeles with her boyfriend, Ares Sakura, and had taken a suite at the Plaza, and she was now lying stretched out on the sofa in the prow house living room. She'd just finished her sound check, and had stopped in to visit for a bit before going back uptown to the hotel to do her usual pre-show rituals. She stirred lazily and comfortably, her legs across Ares' lap and her left hand stroking the thick mane of Macduff, who was sitting adoringly beside her with his nose on her ribs.

"The boys didn't want to play three Garden shows like the Stones're doing? I don't blame them, mind, and we certainly wouldn't do three ourselves—not that we could sell out three, maybe two, but *they* could."

Rennie snorted and shook her head. "Turk figured that in this, as in so much else, he'd leave the over-the-topness to Mick and Keith. But he's totally pleased Lionheart gets to go on a week after the Stones, not the other way round. Last act on, last thing in the fans' musical memories."

"Planning something dramatic, are they?" asked Ares.

"Could be, could be." Rennie threw Prax a smug glance; there was a big secret for sure, and they wanted to surprise even Ares. "I've been to a couple of rehearsals. Three-hour show, not counting encores, so more like four. And they're *really* up for it. They're recording it, too, for a possible double album—half live, half studio. They want to end the tour with a bang: they were so upset that the road trip started off so badly, what with the crappy performance at Woodstock and the murders and Turk's poisoning and all; it's only been in the last few weeks that they've been knockin' them dead. As it were," she added hastily. "We do have to watch our metaphor choices around here, don't we…"

Prax grinned and grabbed another handful of M&Ms from the crystal bowl on the table, cramming them into her mouth without even looking at them, just to freak her friend out. Rennie had this weird, borderline-obsessive thing about the little candies: they all had to be paired off colorwise before she could eat them, two by two—green had to go with yellow, tan with red, and brown must be matched only with itself—and it drove her crazy to see people just gobble them up any which way.

"What do you mean 'we', paleface?"

"What do *you* mean what do I mean?"

"Oh, I think you *know* what *I* mean, missy. You're like the rock and roll Black Spot. Rennie Stride has only to show up somewhere and people start toppling over like dead ants, arms and legs waggling pathetically in the air." She suited gestures to words, startling Macduff.

"Well, thank you so much! Just because I'm on the backstage list—"

"Angel of Death's backstage list."

"May I remind you that *I* wasn't the one thrown into the San Francisco slammer three years ago for double murder? No, sugar lips, that would be *you*."

"And I don't seem to recall that *I* bonked the Monterey Murderers two years ago, peaches, nooooo, that would be *you*."

"Hey! I only bonked *one* of the Monterey Murderers, not so much of that plural bonking there, if you don't mind."

Rennie could see that Ares was getting a little nervous at their sparring, though they were all laughing. He'd come into their lives the previous year, bodyguarding Turk and Rennie against a multiple-murdering stalker, and had fallen hard for Prax, as she had for him. Now he lived in Turk and Rennie's Nichols Canyon home in the Hollywood Hills, as resident caretaker, and they were glad to have him there.

As a high-priced, high-security-factor, licensed-to-kill celebrity bodyguard, the founder, president and chief operative of Argus Guardians, Ares had seen it all. But sometimes he didn't always get how Prax and Rennie dealt with each other.

Now his hostess saw that it was freaking him out a bit, so she changed the subject, bragging, "See what Turk brought me from Boston."

Prax eyeballed the pendant—an enormous pear-cut Mogok ruby, like a great drop of blood—that Rennie lobbed over.

"Fabulous. Most guys need a surgical procedure to get the idea into their pretty little heads: Chicks. Like. Jewelry." She punctuated the words with sharp little reinforcing digs of her toes into Ares' ribs. "Did you have to train Turk very hard?"

"No, oddly enough. It came pre-installed, like factory air, him being that, you know, lord thing—it's bred into his ever so jumpable bones. His male ancestors have been triumphantly tossing sparkly trinkets to their concubines since before the Norman Conquest; why should he be any different? A present for the in-house courtesan after a successful little tour is much the same as a present for the in-house courtesan after a successful little war. Anyway, they probably have rooms full of this stuff at his family's place."

"Whole wings full. Yes, very pretty—haven't we always said that Turk has superb taste? And it goes very nicely with that engagement ring you've been sporting since February."

"It's not an engagement ring. Well, yes, it is."

"My dithering friend, I was practically there when he gave it to you, remember? You told me about the accompanying proposal. In greatly delicious detail." Prax grabbed Rennie's left hand, pulled it over toward Ares. "What do you see there, Skippy?"

"Big red stone. Left hand, third finger. Very nice. Yep, sure looks like an engagement ring to me. Actually, it looks like the Astrodome."

Prax released Rennie's hand and reclined on the couch

again, grinning wickedly. "Let's just see here: Stephen gave you a ten-carat diamond to betroth you with, as I recall?"

"Yes? So? I gave it back when I walked out, as you may also recall."

"Indeed you did, very honorable of you. And his lordship's little offering is, what, a fifty-carat ruby? *More*? Huh. Now, even I know that rubies of great sizeness are often worth more than diamonds of similar sizeness, and we all know that Lord Richard is usually not the kind of guy to go for sheer ostentation. So I do wonder what is going on here. A spot of territory-marking, perhaps? Antler-rattling? Cock-measuring? Or merely tradition and yet another little class issue? Because obviously there's been considerable upward mobility in the engagement-ring department."

"Well, it's a family heirloom; his grandmother gave it to him to give his future bride. It was really more like a placeholder," said Rennie with some heat. "Even though he proposed, and even though I said yes, and even though it is our engagement ring, I couldn't be *officially* engaged to Turk while I was still *technically* married to Stephen, could I? No. That would have been…wrong."

"If you say so, cupcake. And now? I notice that with great and careful precision you use the past tense throughout: you say 'couldn't' and 'was' and 'would have been', not 'can't' and 'am' and 'would be'. So I must assume that place is no longer being held. And that would be because —?"

"Because not married to Stephen anymore." She rolled her eyes at Prax's pretend death swoon. "Right, very funny. But we finally signed the papers and the annulment is a done deal. So, yes, officially engaged. Finally. As of four days ago I am a free woman. Actually, in the eyes of the law, I am a never-married woman. Spinster of this parish. Or some parish. In any case, I'm Rennie Stride and going to stay that way."

"Not Rennie Wayland?" asked Ares innocently. "That would look nice in print, atop your stories. I bet your crazy publisher Fitz would like it too."

"Not a chance, you long-eared bunny! I wouldn't dream of writing about rock under his name. Perhaps other stuff, a long time from now… Anyway, it'd be Tarrant, he's never legally changed it. Because of the title and all. 'Turk Wayland' is just his stage name. Besides, I'd miss being called Strider."

Prax had been dutifully nodding her head all through this remarkable recital of denial. "I see. No, I swear. I really do. How *is* Stephen, by the way?"

"Same as ever. He said to say hi, and to remind you he always liked you even though you always scared him a little. Well, a lot. He and Ling are getting married in San Francisco as soon as they can get the license and as soon as Motherdear can seize the cathedral and her favorite caterer; then they're planning a big fancy Hong Kong religious wedding, christening and dual-purpose reception in the early summer, after the baby's born. That should make all their parents happy. Especially Marjorie. Or at least as happy as the idea of a one-fourth-Chinese grandchild can make her, the racist bitch."

"Surprised she's not freaked out more about the one-fourth French part," remarked Ares. "I sure would be… So, tell us: what did Turk say when you informed him you're now a—well, not a divorcée, an annulée I guess it would be? Did he have to propose to you all over again? Oh, congratulations, by the way."

"Thank you. But haven't. Not yet. Waiting for right moment."

Prax drummed her heels on the sofa in anticipatory glee. "Oh, I *so* want to be around for *that!*"

"Yeah, yeah, nothing to see here, people, move along. Maybe Turk and I will go over to Hong Kong for the wedding. He could bring the band to play at the reception and I could give Stephen away…"

Rennie was silent for a while. "I'm not the tiniest bit unhappy or sorry about it, you both know that. I'm in love with Turk like I've never been in love with anyone else in my life and I'm going to be with him forever and ever yea even unto the ending of the world and beyond. Stephen and I were never in love, and we were totally over even before I left him, and we should have taken care of this back then. But it *is* a weird feeling, I won't lie to you. It's strange to think of myself as not married to Stephen anymore, when I never thought of myself as married to him when I was… and now I've legally never been married to him at all, which is really—just about right."

She stretched hugely in her chair. "Anyway, I can't wait till you guys move down here from the Plaza. I've given you the Victorian suite, I totally love saying that…I certainly loved decorating it."

"And we thank you, and we will, and we shall, but not until after everybody's shows are done with. You know that before gigs I'm not fit for human company—Ares doesn't count," Prax added, to general laughter. "And Turk won't want the distraction of houseguests either. It's been hard enough on him and the guys this tour. But after the Garden we'll come and stay for a while before we go back to L.A."

"As long as you like."

After they'd gone, Rennie went up to her office and sat down in her writing chair, staring out at the street bathed in slanting winter-afternoon light. Prax was right: Lionheart's current road trip had been a much, much more rugged one than usual, maybe their hardest ever. The album it was originally in support of, *Cities of the Plain*, had not been well supported in turn by the label, nor had it been well received by the public and the critics. It had long since died the chart death, and advance ticket sales for the tour had been sluggish, to say the least. Lionheart weren't on the level of the Beatles or the Budgies, say, but they were a legitimate superstar group, and this was something they had never had to contend with before. Sure, the album was heavily orchestrated and nothing like their usual, but it had some lovely cuts, and it hadn't deserved the blistering scorn heaped upon it by critics and fans alike. Once Centaur had bailed on working it with ads and airplay and radio spots, it had fallen off the charts like a pebble down a well.

But the tour was booked, and it had to continue. Faced for the first time since their green years with unsold-out arenas and halls, and, more to the point, deeply stung by audience apathy and critical barbs, Turk had fought back by writing on the road, something he'd always thought he could never do, and the other guys had loyally backed him up, working out arrangements on the fly, using the sound checks to give the new material a shot. They'd been slipping in the new songs as they went, a baker's dozen so far; he and Rardi, the main writers of the band, had twice as many more they hadn't even tried out yet, and even Shane and Jay-Jay had kicked in a couple apiece.

The results had been amazing. It was like the old Lionheart days, everyone said, marveling, those earliest scuffling exciting days — the ones before Rennie's time, the ones that she had been around for only at a distance, as a young fan. The band had been newly fired up, and as word of mouth got around about the great new songs and surprise reinvigoration, the last half of the tour was a sellout. They'd even added dates, so many that some nights they were so tired they could hardly drag themselves onstage; as Eric Lacing had mentioned, Turk had actually collapsed in mid-riff at the Cow Palace, from exhaustion, the flu and creative self-medication.

But it had paid off big-time. They had even managed to garner a completely positive critical rethink in reviews. Turk had exulted in one of his thrice-daily road phone calls to Rennie that he couldn't remember the last time so many critics had liked them so unqualifiedly. Maybe never. At least not since *Clarity Road*. Or maybe not since their big breakthrough *Sgt. Pepper*-class album, *The Little Gentleman in Black Velvet*, the one that, combined with their dazzling Monterey Pop Festival performance in June of 1967, had shot them to superstardom.

Thanks to the tour rebirth, *Cities* was respectably repeat-charting, though not ascending to anywhere near the heights that Lionheart was accustomed to occupying. But the rush-release greatest-hits LP, *Local Politics,* their first—and Turk had chosen the tracks very carefully indeed, especially the three new ones to keep the fans happy—was topping the charts, bullets in every trade. And now the Garden concert, which they'd been planning for almost a year, and which they'd arranged two weeks off preceding, to make sure they were well rested and at full strength. It was going to be *epic.*

Rennie smiled to herself, and began to type.

She told Turk about the annulment at supper that night. She hadn't really thought what he might do or say, but he was annoyingly serene about it. No big dramatic scene, just Right, about time you and Stephen got around to it, glad to hear I'm no longer sleeping with another man's wife, oh wait, if you're annulled then you never actually *were* another man's wife, were you, well that's fairly paradoxical but hey, it works for me.

No renewed proposals either, which, perversely, irked her, though if he had dropped to one knee and passionately declared himself yet again she'd have been perversely irked at that too. It just seemed to be taken for granted that now their engagement was both official and lawful and remained only to go public. She could see Country Life looming darkly down the road.

The next night, booted against the snow that lay deep on the ground and bundled up against the bitter cold, Turk in his shearling and Rennie in her silver fox—the mink stroller from Harrods just wasn't right for the neighborhood—they walked the few blocks south on Second Avenue to the Fillmore East. Passing under the bold neon-lit marquee with EVENOR top-billed in big black letters, which Rennie proudly and possessively beamed to see, they went around to the backstage entrance halfway down the block on the Sixth Street side, where they were cheerfully waved on through.

The pocket act—second on the bill of three—was deep into its set. Turk and Rennie took care not to get in the way of the roadies as they crossed behind the lightshow backdrop, eeling over to the far side of the stage and up the rickety dressing-room stairs. No matter how many times Rennie came here, she never failed to be thrilled by the backstage vibe: the amazingly efficient crew, the lightshow paraphernalia, Bill Graham surging like a mighty tide to the stage and back again—the man never just *walked*. Maybe the punters out in the plush-covered seats couldn't see most of this, but they sensed it—it was all part of the show. Like an iceberg: even though you didn't see the vast, complex mass below the surface that held up everything else, you darn well knew it was there. Especially when it hit your ship.

In the headliner's dressing room, Prax greeted them with distracted delight, hugging them, kissing them, telling them to sit for a while, she didn't have to go on for half an hour yet, then promptly shifted back into her pre-concert angsty sulk mode. Her friends, well accustomed to it and not offended in the slightest, equally promptly went over to hang with the other musicians, whose own pre-concert policy was 'Company and plenty of it!'

When the band finally headed downstairs, Turk and Rennie went down with them to stage level, where they then hung a sharp left, going up a short, twisty staircase to the visiting-celebrity perch in the box on the right-hand side of the house, screened by a velvet curtain and a bunch of sound equipment.

Evenor's set was killer, band and audience both ferociously into it. Final-night late sets were often like that: the band knew that they didn't have to save anything and could do whatever they liked for as long as Bill felt like letting them do it. Which was why you always got the real diehards at the last Saturday show: the fans appreciated the effort, and came prepared to stay until dawn—and often did. Two-thirds of the way through the set, in front of the liquid-jewel dazzle of the light show, Prax looked straight up the spotlight beam and brushed her hair out of her eyes.

"This one's for Strider and Slider," she said softly into the mike, not glancing their way, and up in the sound booth Turk and Rennie, not taking their eyes off Prax, reached out to hold hands. There was a ripple of applause among the better-informed—or more fannishly obsessive—audience members, the ones who actually knew who the hell Prax was talking about, and then Evenor launched into the gorgeous Lionheart ballad "Love at First Light", written last year by Turk about his and Rennie's first night together, one of his peace offerings to get her back after their break-up.

Though she was primarily a melodic belter, Prax's contralto was exquisite in the softer registers, and she wrapped herself around the song like an embrace. She was singing not only *about* her best friends but *to* her best friends, and when she was done both Turk and Rennie had tears in their eyes. Careless of who saw, they both leaned forward to applaud her, and Prax bowed and blew them a kiss.

"What a wonderful surprise," sighed Rennie as they sat back. "I never knew she could cover your stuff as well as that."

"It was a gift," said Turk, raising her hand to kiss it. "Love to love to love."

A few days later, on Thanksgiving Day afternoon, Turk and Rennie walked into the Fillmore East again, this time through the side door, turning right, into the lobby that had been filled for the occasion with long banquet tables decked with flowers and china and cutlery. Every year Bill Graham did this at both Fillmores: a feast originally intended for musicians who were playing his theaters over the holiday and who would otherwise miss out on drumstick day, but the guest list had soon expanded to include local friends — press and musicians and people in the biz. Rennie, when she'd been invited for the first time in San Francisco three years ago, had been so thrilled and nervous that she couldn't even eat anything, and just nibbled, gazing proudly around; she'd felt that she really belonged there, a card-carrying member of rocknroll.

Immediately on their entrance, they were greeted cheerfully by friends and associates. While Turk conversed with Bill about some future dates at the Graham theaters — even though Lionheart could sell out the Garden three nights running, Turk never wanted to give up playing smaller venues, and Bill, hurt and angry that too many acts snobbishly turned their backs on his places once he had given them the exposure to really make it, appreciated Lionheart's loyalty — Rennie checked out the scene.

Well, look who's here! Janis, most of the Airplane, oh, that cutie-pie John Sebastian, he shows up *everywhere*, Chris and Nancy Sakerhawk in from L.A., Tennessee bluesman Vonnie Lee Nash, even some Velvet Undergrounds, how strange, not their scene at all you'd think but they *were* local and maybe they were just hungry — tons of other musicians, all their favorite writers and record company people and Fillmore East family and very few people they couldn't stand. Hey, that was a lot to be thankful for right there.

They sat down with Janis, and were soon joined by Jack and Jorma Airplane, Vogue fashion writer Zsa Zsa Briscoe and Belinda Melbourne, who lived around the corner from Turk and Rennie and who had lurid stalker tales to tell them now that she'd hooked up with well-known lunatic Diego Hidalgo, the lead singer of Cold Fire — Rennie had fixed them up after Woodstock, and had happily watched the chips, and the clothes, fall where they might, by all accounts most successfully. A couple of other Lionhearts showed up, though not Niles, and everybody tucked into a surprisingly good dinner.

Rock and roll never sleeps: after a stop at the prow house to change, they headed uptown to pick up Prax and Ares at the Plaza and go over to the Garden to catch the first of the Stones' three shows. Of course there had been the, ah, unpleasantness at the Stones' Hyde Park concert back in July, which Rennie had handled with her usual murder aplomb: she and Turk had flown over for Brian Jones' memorial service and, natch, someone had been murdered backstage, necessitating her involvement. Brian had been Turk's first real friend in the London music scene: sadly, they'd grown apart as Brian began to fall apart with drugs and personal difficulties, though Keith Richards and Turk had been close and still were. Brian had been a friend of Rennie's and Prax's as well, and they'd all been devastated by his death. She'd solved the murder for his sake, not so much for the other Stones. So really Mick owed her, the little ratbag. She must remind him.

After the hour and a half set, they all trooped backstage to pay respects and scope out the facilities with an eye to the following week's Lionheart gig. Turk and Keith greeted each other with warmth, though Mick and Turk were on cooler terms — apparently there had been an Incident once — and so merely exchanged the mutually recognizing nods of royalty passing in the night.

But it was a nice half-hour with Keith and Bill and new guy Mick Taylor, as they listened to Keith tell them about this free concert they were planning in Golden Gate Park, to be held next Saturday, the same day as Lionheart's Garden gig. Just to "give something back" to the fans, as had been announced rather imperiously at yesterday's Rainbow Room press conference. The Stones had actually provided a string quartet to keep the rabble entertained until they deigned to show up, and it had indeed been entertaining, though probably not quite in the way the Stones had intended. Rennie, who had attended the conference purely for amusement value, had found it hilarious, and she now forbore to laugh right in Keef's face, though she did arch the Eyebrows of Meaningful Non-verbal Spousal Commentary at Turk.

Oh yeah, we'll just see how that plays out... Already there were impassioned San Francisco city officials swearing that only over their cold dead civic bodies would the Stones be allowed to roll into Golden Gate Park, so the concert had had to be moved elsewhere, some racetrack or speedway outside the city, place called Altamont, and there had been talk of using the Hell's Angels as crowd control, yeah, right, *that* made sense…

Over in one corner of the room was a tall, brown-haired girl with amazing bone structure, looking every bit as shy and nervous as Rennie had once looked, so she went over to talk to her, and they hit it off right away. Nice girl, nice name — Carly, like Rennie's goddaughter. She was a scion of a famous New York publishing family and a friend of Keith's guitar tech Danny, which was how she came to be in the Garden dressing room in the first place. In a burst of candor she confided to Rennie how staggered she was to be here, even though from childhood she'd been used to meeting people like Charles Addams and Oscar Hammerstein at her family's home, and how she was too shy to even *look* at the Stones so was spending all her time staring at the floor, and how she was working on an album herself, hoping to get her own solo singing career off the ground one day soon. Rennie hoped she did, and they promised to stay in touch.

The concert itself had been okay, though not epic, and the setlist rather lackluster — not many of her favorites. From Mick's first drawled onstage words, a precious little tease about how he'd busted his buttons and his trousers were falling down you wouldn't want that now would you — cries of No! (and Yes!) — the Stones had been on, but the big surprise moment had been Janis Joplin, still wearing the big white fur hat she'd had on at the Fillmore East Thanksgiving dinner that afternoon. Leaping onstage and electrifying the audience, once they figured out who it was, she sang in with Tina Turner during the opening act. Rennie had scowled for a moment, thinking Janis had somehow got wind of Lionheart's secret plan and was trying to preemptively upstage them, but reassured herself. Great minds thinking alike, was all. To her surprise, she learned later that the Stones had been annoyed as well, thinking Janis was trying to upstage *them*. Oh, rock divas! Can't not enjoy 'em, can't kill 'em… Well, you *could* kill them, actually. As they'd all seen.

Thanksgiving Friday Rennie and Turk hosted Prax and Ares and members of Lionheart and Evenor for dinner at the prow house: official consorts only, no groupies allowed. Rennie had made an enormous and spectacular roast turkey with all the fixings, and after dinner most of them trundled on over to the Fillmore East yet again to see the Airplane.

"It seems like a strange way to spend the last week before a major gig," remarked Rennie on the way home after the show, when the four had stopped off at Gem Spa and she'd bought them all egg creams, to which they were all passionately addicted, and nobody made them better than Gem's. Turk grabbed early editions of the local papers and last week's lone remaining Sunday London Times, and they proceeded up Second Avenue, sipping their chocolate-syrup-milk-and-seltzer confections as they went. "Going to *more* concerts, I mean, and friends' concerts at that."

"It takes my mind off it," said Turk firmly.

"Really? It doesn't make you think hey I could steal that fuzz riff of Juha's and use it somewhere and Niles would like what Jagger did with that tonal stuff and maybe Jay-Jay could do that drum fill Charlie does only he could do it better, and other things along those lines?"

"Of course it makes me think that. Musicians are always looking for things to steal. Just like writers." Turk and Prax both grinned at her outraged expression. "Believe it or not, that really does take my mind off our own show. It helps me focus. I wanted time off from the tour before the Garden, for all of us to rest up, but it's been a little too *much* time off, perhaps, and I don't want us losing our edge. If we'd gone to the movies it wouldn't have distracted me enough, and if we'd stayed home I'd be obsessing. This was perfect—keeps my head right where it should be."

"Well, anyway, three down, two to go," said Prax as they went up the steps of the prow house. "Us, Stones, Airplane. Next up, Sledger Cairns and this axe murderer and his so-called band."

Rennie nudged Turk sideways with her shoulder. "I don't know, Flash, everyone's been playing *miles* above their game—Keef, Jorma, this one here...the bar's set pretty high."

Turk loftily refused her gambit. "Well, we'll just have to do what we can, then, won't we. Our poor pitiful British best."

"And our good friend Sledger too will have her work cut out for her," said Ares with a grin. "Interesting. But then she always is."

Interesting probably wasn't quite the word. Sledger

Cairns, eldest daughter of legendary blues guitarist Galt Cairns, at whose irascible mountain-man feet even Turk humbly worshipped, was the only famous female lead guitar player in all of rock—no, make that pretty much the only female lead guitar player at *all* in rock—and she was incredible. She had gotten her nickname from her trademark chording action—like a sledgehammer on the strings, some early critic had said. Trite and predictable, but she could out-riff quite a few of the big boys—not Turk or Jimi or Eric or Jorma, of course, but most of the rest, and even those four she could give a run for their money on a good night. The name had stuck. Still, her Texas driver's license read Veronica Lee Cairns, and the all-girl band she'd previously fronted had been known as Ronnie and the Reloads. And they'd been just as tough as their name.

Sledger and Rennie and Prax and the late Tansy Belladonna had all hung out together in San Francisco before Sledger moved to New York and Rennie and Prax had moved to L.A., and they had renewed their friendship when Rennie came east to set up house with Turk. When Sledger had begun to put together Externity, her current chart-topping outfit, she'd gotten good press from critics and a hard time from the modestly big-name guys she approached as potential bandmates. They all assumed that, as *guys*, they would naturally be the focus and Sledger would be this pretty performing seal off to one side.

Bi-i-i-ig mistake. Sledger Cairns—wild mop of curly orange hair halfway to her famously freckled ass, legs up to her neck and tits out to the other side of the room—was total chick, but she could make the most macho rocker around look yang-deficient by comparison. And she had very definite ideas about who was frontperson in her band. Quite a few rocklords profoundly admired her technique. Oh, and they admired her guitar playing, too.

To ease Turk's fears of slackness, Lionheart got in two more rehearsals, hiring the auditorium of the funky old Ukrainian National Home, just a block away on Second Avenue, to practice in, and Friday night they all went up to the Garden for the sound check before Saturday's show. Prax was there, too, her participation being one of the big secrets everyone was still at such pains to keep. Turk worked them all hard, and himself hardest of all, and when everything had finally been concluded to his satisfaction, he and Rennie headed downtown to catch a bit of Sledger's Friday late show at the Fillmore East before they went home. Well, when your life was music, music was your life...

Hand in hand, they strolled in at the front entrance, too lazy to walk around to the side. Sledger's set was well under way by now, so the risk of fan interaction was minimal, and the little that occurred was friendly and casual. Fillmore East habitués, the coolest music fans on the planet, did *not* hassle artists; in fact, artists considered themselves lucky if they were even acknowledged.

After watching for a while from the back of the house, they went up to the dressing room to wait for Sledger. She came erupting in, a force of nature panting and alive and realer than real, and all the oxygen in the room surged straight over to her. They were used to the phenomenon, though, and sat down to wait, smiling, until the atmosphere had settled down a bit.

When Sledger saw them, she squealed like a dolphin and bore down upon them like a midnight freight. "You guys *came*, oh you are so *sweet*, what a sexy beautiful limey hunk you are, Lord Richard, if your old lady wasn't standing in front of me I'd ball you right here on the floor, maybe I will anyway, she's welcome to join in—"

She grabbed a horrified Turk and kissed him thoroughly, laughing at his shock, then transferred over to Rennie, who was laughing herself at the look on Turk's face. Flinging an arm around Rennie, Sledger drew her aside.

"Listen, Strider, you clever gorgeous thing, I know it's weird and sucky, but I need to consult you professionally. Privately. *You* know."

Rennie felt her heart sink into her brown leather bronze-buckled square-toed witch-heeled Pilgrim shoes, but before she could do more than open her mouth to protest Sledger shook her head reassuringly.

"Oh no no no, not that, babe, nobody's dead, well, not yet anyway, though I *may* have to kill *someone*—but it's a major bummer and I need help from somebody who knows about this kind of crap. And here you are and who knows more about it than my dear friend Rennie Stride?"

Oh, thanks a bunch, Sledge…

Sledger pulled Rennie out into the hall and then into the farthest corner of the staircase leading to the upper dressing rooms, carefully checking to see that no one was lurking nearby.

"I've had some death threats," she said, casually and confidingly. "And I thought you'd be the one to talk to about them."

"Oh, Sledger, dear God —"

"Never mind that, hon, it gets worse: someone's kidnapped the Duchess."

The Duchess...for a brief and confused instant Rennie's mind swam with images of her future mother-in-law. Still, this was Sledger, so obviously Turk's mum wasn't involved. And it wasn't a girlfriend, probably, either.

"Your dog," ventured Rennie. "Your *cat.*"

"My GUITAR! My best and most favorite work guitar. There was a note, I don't have it here, but they said they were taking Duch and I could get her back if I paid them a thousand dollars. Which of course I will."

"That's a lot of bread."

Sledger waved beringed fingers. "I'm hip. I could score ten crappy guitars, three decent ones, two good ones or one great one for that. But there's nothing like Duchie. My daddy bought her for me; I compose on her, we've been together since I started, and I damn well want her back."

"Yes, but about these death threats, Sledger —"

Again the Fluttering Fingers of Dismissal. "Later for that. I just wanted you to know about my axe. I *don't* want to go to the fuzz. I'm going to leave the money just the way they told me."

"Okay, fine, but I still would mention it to Bill or Kip. They will *not* be happy about something like this happening here. And once you've paid..."

"Yeah, yeah, yeah. But don't tell anybody else. Well, you can tell Turk, and Prax, oh, okay, and Ares too, he might be able to help. But nobody else, not yet anyway. It could be someone we know, someone here at the Fillmore, someone in my band, even, and I don't want it to get back to them that you and I talked."

"Veronica Lee—"

"Not tonight, bunnyface. It's not really life and death, you know—not like you're used to. Nobody's been offed. Turk's Garden gig is tomorrow night, right? Yeah, and I have the two shows to do here. So I'll call you on Sunday. We'll talk."

But by then people *would* have been offed. And it *would* be life and death.

CHAPTER FIVE

OODED CHINCHILLA CLOAK — AN extravagant early Christmas gift from Turk — draped loosely round her shoulders, Rennie sat on a tweedy sofa in a clean, warm and utterly charmless Madison Square Garden locker room. Ten feet away, Turk was suiting up for the show, and she was watching him. On the short walk from the cab to the backstage Garden entrance — no limo, yellow cabs just like everybody else were fine with him, and Rennie had taught him how to scout them from five blocks away and to ruthlessly "upstream" competitors, the mark of a true New Yorker — he'd shifted effortlessly into pre-game mode. She'd actually seen him do it, between one step and the next, like changing gears on his Porsche — shutting down Richard and turning on the Turkness. He was a pro, and that's how pros did it.

And that mode was so removed from everyday consciousness, Rennie considered, though not in a bad way: to get your head into a place where you're not just going to perform your art and display your craft — harrowing enough — but you're going to do it out in front of twenty thousand people, naturally and instinctively and excitingly for both you and them, giving them what they came hoping to see, and all without hitting one wrong note. That required an active headshift, a deliberately altered state which always amazed her; it was something she herself could never do in

a million years. And he just *did* it: one minute he was a guy
walking with his girl, the next he was a superstar on his
way to work…

It never took him more than a couple of heartbeats to get
deep into it, the zone, the inner focus, gearing up, enlarging
and expanding himself for the stage by going deep within.
So now, with royal disregard for watching eyes—not to
mention the couple of movie cameras shooting footage for a
Lionheart documentary—and wrapped in a totally absorbed
awareness that was somehow as far from self-absorbed as
it could possibly be, Turk stripped off his street clothes to
change into tonight's stage costume. He stood there naked
and godlike for a moment—not preening or posing but
totally unselfconsciously, preoccupied, a man with more
important things on his mind than getting dressed—then
began to encase himself in a close-fitting whipstitched
leather outfit, doublet and trousers and laced-up triangular
fly, a garnet-red version of the sapphire-blue stage costume
that Rennie had hand-made him for the Whisky A Go-
Go gig last year, as she'd made this one for tonight. *The
pants look terrific on him…they'd look even better on our
bedroom floor…*

He grinned as he caught her speculative gaze on him,
and she smiled back. "What the well-dressed rock god will
wear, my lord?"

"Please! Sex god, thank you ever so. And only if the sex
god's equally sexy goddess has sewn it for him, my lady."

"I see. But who says you're a sex god?"

Turk was packing himself into the skin-tight leather
trousers. "You, if your fervent outcries to my divinity last

night are to be believed."

"Oh, those." Rennie blushed slightly. "Well, you needn't be so smug about it. Still, I think we can take my word for your godhood. Miraculous indeed. *Quod erat demonstrandum,* and, indeed, *quibus vidimus.* On occasions beyond counting."

"Nothing like a classical education." With perhaps just the teensiest reminiscent smirk bringing out his dimples above the beard, Turk returned to fastening up his doublet over his bare chest, back in his little bubble of preparation again.

Smiling slightly herself — *There! Got him relaxed, or at least thinking about something else, job well done, Ren-Ren, and yes, it had been* quite *a divine night —* Rennie got up to fetch herself a glass of wine and strawberries from the catering table, one of which stood in each dressing room, laden with fruit and cheese and pastries and sandwiches, beer and wine and tea and coffee and soft drinks. Though the musicians themselves rarely partook of refreshment before a show, except the odd cup of tea or glass of water, the crew, who had been there all day long and sometimes the preceding night as well, needed to be fed; hence the lavish buffet.

And the ever-starving rock press corps was always grateful to be tossed a few crumbs, literally: as a former starving rock press corpswoman herself, Rennie knew how it felt to depend on such largesse. Sometimes a press party or concert catering table was the day's only meal for hungry underground journos, so in her position as leader's mate — the de facto lady of the manor, in more ways than one — she always made sure Lionheart had good stuff out. And a supply of plastic baggies so people could take leftovers home—it would just get thrown out otherwise. Sure, it was noblesse oblige, to a certain extent, though she preferred to think of it as maternal concern.

But there were no over-the-top demands like no red M&Ms, or *only* red M&Ms: Lionheart and Evenor and Turnstone and Bluesnroyals and all her other band buddies weren't on prima-donna trips in the slightest. Gray and Prue Sonnet, as a former Budgie and a former queen of the singles charts, were arguably the most entitled to behave so, and they wouldn't have *dreamed* of being so obnoxious. Rennie had seen stars of far lesser magnitude put outrageous clauses into their concert riders, like when they walked past backstage, everyone had to turn around and lower their eyes and not look upon them. Presumably to show slave-like submission. Yeah, right; who did these twerps think they were, the Czar of All The Russias? Turk, who certainly deserved such homage, would never even *think* of such a thing, though perhaps Niles might.

No, all Lionheart cared about was that the equipment, their own and the hired gear, was in perfect shape. The only commandment the group had was no nuts in any food items, which, considering what had happened at Woodstock, made perfect sense. Otherwise, they didn't give a damn, and were happy to leave the catering specifics to Rennie and Christabel Green, Lionheart manager Francher's wife, who knew what the boys liked and arranged things accordingly; Francher, who as manager would ordinarily be expected to see to all this himself, was grateful that the two relieved him of the task.

Heading back to her seat on the couch and her Turk-watching alike, she ignored the cameraman and sound guy trying to get a better bead on them both. She did frown slightly: as pleasant a sight as she always found it, perhaps Turk being starkers in a documentary wasn't such a good idea. She really didn't care for the fans seeing him nekkid, though on the other hand she rather liked the thought that they'd be envying her even more than they already did, once they actually got to see what they were missing. Which would of course be the only way they ever *would* get to see it...well, perhaps she could make sure it got edited out. Though saved on a tape for her personal home enjoyment, of course.

Turk didn't allow either the camera's presence or Rennie's to interrupt his process, which was rather like that of an actor getting into character for a play, or a veteran knight arming for a tournament. All the armor went just so, then when he was satisfied that he felt comfortable and protected in his mail, he would pick up his weapons and make sure of them. Glorious and gleaming, all different, they were laid out like jousting lances on a table across the room: the guitars he would need for the show, which Pudge Vetrini, his devoted guitar tech, had been bringing in two at a time as he got them set up.

"It's never scary for you, this?" she asked curiously. "After all these years you've been doing it?"

Turk glanced up, surprised. "It's *always* scary. It *should* be scary. That's what people pay for, that's what they come to see: the chance to observe public terror on a nightly basis."

"Oh, I think they come for just a *leetle* bit more than that."

He favored her with a grin and sat down to pull on his boots. In the other dressing room across the hall, there was a sound of revelry this night, at least judging from the noise level. Which was unusual: with Lionheart, as a rule that kind of stuff didn't happen till after the gig. Rennie hoped the unaccustomed looseness didn't bode ill for upcoming tightness onstage—nerves often served them better, pre-performance. All the other guys were in there with their ladies and the usual hangers-on and guests. Shane and Rardi had companionably shared this room earlier with Turk, but once they were dressed they'd left him to get into his game face, as they went off to do whatever they did to get into their own.

She'd seen it happen a thousand times with a thousand different acts, not just Lionheart: the sudden concentration and remove, as the performers pulled away from the everyday and went deep within, stoking themselves, getting into that concentration and focus, that performance place they needed to be in to go out onstage and play. It wasn't inappropriate that the locker room was also used by sports teams playing the Garden—though one wondered whether the Garden was *ever* appropriate for rock acts. But it was all the same thing. They were all gladiators for the crowd.

As Turk, now dressed, was testing the tuning on the Les Paul he always started off using, Niles came in, wearing surprisingly sedate, at least for him, grass-green velvet—a cutaway coat, of which he would divest himself in his usual showy fashion over the course of the evening, and matching trousers, with a skin-tight, sleeveless gold lamé t-shirt underneath, v-necked to his waist. The air frosted over noticeably in Rennie's corner — *Well, hello there, Aladdin!* — and Niles checked visibly when he saw her sitting there enthroned like Lincoln in his Memorial, but they exchanged brief civilities and curt nods, and Rennie offered luck for the performance, managing not to sound sarcastic. Niles and Turk conferred briefly over the final set list, each of them moving around a number or two, and then Niles left to fill in the others on the switches.

Turk went back to his work without missing a beat, until every instrument he planned on possibly using that night — two Gibsons, two Strats, a Telecaster and a vintage Martin acoustic, and backups in case he broke strings — was adjusted to his liking: open-tuned in different keys, regular tunings, tunings of his own devising. He'd still have to tinker onstage, and the acoustic always had to wait till the very last minute before he needed it; the gut strings went out so fast, especially in a huge arena setting, but he only used it for a couple of songs in the encore, so that was fine.

Pudge had done a perfect job, as always, but this totally unnecessary tweaking was part of Turk's pre-game ritual, a sort of personal rock Zen, and he'd no more have thought of skipping it than he would of asking Rennie to stay home on concert night. It was as if he was waking the guitars up, getting them out of bed and ready to work, psyching them up for the show as he was psyching up himself.

Finally he laid down the last axe for Pudge to take out to the wings and array in order of use, then came over and pulled Rennie up off the couch and into his arms for a kiss and cuddle, back to his everyday self for a last brief moment before going on.

"Do you want me in back or in front?" she murmured into his chest, and he ran his hands down to her rear end, pulling her close against him.

"I take it you mean for the show? How very disappointing. Perhaps we can manage both when we get home. Well, wherever you like, of course."

She shook her head, smiling. "No, my friend, wherever *you* like."

Turk appreciated the fact that she was both professional enough and personal enough to ask. Having her watch from backstage was nicer for him: he could glimpse her if she was in the wings, even talk to her between songs if she was lurking behind the stacks—she was his instant barometer for how the show was going. But he knew she felt that she was intruding on band turf, or, worse, distracting him from his job, breaking his concert-pitch concentration. In the house was nicer for her, because she was after all a reporter as well as a fan, and she liked to see the show as a whole, as a regular audience member would see it, to pick up on things—how the crowd was reacting, if certain ideas had or hadn't worked, if the sound was off, things he couldn't judge for himself, things she'd tell him about later. But if she was out front, he missed the instant feedback and the comforting sense of nearness that she supplied between numbers.

Still, they had agreed when they first became involved that Lionheart concert nights would be about his work, not hers, so Rennie was happy to do whatever made Turk happy, which meant she usually spent most shows watching from the wings, hanging out by the monitor board just out of the audience's sight. Part of Niles' grudge against Rennie was that she was the only band consort allowed onstage during performances; the others had to either sit in the house or watch from the greenroom on closed-circuit TV.

Niles seemed to feel this especially keenly on behalf of his own lady, Keitha, and had openly complained that Rennie was getting preferential treatment. To which Turk had coldly replied bloody right she was and when Niles was the leader of Lionheart and when Keitha was a renowned journalist with a huge readership then she too could hang around in the wings. Turk's attitude hadn't exactly helped to further endear Rennie to Niles, but at least the little crapweasel had shut up whining — in public, anyway.

"I'll split the difference!" she said finally, laughing, after they'd gone round the barn a few times. "Five songs backstage, five out front, all night long…" She hesitated, looked up at him, gently touched his cheek. "You up for this? Really?"

He smiled. "Got my playing shoes on. It's going to be a good night."

Since they'd been together, Rennie had developed a pre-show ritual of her own, giving him something new to take on stage with him; not for every gig, just the big huge hairy significant ones, as which tonight certainly qualified. Rings were a worry — Turk felt they affected his finger work, and he never wore them when he played, though most guitarists didn't think it made a lick's difference — so her gifts were either small pocket pieces or something that he could wear and not have to think about.

As usual, he had on the massive silver bracelet she'd

given him a year and a half ago for the already legendary Whisky show. Right, half a pound of solid silver shackling his pick hand wrist, no problem; a little tiny ring on one fret hand finger, all of a sudden it was the Prince and the Pea. Oh, the humanity. But, whatever worked for him; and now, every inch the fair damsel bestowing a token on her chosen knight before the big joust, she slipped over his head a strand of ruby beads she had strung for him herself, so that it hung against his chest, below the little jade phoenix disk he never took off, and the facets on the tiny stones sparkled as they caught the light.

God, he looked spectacular; the red leather outfit was *incredible* on him, even sexier than the blue one, and his hair and beard were great. She felt the usual glowy surge of pride — not that he belonged to her but that she belonged to him. But she didn't look so shabby either: she had taken extra care with her own attire tonight, knowing there would be eyes and cameras on her and Turk together and feeling that she owed it to them both to put up a good fashion appearance. As a rule, they didn't dress up much, but they were both very pleased with tonight's unwontedly fancy threads; every now and then it was nice to dress to suit one's station, present *or* future.

So here she was in — well, barely in — a clingy jersey dress with a neckline that plunged to her waist and flowing crisscrossed tiers of skirts that were micro before and maxi behind, her hair streaming loose and half caught up with combs. By her design both she and Turk were wearing the same deep dark red, as if they'd been dipped in a vat of Burgundy. At her throat on a velvet ribbon was a jewel she had designed and had made earlier this year: a gold rampant lion holding a small ruby heart. It had become a talisman for them both, and she wore it every time she came to watch him play; tonight the new ruby pendant hung below it, between her breasts. The unpiercing Victorian nipple rings he'd given her on their reconciliation last Christmas were clearly visible through the thin stretched fabric, and as she sat down again, she smiled up at him and casually flashed him, uncrossing and recrossing slim legs under the tiny frontal scrap of skirt.

Just a spot of positive reinforcement to rally the troops, remind him what he's playing for; no doubt the docu-dudes will appreciate it too…

Turk caught a brief gleam of gold, and realized, dumbfounded, that she was wearing the other, nether adornment that went with the rings, and not a damn thing on over it. In spite of his astonishment, or perhaps because of it, he felt himself appreciating the fashion effort she'd made on his behalf.

She noticed, and grinned approvingly. "Now *that'll* look nice onstage. Good thing that fly is expandable. And just think how good it'll make *me* look."

"Wow," said Prax, coming in with Ares. "I'll say… sure you can get your axe in front of that, Turk? And so a little — make that a *lot* more is added to the legend. Fans'll love it. Not too close," she added as he hugged her. "I hear your old lady gets insanely jealous, I don't want to set anything off."

"Too kind, Mary Praxedes." Turk kissed her on both cheeks and passed her over to Rennie.

Prax eyed her friend up and down. "And yet you say

you want to be taken seriously as a journalist."

"And don't you forget it, bright eyes! But tonight I'm just the lead guitarist's bit of crumpet. Anyway, you should talk," added Rennie, gesturing at the other's own attire: red fox-fur vest worn open over nothing but Prax, denim miniskirt, brown suede boots, the Mexican silver-and-amethyst collar that had been this year's birthday gift from Rennie, newly blonded hair tousled and tossed. She was so cute; the fans were going to love her too.

"I don't remember ordering an armed guard?" Turk asked, as he and Ares exchanged suitably manly forearm clasps and one-arm bear hugs.

"Off duty tonight, my brother. Though I *am* carrying, of course, as always. But really I'm here only as a music-loving civilian," Ares returned, smiling, and gave Rennie a kiss and hug in turn.

Rennie scoffed. "So you say now, but how many times have we heard *that* before! Not to jinx anything," she added hastily, casting her eyes up to heaven. "I'm just saying."

Blind Faith, Hendrix and the Doors had played the Garden earlier in the year on separate occasions, and Rennie had of course attended, not just as a journalist but as an advance scout for Lionheart, to see how things worked and how it all sounded. Everybody knew that the Garden was hell for music: the sound could be a nightmare backwash unless everything was set up just right, so heeding Rennie's reports, Turk had had it nailed down in Lionheart's contract that there would be a real proscenium stage — complete with wings and backing curtains, not just an open platform — at one end of the arena, with huge speaker stacks on each side and the PA system flown on wires above. Still not ideal sound circumstances, but the best they could probably hope for.

Not a central stationary boxing-ring style stage like the Doors, and certainly not a central revolving one like Blind Faith, who in their all-important American debut last summer, right after Woodstock, had been totally done in by the rotating setup. The mechanics of revolving stages were not yet entirely worked out: some idiot had put the monitor speakers on the Garden arena floor, not on the stage, so that the band could hear themselves only every couple of minutes when they went spinning by, like carousel horses going past the brass-ring pole, and the show had ended in a small but quite real riot. By the fans, not the artists, but still. The mood had not been of the merriest from the start: if Eric Clapton and Ginger Baker had had guns, they'd probably have shot each other. Or themselves.

Nothing like that tonight, though. Another of Turk's dictates had been no seats sold behind the stage: less money for the group and the venue, but guaranteed decent sight and sound for the audience, and to Lionheart, that was what mattered most. It wasn't just noblesse oblige, either: they were recording everything and filming it as well, and they wanted it to be as perfect as they could get it. But the attention paid to detail had obviously paid off: filtering in from outside, the vibe of the house was happy and buzzy.

The backstage loudspeakers crackled suddenly, "Lionheart to the stage, please"; and Rennie took a deep indrawn breath. As the band started down the corridor to make their entrance, the other guys falling in behind Turk, forming on him like a fighter wing, Rennie could see that they were all now in the same headspace as their leader. Hi-ho, hi-ho, it's off to work they go... All of them clearly shared the audience's excitement: this was the end of a long damn tour that had begun badly and now was winding up brilliantly; tonight they didn't have to pace themselves or hold back, they could let it all out at last.

She followed them at a discreet distance, never taking her eyes off Turk, herself excited now for the show about to begin, and she breathed a prayer to the music, or whomever: *Just let it be okay for him. No, let it be GREAT for him. He so deserves it...*

Usually by this point he'd forgotten all about her, and that was as it should be—the only thing on his mind was waiting for him onstage. But now he turned around on the steps to the rear stage platform, paused silhouetted against the brilliant blue-white light to let the other guys pass him, and threw her a smile like sunrise, a smile that said See, everything's good, everything's fine, don't worry about me.

Rennie smiled back and blew him a kiss, whispering the good-luck line she always gave him before a performance.

"See you out there."

CHAPTER SIX

STANDING IN THE WINGS just outside audience sight range, as Lionheart took the stage to a deafening roar and a tidal wave of flashbulbs, Rennie watched Turk recede from her into the blinding spotlight glare, feeling like the whaleboat captain's wife watching his ship put out to sea. Out where there be dragons. Or pirates. Or sea serpents. Out where if somebody decided they wanted to achieve immortality by taking him down, no one could protect him—not the ring of rent-a-cops, not her, not even Ares—and he'd never come walking back out of that blaze of light.

Oh, she didn't dwell on her fear, and it certainly didn't impede her enjoyment of Lionheart concerts—though she was damn glad there wouldn't be anyone sitting behind the stage tonight. But neither had she forgotten how her heart had almost stopped, what her instant thought had been, when Turk had collapsed in mid-show at the Cow Palace back in September. And she'd never, *ever* forget the sound the crowd had made—or the sound she had. It had taken two hulking roadies to physically restrain her while Pudge Vetrini and two more roadies carried Turk offstage.

They'd gently laid him down on the floor in the wings, and Rennie had fought free of the roadies' grasp and rushed to kneel beside him, and the band had played desperately on, with rhythm guitarist Mick Rouse taking over lead.

Though a little woozy, Turk had been good to go again fifteen minutes later, show must go on and all that. He'd received a huge standing ovation when he came back onstage and explained about having the flu, and his only concern had been that his fall might have cracked the neck of his favorite Telecaster. He'd gotten a hero's tribute at the concert's end, of course. And then Rennie had whisked him off in a waiting ambulance to the nearest ER.

All the same, she had only once confided to him—and he'd understood her fear, shared it, as did other artists of his stature and out-thereness, and they'd never spoken of it again—that one overriding, not so very irrational terror of hers: the paralyzing dread that one night when he was out there in the follow spot doing his job, some right-wing wacko or left-wing nutter or crazed fanboy or -girl up in a dark corner of the balcony would get him in their gun sights and drop him right there onstage.

It wasn't all so far-fetched, rock assassination. Just the next step up from rock murder, really, and they certainly knew all about *that*. As Ares had told her once, such attempts happened with a terrifying degree of regularity, but the public just never heard about them; he'd thwarted three himself in the past year alone. He'd discussed them with her, candidly and somberly, when she asked, straight out, as one who needed to know, and had never breathed a word to Turk of what Ares had said, too frightened to even think about it. She never knew that Turk in his turn had spoken to Ares on the same topic, and had never told her, not wishing to scare her.

One day, though, some counterculture Lee Harvey

Oswald was going to get what he wanted. Not Turk, please God never ever Turk — she touched her lion pendant superstitiously or religiously, she wasn't quite sure which, perhaps both — please God not anyone. But sooner or later, it would be someone. And though none of them ever mentioned it, nobody had forgotten Malachite.

That was how close it could come, Rennie reflected, staring fiercely at Turk smiling and chatting with Shane and Mick as the band plugged in and tuned up. They had all trusted her; they had held her deep in their counsels and confidences and friendship, and she had repaid them by killing five people, and almost killing Turk and Rennie twice each. So, if she, whom they had known and had faith in, then how much more so strangers?

With an effort she turned her mind back to the moment. *Trust the music. The music will protect him, the music will keep him safe…and if that's not a prayer to a Power I don't know what is…*

Turk had the beautiful sunburst candy-apple-red Les Paul on, the one the fans had nicknamed "Sparky", with the new turquoise-studded strap Rennie had had made for him by a leatherworker on East Ninth Street. Now he waved once to the roaring shadowy dimness that was the crowd and spun around to face Niles, hair flaring like a comet's tail with the speed of his turn, and without warning the Garden walls blew out like a giant concrete exhale with the famous nine-note opening riff of the current chart-topper, "Walking with Tigers".

As he repeated the riff, expanding, and the bass and drums and piano kicked in behind him with Niles on maracas and Mick on rhythm and it all began to happen, Rennie felt it pick her up and carry her away, the old familiar rush and thrill. Here in the wings she didn't get the full effect of the sound, it wasn't aimed her way, but she felt her solar plexus quivering like a trapped hummingbird with the vibrations coming up through the floor.

It was always so trippy when he was onstage at work: it seemed as if he were not her guy at all but was suddenly revealed as the king of some far and secret magic country — removed, commanding, masterful, but also somehow right there in it, as here and present as anyone could possibly be. He certainly *looked* like a king, if perhaps a medieval one, or an Elven one, at least going by hair and clothing. Attended like one too: his loyal subjects were all present to cheer him to the rafters, his helpful advisors and servants lurked within reach in case he needed assistance, and his loving consort and as-yet-uncrowned queen hovered like a dutiful handmaiden, ready to perform whatever service his royal whim might require. Rennie grinned; sometimes such service could be very interesting indeed…

She'd gone out onstage once, at His Majesty's invitation, while they were playing a sound check full on and flat out, just to see what it felt like. In her first days of rock fandom and then reporterage, she'd spent her share of concerts happily parked in front of the stacks with her elbows on the stage, for *hours*; she'd have ringing ears for three days afterward, and it was totally worth it. But this was different. It was loud enough to blow her clothes off. Well, maybe not quite, but she'd had to leave, stunned, when she actually felt the air in front of the amps pushing back at her like an invisible hand, *blowing her hair around*, just as Turk had promised it would. Cool.

But that was just machines, and just to show her how loud it could get. Though they certainly were loud, Lionheart didn't usually play at that run-for-your-life Blue Cheer curdle-the-air-like-cottage-cheese decibel level, as someone had described it, not even in performance. That wasn't their point, or even where their real energy boost came from. Listening to Turk play at home, or at a check or rehearsal, was one thing; but out in front of a hall full of people, who fed back into him the same way his guitar fed back into the amp, and not just into him but Shane and Niles and Jay-Jay and Rardi and Mick, and then them feeding back into each other and out again into the crowd — now that had to push back harder than a whole *wall* of Marshalls. No wonder he was always so wired after a show.

That energy exchange was one of the reasons she liked to sit in the house for concerts: to feel it coming from behind her and beside her and around her and off the stage in front of her, the flow and surge of vibes. She'd go out front after a while, if things were going well; she had a center aisle seat about eight rows back, close enough to see subtleties of technique and get a nice balanced sound, but not so close that Turk could see her. Once he was onstage he never saw anything past the monitors in front of his feet, but she didn't want to take the chance.

She exchanged a smile with Pudge, who was standing by the board with the next change of guitar and a spare for the Gibson in case Turk blew a string. Even if he did, he was a good enough musician to finish the song on five strings alone, of course, but Pudge was ready in any case. She and Pudge didn't see a lot of each other, but they were on friendly terms. Guitar techs were a new phenomenon, a natural outgrowth of "the guy who hands me my axe when I'm onstage", and only a very few very major players had them as yet. Pudge had once confided to her that all the other quippies and roadies were sick with envy that he got to work for Turk Wayland and they didn't: his lad, as he fondly called him, was demanding, sure, but only in service of the music, not his ego, and as they were both dedicated to obtaining the best sound possible they got on fine. Rennie was glad of it; just one more thing Turk didn't have to worry about.

They had set-listed carefully and well: a nice balance of old and new, hard and slow; plenty of greatest hits—even "Svaha", which always brought down the house. It was weird to listen to a song your lover wrote to win you back after a breakup being sung by him in front of twenty thousand strangers while you're right there listening, knowing that everyone there knew all about it—almost like being naked in public. But that was part of what they had with each other; it was just odd and shy-making to share it, and him, with the audiences. It would probably never change, and she would probably never get used to it.

After a while she went out front, to sit with a friend—Prax had remained in the dressing room, to psych herself up for her surprise performance—and watch Lionheart as any audience member might. Well, okay, maybe not *any* audience member. The band had just started their huge hit "Clarity Road", the monster title track off last year's monster album—the roar as Turk unslung the Gibson, sat down at the baby grand and chorded out the lead-in had been the loudest of the evening so far—and she leaned back and let the song, and Turk's rare lead vocal, have its way with her.

"Come stand by my side when the night draws in near
There's no map to where we're going, no guiding star to steer
The safe way through the wilderness hasn't yet been showed
Take my hand and walk with me down Clarity Road..."

That was the nice part of being off-duty; off-duty as a working reporter, anyway—she was still very much on the job as observer for Turk. Four years as a reporter and almost two as a rock consort hadn't ruined her pleasure in the music, or dimmed it for her: of all the bands she knew and loved, this was still the one band she wanted to listen to forever, he was still the one musician who never bored her, the one singer whose voice she never tired of hearing.

"It's hard to stand tall when you can't find the path
When your boots are worn through in the long aftermath
But the tracks they go deep where the heroes once strode
Just step where their feet bled on Clarity Road..."

It was a two-edged sword, having a hit of that size and caliber, a signature song; you were pretty much doomed to sing it at every concert you performed for the rest of your life: "White Rabbit", "Light My Fire", "Satisfaction". So you had to be careful about what you might get stuck with, since it would be with you for a very long time, and you got over yourself very, very quickly. But Lionheart didn't have to worry, at least not with this one. It was one of Turk's best lyrics, and his voice and playing set it off to perfection. He'd written and recorded it before his arrest for

Tansy Belladonna's murder, almost two years ago, but she could hear in the shading of his voice what weight of new authority he could now bring to the words, and she wasn't the only one in the Garden to whom that thought occurred.

"Take yes for an answer — the question's been asked
The long knives are out, but the truth's been unmasked
I'll pay any price and I'll lift any load
Let me lean on your shoulder down Clarity Road..."

He was deep into the bridge now, floods of silvery notes redoubled and achingly self-echoed, Rardi's violin riding on the sound like a ship on a rising tide. Oh man, they both were so, *so* good — that violin could tear your heart out, and Turk was as superb on piano as he was on guitar. Then there was Mick Rouse, playing lead guitar for this one, his solo here was one of the best things he did, and some shimmering cymbal work from Jay-Jay Olvera. But in the end it all came round to Turk again, as it always did. As it always should. And that was the critic talking, not the consort.

"The confusion's been lifted, it's all down to you
Your hand pulled me up and your heart pulled me through
I'll love you forever, it's due and it's owed
Come lay down beside me on Clarity Road."

Applause like thunder; that was the last verse, as everyone in the Garden well knew. But the band hadn't stopped playing, had in fact upped the volume and slowed the tempo and played a few extra bars to cut through the clapping and bridge to, apparently, a new closing verse. Rennie straightened in her seat, herself surprised and wary, as the audience applause uncertainly faded — hey, what's this, song not over!, what the hell? — and the music dropped away behind him and Turk's voice grew harsher as he went into a verse she'd never heard before.

"Make an end of the hurting, put paid to the pain
Walk home in the tempest, in the cold wind and rain
Through the storm you can see where life's fires once glowed —
As you follow my coffin down Clarity Road."

He finished not on the usual soft fading run but on a ringing chord that was sorrow and anger and defiance and scorn together, and Rennie herself didn't know everything that went into it but it was all there. There was a scattering of renewed, if uneasy, applause, and a sense that the wind had left the evening's sails for an instant. No uncertainty about how Turk felt, though: there was a brief, cold, very private flash of a smile on his face that startled even her.

But it was over in an instant, and they moved on into the next phase of the show. Strapping on his Telecaster for the rolling sprint to the finish, visibly recharged now that he'd said what he'd felt he'd needed to say, Turk began changing the set list to follow the changing vibe, calling audibles now, bringing out songs he and Rardi had written on the road, none of them yet recorded, some of them never before played for a paying audience, some of them barely rehearsed, all raw and sloppy and electrifying as only the very best rock can be.

Rennie glanced around at the rapt faces nearby, then up at the tiers of packed seats right to the top of the Garden. Her guy had them in the palm of his hand: he had bagged this thing and sent it home like a pro. But he always did: he and the rest of the band had mastered their craft, and now could bring it forth at their pleasure, or their leisure. The audience knew it, too: they were as into it as she was, thrilled to hear something new from Lionheart, even more thrilled that it sounded like something old from Lionheart.

That was the successful rock band's eternal dilemma: how to give 'em new stuff, but at the same time make sure it doesn't sound too far off the old stuff that made them like you in the first place. Just enough change and difference to keep yourself artistically interested and let your fans know you're growing, challenge them to come along and grow with you; but not *so* much change and difference that they feel scared or sold out or left behind. God, it was tricky. She didn't know how the hell he stayed so sane. Look at all the people they knew who didn't.

They had been playing three full hours now and were heading for four. Turk had scorned the idea of an opening act, wanting it to be all Lionheart all night long—this show was for the band as much as it was for the fans. Rennie gave him a quick scan: not to worry, he looked fine, going strong, plenty in reserve—not tired, happy again, really enjoying himself. He could probably play until dawn; the other guys too. But the show was beginning to wind down now, so she took advantage of Rardi switching off violin and the exit of the small horn section they'd added just for a few songs tonight to make her own exit.

She reached the wings just as they started on the set closer. Something brand-new, she'd heard only bits and pieces as they'd rehearsed it; she didn't think she'd ever even been told its name. But whatever it was called, it was mighty: huge tidal shifts and swings of anthemic sound,

Rardi surprisingly scary on accordion of all things, high ringing exchanges between Mick and Turk over a crackling rhythm from Jay-Jay on snares and Shane's deep rumbling bass line, Niles abandoning all stylings and just singing from his toes on up. The song had a long instrumental coda, and as Niles finished the vocal and faded back into the shadows to a rumble of applause, Turk stood there like a rock in the sea and bent over his guitar and just played on and on and on.

And as he did, Rennie couldn't believe what she was hearing. She felt herself being pulled forward into it, into the exalting hugeness, the yearning stillness at the heart of the melodic storm, as if it had its fingers hooked in her collar and she had no choice but to go where it wanted her to go. Her face grew still and taut and more sharply focused, as if it were hit by a spotlight from within, luminous and clear.

And she knew that everyone else in that whole vast hall felt exactly the same, as the music said to her, to everyone who listened — and to him too, to him most of all, first of all, first and last and always — in his voice and its own, "*This is what it is, this is what we know it is, you and I, at the time when I need to say it, on the day when you need to hear it, in an hour when it counts, in a moment when nothing matters more…*"

When the last notes had soared and crashed and faded, he stood there spent, guitar raised, shoulders bowed, head dropped. For two full seconds there wasn't a sound. And then there was a roar so loud that the ear rejected it and made it read like silence.

It was as if they had been privileged to watch him doing something which normally no human being ever gets to see. Not like sex — people watch other people doing that all the time. But something far more intimate, as if they'd been witness to him facing up to his own vision of the universe, facing up to his own soul.

They'd had no share in it, it wasn't for them. He hadn't done it for them, hadn't been thinking of them at all while he was doing it. Nor of the band that had kept pace with him, not so much behind him as beside him, alongside him, around him — though he knew they were there, he hadn't heard them. In front of twenty thousand people, he'd been away, alone with himself and the thing that was working back at him, giving it its voice through him, finding his own through it. That was the only thing he'd been aware of, and now as he came back, raised his head and saw them there, remembered where he was, he was surprised.

And they saw that too. That two-second silence, that was the *real* tribute to his art, not the storm of applause; that was what meant most to him as an artist, not the easy uncritical adulation or the inane fannish graffiti promoting Turk Wayland for president/king/emperor/God.

He didn't say anything to Rennie as he came offstage, didn't smile, even, just looked. And she looked back at him, not smiling either, not saying anything, but letting him see what was in her heart, her face alight, and she nodded in answer to what he hadn't asked aloud, not willing to trust her voice. It had been something amazing, astounding — yes, something magical. Words that reviewers and ad writers toss off promiscuously twenty times a day. But sometimes they're the only words, and the right words, and the only right words. This, here, now, tonight, was why they both did what they did. And man, he hadn't done anything wrong there, had he. No. He hadn't.

The crowd was screaming for an encore, and had no idea what they were about to be given. But there was a minute to spare. She handed him a bottle of water and a towel to mop his face, a quick drink and wipe, a few seconds more to catch his breath, and then the band ran back out into the howling, stamping thunder. Turk slung on the glittering gold-plated Strat he always used for encores, Jay-Jay crashed out the drum intro to "Sleeping Dogs Lie", one of their best songs, and Niles pulled his mike off the stand, for the yo-yo tricks he only did when he was feeling good, coming in dead on the beat with all the force of a fist.

"Never trouble tired things
Let them rest in peace
Faded art, a jaded heart
Merit kind release
Angry words you spoke to me
Like poison darts that fly
The love you lack
Can't take them back
Let sleeping dogs lie…"

A red wash light fell over the band as the song progressed, sparking gold flashes off the blindingly metallic Strat and then gradually fading, so that everyone else was silhouetted against a pale blue gleam and only a white pin spot lit Turk down to guitar level. His dark-red leather outfit glowing like rubies, hair blazing as gold as his axe, he and Shane and Jay-Jay took the ride section to the last verse; then the spot faded too as they finished. The crowd was cranked to a pitch

such as even Rennie had seldom witnessed, and she hugged
herself, shivering with delight, knowing what was coming.
Rock audiences had started acting self-entitled about
encores lately, piggishly demanding moremoremore even
after a band had flat-out given everything it hadhadhad; Bill
Graham had even publicly chastised the fans for it, calling
them greedy spoiled brats. But Lionheart wasn't even near
that place so far tonight, and nobody'd heard nuthin' yet.

They did a cover of one of Evenor's songs, by way of
gracefully returning Prax's compliment of last week. Then,
for a change of pace, they shifted gears all the way back to
their roots, beginning with a startlingly pure instrumental
version of the old spiritual "Wayfaring Stranger", played
fast and poundingly up-tempo with Turk on banjo, Rardi
on violin and Mick on Rickenbacker twelve-string.

Still folked-up instrument-wise, they played a surprise
for Rennie, one of her absolute Lionheart favorites, which
she had first heard them do at Monterey three summers ago
and for which she herself had even suggested the name:
an eerie morris-dance tune called "The March to Atlantis",
Shane doing the bass line on a tuba he'd borrowed from the
brass section and Mick echoing Turk's banjo on melodeon.
Then they seamlessly segued into a lovely and seldom-
heard-live number, "Knight of Ghosts and Shadows", the
title track from their very first album, with Turk taking
lead vocal for the third time that night, which was a record
number for recent years and it was going to sound terrific
on the live LP. In the wings, Rennie exchanged a glance with
Prax, who had just joined her, ready for her own entrance:
yeah, if the pissant Niles did leave, Turk could manage the

singing chores just fine. He hadn't done anything wrong there either.

Now Turk had the gold Strat on again, and he and Mick and Rardi, also back on their usual instruments, were retuning quickly, not wanting to lose the momentum. Niles and Turk conferred with one another, laughing, and Rennie laid a hand on Prax's arm. She could feel how performance-tuned her friend was: the bowstring tautness, the eagerness to go, the intense focus that excluded even Rennie. Up on her toes like an Olympic sprinter in the blocks, like a Derby runner in the gate, Prax McKenna was ready to roll. This was what they did, she and Turk both, this was their job and their calling, their love and vocation, it was what they'd been born for…

"You're up, Mary Praxedes. Go get 'em."

The intro cut loose, the house lights blazed on, and Prax took Turk's cue and leaped out onstage, grabbing the mike from the stand in front of Shane; they hadn't wanted to tip off the crowd that somebody special — well, two special somebodies, actually — would be joining them. She yanked on the mike cord, cracking it like a whip, and got herself all the way across to center stage next to Niles before the crowd realized who it was and went wild.

They went wilder still when they recognized the unmistakable riff that was going on under their uproar, and as soon as they did they settled down immediately. This was more than rare and special, this was legend: Lionheart only ever did this live, and only when they were feeling solid and happy — their spectacular fifteen-minute cover medley of "Peggy Sue", "I'm A-Gonna Love You Too", "Not Fade

Away" and "Who Do You Love" — and nobody wanted to miss a note, especially not with Prax McKenna singing in.

The band was well down into the familiar chugging Buddy lead-in, considerably rocked up Lionheart style, when the evening's other surprise stepped onstage, with Turk's custom white-pearl Flying V on, and the audience exploded all over again. Black jeans and black T-shirt rumpled as usual and dark hair shaggy as ever, no flash leathers or velvets for him, Graham Sonnet slid from between the Marshall stacks to stand beside Turk, plugged in and picked up the riff. Grinning at his friend, Turk took everybody around one more time just because he felt like it, Prax whooping it up before the verse, hit it, boys! Then the vocal cue came rushing up, and Niles moved closer in, facing Prax, and the two singers put their ears back and opened their mouths and wailed.

As the band churned behind them, Niles and Prax began moving downstage, singing their lungs out straight into each other, smiling, challenging, until they were face to face a few feet apart with Turk and Gray just behind. When the vocal finished and Turk's Strat ran out into a screaming solo, they backed off and gave him the stage, then Rardi took an extended organ improv. After the next song, Gray spun off with a solo of his own, the V looked so cool and sounded great, and then he and Turk cut loose with an unplanned blues jam, trading fours and eights — echoey, hammering on, pulling off, heavy with distortion. Shane and Jay-Jay picked up the pace, pushing faster and faster, and the guitars ran before it, the crowd more and more delirious with every new building riff, until it all tumbled down in a mass of feedback and fuzz and spun back to Turk's long, filigreed, singing segue to the unmistakable riff.

"Walked forty-seven miles of barbed wire
Got a cobra snake for a necktie
Brand-new house by the roadside
Made out of rattlesnake hide…"

Rennie was dancing like a maenad with Prue Sonnet, with whom she'd been sitting in the audience and who had come backstage when Rennie did to be near her own old man— all consorts were allowed in the wings for encores, even the groupies du jour. She could see Niles' face and Turk's and Rardi's but nobody else's, either their backs were to her or they were out of her sightline. But judging from the way those boys were smiling, and the way Prax was sounding, and the way the audience was standing on the seats waving back and forth like wheat in a windstorm when they weren't tsunami-rushing the front of the stage, they were as happy as she was herself. She felt a pang: *God, why can't it always be like this…* The energy coming off that stage could power the Garden's lights; hell, it could power half of Manhattan Island.

Finally Shane and Mick and Jay-Jay began the pounding rhythm duel that signaled the move to close, bass throbbing like a paper-cut thumb. Turk and Gray laid down sinuous riffs over it, drawing the singers back in for a big double vocal before the instruments fell away and everyone onstage began chanting "Who do you love" to a handclap beat. Audience too. And then, from high above, rose petals began to fall from the nets that had held them, lightly at first, then like a pink and red and white and golden blizzard.

Petals storming around them like colored soft rain, Niles and Prax picked up the verse again, singing into each other at the top of their voices, while Gray and Turk stepped forward and joined them at the mikes, with Rardi's violin descanting over the top as the instruments all came crashing back. And then everybody came together as Turk single-handedly carried them all back to the major for the towering windup to what had turned into the half-hour closer to a one-hour encore to a three-hour show, rock marathoners with the finish line in sight.

It was like hitting a wall. Not even a millisecond's silence this time: as the last note slammed out, the audience noise was already cascading down like a chain-reaction collision on the freeway — wave upon wave of rather terrifying approval. Turk lifted his head and flung up his arm, flushed and triumphant, saluting the standing crowd as the petals continued to fall, a victorious gladiator at the games; then he and Prax and Niles and Gray threw their arms around each other, bowing and smiling and waving with the rest of the band, scooping up flung flowers and flinging them back to the front rows, clapping their own approval to the audience for having been such a good one.

At last they all went offstage again, a lot more slowly this time, and both they and the crowd knew they wouldn't be back, not after that. But the cheering and stamping went on for a long time all the same.

In the wings, Prax had already been grabbed by a delighted Ares and swung off her feet; Gray and Prue were happily hugging everyone within reach. Rennie, waiting over to one side, saw Turk looking around for her; then, when he saw her, she smiled and went to him, heedless of the cameras.

"Hi, honey," she said, reaching up to kiss him on the throat, beneath the beard. "Good day at the office?"

CHAPTER SEVEN

TURK CAME OUT of the shower all dripping and steamy and warm. Wrapping himself in a couple of towels, he began to dry off, secure in the knowledge that it was indeed good to be king: either everybody would be patiently awaiting his clean and leisured emergence or else they'd have taken all the limos but one and gone on ahead to the restaurant. Either way he and Rennie had wheels at their disposal, and if the others did go ahead and it wasn't too late, maybe the two of them could cut out with Prax and Ares over to Peter Luger in Brooklyn, for his favorite, porterhouse for four.

But yes, king was good. And they had all been kings tonight. What a trip. Three-hour show, another hour of encores, fired up and cheered on by the most amazing audience ever. They would incur staggering overtime from the union guys, not to mention cleaning up all those rose petals, but it was worth every penny. Anyway, the label was picking up a big chunk of the costs, not shifting them along to the band the way it usually went—part of Turk's contract terms, and Centaur was getting a bargain even so.

They had played better tonight than maybe they'd ever played in their entire Lionheart lives, even their raw and exhilarating club days. The crowd had even liked the acoustic stuff—though they'd been so into the whole trip that they'd probably have gotten off if the band had jammed

on "The Farmer in the Dell". Thanks to Prax and Gray—
Christ, what a voice she had, and how amazing had Gray
been, they should all play together more often, maybe they
could do a joint album on one of the labels, if they could
work out the legalities—thanks to them, the encore medley
had been epic, even better than planned or hoped.

It had all been recorded for the two-disc album they
planned on slotting in next year; they'd had a remote
truck stationed on the inside Garden ramp, equipped
with a custom-built console and all the latest equipment,
and a sound board inside the stadium with their producer
Leo Rafferty and their genius engineer Thom Courtenay
sitting at the controls. And, at Rennie's suggestion, the
whole thing had been both filmed and videotaped for some
future use, they didn't know what: maybe a short film or
TV documentary, maybe just to have a record of this night
for themselves, something that they could watch when
they were all ninety and doddering around the Woodstock
Nursing Home for Aged Rockers, getting medicinal-
purpose acid from the longhaired staff.

He sat down on the locker room bench to employ a hand
dryer on his hair; ordinarily he wouldn't have bothered, just
toweled it dry and brushed it out and gone home, but they
had a fancy Centaur dinner to attend and trade-magazine
pictures to pose for and Rennie would be sad if he wasn't
nicely groomed. By all rights he should be exhausted, they
should be blotting him up off the floor; but he wasn't tired in
the slightest. *Au contraire*: he was totally energized—amped
to the teeth, just not on speed. Well, with a crowd like that
shouting your name and feeding you vibes for four hours

straight, that was hardly surprising. That audience had deserved Lionheart tonight, and Lionheart had deserved that audience. Each had given it their absolute best. Anyway, he felt ready to ride out to conquer the world, or at the very least jam for another four hours, he could always crash later, at home; but the sure signal that it had been a superconcert was that he was even more ravenously hungry than he usually was.

His mate called it soul starvation: she said that he put out so much psychic energy onstage that his chakras got depleted and hunger was the symptom, that he was always so famished after a show because he needed to ground himself again, like taking on ballast. Made sense. If the four of them did manage to escape to Luger's, though, they were ordering steak for *six*, and he wasn't sharing the two extra portions with anyone. What he really wanted to do was take Rennie home and tie her to the bed and fuck her senseless; that was the way he always felt after a gig, especially a successful one, and he knew she felt the same—why else had she worn that outrageous little dress and those even more outrageous little trinkets? But all in good time.

Turk finished with his hair, set the dryer aside and began to pull on the clean clothes meant to be worn to dinner, a black cashmere v-neck sweater and black suede pants and black boots—his Hamlet look, as Rennie, who was always totally turned on by it, had enthusiastically dubbed it. The band and their ladies were all being hosted to dinner by Centaur Records president Freddy Bellasca, who'd flown in from L.A. with other label brass for this big-time rock occasion, and if he had to be paraded around like a prize poodle, he'd wanted to at least be comfortable.

Someone had hung everything neatly in an open locker, ready for when he came offstage. Later, when the band was gone, someone else would collect the clothes he'd worn in from home and drop them at the prow house, and take the leather outfit and all the other guys' costumes away for cleaning—his doublet had been soaked through. And Pudge would carefully check all his guitars for needed repairs and then clean them and pack them away. He didn't have to lift a finger.

These days none of them had to worry about picking up after themselves—one of the many pleasant things about being superstars was you got to have minions. Not to mention you also got to actually have stuff that had to be picked up and looked after. Stuff was good. When they'd first started out, in tiny, grotty English blues clubs in the dodgier London and Bristol and Midlands boroughs, they'd played in their street clothes—the only ones they had—and had cherished and cosseted their second- and third-hand instruments and equipment like first-born children.

They hadn't had much of anything then. Even Turk, who'd been heavy into rebellion in those days and refusing to touch tuppence of his family's money—not that they were offering any pence at all, hoping to literally starve the wayward heir back into the ducal bosom—had had only two guitars, his treasured Gibson and the equally precious Martin dreadnought; and that only because he'd owned them from his Oxford days; otherwise he wouldn't have been able to afford them. His first Strat had been received gratefully as a hand-me-down from his good friend Graham

Sonnet, who was upgrading; it was only recently that "second-hand used" had become "vintage pre-owned", and much sought-after. As for his parents, they had long since come around, and now attended Lionheart gigs with pleasure; even his grandparents the Duke and Duchess had shown up for a big London benefit at the Royal Opera House in Covent Garden, with several members of royalty in the audience. Though, thankfully, no family members had been present tonight, or royalty either, at least as far as anyone knew.

But he and the other guys had worked like galley slaves back then, and since then too: every step of every road trip and every hour in the studio and every night of their performing lives, they'd chained themselves to their oars and pulled as hard as they could. Ramming speed. Nobody could say that Lionheart had had it easy, hadn't totally paid their dues: they'd given the same flat-out full-on effort when they were getting five quid a night as they did now when they were getting fifty thousand; no reason on earth for them to feel guilty about having minions to do their housekeeping.

And now the tour was finally over. After three months on the road, tonight had been the last hurrah, and he didn't have to *look* at another guitar — except for his daily practice hour, of course, which counted as meditation, not performance. At least not until they started laying down tracks for the new album. They'd have six or so weeks off; he and Rennie had talked about getting out of town for a while, as they'd mentioned to Eric and Petra. Or, depending on how they felt, maybe the band would just start right in recording after New Year's. Nothing was set in stone, and he didn't have to think about it now anyway.

He'd take her away anywhere she wanted to go, of course, but what he really wanted for himself was a nice chunk of downtime to settle into the prow house; he'd been on almost continuous tour since Woodstock back in August and hadn't had much chance to just live in the new place with Rennie and enjoy it, arrange his books and pictures to his liking. She'd done an amazing job: once he'd gone on the road, she'd had to handle the renovation single-handed, in addition to everything else in her life and his and theirs together, like his grandfather's death, and he himself getting one step closer to the big title, and their upcoming wedding, not to mention her usual murder trip — the stuff she'd had to deal with at Woodstock and Big Pink. And she hadn't complained once about how *she* had had to do everything and all *he'd* had to do was sign the checks. Actually, he hadn't done even that: the duchy estate managers had taken care of it. So she really deserved him carrying her off someplace nice for a romantic holiday.

The rest of Lionheart was heading home for Christmas, to London or L.A. or wherever, and coming back to New York in late January: he'd managed to persuade the band to record here for a change, and the famed Record Plant studios on West 45th Street had already been tentatively booked. The last album had been a big departure from their usual sound and style, but the next one would be more of a return to form, and Turk wanted to work with a new producer in a new studio — someone who wasn't locked into the Lionheart paradigm and would be open to new ideas. Besides, he had a brand-new home studio of his very own, down in the prow house cellar, and he was eager to try it out.

Because he had quite a lot of new ideas. If *Cities of the Plain* had been a different kind of sound for them—lush, dense strings and horns and woodwinds, extra guitars and keyboards, even some chick backup vocalists—this new one was going to be different in a whole other way, and he didn't want to record with the same old gang they always used. It would be back to hard blues-rock, but in Lionheart style and with New York production values; he was really excited about it.

Of course, Centaur was already worried—their eternal mantra was "Hooks! Singles! Airplay!"—but they'd just have to take what the band chose to give them and trust Turk's judgment. Like *Cities*, the new record might not be as successful as their previous albums, or it might well be more so. He'd seen how it worked for other bands when they tried to break the mold, even a little: the Stones, the Airplane, the Doors, Stoneburner, Bosom Serpent—none of them could catch a break lately. See how it had been for themselves with *Cities*, they'd been absolutely crucified. Well, *he* had been, mostly—the perils of being the founder and public face and chief creator of Lionheart. Fans could be incredibly fickle: they might be disappointed or they might be knocked out, but they were always vocal. As for critics, they could be scathing or they could be utterly wowed. You just never knew. But man, you had to try, every time; otherwise what was the point? You could only do it for yourself—not for the label, not for the critics, not even for the fans. Just for you, because it was *your* name and *your* face and *your* sound out there.

And you had to give your absolute best every night, no matter what, because there were always people there who'd never seen you perform live before, people who'd been fans for years, who'd maybe saved up their bread for the album and a once-in-a-lifetime concert ticket for weeks beforehand, and who totally deserved the same show, or as close as the band could get it, as the show they'd given tonight. There wasn't room for laziness or sloppiness. No repeats onstage: it had to be One-take Wayland, One-take Lombardi, One-take Clay, one-take everybody, all the way, all the time. Onstage, you didn't get do-overs the way you did in the studio. It was perfection or nothing. And it had better be perfection.

Because the fans supported you. They made you famous and rich, they let you do what you loved doing—and in return you owed them the best you *could* do, even if it meant you got up after you collapsed unconscious onstage and you went back out and you finished the show full-strength knowing there was an ambulance waiting to take you to the hospital the second you unslung your axe. That was the deal—as he saw it, anyway, though others of his peers didn't necessarily agree.

But he didn't have to think about that now either. The show was over, the tour was over, and all he had to do now was to chat up the distributors and promotion guys and critics outside in the dressing room and then sit through Freddy's annoying bloody dinner with the rest of the band and the label brass who'd been invited.

For all his wistful hopes, Turk knew perfectly well that he couldn't sneak off. That was the price you paid for being the leader, the creator, the frontman. The one everybody wanted to meet, to talk to, to hang out with, to have a beer with, to go to bed with. Because that too was part of the deal — though not that going to bed with part, not anymore, those days were over. They had never really happened anyway, not the way they did for other people on his level, and he was glad of that — it was a question of personal standards, and he wasn't much like his colleagues in that area anyway. But he'd always been glad of what he'd been able to find for himself in his music, and in his heritage too, once he'd come to terms with it. He'd just never thought he'd ever manage to find anything of worth in his star status. And it wasn't an ego thing, and he wasn't ungrateful; it was just that there were demands he didn't always feel like meeting. One did what one could, and tried not to let it get overly wearisome, over and over again — not the music, not the heritage, but the fame part of the job. But it had brought him some real rewards; and now it was time to go outside and join her.

Sitting on the bench, he refastened the silver bracelet onto his right wrist and his watch on his left, then slipped the new necklace his mate had made him over his head again — a strand of tiny ruby beads, the twin of the sapphire beads she'd given him last year to go with the blue Whisky stage leathers.

After Tansy's death, for reasons of her own — maybe reasons even she was unaware of — Rennie had taken up making jewelry. As Tansy had done, she enjoyed fashioning intricate bead necklaces with her own nimble fingers, to wear herself and bestow on friends and even sell in the boutiques of other friends, and designing other pieces to have made up by pros, like her lion pendant. Turk was glad of all the things she made him: the clothes were armor and protection, the jewelry weapons. It all felt like her hands on him, like herself interposed between him and harm. Couldn't hurt. Now he tucked the beads inside the sweater's v-neck, beneath his jade pendant, and went outside.

After the shower room's damp warmth, the air felt shockingly cold. Guests were happily thronging the locker rooms and grazing the restocked buffet tables and spilling out into the hallway; Rennie and Prax, together with Gray and Prue Sonnet, had been fending them off while he changed. When he came up behind her and put his arms around her, slipping his hands inside the open dress front to cup her bare breasts, Rennie sighed with relief and leaned back against him, sliding her hand between them to grab him through his pants.

"Problems?" he murmured, bending his head to bite her ear.

"Not now...it's always fun copping a mutual feel in public, makes me feel very groupie-ish. They want *you*, though. Well, who doesn't? You're not off the clock yet: you need to talk to half the people here, I'm afraid."

"Not my favorite part of the job, this." He grinned. "Although, lately, there have been some perks." He closed his hands on her a little tighter.

She moved her own, more discreet grasp. "No doubt."

"It won't take long. You have chores to do, too."

She reached up to touch his face; then, despite the many covertly, and overtly, watching eyes, she ran her hand into his hair and pulled his head down to kiss him—something they seldom did where others could see. But just now it felt right.

"I know. I'll go talk to Freddy and the guy from the News and the trade writers, shall I? You make nice with the distributors. And don't forget to say hi to Fitz and his wife."

"Lady Alexandra Fairfax," said Turk promptly. "I hadn't forgotten. Sister of the current Earl of Whitstell. We met her at Tarrant House."

"We did, and you both worked out that you're fifth cousins thrice removed or something... And then there's dinner with the label monkeys to get through. It'll all be over before one. Gray and Prue had to leave, but they said they'll come stay with us from Monday, before they go back to London. Oh, and don't be thinking we can hijack the limo and slope off over to Luger's instead. Not gonna happen, my lord!"

Turk shook his head, laughing. "Damn, you're good!"

"Why, yes, I am. But really I just know my guy."

She watched out of the corner of her eye as he walked across the room and courteously introduced himself—yeah, right, as if they didn't know who he was—to the distributors, who were all visibly thrilled that he actually knew who *they* were, and what they did for him. On these occasions of Turk at work, whether it was meeting his "employees" the label folk, or his "employers" the fans, Rennie was completely happy to be in his shadow. He was the star, she was the professional observer: she looked on with pride, was delighted to stand aside for him, and did indeed have work of her own to do, as he had reminded her.

His rock stature in itself had never been a problem for them, though there had been a few darkly jealous mutterings from outside sources about conflict of interest. To be sure, bedfellows could make strange politics; but she had always scrupulously kept favoritism out of her professional life, and had now entirely given up covering Lionheart, though Evenor and several other groups she was friendly with remained within her writing purview — well, she couldn't stop writing about *everyone* she was on cordial terms with, she'd be reduced to covering bar bands in Dubuque. Besides, she was by no means the only reporter who was entwined with a subject, in love, sex or friendship; she could think, off-hand, of at least a dozen others, female and male alike, and probably there were a whole lot more she didn't know about.

No, it was Turk's future dukely status that had proven to be so much more problematic than his rock stardom, since it involved, inevitably, her own future duchessly status, and she had been badly spooked by that from the moment she'd found out about it. But over almost two years now, as they had lived together in L.A. and now here in New York, they had painfully, painstakingly, hammered that out between them, and had over the past spring, summer and fall — a time that had seen Turk's grandfather die and Turk himself elevated in title — come to terms with both issues. It would be fine. It *was* all fine. It couldn't not be.

By the time they left the Garden, a surprisingly large fan

contingent still lingered outside—fans who had patiently watched all the other members of Lionheart come out and who knew there was one who had yet to emerge, and that he'd have an equally famous friend with him.

So perhaps a hundred fervent admirers, held back by cops, stood out there in the bitterly cold night, not caring that it had started snowing again, clustering around the one remaining limousine that was parked on Eighth Avenue, motor running, as near the backstage entrance as it could get. They knew perfectly well for whom the car was waiting, and when they saw Turk and Prax finally appear they made a delighted surge through the police lines and barricades. By dint of much practice, the little group had it all down by now, like a football play being executed: Ares immediately assumed the blocking position, Rennie tucked her hair inside her cloak and hurried ahead to the car, and the chauffeur quickly got out and opened the rear door for them to use for cover.

Turk graciously signed autographs over the hood of the car, refusing to stop until everyone who wanted one had been signed for, as was his courteous practice. Then Ares, whose hard, alert glance had never once stopped moving over the crowd, drew him away and pushed him into the back seat, where Prax, who had been signing autographs of her own, and Rennie were already ensconced, and climbed in after them.

"Well, my legions, not a bad night's work, if I do say so myself." Turk relaxed into the upholstery and unbuttoned his shearling coat, glad of the car's warmth. He well remembered Rennie's account of Jim Morrison dramatically flinging his jacket to the Garden crowd back last January and regretting it afterwards as he shivered in the cold outside, the crowd most uncooperatively not having flung it back — and Turk wasn't about to imitate the gesture in an even colder December.

As the car pulled out and headed uptown on Eighth Avenue, he twisted round for a quick last glimpse of the fans with the Garden walls looming above them, and turned back with a grin that made him look seventeen again. After all these years, that kind of thing still jazzed him as much as it had the first time, he still needed to convince himself it was real, that they were there for him… He turned again to the limo's other occupants.

"Once more, Miss McKenna, thanks ever so. That was a total trip, having you up there with us."

"My pleasure," said Prax demurely, as Turk reached for her suede-gloved hand and kissed it. "I had a pretty nice time myself, thank *you* for thinking of me. And not forgetting our friend Mr. Sonnet, who is not in our midst at the moment but who deserves praise and honor even so."

"Indeed he does, and we do not forget. And thank you Ares, for that nice piece of professional courtesy just now. You may have thought we didn't notice, but we did."

"Hey, man, it was nothing — consider it a very inadequate payment for that terrific surprise from this one here." He dropped a kiss of his own on Prax's head. "Totally blown away…you did great, honey. You were *all* great."

"The fans too. I don't think I've ever heard a crowd as loud as that one," said Rennie. "They worked as hard as you did, your lordship."

Turk grinned. "Rardi said he couldn't even hear me when I changed the set list onstage. He said when I was counting off he and the other guys didn't even know what the hell we were going into."

"Well, the fans quieted down enough to listen, at least," said Ares. "Give them points for being respectful."

Turk put his arm around Rennie—she was looking adorable in the gorgeously soft fur cloak, cuddly and wickedly alight—and bent his head to hers, his mouth against her ear.

"Hard to get *at* you in all that fur... Did I tell you yet how much I like that dress?"

"Ossie Clark. One of your countrymen."

"Oh yes?"

"He says he designs his dresses so you can pull the top down and the skirt up and fuck in them anywhere at a moment's notice."

"My kind of designer. Makes you look good on me..." He moved his other hand. "Nice jewelry—your old man give you that?"

Cries of horror and protest from Ares and Prax. "No, no, friends here, don't want to be seeing that sort of thing! Later at home for that!"

"Hey, I'm English, I'm a rock star, I can do whatever I want—"

But half-reclining as they were on the bench seat opposite, the other two weren't exactly dissimilarly involved themselves, and Rennie pointed this out.

"It's just what you *do* after you get offstage, isn't it?" said Prax, grinning. "All this energy with nowhere to go, gotta work it off somehow with somebody — or some body. It's like you're a Viking and you've put in your pillage time for the day and now you get to have a spot of ravishing as your reward."

Turk laughed. "Exactly! I feel as if I've just sailed in off the North Sea with my longship fleet and taken a Saxon town."

He looked as if he could have, too, Rennie considered — that kind of hair and beard and bearing were probably last seen to such public advantage on Guthrum the Dane. Against whom some of Turk's ancestors had reputedly fought. And at the side of whom some others of Turk's ancestors had also reputedly fought. And who was reputedly a Turk ancestor himself. Maybe Vikings too had had groupies... But the mood of the heart of Lionheart was the one mood that mattered, onstage, backstage, at home, here in this car. Besides being always famished after a show, Turk was also always effervescent, charged by his performance, amped and fizzed, shooting off sparks in all directions, and Rennie loved to see him like that. Not to mention, as Prax had pointed out, more than even usually amorous. And she loved to see him like that too.

He hadn't yet finished dialing himself back down to normal, that coming-back-to-human-size-from-larger-than-life thing rock stars did, though it seemed to be happening more quickly than usual tonight, perhaps because Prax was there and she had to do the same thing herself and there just wasn't room for both their legends in the limo at the same time. Richard and Praxie, fine, sure, no problem. But "Turk Wayland" and "Prax McKenna" weren't going to fit in the same back seat; the same stage had barely been big enough. Good thing Gray — "Graham Sonnet," rather — wasn't there too, or Ares and Rennie would have had to get out and walk…

She stole a glance at Turk as he disputed good-humoredly with Ares. God, he looked great — exultant and gorgeous and sexy as hell. It wasn't an ego thing at all, his mood of triumph. He knew the band had pulled off something amazing tonight, and he had every right to be proud — yes, and she hadn't worn those nipple rings and that other thing in vain, had she, no, she hadn't.

"So that would make Ares and me the villagers to reward the pillagers?" she asked, cuddling closer against Turk and putting one hand on his suede-clad thigh, drawing his free hand into the warmth of the chinchilla cloak to entwine with her own, or with whatever hidden else he wanted it to entwine with. "Well, I guess it's not such a lot to ask, Ares, is it, enduring an occasional wench moment for these two, they're pretty much worth it…"

"Beats tossing TV sets out of hotel windows."

They were companionably silent for a while as the limousine swept north through a dark and snow-filled Central Park, on its way to the Upper East Side restaurant. Then Prax:

"Turk, what the hell is Niles' problem?"

Turk never moved his head from where it was resting against the top of Rennie's. "Meaning?"

"Well, I didn't rehearse all that much with you guys, but even I can see that something's going on. He seemed to be — distancing himself? Is that the word I want?"

Turk felt Rennie's hand tighten on his thigh in warning, and got her message: Don'tdon'tdon'tdon't*DON'T* get into it now, we have to sit at the same table with Niles all through dinner, you can talk to her about it later…

Rennie fixed her best friend with an unreadable glance. "Praxie. Niles is just going through some—trips. Yes. Trips." A glance unreadable by their men, at least: after an apparently telepathic moment Prax gave a tiny nod of solemn comprehension in return, and that seemed to be the end of their conversation. If you could call it conversation.

Turk and Ares exchanged a glance, too, but it didn't clear up a damn thing for either of them. Turk was just as baffled as his friend: he knew how it worked for him and Rennie, but now he suddenly found himself wondering how it worked for Rennie and Prax. He had seen it so many times, where one of them would say something brief and cryptic, or even just look, and the other one somehow knew exactly what was going on. The band had a rapport that was not unlike it, especially when they were onstage or when they were working out a new song. But he had never had a friend like that in his life, though Ares was becoming one, and Gray Sonnet was even closer to it—and only since Rennie had come along had he ever had a woman like that in his life.

But the woman in his life looked up at him now, and saw what she saw in his face, and then began to talk loudly about how sure, yeah, the Stones had been amazing but Lionheart had wiped the Garden floor with them, and what a good thing that Mick and the boys had already left town so they wouldn't have to kill themselves in the face of the shame and humiliation, and since McCartney was "Macca" and Clapton was "Slowhand" and Turk was "Slider" and Rennie was "Strider", what should Prax be called ("Your Majesty," that lady suggested, only half in jest), and the nicknames started flying, as thick and fast as the snowflakes outside.

The Centaur duty dinner for forty, including the band and their ladies (official consorts only, no pickups allowed), in the private dining room of the snob-infested upper East Side French restaurant, was so predictable it might have been scripted—as, indeed, it pretty much was. They all had their parts by rote: the label boys were terrifically impressed with themselves for having dinner with big-time rock stars, and the big-time rock stars were gracious and dutiful. Freddy Bellasca was overenthusiastic and fake-hearty, while Turk was amused, detached and wary—though like the other guys he knew perfectly well what was expected of him, and as long as he was signed to Centaur he would continue to do his job. It was always the same deal after a big concert or TV appearance: Freddy would use proximity to the band as both a carrot and a stick for the lackeys, Come have dinner with Turk and the boys—a little reward for efforts rendered. Plus it made the uninvited work harder so *they'd* be asked next time.

By this stage of their career, Lionheart was well used to this kind of dog and pony show, and they were usually very good at playing along, taking one for the team. But tonight Niles Clay seemed to have lost all his team spirit and was playing up instead—from the starter course on, he'd been by turns boorish, patronizing and, yes, borderline offensive. Freddy was hurt and bewildered: not knowing what to do, he pushed Niles harder to make nice, so of course the more he pushed the worse Niles behaved.

Rennie could see Freddy clearly thought that Niles' surliness had taken away all the extra points that having Prax McKenna there had won him, Freddy, in his lieutenants' eyes. A huge star in her own right and *not* a Centaur artist, it was pure gravy that she'd come along to dinner, let alone contributed so memorably onstage. The fact that she'd done both out of love and friendship for Turk and Rennie was lost on Bellasca; as such motives always were.

But somehow they all got through dinner without anyone sticking a fork into anyone else, though it came dangerously close a few times; Turk himself, or more accurately the Marquess of Raxton, and, somewhat surprisingly, Prax were the chief smoothers-over. Still, by dessert Turk was completely fed up: between them, Niles and Freddy had managed to almost ruin his beautiful mood. Time for a tiny bombshell over the chocolate *pêche Melba*, sycophantically renamed *pêche Ravenne* on the pretentious souvenir menu — what a clever boy he'd been to prearrange the detonation. He dropped a casual kiss on Ravenne's neck to cover his whispered instruction in her ear — "Go for it, sweetheart!" — and she was away.

"You know, Freddy, you *could* always sign Niles as a solo act," Rennie mused a few minutes later, as if the idea had only just occurred to her, in a lovely clear carrying voice that no one could possibly avoid hearing. "If Turk takes the band somewhere else, I mean, after the contract's up and if Niles doesn't want to come along. Or is it like baseball? Maybe you could trade Niles for Stephen Stills and a bass player to be named later."

Aaaaand we're done! She took a big bite of *pêche* and held back an evil grin as she felt Niles' narrow-eyed glare, heard Prax's barely suppressed choke of laughter, didn't dare look at Freddy. Turk had coached her on exactly what to say — the baseball line was ad lib — and she was only following orders. Anyway, he would have carefully observed all the reactions he needed to see. He'd tell her later how everyone had responded. Hey, that alone almost made up for not being able to go to Luger's.

After that, no one was much for lingering. Turk let Lord Raxton make Turk's and Rennie's farewells, which he did charmingly, as only a bored English nobleman who doesn't want to appear bored can do, and Rennie pulled on her furs and headed for the door. Niles muttered something about going down to the Fillmore East to catch Sledger Cairns' last set, which had Rennie worried for a moment: he better not be expecting her and Turk to offer him a lift, since they were headed home and home was only a few blocks north of Bill Graham Central. But he left on his own, saying he wanted to walk for a while and get some air, and then he'd catch a cab.

Rennie and Turk were glad of the quiet ride downtown, and instructed the driver to go the long way round and through the park several times, taking advantage of being alone in the limo to indulge in a spot of Viking-and-wenching. Prax and Ares had already departed by cab for the Plaza, and would no doubt be out of touch for a day or two, if their pattern held.

"So this is what bigtime rock stars do after big huge important concerts," she teased, a little out of breath, her forearms resting on his thighs where she still knelt in front of him on the limo's thick carpet, his fingers twined in her hair. "Do they go out partying their nice suede pants off with their bigtime rock star pals? They do not. They go home with their old lady and sit in the kitchen eating scrambled eggs. Though pants off will certainly figure into it at some point, one would hope. Oh wait, they already have."

"Did you want to go out?" asked Turk, surprised. "We can still go somewhere—it's not late, I'm not tired at all. Actually, I think I'd really like to celebrate a bit—"

"I thought you might," said Rennie with pardonable smugness, leaning forward again, "and it's already taken care of. There's some company coming—lots and lots of people in town, very convenient—and I invited a whole bunch of them to slouch on over any time after one. Which is, let's see the watch there, hmm, not too far away now. If they show up early, Hudson will take care of them. Mick and Shane thought they'd turn up if they can't find any groupies, yeah right, like *that*'ll happen. Sledger said she might stop by when her late set is done. So you, bigtime rock star, will get to party with bigtime rock star pals after all."

Silence in the back seat for several minutes, or mostly silence. Then Turk, a little hoarsely: "Yes, well, after I've had something to eat to keep my strength up, now that you've worn me to a complete frazzle. Can we still have scrambled eggs before they come? Can I have a *steak*? I didn't get nearly enough to eat at that pretentious greasy spoon, you know how hungry I am after a gig—"

"Always something to eat at home. Pants on or off. Aren't you glad I made this pair so conveniently...accessible? Speaking of getting enough to eat—"

"—At this particular moment, very glad indeed."

"Happy to take care of your problem, Flash, all you have to do is ask."

He pulled her up onto the seat, leaned down. "And speaking of pants off—no doubt that would be why you wore this charming, ah, bauble?"

"Well, you're the one who gave it to me," she murmured against and around him as he pressed her into the upholstery. "God, you're so easy."

"Only with you, madam. Only with you."

When they woke up well into Sunday afternoon and came yawning their barefoot way downstairs, Hudson, who'd stayed up late herself to help with the party—again catered by the Second Avenue Deli, nobody had to assemble so much as a sandwich, and Turk had gotten his hoped-for steak and eggs—came to meet them and quietly delivered a somber message.

They stared at one another, shocked and disbelieving. But it was on the radio, and all over the papers spread out on the kitchen table, so it must be true. Being local, it was even nudging out the other shocking rock news of the day: the onstage knife murder that had incredibly taken place at the Stones' thank-you-fans concert, the one Keith had told them about, held yesterday at some dusty San Francisco

Bay Area auto racetrack called Altamont.

Not to mention the announcement that the savage Hollywood murders that had so shocked the nation last summer had been committed by one Charles Manson and a band of killer zombie followers, who all had connections to the L.A. music biz as well, and whom they all had heard of, seen around the scene. or even spoken to. Lionheart itself had actually been in their sights for a while: Rennie remembered them very well from an Aquarius gig last year, where they'd homed in on Turk like heat-seeking missiles, how she'd protectively kept Ares and herself in front of him like human shields. Both of them, and Francher as well, had sensed the vampire vibes instantly and had taken steps to neutralize them, and after a couple of weeks of trying to break into the band's circle, the psychos had departed in defeat, aware that Lionheart was not in the cards for them. Thankfully. But horrible to think that they'd turned elsewhere, to other musicians and actress Sharon Tate and her friends... Must be some big mean dark star shining down on the rockerverse this weekend.

But if all that was true, then obviously the hometown horror story was also true: Sledger Cairns' sound guy had been found dead with a groupie, in a tiny cemetery several blocks downtown from the Fillmore East.

Quite a weekend for rockdeath, as Hudson sadly observed. The speculation was that the two unfortunates might have OD'd, or they might have frozen to death; it had been snowing hard in the early hours, the worst night yet of the unseasonal cold snap. Maybe it was both: maybe they'd gotten stoned in the privacy of the little graveyard,

then, zoned out on snow, they'd zoned out *in* the snow —
just peacefully, well, chilled, under a pristine white blanket
that had had no warmth in it for them.

"Poor sad buggers," said Turk fervently, setting down
the Daily News. "At least it didn't happen in front of the
audience, like Altamont. And aren't we glad we've got a
cast-iron alibi."

He turned on the small kitchen TV set to wait for the
early-evening local news program they favored, and
counted off on his fingers. "Onstage in full sight of twenty
thousand people all evening long. Late supper in a public
restaurant — probably a hundred diners saw us there. Then
blamelessly *chez nous* with a bunch more people, let's see
now, who can vouch for us: the Harrisons, the Dylans,
two-thirds of Cream, Prisca Quarters, John Sebastian, most
of Evenor, the Sakerhawks, Shane and Jay-Jay and Rardi,
most of our crew, bunch of your rock scribbler pals, Diego
and Belinda, some Centaur people including your old
schoolmate Gerry Langhans and his wife, and, well, I don't
really remember and who else, until just about dawn, I
believe it was? Right. Great idea of yours to ask them all over,
by the way — I usually don't like a lot of company after a gig."

"I just had the feeling that last night you somehow
would."

"Useful, too, that they were here," said Turk, pursuing it.

"Yes, wasn't it."

"Almost as if you knew we'd need an alibi and so you
deliberately kept us public all night long."

"Now how the hell would I know *that*?"

"This is what I'm always asking... Well, either way,

we're off the hook for this one, and I must say I am quite glad of it."

"It is a most pleasant change," agreed Rennie gravely. "But very sad and terrible for Sledger. We must comfort her."

"Game on, then. But since we're not involved in the murder—if indeed it *is* murder and wherever you're in the vicinity it generally is—we don't have to *get* involved, do we? Or rather, I mean, do *you*? Rennie? *Do* you?"

Before she could answer, the doorbell rang, and Hudson went to answer it. She came back flustered, and holding on by main force to the collar of a lunging, barking, snarling, fangs-bared Macduff, Thane of Gondor.

"Sorry, he just—I couldn't—"

Before she could get anything else out, Niles Clay pushed past her and the furious collie and stood at the top of the kitchen stairs. He looked as if he hadn't been to bed and had slept out in the park in the snow, and that would be because he hadn't and he had.

"Niles?" asked Turk, his initial flare of annoyance dying away at the obvious distress his singer projected. *God, he's shaking like he needs a fix, and he isn't even into smack...* "Macduff, quiet! Niles, what is it, man?"

Niles wasn't looking at his bandmate, though, but straight at Rennie, with bleak and desperate eyes. Finally he spoke.

"Help me. I don't know who else to go to. You have to help me. I think I killed them."

CHAPTER EIGHT

NILES WAS HUDDLED miserably in a big leather armchair in the triangular living room. The windows to either side showed fine dry snow slowly falling in the glow of the streetlamps; it was dark out by now, very cold but not windy, and the people trudging by below the windows were all bundled up like little Russian dolls.

Rennie, to whom an honest appeal for help was always grounds for canceling attitude debt, or at least deferring it, had decreed that there would be no discussion of the situation, however dire it might appear or in fact actually be, until Niles had been taken to the kitchen and warmed up and given something substantial to eat.

So she and Hudson had put together a pot of tea and a plate of untouched party leftovers: overstuffed roast beef sandwiches and chicken soup with dumplings. Niles, sitting at the oak table wrapped in one of Rennie's grandmother's "affagans", had hoovered it all up as if he hadn't eaten in days, shivering the whole time, while the others resolutely kept up a stream of inconsequential chat.

Having been sternly commanded by his master to silence and the floor, Macduff had contented himself with glaring at the new arrival from his nose-on-paws guard post at the top of the four room-wide steps leading down from the dining room. It was obvious that only orders prevented him from continuing to say pointed things at the visitor, but being a well-mannered dog he kept it to himself for now and hoped for better times to come — *bad vibes going on here, you're a nasty man, I can tell you're afraid, Pack Leader may be okay with you but Leader's Mate and Beta Female are definitely not and neither am I, my ancestors chased off wolves, I have really sharp teeth…*

When Niles had stuffed as much as he possibly could, they all went up into the living room, where a wood fire burned in the big white-marble hearth, to sit and talk and hear and consider what should be done. Hudson handed him a mug of tea laced with honey and echinacea, and Rennie passed him a Valium, and Turk set a crystal tumbler of single-malt on the table in front of him, and they waited for him to tell his story at his own pace.

"After I left the restaurant last night," said Niles hoarsely, after a while, "I was in such a foul mood I decided I wasn't fit to be around anyone, so I left Keitha to go back to the hotel on her own, not very nice of me, I know. I walked in the snow for a while until I found a cab and then I went down to the Fillmore East. In fact, I saw you two getting out of the car here, in front of the house, when my cab stopped at the light on the corner, and I thought I'd been snotty and stupid and I should get out and come over and have some fun at the party, that maybe you'd even be glad to see me." A tiny hopeful pause, as if he expected some reassurance there, like Oh absolutely old boy, we're always glad to see you, but they were silent, and he continued, a little deflated. "Anyway, I didn't. I went on to the Fillmore and just went in. Sledger wasn't on yet, so I went up to the dressing room and we all did a little coke. Anyone who didn't have to be on stage for her set stayed right there, and we all did a lot more coke."

"You stayed there the whole set?" asked Turk. "When did you leave?"

Niles was clutching the pottery mug in both shaking hands, trying not to let the tea spill. "I don't know. I reckon the show was over. Well, it must have been, mustn't it, because the sound guy left with us, and if Sledger had still been on he couldn't have done. Anyway, I remember leaving the theater with him and this groupie, all three of us wired to the gills on coke, running down Second Avenue all crazy and wild in the snow and finding this little cemetery tucked away on some side street with houses all round."

"Marble Cemetery," said Hudson, from her seat on the couch next to Rennie. Her face was impassive, her tone severely polite: she was struggling, for Turk's sake, to conceal both her great dislike for Niles and her equally great delight, for Rennie's sake, that Niles now found himself in such a sticky situation. "One of the oldest in Manhattan. Though that one"—she pointed out the window to the cobblestoned graveyard that surrounded St. Mark's Church across the street—"is even older. Nobody new ever gets in either one, though I think relatives of incumbents, or recumbents actually, I guess, can still be buried in the one you were—in."

"Yes?" said Niles doubtfully. "Well, it was very pretty and very quiet and the snow kept falling, and we were as I say very stoned, so we climbed this big wrought-iron fence and went inside."

"And then?" prompted Rennie.

"Did some more coke. That's all."

"What do you mean, that's all?"

Niles picked up the Waterford tumbler of whiskey and drained it in three gulps, and Turk silently refilled it before he started shaking again.

"I mean that's all. If there was more, I don't remember it. I don't remember anything. I woke up, or came to, on a bench in Tompkins Square Park about ten minutes before I was here pounding on your door. I don't think I'd been there long, because I wasn't cold and there wasn't much snow on me and nobody'd mugged me. But I have no idea where I spent the night; somewhere, obviously, or else I'd be frozen to death just like—just like—"

He was shivering violently again, and Rennie, without comment, passed him another affagan that had been lying on the sofa, which he huddled into immediately and then resumed the story. "Well, I had money and I was famished, so I figured I'd get something to eat at that Ukrainian coffeeshop across from the park, and catch a cab up to the hotel after. But as I was sitting at the counter, I saw the local news on the TV set; they had the whole story."

He ran a hand over his face and looked up. "I knew you two were only a couple of blocks away. I ran all the way over. So here I am. And they're dead. And maybe I killed them."

There was a long, incredibly thoughtful silence. Niles peered hopefully over the rim of his tumbler at the impassive faces, but nobody met his glance. A log snapped in the fireplace, but still nobody stirred.

Then: "Rubbish," said Rennie, so bracingly that Niles

jumped and everybody started breathing again. "It's just another stupid damn OD. Which is certainly, yes, stupid, but equally certainly not your fault. Unless you held them down and forced the stuff up their noses until they died?"

"I don't think so," said Niles, startled. "I think I'd remember *that*."

"Who were they?" asked Turk. "The police didn't give out any names; the news stories said they're still waiting on notification of next of kin. Do we know them?"

Niles nodded, and took another hit of Scotch. "Sledger's chief sound guy, Biff Nydborg, you remember him, he helped us out at the Cow Palace the night you went down onstage. And the girl — when I saw her in the dressing room, I thought for a minute it actually *was* Sledger." He laughed mirthlessly.

"Well, who was it?"

Niles was relaxing visibly as the Valium and single-malt kicked in. "That groupie bird, I don't know her real name, she calls herself Scarlett — you've seen her around. She comes to our shows sometimes with Jeffie and Maryanna. She looks a *lot* like Sledge, the way that other chick we always see around looks a lot like Janis. And you know how both of them play it up to the hilt, clothes and hair and makeup. She has — had — orange hair like Sledger, though not the big bristols, and she was wearing a black leather jumpsuit and a ton of silver bracelets on both arms, the whole trip. All just as Sledger does. It was rather creepy, really."

Turk and Rennie exchanged glances, both of them instantly identifying the girl he was talking about. Like the Joplin double, who looked so startlingly like Janis that even

Rennie had mistaken her on more than one occasion, Scarlett was oh dear a *dead* ringer for Sledger, and always around on the New York rock scene. The Jeffie and Maryanna that Niles had mentioned were two longtime Lionheart groupies who had at last achieved the friend-of-the-band status to which they'd always aspired; they weren't interested in balling the guys anymore, just in hanging out with them, and neither had ever laid a hand, or anything else, on Turk. Rennie hated them anyway. But both she and Turk were remembering two other groupies, almost two years ago now, who'd also looked like other people…

"I can imagine," said Turk after a while. "And Sledger?"

"Laughed like a drain when she saw her backstage between sets. Doesn't give a toss, she thinks it's hysterical. Oh, you don't think *Sledger*—" Niles' eyes widened. "Oh my God you do, don't you?"

Rennie made an impatient face. "We don't think anything just yet."

"But you believe me?" Niles stared at her imploringly, trying to read if she did or not.

"Why wouldn't we? We've all been there. Prax. Turk. Gray. Roger Hazlitt. Ned Raven. I believed them, didn't I?" Only Turk noticed that she very carefully did not say that she believed Niles as well.

But Niles had not noticed, and now he was nodding, shakily but sincerely. "That was why I came here. You don't have to help. I wouldn't blame you if you didn't. But please help me. Please."

Rennie was silent for a long, long moment—volcanoes built new islands, fish grew feet and climbed onto dry land, in distant galaxies stars burned out—and she could feel the needle on Turk's tension level moving deeper into the red the longer her silence lasted. She knew perfectly well what she was going to do, of course, but she was damn well going to take her own sweet time about doing it. And it had not escaped her notice that so far, either earlier in his first or now in this second impassioned entreaty—well, at least he'd said 'please' this time, which was some improvement—Niles had not once spoken her actual name.

You pissy ungrateful little ratbag. You snip and snap at Turk every chance you get, and you stabbed him in the back and sold him out to Freddy last year—only your evil scheme didn't come off, because Turk is a million times smarter and classier than you'll ever be, and no not because he's a lord but because he's a fucking PRINCE—and you've been taking bitchy potshots at me ever since I moved in with him, but as soon as there's blood in the streets and the cops are crawling up your bum you come running to Murder Chick begging for help...well, if I do help you, you pathetic worm, the price tag will be the biggest damn quid pro quo you've ever seen in your LIFE...

"I know I don't *have* to," she said at last, evenly, and Turk and Hudson both shot her a glance. "But I will. At least—I'll do what I can. Whatever. For the band's sake."

"It's family," said Turk, breathing again, and Niles dropped his head, almost collapsing with sheer relief. "What do we do now?"

"Well, the first thing," said Rennie briskly, "is we talk to the fuzz—the Ninth Precinct stationhouse down on Fifth Street. I don't really know anyone there yet, and they weren't in the least bit helpful when a writer friend—well, you know her, Belinda Melbourne, she lives around the corner on Stuyvesant Street—had a problem with this lunatic fan from Italy who won't leave her alone now that she's dating Diego Hidalgo. They just blew her off, wouldn't even take a complaint. But the cops'll be all over this by now, and they're already looking for Niles, you bet they are. They seek him here, they seek him there, those piggies seek him everywhere... By this time someone has surely mentioned seeing Niles leave the Fillmore East with the victims, and they'll be wanting very much to sit down and have a little talk with him."

Turk nodded. "We should be the ones to call and tell them he's here, though. Nothing to hide. Cooperating with the authorities. But let's wait till morning, and let's make them come to us."

"Damn straight! What's the point of being rock gods if you can't make it work for you every now and then?"

Rennie stood up, put a tentative hand on Niles' shoulder; he was fading fast, and she felt a tiny, and infinitesimally brief, pang of sympathy before she snatched the hand away. "Niles. *Niles.* Go upstairs and take a shower, get comfortable, have a liedown. We'll find you something to wear. And I'll call to see if Berry Rosenbaum"—her longtime lawyer friend, who had handled both Prax's and Turk's murder-related difficulties, and knew everybody's secrets—"can recommend someone at King Bryant's New York office. Just in case we need them."

Hudson got up to show Niles upstairs to a guest room—escorted closely by Macduff, who was plainly still hoping his muscle might be required—and she and Rennie quietly exchanged glances. Set aside the clothes he was wearing, was their unspoken thought, the cops might want to take a look. But Niles, just about asleep on his feet by now, didn't pick up on it, and, following Hudson, trundled happily off to do as Rennie had suggested.

The householders sat silently for a while, watching the light flickering in the fireplace, listening to the snow hissing against the windowpanes. The house was very still, wrapped in that special silence peculiar to New York in a snowstorm. Presently Turk got up and went over to the piano and began to play some Bach—slow, elegiac, a small lamentation.

"That's a very nice thing you did," he said after a while. "You didn't have to. Thank you."

Rennie shrugged, a little embarrassed, and absently stroked Svaha, the new Himalayan kitten, who was purring thunderously in her lap. Furry and warm and ridiculously affectionate, the tiny creature was a Christmas gift from Gray and Prue Sonnet, offspring of their regal championship cat Piggy, whose acquaintance Rennie had made last Christmas at Pacings Castle. She was named for the beautiful and desperate and hard-rocking love song Turk had written for Rennie after their breakup a year ago, which had helped bring them back together and was already a rock classic and was going to outlive them all.

"Don't thank me just yet, blondie! My motives are far from pure, I promise. I'm doing it for *you*, you know. Just you. Well, you and Lionheart. Not him. Not him at all. Even though he's part of Lionheart. But I was thinking, if Niles feels he owes you for this, even if it's through me, maybe—"

Turk watched her, continuing to play, but she left the thought unfinished.

Hudson came downstairs to report that Niles was crashed in a second-floor guest suite, then bade them good night and headed off to her husband Daniel and their flat at the far end of the north wing. Turk and Rennie had a light supper of more leftovers and then spent a quiet evening: watching TV, talking somberly to friends on the phone about not only Sledger's misfortune but the Stones' extremely bad day at Altamont. What with the knife murder of an audience member right there onstage as the concert was being filmed, and Marty Balin of Jefferson Airplane being decked and rendered unconscious by a Hell's Angel, and the Grateful Dead just turning right around and choppering straight back home again without playing a note, Saturn must be *seriously* retrograde. They made sure to ring up Sledger with their condolences and offers of help, and Rardi and Francher, to let them know the whereabouts of their lead singer, and likewise Niles' wife Keitha, who was flipping out at the Plaza because she didn't know where her husband was, or with whom, and had been fearing groupies—with good historical cause. So probably a mere murder suspicion came as a huge relief to her.

Keitha's spouse was obviously wiped out, since he slept straight through. The sleep of the blamelessly innocent? Rennie wasn't so sure: maybe just the result of an empty tummy suddenly full and overstrung nerves suddenly slacked off with Scotch and Valium and the relief of her promise to help. When she and Turk retired around midnight—ridiculously early for them, but they were exhausted—Turk detoured to check in on their castaway. Out like a light, he indicated to Rennie, firmly closing the door against the Thane of Gondor's conscientious nighttime patrolling, and went with her down the hall to their own rooms.

After a long, relaxing, shared shower, Rennie got quickly into bed, pulling the sheet and blankets and down comforter and fur bedspread up over her bare shoulders before she lost all the good of the shower's warmth. Rather medievally, she and Turk liked to sleep naked under a ton of bedclothes in a cold room, even in the summer, and the big, high-ceilinged bedroom, with a window open a scant inch and snow drifting onto the sill, was already too frosty for most people's comfort. She held open the covers, and he slipped in beside her, pulling the bedcurtains closed behind him, to make a warm, private, enclosed little space for them in the vast fourposter.

She cuddled up to him, soft and sleepy from the hot water, her head on his chest and one leg twined through his. But neither of them was in a mood for romancing, at least not just yet; there was too much on their minds.

"Sing hey for the quiet life!" she said drowsily. "I tell you, you come home for the big concert and the end of the tour, you think it's going to be all tranquil and vacationy, maybe you can even flee with your honey for a couple of weeks, and boom! Somebody turns up on your doorstep with a tale of two dead bodies and snow in the snow. And lo, we find ourselves in Murderland, that same old familiar place, once again. Or still."

"Do you think Niles is telling the truth? About not killing them, I mean."

But Rennie, tempted though she was to cry out "No!" in a mighty voice—well, Niles wasn't the nicest member of Lionheart, was he, no he wasn't, and he'd certainly not been the best-disposed to her since she and Turk had been together, had he, no he hadn't—on the whole thought he was innocent as self-proclaimed. Still—

"You've known him a lot longer than I have," she said after a lengthy and eloquent pause. "Do *you* think he could have done it?"

Turk shrugged. "What have you been telling me ever since we met—anybody *can* kill? Sure, I expect he could have done it. Do I think he actually did? No. No, I don't. Why would he?"

"Why indeed? —Well, in case you're wondering," she said at last, "*I* don't think he did either. But it just doesn't *feel* right. There's so much we don't know yet. Let's wait and see what the cops have to say about it. By now they've probably found out a lot more. Maybe they'll even share."

"And by 'share' you mean maybe you can winkle something out of them with clever questions that they'll be too stupid to avoid falling into."

"I do mean that."

"Thought so. And then?"

"And then—and then I think I need to have a serious little talk with Sledger. I'm sure it hasn't escaped your notice that she was the real target."

She felt him go very still against her. "Apparently it had," said Turk then, sounding a little chagrined. "You mean somebody killed that groupie thinking they were really killing Sledger?"

"Well, who's the one who got the death threats I told you about? Not Scarlett, that's for sure. No, I think it's entirely possible they hit the wrong girl. And where have you and I seen *that* before?"

She sat up, rearranged her four big fluffy pillows apart from Turk's four, lay back down again and lapped them both up to their noses in duvet. "I think it might be a tad nippy in here tonight even for us—cuddle up there, Flash." As Turk obediently drew her closer against him: "I did warn Sledger again when I talked to her earlier that they might try to get to her and she should be extra-extra-careful. Though of course she won't, the stupid cow."

"You've explained it all to her, I presume."

"Oh, sure. But you know how she is."

Turk kissed her between her breasts and turned over; she spooned up to his back as they invariably fell asleep, drowsily rubbing her cheek against the astonishing warmth of his shoulder blades—he was like a heat sink, almost as good as a cat. Though of course a hell of a lot sexier, and with the delicious clean scent of Ivory soap from the shower to inhale off his skin.

"Unfortunately, I do," he murmured. "I just never thought rock was such a high-risk occupation. Well, not like that, at least."

Her arm arched over him and drifted slowly downward. "Have you learned nothing over the course of our time together, o flower of English manhood?"

He turned back over. "I've learned this…"

"Ah. And what a very good student you've been."

CHAPTER NINE

AS GRAY DAWNLIGHT DIFFUSED by yet more snow began to sift into the room, Turk stirred in the warmth of the curtained bed, and without opening his eyes he reached out for Rennie. Pulling her onto her back, he rolled over on top of her, not a word spoken, one hand pinning her arms over her head, the other sweeping her long tangled hair out of his way and wrapping it around her wrists, one knee pushing her thighs apart. She liked him to make love to her like that sometimes, forcefully, heedlessly, when they were both half asleep: she either fought back or lay still for him, as the mood struck her—they enjoyed it either way. This morning he was quick and insistent and thorough, and she was happy to let him do all the work—a change of pace from their usual epic style.

When they were done, Rennie tightened her arms across his back, sliding her legs down his, and held him there on top of her for a few moments—she liked that, too, to feel the full drowsy weight and warmth of him upon her, both of them spent—before he bit her shoulder and moved off her still holding her in his arms and they fell asleep again.

Coming downstairs at last around noon, the first person they saw was Niles, and Rennie smothered a laugh. *Hey, it's rocknroll Goldilocks!* Niles Clay in a too-short pair of her loose black yoga pants and a too-long shirt of Turk's and a just-right pair of Hudson's tabi socks, all fresh and clean from the laundry basket. He was sitting in the living room talking cheerfully and earnestly to Prax and Ares and Berry Rosenbaum's lawyer colleague Shea Laakonen, who had all hit the doorstep together twenty minutes ago. No one had wanted to wake Turk and Rennie up, so had accepted tea instead while they waited for them to descend. Prax and Ares had spent the hours since the concert cocooned behind a do-not-disturb sign at the Plaza, and didn't have a clue about what was going on, while Shea had shown up in response to Berry's transcontinental SOS. And all of them had to be brought up to speed immediately.

Shepherded by an interested and excited Macduff, his suspicions about Niles allayed for the moment and pleased to have his flock suddenly expanded by so many new arrivals, everyone headed down to the kitchen. While Rennie got out the breakfast china and explained to the newcomers the dire circumstances that prevailed that morning, Turk set himself to the big professional-quality Aga range he'd had shipped over from the homeland, fixing a substantial morning meal for all comers. To much amusement.

"What, you've never seen him cook before?" asked Rennie, who having helped with the prep was now efficiently waitressing, passing along the platters full of hot food as Turk turned it out at diner-level speed and quantities—pancakes, bacon, sausage, eggs, hash, home fries. Good thing the stove could handle it all.

They all solemnly shook their heads, trying vainly to keep their faces straight even as they eagerly stuffed them.

Shea waved a fork. "It's just that it's, you know, *Turk Wayland*. Slinging hash. *Literally* slinging *actual* hash. Not what usually comes to mind when his name is mentioned."

"I do not for the life of me see what you all think is so damn funny," said Rennie with some asperity. "He can cook, I can't. Kneel before your king and be grateful! Your Majesty, step away from the stove, they don't deserve to be fed."

"Actually, I *have* seen him cook before," said Niles reminiscently. "When we were on the road in England, summer five years ago, that first tour after I came on board — you remember, Turk?"

"I do not."

"Oh yes you do!" Niles winningly addressed himself to the table, including everyone in, laughing. "Back then, we were much too poor to eat out — spent all our pocket money, when we had any, on guitar strings and amp fuses — and our idea of a lash-out meal was a grotty fish-and-chipper. It wasn't a fun time, though the fans love to hear about how we struggled and suffered. Anyway, to keep from starving, we'd pool amongst us whatever pathetic few pence we possessed, and then Jay-Jay and Shane and I would go food shopping."

A scoff from the vicinity of the Aga. "What Niles really means to say is Jay-Jay would frugally and law-abidingly shop, while Shane and himself would feloniously though discriminatingly shop*lift*."

Niles crowed in triumph. "I *knew* you remembered! Anyway, when we were on the road, we couldn't usually afford places to sleep, either — we kipped in the van, not very comfortably, on the ratty old mattresses we kept in there to protect the amps. But whenever we were a bit more flush, we stayed in these dreadful little backstreet places, quid a night, four of us to a room—but, both necessity *and* luxury, access to a hot shower. 'Fleabag' is too dignified a term. Low-end B&B's, high-end flophouses—but there was usually a cooker about, and a teakettle and an old pot or two, and whatever we could score, lawfully or un-, Turk would chef up. We ate pretty well, as I recall."

"Only because you blokes were so bloody brilliant at petty theft." Turk was laughing now: his turn to appeal to the room. "You wouldn't *believe* what those two nicked! They were the most epicurean pilferers who ever pilfed. Their menus were impeccable. Steaks, chops, veg, puddings—once they even stole a monstrous great goose for our Christmas dinner, I don't know how the hell they got out of Sainsbury's with it. They gave 'takeaway food' a whole new meaning."

Niles bridled with mock indignation. "We paid for most of it. It was only when we didn't have enough money to feed us all. And when we hit it big we funded that food pantry for starving artists, as you well know."

"Making us karmically square with the Horseman of Famine as well as the god of thieves, yes, I do know. So we can now enjoy our bangers guilt-free."

"I seem to recall that scruples didn't keep *you* from stuffing yourself with our ill-gotten swag."

"No, well, I was just as poor and hungry as the rest of you, wasn't I." Turk handed off another loaded platter and grinned at the memory. "I remember once, we were playing a little club on the south coast, Hastings or Rye or someplace. We got off the gig in the wee small hours, but it was a bank holiday in the morning and all the shops would be closed. Our bastard then-manager had scarpered back to London, abandoning us with no money to speak of and nothing to eat except some bread and cheese and a dozen bottles of cheap wine that the club had given us in lieu of actual money. We figured we were just going to starve to death right there; but, on the positive side, at least we'd die blind drunk, so we probably wouldn't mind too much. Anyway, Shane and Niles went out foraging and came back around dawn to this absolute dump of a place with a bushel of live and extremely kicking lobsters. To this day they've never told the rest of us how they did it."

"Oh yes, and what about you?" said Niles, though he still didn't tell how they'd done it. To the rest of them: "His lordship, only of course we didn't know he *was* a lordship then, charmed some cream and eggs and butter out of the gorgon landlady, and made us a sumptuous feast of lobster Newburg on toast points. We ate up every bite. First time we'd ever had it—well, except for the Marquess, of course, who no doubt grew up on it from birth—and damn tasty it was, too, especially for breakfast. So, Turk, you're as good a cook as you are a guitarist."

"So, Niles, you're as good a thief as you are a lead singer," said Rennie, who even as she spoke couldn't quite believe she was actually saying it. "How very Oliver Twisted of you. But apparently not a murderer. I suppose that's something to be going on with."

Into the shocked silence, with Niles looking ready to burst into tears, Ares spoke quickly and diplomatically.

"Most likely he was *liberating* the food, you know, not stealing it. Power to the peckish, right on... Well, well—

Turk Wayland, guitar god, kitchen god—whatever would the fans say if only they could see you now?"

"They'd say how amazing is *he*," said Rennie, appalled she'd said what she had said, and more appalled still at not knowing why she'd said it.

Actually, she was more surprised at Niles' casual confiding: she'd never before heard him talk as easily as that in her presence, and she was a little sorry she'd been so bitchy in return. But only a little. And too damn bad but she didn't feel like apologizing, either, and she wouldn't, not even if Turk begged her on his knees. Or other things on his knees.

Listen, if Nilesy expected her to help him out, he owed her a *lot* more shots than that—two years' arrears of bitchiness, in fact—and if he thought she was going to forget about his behavior to Turk, he had several, no, *many*, thinks coming. Attitude-debt forgiveness went only so far. Anyway, deep down, all of them were cross with each other and no one wanted to be nice. But she could tell that Turk, though he'd sooner be dead in a ditch than show it in front of guests, was annoyed with her. Well, too damn bad about that too.

"Richard, your breakfast is getting cold, please sit down and eat," she commanded, and to her surprise, Turk, whom she never addressed as Richard except with subtext, silently obeyed. To cover her confusion, she shooed away the mutely imploring dog and kitten—oh please, nobody ever feeeeeeds us, our kind don't have the ability to use can openers, you're the ones with the opposable thumbs, have pity on us—though, pushover that she was, she did sneak Macduff the leftover sausages and a piece of toast, graciously accepted, and Svaha some soft, tiny bits of scrambled egg.

Across the table from Prax, Shea Laakonen held out her plate for more pancakes, and Rennie obliged, smiling. Dark-haired, not tall, by ancestry half Finnish and half Irish, a younger law-school associate of their lawyer friend Berry Rosenbaum, Shea was based in the great Kingsford Bryant's New York offices, and she came highly recommended. "She's a go-getter," Berry had said on the phone from L.A. the night before. "Utterly fearless, utterly honorable. She's like a little bulldog, a little terrier. Nobody I'd rather have on my side if I needed help. And it sounds as if Niles can use some. Dear God, what *is* it with you people and dead bodies?"

Damned if Rennie knew. But breakfast was barely cleared away when a couple of detectives from the Ninth Precinct came knocking, stamping the snow from their boots outside the front door like peasants coming in from the steppes. Shea had made the call earlier that morning, before leaving her office and coming down to the prow house, and for once the cops had not been slow to respond.

Rennie saw immediately, when Hudson had ushered the visitors into the living room, that the cops were completely unimpressed that the not-so-tall dark-haired Englishman sitting rather uncertainly in a big leather club chair was Niles Clay and the very tall blond Englishman who'd just stood up to courteously welcome them to his home was Turk Wayland. Well, they were rough tough NYPD detectives — she hadn't been expecting them to go all wibbly and ask for autographs. But still…

It was that total New Yorker expression on their faces of they'd seen it all before and they *really* didn't want to be seeing it again. Rennie knew the look well; indeed, she had employed it herself, and often. From experience, though, she knew that the indifferent pose went only so far, and she also knew from experience how this part of the crime process went. So did Prax and Turk, for that matter, by now, and Ares was not altogether unfamiliar with it either.

It was Shea's job, as it had previously been Berry's in other, similar situations, to hustle things along, and it was Rennie's job, as always, to find out whatever she could by whatever means she must. But of course they were all concerned to make it as easy for Niles as possible, yeah, yeah, even Rennie, so to that end Ares and Prax wisely decamped to their suite to unpack. At the detectives' rather surprising request, Rennie and Turk stayed, sitting side by side like well-behaved Victorian children on one of the Chesterfield sofas, and Shea sat next to Niles on the other; the cops settled into armchairs, and everybody was ready to, as it were, rock.

The cops, who introduced themselves as Detective Nicholas Sattlin — Brooklyn Irish — and Detective Bob Casazza — Bronx Italian — were annoying but thorough. Oddly casual in their questioning, too, which visibly surprised Turk and greatly relieved Niles, but Rennie and Shea exchanged glances, which read as Oh yeah, we've been here before, we know how *this* goes...

Niles' account was as he had told it the previous day, and the cops took careful notes on everything everyone said. Rennie and Turk were questioned as well, scarcely less intensively; Hudson and Prax and Ares were recalled to answer a few things. Stuff like when was the Lionheart concert over, when and how had all of them left the Garden, how long had they been at the restaurant, when had they arrived back here or where had they gone instead, what had they done all day Sunday, who had been at the party, who were the house guests, when had all the party people left, could they be located, would they corroborate everyone's statements. Rennie watched closely as mighty names were dropped like clanging anvils, but the collective police game face remained impassive. Damn, they were good. But maybe...

"Have you found out anything more about the victims, Detective?" she asked casually, as soon as she and Turk and Shea were alone with the cops—Niles having fled upstairs as soon as the detectives said he could leave—and the senior shield cut his glance across to her and didn't reply right away.

Nick Sattlin had done his homework on Rennie Stride. His precinct commander, who had connections, had filled him in, back last spring when she and her rock star boyfriend had bought the three houses in the Ninth and commenced extensive renovation and public cohabitation. You wouldn't think they'd want people to know they were shacked up together and not married—nice local girl like that, born in Brooklyn just like him, same parish as his cousins, and Wayland had a title and was the Queen of England's godson, for pete's sake—but these hippies didn't seem to care. Anyway, it was only good cop practice to keep track of famous people moving onto your turf. For one thing, they were far more likely to cause you major aggro than street scum was, and for another, you never knew if some crazed fan was going to take a shot at them or burgle their home — so it was wise to keep an eye on not only them but their places of residence.

But Sattlin, a couple of years older than Turk and, since being posted to the precinct containing the Fillmore East, a huge fan of the music, had gone further. He'd actually checked up on them on his own time, talking about them to a friend who was in the Monterey police department and one who had worked with that agent Marcus Dorner on the Tansy Belladonna investigation in L.A.; he'd gotten a further earful from a brother detective in the Ninth who'd had to deal with that other local writer Belinda Melbourne's recent stalker complaint — she was good friends with Stride, no surprise there — and several earfuls more, and very thoughtful ones too, from Sheriff Caskie Lawson of Sullivan County, who'd had to deal with Stride at Woodstock, back in August.

He'd even read Stride's commentary pieces in the Sun-Tribune, so he already knew more than enough to go on with — she was a stylish, informed and passionately opinionated writer, typical liberal sensibilities but sprinkled with occasional and quite logical conservatism. Stringent and astringent. He'd always admired this house, too, so when the call had come in earlier he'd asked if he and his partner could take it. Nobody else wanted to spend a freezing cold Monday afternoon coddling some limey aristocrat rocker and his reporter popsy and his possibly murderous lead singer, not with all the major press that was guaranteed to come down on this story — he was surprised they weren't sniffing around already — so the brass were only too glad to push it off on Nick and Bob.

In any case, he considered the people here big trouble, with the lady of the house at the top of the list. Something of a murder magnet, apparently, or else just meddlesome: those files telecopied from the Coast and upstate had been interesting, to say the least. But weighing Rennie's glance as it met his, all at once Sattlin switched over to trusting that New York instinct, and told her what they knew.

Which admittedly wasn't much: cause of death would have to await the coroner's official report, but it seemed as if they'd been doing coke just as Clay had said; it hadn't yet been determined if the drug itself had killed them, or something the drug had been cut with, or if they'd died of hypothermia first.

Rennie raised an eyebrow and forbore to point out that Niles had already admitted he'd been snorting out of the same stash and he was just fine, but she and the cops both knew that that intriguing little detail hadn't gotten past any of them, and they tacitly left it for the "later" they all knew would inevitably be coming down the pike.

"The guy was lying on a marble step, at the foot of one of the larger monuments. The girl was curled up next to him." Sattlin tried to keep out of his professional voice the personal sorrow he'd felt at seeing them: they had looked like two kids who'd been tired after a long day and had just lain down together and gone to sleep, under a blanket of white.

"Footprints?" asked Turk after a moment, breaking the

sudden little silence.

Casazza shook his head, taking the cue from his partner. "Mostly messed up, and what wasn't messed up was covered over by the snow. It snowed for at least four hours after the Fillmore East let out."

They went over a few more things—why, yes, we *would* like to see Mr. Clay's clothing from last night, clever of you to think of keeping it aside for us—and re-asked a few questions, the significance of none of which was lost on Rennie. The cops gave Niles' clothing a quick professional scan, found nothing of note—and Rennie was watching closely to see if they did, even if they didn't share—then took their leave, with thanks and the usual cautions, three hours after their arrival.

"Well!" said Rennie lightly, coming back from closing and locking the front door after the fuzz. "That was—interesting."

"At least they didn't arrest me," said Niles, who'd changed back into his own clothes once the garments were free of suspicion, and had come back downstairs after ascertaining that the coast was clear.

"They wouldn't have, not at this stage or on that evidence," said Shea. "But you notice they did caution you all to stay put, and you specifically, Niles, not to even *think* about leaving town."

"And very tiresome it is, too," complained Rennie. "Turk and I aren't personally persons of interest—yes, yes, for a change, I know, you don't have to remind me—and we'd been hoping to get the hell out of here for the holidays."

Shea laughed. "And you still can. They have no legal right to insist you two stick around; they just said they'd really like it if you did. Of *course* they'd like it! They're *cops*. They want it all easy and nice for them, laid out on a silver platter with chocolate-chip cookies and tied up in ribbons. With glitter. But they can't make you. Besides, what's the problem? The tour's over, you two live here and Berry told me that Lionheart is recording the new album here. Staying put shouldn't put a major crimp in anyone's plans."

"The sessions don't start till almost February, as it stands now," said Turk gloomily. "But the rest of the band's not hanging around until then; we have a meeting up at Centaur on Thursday, when everyone's had some time to recover from the show, and then they're all going home and not coming back until we start recording. So that leaves six or so weeks where Niles will be stuck here in town like a raisin in a bagel, most unnatural. And if we scamper off to Banff or Cortina, he'll be stuck here all alone."

"Listen, Niles, I just this minute had an idea," said Rennie brightly — a big fat whopper, as she and Turk had discussed the idea at length last night before they fell asleep. "Why don't you crash here with us? Keitha too, of course. You can stay as long as you want, or until you can find an apartment or a hotel you like — the Chelsea, the Navarro. The Gorham even has suite kitchens and pots and pans, just like the old days at — Hastings, was it? Right. But much, much nicer. English bands stay at the Gorham all the time, I just interviewed Jeff Beck there; he even made me tea. But here would be better. There's plenty of room, and the studio's right downstairs — you and Turk could start working, take your mind off things. Prax and Ares are here, and Gray and Prue Sonnet are coming tonight to stay for a bit. It'll be like an English house party. Fun for everybody, and a lot nicer and more private for you and Keitha than a hotel."

A lot safer than a hotel, too. But that thought she kept to herself. If that sound guy and groupie *had* been killed for a reason, maybe the reason might spill over to Niles. Sure, it would be a major pain in the behind having him skulking around the house like Marley's ghost, but if she drove him out into the snow and then something happened to him...

Okay, yeah, *maybe* deep down inside she'd be doing a little dance of grief and bereavement, oh so very very sad, ya-ha, serves the little pissant right, but no—it wouldn't be a good thing at all, for anyone, in any way. Not to mention the fact that it would destroy Lionheart—and devastate Turk. It would mean the flaming fiery end of not only the band, Turk's creative fount and source, but of one of the oldest and most cherished relationships he had. He didn't deserve any more grief: he'd been through enough this year and last; they all had, really.

Besides, being in such close proximity might give Rennie and Niles a chance to work things through, even get to be friends. Okay, probably never nice happy shiny *friends*, no, that was a lot to ask, but at least maybe not so much antagonists anymore. It could happen. A lot of things *could* happen—manna could fall from heaven, unicorns could gambol around Central Park, Pegasus could roost on the top of the Chrysler Building. Pigs could fly. Well, they could if they booked early enough. You could never tell. And it would make Turk very happy, Rennie knew, if she and

Niles made peace—his bedmate and his bandmate. God in heaven, lead singers were *such* a pain in the ass…

As for any other threats, a houseful of world-famous rock stars would all be as safe here as they could possibly be. Safer than just about anywhere else, probably. There were security measures all over the place. Outdoor concealed cameras. Gates and grilles and alarms and fences. Bulletproof glass. Macduff was eternally vigilant. And of course Ares would be in residence. It was good to have professional muscle as a houseguest. Not to mention licensed firepower—he had a permit to carry loaded in New York, not an easy thing to get. No, this was a *fine* idea.

She set herself to charm and convince, and so great was the persuasive power she exerted that two minutes later Niles, who'd been huddled over rather sad and small, looking lost, was quite perked up and happily agreeing, thinking it was all his own idea and a damn good one too. After Niles had headed uptown with Hudson to fetch Keitha and his other belongings from the Plaza, Turk surveyed the living room and ostentatiously chafed his hands and rubbed his arms through the sleeves of his sweater.

"Is it getting chilly in here all of a sudden?" he inquired with mock puzzlement. "Could it be, oh, I don't know, maybe hell freezing over? Oh look, there's Satan, he's ice-skating…"

"That's not a very productive attitude, my lord," Rennie informed him. "I thought you *wanted* me to be nice to Niles?"

"I did. I do. It's just creepy to actually *see* it. Are pigs flying yet? Should I alert air traffic control?"

"Cute. Well, you'll have to get used to it. As will I.

Because there's going to be a lot more of it around here before I'm done."

Ares was eyeing Rennie with new respect. "Now I know the true meaning of the word 'blarney'. I don't think I've ever seen you in action like that. He never knew what hit him. Nothing like being worked over by a pro. But won't all this company be too much — us, Niles and Keitha, Prue and Gray?"

Rennie acknowledged the compliment, but shook her head to the question. "No, it won't, because we'll never see you except at meals. Or perhaps at the jolly little communal group sings and nightly marshmallow roasts. No, just kidding about those. There's acres of space; we won't impinge on one another's privacy. If you have to conduct business, there's a nice little side parlor you're welcome to use. If you get bored, there are TV sets and stereos all over the house, two libraries full of books and a billiards table in Turk's attic playroom. All Manhattan is right outside the front door. If you get hungry, you know where the kitchen is. Otherwise, breakfast is whenever someone gets up and makes it, lunch is usually sandwiches on the fly if it happens at all, tea is at four, supper's at ten. If you're still hungry at inopportune moments, Chinatown's five minutes away by cab and this town has oodles of restaurants. Hudson will give you the key codes so you can come and go as you please. You're all entertainers, right? So — entertain yourselves."

"Well, that seems easy enough." said Ares. "Makes *my* life a bit simpler, at least, if everybody's here under one roof. Yes, I know, I'm not officially on duty, but even so."

Rennie made a shushing motion, and Ares laughed, and

she continued.

"We have a housekeeper who will tidy up and do laundry and shop for any particular foods you may crave or require. She also does some cooking, as does Hudson, but usually Turk and I handle the meals. Or you can cook for yourselves: there's a weekly menu posted on the fridge. If you need anything special—drugs, guitar strings, bullets, drugs, shopping advice, getting on backstage lists, drugs, restaurant reservations, I did mention drugs?—ask Hudson. The cardinal, unbreakable rule is don't ever, *ever* wake Turk and me up before both the clock hands are on the twelve, unless the house is exploding or the world is ending. Oh, wait, none of you lot wake up before noon anyway. Well, that was easy."

Turk grinned. "Can't tell *me* you don't love laying down the law, lady of the house."

Rennie sighed, then publicly addressed what they were all privately thinking. "Okay! I just feel that Niles is better off here. Yes. That's right, you heard me. Right here where we can keep an eye on him. Many eyes. My eyes especially. Oh, don't look at me like that, I know every single one of you shares my nasty discreditable thought."

"And here I thought we were all being so subtle." Turk stretched lazily; his earlier annoyance with Rennie had long since evaporated under the heat and light of the police inquiry—they'd had to present a united domestic front to the lawmen, form a shield-wall to repel attackers—and now he smiled at her. "You've got it right on both counts, though: he's better off here, and we're all thinking alike... So what next?"

"I need to go up to the Sun-Trib and talk to some people. The reporter who broke the story, obviously. Who, as it turns out, is none other than my old San Francisco pal Ken Karper. And of course Fitz. Maybe they can help me out with some local contacts."

Turk rubbed a hand over his beard. "You mean Paranoid Little Me can take a figurative nap? Well, that *is* good news. I say, Prax old thing, let's go guitar shopping — Henry called from Manny's Music and said they just got a new shipment in, with this sweet old Gibson I've been wanting."

"Oh?" inquired Prax. "Let's hear. I may have to fight you for it."

"A 1931 L-5, in pristine condition. And I'll thank you to keep your little picking fingers off it, missy. It's mine. Mine mine mine. I want to grab it before Gray hears about it, he's such a guitar hog, he wants everything, the greedy brute —"

Rennie rolled her eyes. "And all those axes downstairs just followed you home? Listen, I'll give it to you as an early Christmas present if you'll wait till Niles gets back and take him with you. Maybe you can buy him a glockenspiel or some other shiny noisy thing to distract him. Just make sure he doesn't ever leave the house unless somebody knows where he's going."

She dropped a kiss on Turk's head in passing. "I'll have tea with Fitz, talk to Ken, do some uptown stuff and be back in time for supper. Your turn to cook tonight. I'm fancying boeuf bourguignon with potatoes Anna, so you might want to get moving now. Send Hudson or Galina out for supplies if we don't have the fixings."

"Not so fast there, Daisy Mae." He hooked her thigh and

pulled her off her feet and into his lap for a real kiss. "So I guess we don't get to go to the Dolomites."

"Not just yet. Come on, don't pout, you weren't all that into it in the first place. Nothing worse than a pouting Englishman. You just came off three months on the road— you've been whining for the past two weeks that all you wanted to do once the tour was done was stay here and put your feet up and mess about with your books and pictures and records. And now you can. Besides, what's all this anyway, you *hate* traveling."

"Some line of work *you* picked," said Ares.

"Murder karma, the gift that keeps on giving! Hello, darling girl, how nice to see you; even nicer under these circumstances, as always, if you know what I mean and I have every confidence that you do..."

Oliver Fingal Flaherty Fitzroy, first Baron Holywoode— pronounced Hollywood, and yes, he'd heard all the jokes— came around the huge glass-and-steel power desk, took Rennie's hands and kissed her on both cheeks with great enthusiasm. Rennie responded with equal enthusiasm; she liked Fitz, as he was universally known, very much indeed. Well, he was very likable. For a tabloid king and a press lord and a self-made baron, anyway. It was just that she didn't trust him for a heartbeat. It was an unusual friendship, a reporter and her publisher, and it could have led to major problems. But there was little about either of those two that *wasn't* unusual, and so far the problems had been minimal.

" 'lo, Fitzie." She kissed him back. "And isn't that what you hired me for?"

Fitz laughed, then led her over to a Barcelona chair by the floor-to-ceiling windows with the sweeping Central Park view, sat her down, ran his hand through his impeccably Beatle-styled brown hair and rang for tea.

"Well, let's just say it doesn't make me weep bitter salt tears that you keep on regularly finding yourself in the middle of murder investigations. Oh no it doesn't! If rockers insist on popping their clogs under sensational circs, I want to know why, and I *absolutely* want to know why before anyone else does. That most certainly *is* what I hired you for, Suzy Creamcheese. Remind me to give you a pay rise. Or perhaps a bounty would be more the thing. One major piece of jewelry per murder, does that sound like a good going rate? I know you like your trinkets, and that way you'll stay properly motivated…plus laying in a stock of baubles for future marchionessly need. Oooh, I'll be Mother and pour, shall I?"

He poured out from the Georgian silver tea service his secretary must have been lurking behind the draperies with, so swiftly and unobtrusively had it arrived on the low marble table. The tea ritual was part of their every meeting, and Rennie enjoyed it as much as Fitz did.

"Milk and sugar, yes, I remember—there you are… Speaking of tiaras, how's that gorgeous rock lordship of yours?"

Rennie sipped her tea. "Him? He's fine. He's gorgeous. Well, you were at the Garden with the lovely Lady Alix, in those nice expensive second-row seats he supplied you with, free, gratis and for nothing, you got your picture taken with him backstage for your tacky gossip columns—

you saw for yourself how fine and gorgeous."

"Yes, he was splendid, wasn't he," said Fitz appreciatively. "And your pretty little lesbian friend too."

"Her name is Prax McKenna. She's a *superstar*. She likes girls *and* boys. Surely you can remember that, from the Fillmore murders if nothing else. She helped you out so much, her being a suspect and all. Helped you out circulation-wise, I mean."

Fitz waved the silver jam spoon and went for the clotted cream. "Yes, yes, I know, I'd say I'm eternally grateful only you'd hold me up for a still greater pay rise…oh, and the other guitar player, that Sonnet chap, *loved* him with the Budgies. It's so good that you have such hugely famous friends. In fact, it's all good. But this is better. Now tell me what you know."

"I was rather hoping you, or your hired gun Ken Karper, who wrote it all up, would tell me what *you* know."

"Ken figured you'd say that; you can go talk to him when we've had our tea. Nice to see you two together again…" He passed her a plate bearing a warm scone dripping with clotted cream and raspberry jam. "But you mentioned on the phone that Niles Clay, currently sought by the local plod to help them in their inquiries, is staying at your place and you'd had a pair of tecs over just now to speak with him. So?"

"Yes to all of that, but they weren't terribly forthcoming," said Rennie around a mouthful of scone. "God, this is good… Well, they did say the deaths were almost certainly due to an overdose. Which I'm sure they were. But…"

"But you think there's more to it," said Fitz happily.

"Yes! You always do. And—I do so love this part—you always seem to be *right*."

"Only 'cause I've got a nasty suspicious mind. Well, there was one odd thing: the cops said the sound guy and the groupie had been snorting coke, and that it was probably the purity of the stuff that killed them."

"And why is that odd?"

"Our Niles had been snorting from the very same stash, and as we've all seen, he is still very much quivering with us."

"So?"

"So…either his tolerance is remarkably higher, so to speak, than theirs was—possible, he's a coke pig—or he didn't snort as much as they did—also possible, but not likely, did I say he's a coke pig? *Or* they did some stuff that he didn't do and then it did them. In. And the cops knew I'd noticed that little detail, and they knew I knew they knew I knew. If you can follow that."

Fitz's sherry-brown eyes sparkled. "That's my lass! And I actually did follow, clever old me." He sat back, watching her with pride over the rim of his teacup. "In the meantime, what delicious gossip have you got for me out of the rockerverse, as you so delightfully call it?"

Rennie reached for another scone. "If you think I'm selling out my friends so you can pass it along to your sleazy gossipmongers—"

"Not your *friends*."

"Oh. Well, in that case…"

CHAPTER TEN

THE NEXT NIGHT it was snowing again, small fine dry driving flakes like armadas of tiny ghosts, streaming past under the streetlights; in the prow house, it was warm and quiet. Niles was now safely in residence with Keitha, in the room with the wonderful oak furniture that Rennie and Turk had collected upstate in October, when Turk had had six whole blessed days off from the tour and she'd met him in Buffalo. They'd driven leisurely home through blazingly beautiful autumnal rural New York State, antiquing all the way, stopping off en route in Sullivan County to have Sunday dinner with Sheriff Caskie Lawson and his wife — who had been invited to the Garden show, as promised, and whom they'd entertained to dinner beforehand, also as promised — and to claim the Mission table that now stood proudly in the foyer.

Niles came upstairs into the kitchen from the studio, and balked when he saw his hostess sitting alone at the table, eating vanilla fudge ice cream out of a handsomely crafted bowl from a local potter's shop.

Ah, a reprise of our last little convo, only then it was tea, not ice cream — well, let's see if we can make it go a tad bit better this time, otherwise next time it really might have *to be pistols for two and coffee for one...*

She smiled at him, though the smile was just a little too bright and just a little too effortful, and got another bowl and spoon, and he sat down across from her and tucked in.

"Snow always makes me want to eat ice cream," she confided. "I don't know why, it just does."

"I've never noticed. Why is that?"

"Nobody knows. I'm told that the urge to consume dairy products at low temperatures is a well-known phenomenon. Sometimes it's milk, sometimes cheese, sometimes ice cream. Obviously weather-related. Or possibly genetic. A throwback to our Paleolithic ancestors, maybe. Though they wouldn't have had ice cream."

"Most likely not, no."

"Where's Fearless Leader?" she asked after a slightly uncomfortable ice-cream-filled silence, shading her tone with just the right degree of amused affection. "I'd have thought he'd have surfaced by now—he likes ice cream in the snow too. Still downstairs obsessing over his faders?"

Niles nodded. "I thought he was fussy when we just record, but *this*… We're just doing scratch tracks, but he treats them like masters. If he ever wants to give up guitar he could be a damn fine producer."

"Yes, he does get into that whole editing trip. But that's good."

"More than good." Niles had to work really hard to avoid showing Rennie how enthusiastic he was about the session, and she could tell he was annoyed that she saw it anyway. "He has the most amazing ear—well, *you* know. We were trying to bounce two bed tracks together just now and there was this extra beat messing everything around. Thirty-secondth beat, sixty-fourth beat. It was so small and quick I couldn't even figure out where it was coming from, but he went right in after it and cut it out, and I couldn't believe what a difference it made all cleaned up."

"He does that... How are you feeling? All settled in upstairs? Keitha happy?"

Niles belatedly remembered his manners, or at least some of them: this woman was after all providing him and his wife with free room, board, armed protection and legal aid—it would behoove him to show some gratitude. Besides, Turk might toss him out if he didn't.

"Yes, very, and ta again for having us to stay—it's been a huge relief. I think she's out shopping with her old schoolfriend Audrey, who lives here now. They wanted to go hit a few boutiques over in the West Village—they hired a limo and driver and guard from Ares' place. Overly cautious, I thought, but better safe, and all that."

"Indeed." Rennie groaned inwardly, hoping Niles didn't notice how much of a slog she found it, making nice with him. If she'd known when she agreed to take the Clays in that it was going to be so freaking stressful, she'd never have done it, not even if Turk had lain down before her and wept. And whenever she remembered Mr. Clay's appalling pre-Woodstock rudeness to her right here at this table, and his equally appalling behavior at the festival itself, both to her and to his own band, all she wanted to do was drop-kick the little bugger through the kitchen window and out into the street. Without opening the window.

For Turk, for Turk, I'm doing all this for Turk, I can do it for him, yes I can...and he'll owe me bigtime, yes he will...but he knows that...

Really, it was like digging bricks out of a wall with her

fingernails, trying to carry on a conversation with Niles. No surprise: their previous interactions had been limited to brief encounters, backstage before and after Lionheart gigs, in restaurants and at press parties for the band, in the studio during recording sessions. They'd never before been in a situation where they had to be in each other's presence and be cordial to one another twenty-four hours a day. The fact that Niles was Rennie's guest and the reciprocal fact that she was his hostess put a damper on overt hostilities, but it still didn't exactly bring them together in good fellowship and song, *vive la compagnie*. Or anything remotely like it. Not to mention the murder suspicions...

"So what else happened, Niles, in that snowy little graveyard?" she heard herself asking, to even her own surprise, and saw Niles' shock. *Okay, that's it, enough pussyfooting around, it's cards on the table time...* "Oh, you surely don't think I bought your little tarradiddle the way everyone else did? Of course not. You know there's more. I know there's more. You know I know there's more. I can't help you until I know it all. Spill."

"I didn't lie," he said hotly. "I swear."

"I believe you. But I also believe you didn't tell us absolutely every single little thing that went down. And you certainly didn't tell absolutely every single little thing to the cops when they were here. Still, I'll be charitable and call your omissions, oh, let's say, 'things you didn't quite remember at first that maybe you do now'. Even though we both know that it's really not like that at all. Or would you rather I call the cops back?"

He shrugged. "Whatever you like. It's not my funeral."

"No. Someone else's. Let's have it, Niles."

The usual expression of faint scorn that Niles generally wore when he looked at Rennie had returned, and she noted it faithfully in the tables of her memory.

"Murder Chick on the job as usual?" he sneered.

"The very same Murder Chick as has promised to try to save your pale scrawny sorry English arse," she said evenly. "Remember that. So. Talk."

Niles sat silent and mutinous for a few moments, the ice cream melting in the dish in front of him. Then:

"Somebody came into the graveyard as I was leaving. A bloke. Older. A real straight, not like us. He was wearing a big camel-hair coat and a hat and scarf, fancy dress shoes. I remember thinking he wasn't properly dressed for a blizzard, but then we weren't either."

"Who was he?"

"No idea. I didn't really scope him out to that extent. I didn't recognize him straight off the bat. Anyway, he had the hat on, and it was snowing; hard to see his face, and he didn't say anything to me as he came in."

"It didn't strike you as odd that he was coming to pay a visit at that hour of the morning? In the snow?"

He smirked at her. "Now that you mention it, of course it was odd. But I was stoned, I wasn't thinking. The three of us were there too, in the middle of the night in the snow, which was equally odd."

"And he too scaled the wall to get inside?"

"No—he came in at the gate as I was letting myself out. I could unlatch the gate from the inside; so I didn't have to climb over again."

"Do you think he might have been waiting for you to come out, to let him in?"

Niles stared, nonplused. "I never thought of that...I mean, it was three in the morning and snowing like mad—there was nobody else out on the street, nobody at all."

"He was coming to meet up with your two happy cokehead friends, one might think. Well, now we're getting somewhere. What did Biff and Scarlett do?"

"It's hard to remember—no, really it is—well, they stayed behind, obviously. At least I think they did. At least for a while. I didn't look back to see what was going on. So I've no idea." His eyes widened. "Do you think he was the one who killed them?"

"Could well be, yeah. As you and I and the cops all are aware, you were snorting from their stash, and you're not dead and they are. So whatever killed them, it wasn't in the coke they had."

"I hadn't thought of that either." He looked across at her. "But I can't remember any more than that...and that's the truth, I swear it is."

Rennie looked at him. He probably *was* telling the truth, or at least as much of it as he could... It didn't seem anything like enough, though.

Turk came into the kitchen then, from the studio stairs. He put on a show of surprised discovery as he saw them sitting there at the table in apparent amity, but in truth he had been standing in the stairwell for several minutes, listening to the conversation and trying to judge the best moment to go in. It hadn't been easy to decide.

Now he covered his entrance by crossing to the fridge

and getting a bowl of ice cream for himself. Sitting down exactly halfway between Rennie and Niles round the table's rim, he began spooning up the snack, but didn't say anything for a few moments more. Then: "Quite good ice cream. New brand, sweetheart?"

Oh good grief…well, if that's the way he wants to play this… "Yes, darling. Yes, it is. I thought I'd lash out on something wildly new and different. Things do need to be changed up around here every so often."

He caught the subtext, of course, but chose not to let either of them see he had. "They do, yes."

Chatting casually about his studio woes, he finished off the ice cream, then collected all three bowls and spoons and took them over to the sink, washing them out in silence.

Niles took advantage of the moment to mutter something, and then fled upstairs. Rennie looked after him, then looked at Turk.

"We were talking."

"So I heard. Something wildly new and different. For a change."

She laughed unwillingly. "It was worth a shot."

"So to speak." He dried the ice cream implements with a dish towel and put them away before sitting down again, aware that she was watching him the whole time. "Find out anything?"

"Hard to say. He did tell me some things he didn't think to tell the cops, though." Quickly she filled him in on what Niles had said about the man in the snow, and Turk listened with quiet attention.

"Well," he said when she'd finished. "That puts a rather

different appearance on things, doesn't it?"

"*Oh* yeah. But I must say I have a hard time believing that it was just a random guy who wanted to plunk down some flowers on his dear old auntie's grave. In the middle of the night. In a freaking blizzard."

"You think this mystery man was meeting Biff and that groupie for a purpose?"

"What else? He didn't seem to care that Niles was there and saw him, and as far as we know there was no one else in the cemetery."

"But why?"

"Dealer? Bringing them stuff? Buying stuff? Stuff that Niles *didn't* partake of, and perhaps that's why he's still alive?"

Turk shrugged. "Seems likely. But it does also seem an odd hour to be making a drug delivery. Or pickup. And in a snowstorm too." He squared up the edges of the placemats. "If it was just drugs, he could have dealt with the transaction in much greater warmth and comfort before Biff and the girl left the Fillmore East. No one would have batted an eye; that sort of thing goes on there all the time. So something else was going on. Something that nobody saw. Something that nobody was meant to see. Or maybe some*one* that nobody was meant to see."

"I'm hip. But where does that leave Niles? He claims he went out the cemetery gate into Second Avenue and left the three of them behind in the dark and deserted and snow-filled graveyard, like some damn thing out of Poe. And that's where he stopped remembering. He says. Nevermore."

"You don't believe him?"

Rennie shrugged and got up from the table, and Turk reached over to pull her to him, running his hands up her obliging form. "I don't know *what* I believe just yet. But I will."

"You always do."

After Turk had decamped to the living room, Rennie went down into the studio to fetch the teacups and plates and cutlery the guys had left there, because they were guys and hence they were pigs and they never picked up after themselves, and as she began tidying, she noticed that a light had been left on in the control booth.

Oh, for God's sake! He never *shuts off the damn lights after he's done, I guess that's what you learn living in a castle, where you have an endless supply of lackeys to do it for you. Now my mom and dad, being Depression-era children, taught us never to leave a room without turning off the lights behind us, seeing as how lights cost money...*

Heading toward the control booth, reaching for the switch, she jumped about six feet sideways as she realized someone else was there on the other side of the glass half-wall.

"Pudge! I didn't know you were down here...does Turk know?"

Pudge Vetrini, Turk's guitar tech, had been equally startled, and had dropped the guitar case he was carrying. "Oh, man, Rennie, you surprised me...yeah, I came over to collect the black Strat he used in the Garden show, the bridge needs tweaking. He says it felt a little loose, but it seems okay to me, so I thought I'd bring it up to my guy on

Forty-eighth Street to have him check it over. Niles let me in, and as long as I was here, I figured I'd see if anything else needed to be repaired. I'm sorry I scared you."

Rennie's heart had gone back to its accustomed pace and place. "No, no, that's fine, you just freaked the hell out of me; neither of them let me know you were here. Idiots. Is there anything I can get for you? Do you want to run upstairs and see Turk? Stay for supper?"

Pudge had been checking the guitar to see if he had hurt it by its sudden drop, and now he closed the case and snapped the locks. "No, but thanks. I'll just be taking this and getting on my way. I'm going home after I'm done uptown, anyway."

"Oh right, you moved here last year, I remember; do you like it there?" Pudge had taken over his grandparents' family apartment in Park Slope, a spacious, seven-room spread on the top floor of a brownstone on Prospect Park West. "I was born there, you know, and we lived not five blocks from where you are now."

"No! Really?" They talked Brooklyn for a bit, then Rennie let him out by way of the basement door that led into Stuyvesant Street, the one that Turk had ordered put in so that anything arriving for the studio didn't have to go through the front door and annoy Rennie. For which she was grateful—the furniture shipments were bad enough. She waved Pudge goodbye as he headed for the subway at Eighth Street, and then locked behind him the heavy steel door, with the thick sliding four-way security bolt that fastened it into the frame in all directions, and slammed shut an accordion steel mesh and barred gate over it, locking that

too. Turk invariably had a good and solid idea of security —
no doubt acquired from having been brought up in castles,
where portcullises were no strangers — but she was always a
bit nervous about the cellar, and when he'd been out on the
road and she had been alone in the house, she'd arranged
several makeshift alarm systems outside all access points to
the underground regions, to supplement the official ones.
Can't be too careful.

By tacit agreement, she and Turk had put the whole
matter of the murders, if murders they were, on hold,
wanting to have a peaceful Christmas and New Year's. But
it was always there, niggling away in the background like
a pot-au-feu simmering on the stove. Rennie, who before
everything had happened had been eagerly anticipating a
few weeks of relaxation — nothing to write, nothing to do
but hang out blissfully with Turk and make him move
furniture and hang pictures and otherwise mess around
with the house — was well aware that at some point she was
going to have to do at least *some* poking around.

Normally, of course, she'd have been on the case with
both delicately manicured hands and in it with both thigh-
booted feet. But at the moment, she was merely cross. Bad,
bad, *bad* timing. Though far worse timing for those two kids
in the cemetery, of course, so she had nothing to complain
of by comparison. And then there was that little matter that
Sledger had confided to her — the guitar theft and death
threat letters. She brightened: now that was something
she could look into right away, and maybe the murder
investigation *could* safely be left to the police. Just this once.

That would make for a refreshing change, really. Unlike

her dealings with the law enforcement agencies of San Francisco, Monterey, Los Angeles, London and Sullivan County, New York State, she had no previous experience of the NYPD; but she had a dark feeling that the city coppers would most likely not be anywhere near so accommodating or easily impressed by her burgeoning legend, yeah right, as those other cop shops had been. So maybe she really should confine herself to Sledger's problem after all; and Turk, when she mentioned it to him after she joined him in the living room, agreed.

"I don't think you actually realize just how lucky you've been so far with your droll little sideline as Murder Chick. You've only ever run up against detectives who've not been totally obstructive of your amateur investigative efforts, and who've basically let you get away with, well, murder."

"You mean that so far no one has actually smacked me down and sat on me," said Rennie smugly.

"If you like. No offense, but I've noticed for myself that the law officers of several different cities and two separate nations haven't been pleased as punch, exactly, to have to work alongside you. Or, more accurately, in your shadow, as you're the one who gets the headlines. Or writes them. You do get results, though, and they're more than happy to accept those, so I can see where that encourages them to be rather more forbearing of your involvement than they might otherwise have been—DCI Dakers in my homeland, Inspectors Devlin and Gilmore at Monterey, our Marcus, when he was still officially a San Francisco and L.A. copper, even good-hearted Sheriff Caskie Lawson up in the boondocks, I very much liked that man. But this is

New York, and the police department here is demonstrably tougher. They might have a distinctly different view of what they'll let you get away with."

"So?"

"So perhaps you might want to stand back from this one a bit, before they toss you off it. You mentioned that Sledger had some personal difficulties she didn't want to go to the authorities about; why don't you concentrate on those, then? I bet you could wrap that up in a day or two."

She stretched in her chair and swooped up the passing Svaha to cuddle for comfort, burying her face in the long, wonderfully warm, soft fur. "I'm glad to see you've learned to have such confidence in my detectiving skills."

"Rather hard not to, when I've seen the empirical proof over and over. You do put things together very well."

"Yes, I do, don't I." She was silent for a moment, stroking the kitten as the tiny creature industriously licked Rennie's hand and wrapped tiny paws around her wrist, purring and kicking in a frenzy of affection.

"I saw Pudge down in the studio just now," she said then. "He said he was picking up the black Strat to have the bridge checked by that guy you go to on Forty-eighth Street, you told him it seemed loose at the Garden show." Only the tiniest questioning tone had crept into her voice.

"Did I? Oh yes, I have a vague recollection. I really hate it when I pick up an instrument and it's not in absolutely perfect shape to go right there. That's what I pay him for."

"You didn't see him? He'd been in the guitar vault, he said Niles let him in."

"Well, that was probably why I didn't see him, then.

I didn't go near the guitar vault." He glanced up at her. "Don't worry, he wasn't stealing the axe. He told me he was coming over one of these evenings to fetch it, and I just forgot. He doesn't have a key or anything. No problems."

"If you say so. It'll be nice to see him on a more regular basis, now that we're living here and so is he." Rennie tucked the kitten against her and rose to head upstairs, and Turk collared his mate's neck with one arm as they went up the glorious front staircase. "Will you be able to give him enough work in between tours to justify keeping him on the payroll?"

"Trivially. There's always something that wants seeing to, especially when we start recording, and he helps Boanerges with the sound system. Besides, he can always pick up work with other bands to fill in, the way he usually does. He did a few days' toil for Sledger before we had to start prep for the Garden show. And before our tour kicked off, he was helping out Bosom Serpent and some other acts. He's very much in demand; I'm just glad I can get him to look after me as much as he does."

Rennie nodded as they flopped on the sofa before the fireplace in their enormous bedroom, setting Svaha down beside her—until the kitten was more used to the house, they'd decided to keep her in their room at night, and there were appropriate facilities in Rennie's bathroom. She could tell Turk wasn't ready to sack out yet any more than she was: they both enjoyed a little cuddle time before bed, just quietly talking and watching the flames in the hearth, so relaxing, at least until idle fondling turned into serious foreplay. Turk said the décor and layout reminded him of his rooms at Locksley Hall, but thinking of that future ducal abode still made Rennie a little skittish. Why couldn't they just stay where they were, and as they were? For at least the foreseeable future? Say, the next thirty years?

"There's always something going on in New York, between the clubs and the Fillmore and the Garden and the Academy of Music. Still, I don't want him neglecting you, your lordship."

"He won't be. We'll be recording for real soon enough and he'll have plenty on his plate. So will we, for that matter."

"Well, for what it's worth, you're probably right. There's certainly enough to keep me busy as well, around here."

Turk heard the subtext loud and clear, and sighed, knowing that she wasn't referring to housework. "Meaning if you should just *happen* to come across something you think may help the various investigations, you're going to check it out until it squeals for mercy, aren't you."

"Pretty much, yeah."

But Rennie was enjoying her present leisure too much to start actively checking out squealing leads just yet, or, for that matter, to spare the energy to worry about Pudge or anyone else. Niles was taking up most of her time, which she hadn't predicted but really should have, based on past form with Prax and Turk and Ned and everybody else. She had had an irritably unproductive conversation with Ken Karper, with whom she had worked in her early days in San Francisco, at the Clarion. They had forged a fine working relationship as well as a good friendship, and Rennie had been delighted when Fitz had noticed Ken's quality and swiftly moved him to New York, to be chief crime reporter on Fitz's American flagship paper, the Sun-Tribune. Ken had been equally delighted with the move, and glad too to know he would still be working with Murder Chick; when Rennie had followed him there, with Turk, Ken had been even more pleased.

Her irritation had not been with Ken, of course, but with the unproductiveness. Try as he might, he hadn't been able to come up with any more information about the two victims than was already known, and Rennie had left his office sadly unsatisfied. For the past day or two, she had been pottering aimlessly around the house, but thinking all the time, and when her brain finally presented her with something, she had taken it straight to the person it might most directly concern. Well, you had to start somewhere. And she'd been delinquent long enough.

"So let me get this straight, Miss Stride. You're telling me that Sledger Cairns, Miss Veronica Lee Cairns as properly is, received death threats and did not report them to the authorities. And her guitar was kidnapped for ransom, and you think it might have been her sound guy. Her now dead sound guy."

Nick Sattlin steepled his fingers and contemplated her over their tips, continuing. "And *you* didn't report it either, even though you think that it somehow has something to do with the cemetery deaths."

"Yes. That is indeed what I think, and I'm reporting it now, after all." Rennie returned his gaze with equanimity.

They were seated in Sattlin's tiny office at the precinct house on East Fifth Street, a closet-sized space with a window overlooking a dingy courtyard; outside the half-glass walls, the place swirled and pulsed with activity, a few curious glances occasionally being cast their way.

"Why do you think this, may I ask?"

"I'm so glad you do ask! Well, for one thing, stealing Sledger's guitar had to be an inside job. Bill Graham runs a pretty tight ship: the Fillmore East may seem like the birthplace of chaos, but he knows exactly what goes on there, and no way was any random thieving junkie, or souvenir-hunting fan, wandering in off the street to pinch Sledger Cairns' favorite axe. But her own guy? Who'd suspect him? Even if someone caught him with the guitar in hand, he could always say he was going to tune it up, or rotate its tires, or whatever the hell."

As that last sentence left her lips, Rennie felt her slaydar, that apparently magical crime sense that had served her so well the past three years, tingle somewhere far away. She frowned, trying to catch hold of the warning, or whatever it was, but it eluded her, and after a moment she let it go. It would come back when it was ready. It always did.

"Frankly, I think the damn thing never left the building," she went on with a sigh. "I think he just took it and hid it in another case, left the ransom note, and returned it when Sledger paid up. She never told Bill, so there would have been no search made for it."

"What did" —Sattlin glanced at some papers— "Mr. Nydborg need the money for? Theoretically, of course."

"Theoretically? How the hell do I know, maybe a cruise

to Cozumel or an operation for his ailing old mother or a first edition of Mark Twain! Oh, for God's sake, do I have to tell you people *everything*? To pay for the drugs that the mysterious cemetery visitor was delivering, most likely! And said visitor was delivering the merchandise in the cemetery — to a girl who looked like Sledger — so Sledge and everybody else at the Fillmore East didn't witness the transaction."

"Why *couldn't* they witness the transaction?" Sattlin demanded immediately. "I know that in your world drug deals of different levels of seriousness go down all the time. As a cop, I have to say I hate it. But there's a huge difference between a lid of pot for ten bucks and a few kilos of heroin, and most reasonable police officers are aware of it, and behave accordingly. And we don't even know that any other drugs were involved but the coke that the two victims and Mr. Niles Clay had been snorting."

Rennie smiled. "Oh yes we do. We know there was something else because Niles isn't dead and they are."

"Uh, *frozen to death?*"

"Not before something else did them in, according to the medical examiner."

He tried, he really did, but he was unable to keep the astonishment off his face. "How the *hell* did you —"

"I didn't. You just told me. Classic."

Sattlin tried to hide a grin, settled for an exasperated sigh. "Be that as it may — and we still don't know for a fact that it was — how do you tie in the deaths? And do you have actual *proof* of Miss Cairns' claims about the guitar? Did she show you the note? Or proof that the dead sound guy was involved? Not that you've shown *me* so far, you don't."

"But it ties *itself* in! It's *Sledger*. It's *her* dead sound guy. It's a dead groupie who looks like *her*, by design—it's all going on around our Ronnie Lee like a little nasty whirlpool. It's not drugs, or not *just* drugs, anyway. It's something bigger and nastier than that. I hope, I pray, that Sledger's not personally implicated. Not to mention stays alive. As for proof, I bet I can get you some. Maybe not the proof you want. And it might be complicated." She beamed at him. "Though not impossible."

Sattlin ran a hand over his face and regarded her steadily. He was beginning to understand why all those other cops he'd talked to had such ungodly mixed feelings about Miss Rennie Stride, future duchess and present nuisance: such feelings were beginning to develop within himself as well.

"Jesus. With you, it probably isn't."

CHAPTER ELEVEN

THE MOST AMAZING SOUND was coming from behind the sofa. It sounded as though a bunch of owls were being sucker-punched right in their feathery little tummies, whooooofwhooooofwhooooof, very odd indeed. *Better you don't even ask*, Rennie told herself.

Instead, she silently scanned the skylighted living room of Sledger Cairns' four-bedroomed suite on the top floor of the red-brick, wrought-iron-balconied, Victorian-Gothic Hotel Chelsea. Externity was staying at the weird and quirky establishment on Twenty-third Street while they were in New York for a month-long engagement at the Café Au Go-Go, down on Bleecker Street. The Chelsea, being tolerant of all manner of weird and quirky, not to mention excessive, behavior, was much favored by off-the-chart bands and off-the-wall acts, from Dylan Thomas to Bob Dylan, from Mark Twain and O. Henry to Janis Joplin and Jimi Hendrix.

So, kind of a fancy flophouse for artistes. I must ask Turk if Lionheart ever stayed here. Maybe we could take a little escape weekend here ourselves, I hear such good stories...

At the moment, several of Externity's members, as it were, were hanging out, so to speak...no doubt a few more good Chelsea stories would come of it. Over against the wall, an Asian groupie who looked startlingly like Keitha Clay except her skin was honey-butter where Keitha's was amber-topaz, completely naked except for her many strands of beads, was on her knees in front of one of the roadies, her black-silk fall of hair brushing the floor as her head moved back and forth. Froggy Livingston, the bass player, had just come in with a triple set of strawberry blondes, all of whom had their hands all over him, so that the quartet resembled one of those merry, many-armed Hindu deities of ambiguous gender. In the suite kitchen, one of the guys was rubbing an ice cube over another groupie's bare tummy, rolling her out like pastry on the marble-topped counter, while she shrieked with laughter and struggled out of her halter top. Just business as usual, on just another rocknroll night.

Rennie hadn't wasted any time. Once she had her plan worked out to her own satisfaction, she'd phoned Sledger and explained how things stood; and, with her friend's enthusiastic cooperation, she had set it all up. Then she enlisted Turk's assistance, though she didn't tell him any real details—it was more like dragging him into it kicking and screaming. Still, he'd managed to help out just fine at Abbey Road last year, with that creep Barney Levine and the fake session with Prax, and he'd quite enjoyed himself, so he wasn't exactly a crime-scene virgin and shouldn't be copping any false righteousness.

Anyway, here she was at the Chelsea, in Sledger's suite, dressed as a pretend groupie in a skin-tight poor-boy top that barely contained her unfettered frontal assets and a leather skirt about six inches long and fishnet pantyhose and thigh-high boots; and if there was anything to be found, it would be found here and she would be the one to find it. She fervently hoped. At the very least, she could check out the vibe. Though just now, as she surveyed the terrain, the vibe seemed all one way, and not her way…as long as no one hit on her, she should be fine. She devoutly wished.

Sprawled like a Byzantine empress on a shawl-draped sofa, Sledger herself was receiving the attentions of four, count 'em, four very cute young fanboys who were probably barely legal and who obviously couldn't believe their luck. Two of them were concentrating their efforts above her waist — Sledger's bosomage being roughly the size of a small Baltic nation, there was plenty to go around — the other two below. No one seemed particularly upset at the sad demise of Biff Nydborg and the groupie Scarlett. Well, perhaps this was their own very special way of mourning them.

Sledger saw Rennie hesitating in the doorway and languidly waved to her. "Strider! Get over here! Take two, they're small…"

Rennie declined politely and flashed her a warning glance — *don't say my name, you stupid girl, don't you remember our plan, I'm supposed to be undercover!* — but it was lost on Sledger. The only comfort was that everyone was so stoned or so busy that it had obviously gone whizzing by several miles above their heads. She sat down on another sofa across from Sledger and the action, and crossed her legs so that her leather microskirt pretty much disappeared, to the sudden attentive interest of half the guys in the room, however occupied they might be otherwise.

"No, thanks, I'll wait for Turk. He's on his way."

"Oh wow, you're here for *Turk Wayland*?" gasped one of the youngbloods, detaching his mouth from Sledger's bare breast to do so, and staring at Rennie in awe. "You're *His* groupie? What's your name, you're so pretty, you must be a supergroupie if you're here for *Him*."

Rennie opened her own mouth, then closed it again, hearing the capital H. Well, Turk was her cover, to put it crassly; his august presence would give her the groupie cred she was trying for and explain what she was doing here. She just hoped nobody here knew that Turk was engaged to a certain New York reporter and was stainlessly faithful; she really didn't fancy seeing this little escapade ending up in the gossip columns of Rolling Stone or Teen Angels...

"Yeah," she said after a moment. "Yeah, that's right. Nefer. I'm Nefer Almond. I'm *His* groupie. I'm here for *Him*."

Sledger pushed aside her devotees and stood up, pulling Nefer with her into the empty corridor leading away to the suite kitchen. "I love this place, it's like the Chateau Marmont, with all its little nooks and crannies... Listen, I did what you said, and asked around, but nobody seems to have noticed anything strange going on with Biff or that groupie. And did I tell you I paid the ransom money for Duchess? But so far she hasn't been returned."

"Really? You're sure?"

"Of course I'm sure, Strider," said Sledger humbly. "I check the empty case a dozen times a day. Oh well, she'll turn up. If not, heads will roll."

I have every confidence that they will roll, roll down to Rio, if Sledge is crossed in this... But maybe the reason the guitar hadn't been returned yet was because whoever had absconded with it was, not to put too fine a point on it, dead. Both Biff and Scarlett would have had access to it, either in Sledger's room here or down at the Fillmore East, they could have pinched it easily…

She was back on the sofa observing, and Sledger was back on the other one with her adhering adherents, when Turk came in. Instantly Rennie was all over him, and after his initial surprise he cautiously reciprocated.

"Hi, I'm your personal groupie tonight. Nefer Almond, here for your participation. I live to serve. Just play along, please, will you?" she muttered against him, as she unbuttoned his shirt and started kissing bare chest, slipping down to kneel between his thighs as she pushed him down on the sofa.

He struggled to contain his laughter. "Pleased, flattered, delighted to help out, must ask *why*?"

She worked her way back up, unbuttoning her own shirt and slipping his double-ring belt loose at the same time, and noticing that no one was showing anything beyond the mildest abstract awareness of her and Turk, all being pre-emptively preoccupied. Well, *that* was a relief…

"Tell you later. God, I hate these stupid damn hippie belts… Come on, I'm a groupie! Here's your big chance to behave piggishly with absolutely no repercussions, at least none from me."

"If you insist." They fell back into the sofa cushions, Rennie straddling his left thigh and hiking up her microskirt, his hands running under it, hers delving down beneath his waistband, feeling him respond under her familiar touch, and for a few minutes they enthusiastically busied themselves, increasingly deep-breathingly. "Ah, are we starting something we should really be finishing up at home?"

"You tell *me*, guitar stud. I want to go check out the other rooms, and this is the plan: get us out of here. But be sure to treat me like a rockslut."

"You're really making the most of this, aren't you. Oh well, far be it from me to deny you."

Turk stood up, Rennie still clinging to his leg. Wrapping his belt around her throat, he pulled her to her feet, kissed her so long that her bones melted, then slung her over his shoulder and headed off to the nearest unoccupied bedroom. To the cheers of the other guys, seeing that action was imminent and perhaps hoping to be invited along.

Once inside, Rennie reached down behind Turk's back and deadbolted the door behind them. "Great! Now we start looking for clues."

Turk offloaded her on top of the king-size bed and grinned down at her, unfastening his pants. "I don't think so, Nefer! Groupies don't tell musicians what to do—they just follow orders. You started this, anyway. What is it your American cops say? Oh, right. Spread 'em."

Several incident-crammed minutes later, Rennie fell back on the pillows, happily out of breath. "Ah yes, the Famous Five-Minute Fuck, rock and roll's contribution to the annals of human sexuality: they're clean, they're over eighteen, he's hard, she's wet, five minutes and off they get—including foreplay, of course. Nice work, by the way, Ampman."

"Not bad yourself. For a groupie. But my old lady's a much better lay than you are." He dodged her flailing hands and pinned her down again; they were both laughing. "Why don't we just reprise that ride section, a little slower tempo this time perhaps…"

They made it half an hour, then Rennie lay there unmoving and languorous, watching Turk put his pants back in order.

"Goodness gracious, great balls of fire. As it were. If you treat all the groupies like *that*, Mr. Rock God, sir, I'm surprised you haven't got more."

"That old lady of mine I mentioned? Doesn't let me have groupies. Well, actually, it's more like she doesn't let *them* have *me*. Not that I ever do groupies. You being the exception, of course. But we're lucky she's not around. You'd be in big trouble. She's been known to beat them up when she catches them coming on to me."

"Smart woman." Rennie sat up and swung her legs off the bed, searching the sheets for her lace bikini underwear and tossing Turk his belt. "How is it you can always charm the pants off me? Literally. Goodness, that was dizzy-making, as the actress said to the bishop — those groupie tramps don't know what they're missing. And they won't be finding out, either… I include rocker lads in that sluttish designation, lest you think I'm picking on the chicks. Sledger too, I'm sorry to say. I'm very fond of her, but still. On the other hand, perhaps I myself should have been more of a rockslut than I, in fact, was. Before I became your betrothed, I mean. Not that I ever *was* a rockslut. Though I did date around a bit at work. As did you, and all the other people we know."

"Of course we did. But, too late, you had your chance. Should've sat on Keith Moon's face when he asked you to. It's all over now, Baby Blue — you're stuck with me. But do you *believe* what's going on out there? I'm sure you know that most bands don't do that kind of—Christ, who am I kidding, of course they do. But Lionheart's like the royal family by comparison, all sedate and boring. As you can attest."

"Yes, you are, and yes, I can." Her turn to dodge a swat. "So unlike the home life of your own dear Queen. Then again—talking about rocksluts—I didn't know you lads personally in your excitingly misspent younger days, but I surely did hear stories. May I remind you of Amsterdam and bunches of tulips in rather—unusual receptacles? So very unusual, in fact, that Led Zeppelin felt they could only outdo you with a red snapper?"

Turk laughed, a little embarrassed. "Good point. And no, please, *don't* remind me—even though it wasn't me with those, uh, flower vases, it was Mick and Niles and a couple of roadies. And with that red snapper thing the Zep pretty much forfeited their status as members of the human race. But tell me again why you're pretending to be a groupie? Well, you haven't told me even once yet, have you, so I guess just tell me."

"Because, with manager Jason Kee's connivance, I'm going to hang around Sledger and the band, in groupie guise, to try and find out about the origins of the guitar kidnap threat and subsequent death threat on Sledger, and why Biff Nydborg, who worked with Sledger, and Peggy whatever her name is, who looked like Sledger, were murdered. Which they were, even though the cops aren't saying so publicly. And maybe someone will let something slip in front of an airhead groupie that they wouldn't in front of Rennie Reporter, or even in front of Turk Wayland's old lady."

"And you can trust Sledger to keep her mouth shut? *Sledger?*"

"Well, I guess I have to, don't I."

"Are you sure the band doesn't know you're a ringer?"

Rennie shrugged; she had pulled on her fishnets and boots and zipped up the tiny skirt, and now she was struggling into her poor-boy top and impatiently gazing around for a good place to start prying.

"They're all young and new. Still blown away by the sheer joy of being able to play music on a regular basis. Or perhaps by the sheer joy of being blown on a regular basis. They're just kids, they're mostly from England or the Ozarks or some damn where—I very much doubt they read my stuff or keep current on who's paired off with whom. I haven't spent all that much time here yet bizzing it up, but hopefully I won't run into anyone I know or anyone who can recognize me before I finish snooping around. Jason'll watch out for me."

"Oh, Lord God of Hosts, this is *such* a not very well thought-out idea on *so* many levels... There's no way people haven't seen us together, and even if they haven't— sweetheart, we're public. Like it or not, we're out there. *I'm* out there. *You're* out there. And you're out there as much because of you as because of me. People *know* about us. If they're into Lionheart at all they know Turk is with Rennie and Rennie is with Turk and they know we don't fool around with anyone else. Even if they're not into Lionheart, they have this vague gossip-page awareness from, yes, your boss Fitz's own rags, among many other places, that Blond English Ducal Guitar Lad is happily and monogamously having it off with Green-eyed American Reporter Murder Chick. Be sure to thank him from me next time you see him, by the way, I'm *so* grateful. And quite selfishly, I don't want people to think I'm cheating on you even with you. It's bad for my reputation, and you know, I won't have it."

"Too late, they all saw us go in here…though if any nasty rumors do get out about Turk Wayland drilling some trollop in Sledger Cairns' hotel suite, I'm sure we can manage to explain to the press and our friends, probably in that order. Something like how we were just, oh, you know, visiting our dear friend Sledger and we were suddenly overcome by tumultuous and irresistible lust, first displayed publicly and then satisfied privately when you kissed me senseless and carried me off slung over your manly shoulder like one of the Sabine women."

Turk grinned in spite of himself. "Both of us looking damn good, I'm sure, my little trollop."

"I should think so! So if anyone noticed us outside they just thought oh there's that hot sexy Turk Wayland making out with some hot sexy groupie."

"Exactly! See, this is what I'm telling you. I don't *want* people thinking that. At first, the whole idea sounds absurd. But then, when you think about it, you begin to realize that it makes no bloody sense whatsoever."

"Though our Veronica did slip up and call me 'Strider' for the whole damn room to hear," said Rennie, blithely ignoring him. "But they were all stoned out of whatever mind they share amongst them, and pretty busy otherwise, so probably they didn't even notice. The only other one who knows I'm snooping around is Jason, and he promised to keep press and record company people away—anybody who might recognize me. As a manager he knows how to keep his mouth shut. Especially if he wants me to keep snooping. Which he does. It's only for a day or two. Hey, maybe I'll wear a wig! I could buy one in that whore store on Fourteenth Street. I could really get into being a Beatlewife blonde."

A wig. Oh, *Luuuu-ceeeee...* "And suppose somebody seriously hits on you, which I'm thinking will happen in less than a millisecond? What do you think you might do then?"

"I think I might have to kill them?"

"Good answer. Now just file that image away for now and call it up later at your leisure. Not to mention—again—that your career as murder magnet has, how shall I put this, thrust you well into the public awareness, and you have to believe me when I tell you that people are more likely than not to know who you are."

Rennie shrugged, suddenly uncomfortable. "Yeah, whatever."

"And you still haven't told me why you think the deaths and the possible framing of Niles and the threats against Sledger are related, you know," continued Turk doggedly. "I swear I'm not impugning your track record, which speaks for itself, and loudly, but honestly, now. What are the odds of you actually finding out anything from this little charade?"

"Just slightly better than the odds of fourteen tiny pink bunnies flying out of my pert little ass? I don't *know* if anything's related! To anything! That's what I'm doing all this *for*, to find *out*. It's not a *bad* plan."

"Plan!" Turk turned to her, amused. "Bay of Pigs, was that yours too, by any chance? Charge of the Light Brigade? Little Big Horn? Now *those* were *plans*... Well, I'm not going along with it any further than tonight, and not even your vast and undeniable charms can make me. I absolutely refuse to be perceived as another groupie-groping rock lout running around cheating on his lady. Because I never have, and I never would—"

"Oh honey, I know that—"

"—and I know it's a nice thing you're doing for Sledger, I know how you hate people mistaking you for a—"

"Yes, yes, she'll owe me bigtime," agreed Rennie, who had finished poking around the desk and dresser and was now rifling nightstand drawers. "And don't think I won't collect—nice fat exclusive story, I have it all planned out. Fitz will be so pleased. Come on, start looking."

"For what?"

"Anything suspicious. To answer your earlier question about why I think things are related: there was a letter that the guitarnapper sent to Sledger on hotel stationery. This hotel's stationery. Like this right here." She waved a folder of letter paper and envelopes. "Big old clue. Which was either very careless and stupid or very clever indeed. I just want to check around to see if maybe I can figure out which it is. Oh, and she told me before you got here that the guitar hasn't been returned even though she paid the ransom."

"Well, that's not good."

"No, it isn't. Though I have a couple of thoughts as to

why… Anyway, this is Froggy's room. Though as we just saw, obviously anyone can get into it. We can probably sneak into the other rooms just as easily, if they're not occupied. Or even if they are. Oh, come *on*, Turk, please, the quicker we search the quicker we're out of here, they'll be pounding on the door before long, wanting to join the fun…"

"You don't do anything in moderation, do you," Turk observed, reluctantly joining her in tossing the room.

"Gosh, Sherlock, when did you notice?" wondered Rennie dryly.

"As we met," said Turk, more dryly still.

The exercise proved as futile as Turk had thought it would, though Rennie was intrigued to uncover a neatly packed set of fur-lined leather collars and cuffs in the room resident's luggage. Too bad they hadn't searched first. She was equally intrigued to learn that Froggy wore custom-made black silk underwear of a rather notable dimension of pouchage. Well, well. No wonder Sledger had hired him. And here was everybody thinking it was just for his great bass playing…

They checked out the other two unoccupied bedrooms—something very noisy and strenuous seemed to be going on in the third, so they declined to venture in—but found nothing of note, and the winds of the desert that whirl away the footprints of time could not have done as quick or amazing a job as Rennie did with vanishing all traces of her unauthorized activities, though she did leave the bed in Froggy's room all mussed up, just to boast. When they re-emerged into the suite living room, Sledger and her harem were nowhere to be seen, but cheers and whistles of admiration for perceived staying power greeted them from the personnel still strewn across the landscape. Turk smiled gamely; Rennie, reveling in her new role, preened a bit until Turk dragged her by her hair out into the hall and a waiting elevator.

"Right, that's it, Neffie, we're out of here."

When the elevator stopped at a lower floor, though, Rennie couldn't resist getting briefly back into character.

"Oooh, I was never with such a famous rock star before!" she squealed. Plastering herself across Turk's front, she quickly dropped to her knees and applied her face to his fly just as a goggling gaggle of Middle American middle-aged hotel guests piled into the car, mouths agape. "You're sooooo sexy, all the other groupies said so…"

Turk's own face was still burning as they got into the cab outside. "I have NEVER been so embarrassed—"

"Oh, lighten up, Britboy, it'll do you good… Did you know you're adorable when you blush? Yes you are! Besides, they were hardly rock fans. It's very wrong for people like that to even *be* at the Chelsea, they belong uptown at the Holiday Inn. Clearly a travel agent's mistake, booking them in here. I doubt they had any idea who you were anyway, they were just dear little corn-fed tourists from flyover country."

"Well, at least there were no children to be traumatized for life by your appalling behavior."

"Hey! I made you look *terrific* just now, you know, even if you didn't appreciate it properly. Though I can tell you did… I bet we made their day. Hell, their whole trip. They'll dine out on it amongst their dear little corn-fed friends back home for *months*, how decadent New York is, people engaging in unspeakable acts right out in public. As if nobody ever gave head in Iowa. If they thought anything, they probably thought you were Plant or Daltrey or Neddy. All you blond limey rock stars that start with R look alike — Robert, Roger, Raven, Richard…"

"I do *not* look like Robert." He cheered up a bit as the cab hung a right onto Broadway and headed downtown. "Still, if they think that—"

"You just hold that thought." She shifted sideways and down. "I do believe that Nefer Almond has some unfinished business to attend to."

CHAPTER TWELVE

ACOUPLE OF DAYS LATER, the weather had broken; the unseasonal deep-freeze had ended and the snow had gone, and it was merely correctly cold for Manhattan in mid-December. In her cozy writing room, fireplace crackling away more for inspiration and atmosphere than actual heat, Rennie sat at her big old rolltop desk and stared across the street, where the ancient oaks in St. Mark's churchyard rattled their last clinging brown leaves in a northwest wind.

She had gone back twice to the Chelsea in her groupie guise and poked around some more, but hadn't found anything of any material help. Nobody had accidentally dropped an incriminating allusion, no hotel stationery pads had been found with the damning impression of a ransom note having been written one page up, the way you see in movies. The only major happening was that Sledger's missing guitar had been restored to its usual home, a battered, velvet-lined case in its owner's hotel room.

Which confirmed Rennie's conviction that the axe-napping had been an inside job all along, and she duly reported the information to Detective Sattlin. But Sledger was so happy to have Duch back that she ignored all her friend's attempts to reconstruct the crime: she just lolled around on top of her bed and played and played and played. Still, Sledger and Externity were going to be around for the next month, so there was plenty of opportunity for Nefer Almond to ride again if the need arose. Though hopefully the case would be solved long before that.

In other developments closer to home, there had been a private, and highly unofficial, meeting down at the D.A.'s office in the big Foley Square courthouse, to discuss what if any charges should be filed in the matter of the overdose deaths, and Niles was unspeakably relieved to hear that no grand jury would be asked to deal with him as a suspect, because he wasn't going to be arrested. Not just yet, anyway.

"Insufficient evidence to go on," Rennie had announced to Turk with deep relief, having just gotten off the phone with Shea Laakonen, Berry Rosenbaum and King Bryant himself, on a conference call. "Just because he was there isn't enough, and they've got nothing else. Purely circumstantial, like Praxie with Tam Linn's murder. Or you with Tansy's. Obviously it's a grand jury matter, murder always is, but they shouldn't even have been *thinking* of putting it before one at this point with such pathetic evidence. I'm glad to see they didn't, but I guess all the publicity made them feel they had to be seen to be doing something. Hence this delicate little meeting, however unorthodox. They don't want to look like idiots going after yet another famous rock star with all guns blazing and then having to back off for lack of support or evidence or anything actually real. There's been way too much of that lately. As we know, to our cost and annoyance."

Turk had nodded in rueful agreement. "Indeed we do. But whether Niles is involved or not—the way I understand your legal system, the case *will* have to go before a grand

jury sooner or later, right? As all felonies do. And that is to
officially determine if there's enough evidence of a crime to
send it to trial? Which it seems pretty obvious that there is,
as you say. Even if it's incredibly disorganized just now."

"That's exactly right. Grand juries just determine
whether it goes to court. But most cases don't come up for
months, sometimes years even. And the later the better, I
say. More time for evidence to be collected, yeah, but also
more time for someone to solve it."

"And by 'someone' you really mean, of course—"

"Well, in all modesty…"

Though Shea and another lawyer from King Bryant's
firm and Gerry Langhans and a Centaur publicist had all
been there with Niles at the downtown meeting, Rennie had
been reluctant to attend in either a personal or professional
capacity, and Turk too had declined, although Niles had
asked them both to come and lend him support. He'd
probably asked her only because he had to, she considered.
It was all much too reminiscent of Prax's and Turk's ordeals
in San Francisco and L.A., and of Rennie's own in London
after the Hyde Park incident, for either Turk or Rennie to
feel happy about being on the spot for the meeting. Not to
mention the hordes of press lurking outside the courtroom,
which had given the Wayland-Strides yet another solid
excuse to stay away—neither contributing to the circus nor
being afflicted by it, but safe at home, pursuing their usual
pursuits.

For some strange reason, though, no one was besieging
them here in the prow house, for which Rennie was
profoundly grateful. Maybe Detective Sattlin's minions

were chivvying them along before they could get well entrenched, but she hadn't noticed any extra people lurking around on the slushy street outside, not press nor fans nor cops. Too cold, maybe, for loitering. It was too much to hope for that nobody knew where they lived.

Now Turk spoke up from behind her, where he lay stretched out on a sofa under a Victorian floorlamp, reading *The Lord of the Rings*. "I'm just amazed they got to it as fast as they did."

"Again, Frodo Wayland-Baggins, that rock god thing you and the rest of the Fellowship have going? Rank hath its privileges...which you of all people should certainly know all about. How many times must I point it out to you, my little furry-footed friend?"

He lifted bare unfurry feet and wiggled his piggies at her, though he didn't take his eyes from his book, and she laughed.

"I spoke metaphorically. If anything, you're an Elf. Tarrant the Golden. Tall, blond, fair of face and form beyond the measure of mortals." Turk was pleased to hear it, and she nodded toward the thick volume in his hands. "And also annoying beyond the measure of mortals. I'm glad to see that you're finally reading The Book, though. Because if you didn't, then we couldn't be friends. But what do you think Niles will do for the interval? He may be off the hook for an indictment, at least for the moment, but the cops still want him around. He's going to have to be here anyway, when you boys start recording."

"Bags of time," said Turk absently. "It's still almost two weeks to Christmas. We don't have rehearsal time slated until the end of January. I booked some provisional studio time the first week of February, and I could always push it back even further. Or shift it up, if we're all bored to tears and clear to go sooner. We've already started downstairs, and we could always move all the heavy lifting over to the Record Plant or wherever else we want. Or even do the whole thing right here. Depends on the sound we decide on."

"How about us? For our Christmas, I mean."

Turk put the book down on his chest and took off his reading glasses — thin gold wire-rims, a new accessory, though he only wore them when his eyes were tired, and then only to read or write. Rennie loved them. She thought they made him look like the hippest, smartest, sexiest, cutest, most adorable grad student in the world, and she'd have made him wear them onstage if she could. It especially turned her on when he took them off in bed before making love with her.

"We can still go away if you want — we could take a couple of weeks after New Year's, before the sessions start. Or go for New Year's itself. But I was rather hoping we might spend actual Christmas here. Our first in our new house."

He was rewarded with an instant burst of delight on Rennie's face. "With a big old tree and Christmas dinner for our friends and God bless us every one?"

"And Uncle Tom Cobleigh and all. Or just us by ourselves. Yes, of course. Whatever you want." He turned to look at her, joined palms with a small clap for emphasis, startling Macduff, who was snoring under the desk with Rennie's bare toes burrowed into his thick coat. "But."

"I know, I know."

'But' meant no relatives — neither his nor hers. That policy had been mutually determined a while back, and so far they'd managed to stick to it even under the guns of the enemy. Oh, by now she'd met most of his close kin and he'd met most of hers: both families were clearly charmed by the prospective new addition, but equally clearly a little chilly about the public living arrangements, going so far as to wonder aloud and pointedly about the wedding plans.

On the Tarrant side, the two of them had visited his family in England last February, at the ancestral palace in Wiltshire, for the big family post-holiday get-together, once the murders at the Royal Albert Hall had been sorted out, and where they'd become engaged. And a brief visit in July, when they'd been there for Brian Jones' funeral and Lionheart's Royal Opera House gig, and again last month for the old Duke's obsequies, of course. His favorite cousin Lord Oliver Buckle had come to visit, one weekend in September when Turk had had a few days off from the tour, and his youngest older half-sister, Lady Felicity Fitton, the stunning fashion model known to all the world as Flick — just Flick — and her race-car driver Spanish nobleman boyfriend had stayed with them in Nichols Canyon, for a fortnight back in the spring. And every now and then they'd have a family occasion, like the recent one here with Eric and Petra and Carly; and her parents and sisters had come to several Sunday dinners as the prow house slowly took shape.

But the big overblown hyped-up holidays, no. It was just too fraught with conflicting factions and emotional tugs-of-war and familial blackmail on a transatlantic scale, and so they'd made the decision to either go away for the days in question or just be at home on their own or with their friends. They both knew they weren't going to be able to get away with it indefinitely, especially once they were married—the specter of Christmas at Locksley Hall was already rearing its ominous Dickensian head—but for the moment they were grateful that they could still do as they liked.

"Who could we ask?" Rennie had happily shoved her writing aside and was already making lists.

"Anyone you like. Anyone who's in town. Anyone who wants to fly in. Anyone neither of us is related to by blood or by marriage. Well, except Eric and Trey and Petra and Davina. They may be family, but they count as friends."

"Eric and Petra can't come. They have to put in holiday time at Hell House," said Rennie, with real regret. "It's like a condition of parole. The deal is, if you spend Thanksgiving and Christmas there, you get a free pass for Easter and Fourth of July. Motherdear's little barter system."

"Ex-Motherdear. Better still, Never-was-Motherdear."

"Yes...so very nice to be able to say that. Feels like unblotting my copybook. Now *your* mother wouldn't do that, I'm sure."

Turk laughed so hard the book fell onto the floor. "No, she has her own little barter system. Well, it plays out more like serfdom. Which historically was not unknown to us. Though we were the serf-ers, of course, not the serf-ees. I'll tell you about it sometime."

"Can't wait... So for starters, Lionheart and ladies, Prax and Ares, Francher and Christabel, assuming they're all still in town and want to come. I'd ask Gray and Prue, but they're only going to be here for a few more days—Christmas at home with the kiddies and all." She rummaged for a pen, began noting names. "Everyone else, it depends on who's free and around. The Dylans, the Ravens, the Lennons—John and Niles can compare their legal problems—"

"Should be good."

"—Sledger, Gerry and JoAnn, Fitz and Alix, Plato Lars, Diego and Belinda, I am *not* inviting Fastbuck Freddy, no groupies either, how many is that, is that even, girls and boys?"

"I can't count in my head."

"What do you mean you can't count in your head? You're a musician! You count in your head all the time. I've seen you do it onstage in front of half a million screaming fans. You just don't want to be bothered."

Turk, who'd returned to his book as soon as his mate began listmaking, nodded firmly, and kept right on reading.

"Never mind, Dimples, I've got it under control… We should ask as many people as we can to make sure we get a full house. Most of them won't be able to make it anyway. It's very short notice and they'll have already made plans of their own."

"What about serving? And do we have enough whatnot to feed them with—all that kit you like to sit and contemplate?"

"Yes, yes, no problem; we're really only limited by dining room space and chair quantity. Let's say fourteen, maybe sixteen. And I'll get Galina to ask her niece and nephew to serve. You'll want to do most of the cooking, I'm sure, but I do the turkey. Either one really humongous one or two smaller big ones, I like lots of leftovers and the Aga can handle it. Honey, this list is *way* more than we have room for...maybe we could have a kiddie table..."

When she got no reply, Rennie glanced up, saw that Turk was back on the plains of Rohan, and grinned to herself. He was right: she *did* like to sit and yearn at all those things. The butler's pantry held several handsome old original built-in cupboards, oak-framed and glass-fronted, and she had crammed them full of Waterford and Wedgwood and flatware, having traded in all the wedding presents left over from the days of Stephen for patterns Turk liked. Similarly in the library: floor-to-ceiling mahogany cases in the process of being filled with a steady stream of volumes old and new, rare and modern, his and hers, making their way over from the second-hand bookstores of Fourth Avenue, all neatly snuggling into green-baize-lined shelves like lost little puppies home at last.

When the mood came on her, she would open the chests and cupboards and sit on the floor, or, in the library, curl up in a big armchair, and gaze with placid contentment. It wasn't gloating or possessiveness, or even bourgeois self-satisfaction, but something much more subtle; in some strange psychic way, it gave her peace. It was like meditation. She thought it somehow made the things happy too, that she visited them and admired them. The Zen of stuff. Oxymoronic, perhaps; hobbits would understand.

Turk had grown up with ten centuries' worth of Tarrant family chattels, jammed into six castles in four countries; not to mention assorted smaller domiciles—villas, palaces, palazzos, chateaux, manors, whatever, though by "smaller" was really meant "merely the size of Grand Central Terminal, not the size of a minor planetoid." He was used to having things around, often annoyed by the sheer extent of their presence, and didn't really comprehend the nature and depth of her feeling for possessions. Maybe it was a chick thing.

The Duchy of Locksley had paid for this house—all three houses, though both their names were on the deeds—as well as all the renovations, of course. It would end up ducal property in any case: they'd most likely keep it, as the Duchy didn't own any other domestic Manhattan real estate, just business properties. And certainly nothing of this size, though down the road they could always sell it to another rock family, or a hotel chain, or some emergent nation needing a downtown consulate to bolster its image. Therefore it had been important to her to bring something to the table too, even if it was just, well, tables—something besides her pretty little self.

So she'd bought all the furnishings, except for a couple of pieces from L.A. that Turk had wanted to have in New York and all her nicer furniture from the Haight pad. Since no normal person had eight king-size beds or a dozen sofas just lying around, and since everything had to be different because she absolutely refused to live amongst common bourgeois suites of stuff from common bourgeois stores the way common bourgeois suburbanites did, she'd gone out and shopped until she almost literally dropped.

She'd also hand-sewn all the curtains and draperies for the house; it had taken months. It had bemused Turk no end—he'd found it oddly disconcerting, and oddly endearing, to see her beavering patiently away night after night at her vintage Singer. But it was important to her, though even she wasn't entirely sure why, and so also to him, though the last dozen sets of summerweight portières had pinned-up hems, not stitched ones, where her energy had finally flagged.

She glanced over at him now. There was no sex in Middle-earth, at least none that Tolkien had openly reported on, but…

"Hey, Elf-prince, kiss me till I faint."

He closed the book on the Fellowship and opened his arms. "No mistaking *that* invitation."

"A woman must have a whole different psychology of sex than a man does," Turk mused afterwards, pulling up a happily inert Rennie to drape bonelessly across his hips on the fur rug before the fire. "Being penetrated rather than penetrating, I mean; being taken rather than taking…"

His mate gave a most indelicate snort. "Only men think like that. Men orgasmically lose themselves by focusing in, women by unfocusing out. But it is true that women think of sex differently. Not like being invaded but more like actively enveloping—we subsume, we draw in, we take possession, we accept and welcome and enclose and encompass you, like the earth or the sea or the galaxy itself… Or does that scare you, darling, make you think of bad fwightening Fweudian things like devouring vaginas with sharp pointy teefs?"

He scoffed right back at her. "Not I! I've always preferred sex to be more like unarmed combat than a poetic stroll through a flowery meadow, as you very well know. And as you do too."

"Very true, and isn't it a good thing we found each other. But if you want poetic…" She grinned and began to wickedly paraphrase. "'The splendour falls/on Wayland's balls/His thighs of steel and ass of glory…' Lord Tennyson, you know."

"Friend of the family," deadpanned Turk, his whole body shaking with laughter under her, though he tried valiantly to maintain the straight face.

"*No*! Really?"

"M'hm. Had a thing for my great-great-great-auntie Maud, reportedly. You may have read the poem he committed for her."

"Huh." Rennie considered this briefly. "I have, actually. Pretty grim it was, too, as I recall. I vastly prefer the songs you write about us. Much hotter stuff."

He laughed, and did some paraphrasing of his own. "'Are you coming, my dove, my dear? Are you coming, my life, my fate?'"

"I thought we both just did."

"Indeed." He shifted her more comfortably across him. "What have we heard about the investigation lately? Anything new about the victims?"

She shook her head. "Not since I talked to Ken Karper, up at the Sun-Trib. He didn't have a lot. They didn't freeze to death. They got stoned first. Then the drug killed them. *Then* they froze. I sprang that on Sattlin, and he almost passed out."

"Not something fed out to the public, I take it?"

"Not hardly!"

"Good guess, then?"

"Again, not hardly. Just putting things together, as is my adorable habit. It was great, to see the look on his face. But now it seems there was nothing super-strong or super-pure about the coke. But there was nothing *but* coke, so it *must* have been the coke. Unless it was something else and it got taken away by someone, and at the moment Niles is favorite. To our sorrow."

"If they didn't freeze to death, what killed them and why didn't it do for Niles as well?"

"That's the big old question, innit." She stretched lithely and nuzzled Turk's chest. "We've been over and over it."

"With only Niles' word to go on. I know. But he was pretty precise in his accounting. And he may be a loathsome little ferret — well, he *is* a loathsome little ferret in many ways, no maybe about it — but I've never known him to be a liar."

"Yes, but he had his dope goggles on that night; he wasn't exactly seeing things in their true light and nature. It's up to us to interpret."

"Up to *you*, madam. Did the coroner have nothing more than that?"

She stretched again and flipped over to straddle him, bending forward to trace his ear with her tongue, and he shivered, holding her hips. "Not a sausage. No needle marks, which we already knew."

"Niles did say no needles were involved."

"At least no needles when he was with them."

"Then later?"

"Would have to have been, if at all. Problem with that is, as has been pointed out and as we keep coming back to, forensics found no trace of any other drugs in their systems. What do we know that doesn't leave a trace?"

"I have no idea."

Rennie rose up and came back down. "Neither have I. But we know people who will."

Gray and Prue Sonnet had duly moved in, bag and baggage, the Monday after the Garden show, two hours after Prax and Ares. They were already apologizing that they couldn't stay for more than a few nights, as both of them were missing their kids and longing to get home sufficiently in advance of Christmas, but they were eager to see the new house. Rennie had proudly put them in the Jacobean suite on the second floor, to show off the fabulous old black oak furniture and make them feel at home; Prax and Ares were in the Victorian suite and Niles and Keitha in the Mission suite, and Turk and Rennie themselves were at the far end on the point of the prow.

"There! We're all within shouting distance, or shooting distance. Very cozy and collegiate. It's nice to be able to provide fancy crash space for friends, with one suite and a couple other bedrooms left over in case any more waifs and strays turn up on the doorstep seeking shelter. I feel like some character in a Jane Austen book."

Rennie had spread out the neat little floor plans that she'd had printed up to keep track of who was where, and now began carefully inking names and dates against the bedroom pages. She had a special loose-leaf binder into which she intended to put all the information for future use: who had stayed in what rooms and when and for how long, their preferences in food, drink, drugs, entertainment and sex partners. Made her feel quite the chatelaine, and it seemed strange and pleasing to her to be so house-proud.

Prax was sitting on the nearby floor, turning over the pages of assorted rock magazines, noting the people in it that they knew, preening or scowling, depending, when she came across a photo or a mention of Evenor. "Good practice for when you have come to your manifest duchessal destiny and are running that giant heap o' history up in Yorkshire. And all the smaller heaps as well. But all the rooms upstairs aren't furnished yet, are they?"

"Well, no, a few are still empty—I needed to leave *some*thing to amuse myself with down the road, when my lord and master is on tour," Rennie admitted. She made some more notations. "It's very hard work, you know, decorating: planning the themes, buying the stuff, moving it in. Not to mention making all those curtains."

"Oh please! You love it." Prax rolled onto her back and began doing yoga, a practice she'd been into since her teen years in Marin County.

They were in Rennie's morning room, a high-ceilinged, charmingly furnished chamber on the parlor floor. Rennie, who had only ever read about morning rooms in nineteenth-century novels and had thought them pretentious until she had experienced Prue Sonnet's, had been finding out, to her surprise, what dear Miss Austen and her contemporaries had always known: morning rooms were incredibly useful little lairs, a combination of study, office, cozy feminine retreat and defensible bastion of privacy, and she spent more time in hers than she had ever imagined she would. Turk had his own inviolate top-story private space, where she never ventured except by invitation, and this lovely little room was likewise hers alone. Fair was fair.

At the moment, she was making lists of what was needed for her guests; later, she would get Hudson in to go over the notes and meal plans for the week. Then Hudson or Galina, and often Turk and Rennie themselves, would go shopping for provisions: the fishmonger and greengrocer on First Avenue and the Ukrainian butcher on Second, the kosher baker on Ninth Street, the Thursdays-only butter-and-egg store on Seventh Street, the century-old pasta place on Eleventh and the even older world-famous Italian pastry palace next door. Fresh was best, as Chef Turk insisted, and the neighborhood had great resources. No big chain supermarkets close by—the nearest Gristede's was on University and Eighth, way out of the province—but who needed them when you could shop local, the way your grandmother did and all the little neighborhood grannies still did?

"I do love it," she said confidingly. "But it takes up so much *time*. I swear, I don't know how housewives manage. I admit it was fun supervising construction and buying furniture, and food shopping is enjoyable, but thank God, and Turk, that we can afford help and don't have to do it all ourselves. He's a musician and has to musick. I'm a journalist and have to journ. Plus all the extracurricular things I find it necessary to look into. Like Niles, and now this whole trip with Sledger."

Prax unfolded out of her plow pose. "Yes, so you mentioned. Have you heard anything more?"

"She told me she paid the ransom for the guitar, and it's since been returned. But as I've told Turk, I still think it's all connected. And my head she is going to explode, or implode, or some kind of 'plode, unless I find out right quick."

"And you will. You always do. No worries about that." Prax reached under her for some ripped-out magazine pages that her back had been sliding on. "What the hell *is* all this?"

Rennie shot a baleful glance at the crumpled paper, a glance of such focused malevolence, like sunlight through a magnifying glass, as could have set it ablaze. "Oh, little teenies' fannish fantasy love poems to Turk, printed in Loya Tessman's buttwipe magazine Teen Angels. He's not their only object of illiterate devotion; just about every cute sexy rocker boy you could think of comes in for the same sort of rubbish, be he Monkee, Beatle, Stone or Weezle. But she puts Turk in there every month to plague me specifically, and gave me a complimentary subscription, the bony-assed harpy, to make sure I see it. I got pissed off and ripped those out to use for kindling in the fireplace; it seemed appropriate. Read them. You'll see."

Prax had smoothed out one of the offending pages, and now was rolling on the floor with laughter as she perused it. "Holy Mother of God, will you LISTEN to this drivel! *'You're wild, untamed and free, they say/Of this I am not sure/ But if I heed your words, I know/I'll share a love that's pure.'* Oh, poor, *poor* Turk! 'Wild, untamed and free', forsooth! What do they think he is, a freaking mustang? I admit I get some pretty strange stuff from teenage boys, and even teenage girls, but *nothing* like that. And I never wrote anything a millionth part as godawful when *I* was fifteen, I can tell you."

Rennie was laughing along with her friend. "Of course not, because you were (a), an artist, and (b), not as nutty as a squirrel hotel. But really one would think that Turk would have become rather less an object of teenybopper devotion, at least over the past few years. He's a grown man, not a kid anymore: he's kind of aged out of their interest range. However wild, untamed and free he might still be, of course. And I do *not* share, even on paper, so the baby strumpets can take their pure love and just shove it."

"And then there's the you factor." Prax was paging through the rest of the Teen Angels issue, an expression midway between hilarity and horror on her face at the sheer awfulness. "Usually once a rock star has settled down and publicly taken a consort, the twinkies tend to lose interest. Well, unless you're Paul McCartney. Even Linda's presence doesn't seem to stop them; Jane Asher's certainly didn't. Though of course Paul and Jane were only engaged. But I like to think that the married Paulie, his track record hitherto notwithstanding, is now as seagreen-incorruptible as Turk is. And I also like to think that it's Turk's aura of complete and shining fidelity that keeps the groupies away."

"*I* like to think it's my aura of complete and shining homicidal menace that keeps the groupies away."

"Oh, that I *can* say for sure. Total groupie repellent, like cedar to moths. What trampy teenage scruff is going to mess with Murder Chick's man? They all fear ending up as the next victim, since a fair proportion of the rockerverse is totally convinced that you're really a brilliantly clever serial killer and not a girl detective at all, and it's only Turk with a whip and chair, not to mention a collar and leash, that keeps you in check. Besides, didn't you thrash a few of the tiny tarts in the Troubadour ladies' room, couple of years back, just to show them you mean business?"

"London Fog. They started it, and it was three to one."

"On paper, anyway," chortled Prax. "Ah, I never get tired of hearing about that…"

"Well, you're not hearing about it again. I have other things to think about. Like whips and collars and leashes, now that you've mentioned them; did I tell you I found a matched set in Froggy Livingston's suitcase when I was snooping around up at the Chelsea?"

"No! I always knew there was something I liked about that boy… But now you know what to buy his lordship for Christmas. Or he you."

"Either way! Well, chief among those things that concern me is the fact that Niles Clay is a guest in my house and I have to seriously start trying to clear his name for a double murder, much as I am disinclined to exert myself in that direction. If only to get him the hell out from under my roof. I'm only doing it for Turk, as you well know; and for the rest of the band too, of course. Plus there's Veronica Lee's little matter of death threats and kidnapped now restored guitar."

Prax gave her a knowing stare. "Sounds as if you're a pretty happy camper, honeychile."

"I am," said Rennie with sudden wonder. "You know, I really think I am."

But others under the same roof at the moment were not sharing her happy-camping mood. Up in his top-floor getaway room, which included a piano and a billiards table and abutted a small home gym that Rennie also used whenever she remembered it was there, at that very moment Turk was confronting Niles, and he was trying very hard to keep it civil. And by "civil", he really meant "not beating my lead singer to death with a billiards cue."

The fierce discussion turned, as usual of late, on Turk's intention to take the band off the road for the whole of the coming year, or at least most of it, and it had only gotten worse from there. It had not been pretty, though still within the parameters of allowable intramural hostility that Lionheart had long since set up, and both men had been exchanging increasingly icy words for some time now.

"You can try to take the band away from me, if that's what you have in mind," said Turk at last. "But you won't get far. I own the name, you will recall. Whatever configuration of musicians I say is Lionheart, that's Lionheart. Shane and Rardi and Jay-Jay all have key-man clauses, and they would never leave me anyway. Now Mick has one too. You wouldn't get any of them to go along with you. None of you is replaceable. Especially not you. And we both know it." He leaned forward in his chair. "Niles. I very desperately don't want you to leave. The band wouldn't be the same without you. But the band would still be Lionheart."

"Would it?"

"We'd make sure it is." He leaned back again, studying Niles's mutinous expression. "What's the *real* problem, Niles? We've known each other, worked together, traveled together, even roomed together, for the past six years. Why wouldn't you want to commit to something you've been a part of all that time? And so successfully too. It's hard out there on your own. So much easier and warmer to have a tribe around you. We've been through a *lot*, and now it's all good for us, couldn't be better, and we're going to keep it that way. I don't really know why you're doing this. Why would you want to leave now? Do you truly hate me that much?"

Turk's voice had not altered from its even, conversational pitch, but his pain was palpable, and Niles flinched as if he'd been shouted at. "No! Of course not! We've always been great as a band, and that's totally down to you. You're the one who brought us all together, it's your lyrics and music. I just—"

"You just what?"

Niles shook his head, baffled. "I just—something."

Turk studied his bandmate's flushed and stubborn face, wondering what the hell was going on behind it. Their disagreement, as usual, was over Niles' refusal to sign the key-man clause no matter how key Turk assured him he was, which was pretty darn key indeed. Turk had felt, reasonably enough, that as he'd assembled over the years the perfect band and bandmates for his purposes, he then needed to do whatever he could to keep them happy and make sure they stayed with him.

So he'd had the Locksley solicitors draw up the contracts.

The partnership terms were more than generous and the shares were lavish: Rardi, Shane and Jay-Jay had been delighted to sign—they wanted to be secure in their jobs every bit as much as Turk wanted them to be, and their mutual trust and regard went back ten years, all the way to Oxford. He had just offered such a deal to Mick Rouse—the delay had been only because Rouser hadn't been with Lionheart as long as the others and Turk had wanted to be sure, not out of any doubt as to Mick's musical importance to the band but only his compatibility and commitment. So now Niles was the only holdout. Was it money? Trust? Resentment? What the fuck?

"I don't have to tell you how important you are to the sound, Niles." Turk was in full seduction mode now; he'd say whatever he had to, to flatter his singer's ego and soothe his ruffled feathers, and the added advantage was that it was all true. "Why wouldn't you want to be sure of that? And properly rewarded for that? What can I say to convince you?" He stilled, struck by a horrible thought. "It's not about Rennie, is it? Because if it is—"

Niles made an impatient gesture. "No, of course not! Though since you mention her—" He saw Turk's face darken, but rushed imprudently on. "Well—she does get preferential treatment to the other wives, and you must know they're not happy. Keitha says—" He stopped, teetering on the cliff-edge.

"What does Keitha say?" Turk's voice was still even, but there was a distinct sharpness to it now. *Easy, don't antagonize him until you have to, you want him to sign that damned contract. Still, I will be buggered sideways if I'm going to let this degenerate into being about Rennie, and the other girls being jealously pissed off at her. It's being going on way too long, and it's bloody well going to stop, especially once we're married...*

Niles had re-grasped his diplomatic abilities, not to mention his duty of spousal deniability. "Oh, it's not Keitha, it's the other wives. It's just that they think Rennie has privileges they don't, because she's your old lady and a reporter..."

"Well, she *is* a reporter and she *is* my lady and she's going to be my ladyship. And she's been nothing but polite to them for the past two years, I might add. So yes, she does have privileges. Privileges that *she* has earned and that *I* allow her. Because I can. And because I want to. What's their real point?"

Niles had remembered by now that not only was he complaining of his hostess and the affianced consort of his employer, he was complaining of, additionally, perhaps the only person who could save him from a double-murder rap.

"I guess—they don't really have one?" he muttered.

"Good, because I would hate to think the girls were slagging off on her, you know, behind her back. Or behind mine. They're very sweet and pretty, and I like them all, but that would not be—wise." Turk paused delicately, to make sure the point had gone well home, and decided to be magnanimous. "So, getting back to what we were discussing—"

Niles appeared acutely relieved. Sometimes staying in the frying pan was indeed preferable to jumping out into the fire. "The clause. Well, it's not that I'm necessarily opposed to it, especially now that everyone else has one. Can we talk about it in a couple of days, maybe, once we know a bit more about what's happening on the legal front? It would make more sense if we knew where I stood."

Turk graciously unbent, knowing he'd gotten about as much of a concession as he was going to get today. "Of course we can. That would be smart, actually. I know Rennie's doing her best."

"She always does." And for once Niles didn't sound snarky saying so. But Turk wondered, after his lead vocalist had left the room, if Niles wasn't just putting things off until Rennie had decisively and irrevocably saved, as she had put it yesterday, his pale scrawny sorry English arse.

Shortly thereafter, the embattled householders found themselves having tea alone in the kitchen for the first time since the Garden gig — everyone else being out somewhere or skulking in their rooms — and they were delighted for the chance. Just like old times in the Hollywood Hills house, when he had first introduced her to his pleasant afternoon custom: for a moment, Rennie flashed on his lordship as a little golden-haired tot, or holy terror more likely, being taught the graces of the elegant tradition at Nanny's knee.

It made a pleasant and entertaining picture, in which angelic scowls and flung scones figured importantly. Still smiling, she filled a plate with some slices of her favorite marble tea loaf and his own preferred raisin biscuits, and Turk poured, and they enjoyed a quiet, leisurely hour at the table, Macduff and Svaha lying hopefully on the nearby floor.

Over the second cuppa, Turk gave Rennie a detailed

recounting of his encounter with Niles, and she nodded, tossing some remnants of tea loaf to the animals as a reward for their patience, raisins being insalubrious for critters. As for Turk's own patience, she could see it launching itself into orbit, waving bye-bye over its shoulder as it went…

"It's nothing new, you know. It's been like that with the other wives since the first night you and I got together. You should have heard what they had to say about us leaving Tansy's wake together. Grace and Janis and Tokie Broken Bow, among others, all got hot earfuls, and they had to tell me just so I'd be warned."

"How very thoughtful of them."

She shrugged. "Which is worse, knowing that people are saying horrible hateful jealous lying things about you, or not knowing? If you know, it can make you desperately unhappy if you let it; if you don't know, you can look like an idiot for not setting them straight, perhaps by force. I'd rather know, and then I can decide what, if anything, should be done about it."

"I think that's the part that most people who know you are afraid of."

Rennie laughed. "What, because I beat up three stoned groupies on the Strip one night? Ooh, what a formidable reputation! Between you and Praxie, I'll never live that down, will I… Listen, my darling, if I wanted to give the Lionheart ladies something to be afraid of, I'd just go ahead and do it. But I don't, because however annoying I find them — Keitha, Sherrie, Lynette, Marchelle and I can't the hell remember the other one's name, Cammie, Pammy, Sammie — "

"Tammy."

A scoff. "Of *course* it is! However annoying I may find them, which I do, and in a quantity so vast it is measurable only in astronomical units, they are still the chosen companions of your bandmates, and I would never do anything to make things difficult for you in that area." She reached across the table for his hand. "Yes, it's true, I'm a living saint and you should be lighting candles to me nightly—"

Turk lifted her hand and kissed it. "I thought I already did light a pretty big candle to you every night...there's worship, if you like."

She smiled triumphantly. "And *that*, Einstein, is what they're jealous about. I've got you and they don't. It's a simple dynamic and I've told you this before. Whether you want to believe it or not. So, given that as the foundation for the hostility palace they've been building, don't you think I can find it dead easy to just ignore the little brats, with all the regal disregard of the duchess you're going to make me one day? It's all relative, Flash. I only wish you didn't have to spend so much time and attention worrying about Niles," she added after a while. "You guys all have such intense relationships with one another, it's almost like polyandry. I feel quite superfluous sometimes. If we didn't have such a great sexual relationship, I'd really be worried."

"Well, yes, it *is* sort of like being married to you both," said Turk vaguely. "You and Niles, I mean."

"What a horrible thought. Take it back at once, sir, or you'll find yourself cuddling up next to Niles in bed tonight."

He did so, laughing, and after a while they tidied away the tea things and headed upstairs as they heard their guests returning. But neither of them put the difficulty out of their heads entirely.

CHAPTER THIRTEEN

THE ENTIRE HOUSE, in unsettled mood—which had radiated downstairs from Turk's lair like a cold fog, thus clearing the place out for most of the day—decided to go out to dinner together that night, to try to all get back in the nice communal groove they'd been enjoying. As neither Turk nor Rennie felt like cooking, the default choice of restaurant destination was of course Max's Kansas City, the unspeakably hip, or perhaps just unspeakable, hangout up just past Union Square. They crammed into two Checker taxis at the corner of Third Avenue and were unloading themselves on Park Avenue South a bare three minutes later. As they all bundled out of the cabs and hurried in off the sidewalk from the cold, Rennie looked up at the big black and white Max's signage and smiled reminiscently.

She'd been coming here ever since she'd been legal, in the company of her Cornell sorority sisters and later her grad school roommates at Columbia. They had been nobodies back then, just teenagers trying for an air of sophistication; but they were young and pretty nobodies, and in those days that was enough to guarantee entrée. Mickey Ruskin, the owner and a fellow Cornell grad, was glad to have girls like them around, as they raised the tone of the place and attracted guys of all ages inside, especially older arty types who drank a lot. They'd been so innocent and ignorant that they'd never really noticed the kind of adult activities that were going on; they'd just sat there at their little tables or booths, right across from the bar, and enjoyed their meals and gazed happily around, content to be set dressing if it meant they could meet cool dudes.

Most of the girls she'd come here with in the past had drifted away over the years, off into marriage and suburbia, or at least the Upper East Side, but Rennie was a downtown chick to the core, and once she'd returned to the city with Turk in tow, they'd become Max's semi-regulars. They both thought many of its habitués were heavy on the pretentious side, but the food was not bad and not expensive and the ambiance was undemanding, while the management saw to it that no famous guest, or, indeed, young and pretty nobody, was ever hassled.

On the other side of the back room from the two shoved-together four-tops where their group had been seated, carefully placed to maximize exposure—Mickey always got the most mileage out of his famous faces—Loya Mailing Tessman, editress of Teen Angels magazine, held court among a small group of well-known phonies, the *crème de la crappe*, in Rennie's book. The tiny, frizzy-haired, intellectually challenged but animalistically cunning Loya was married to the massive, incredibly successful booking-agency magnate Ted Tessman, whose strangely small head sat directly on his hulking shoulders, apparently without benefit of intervening vertebrae. They were one of New York's major non-celebrity rock power couples, which even Rennie, who detested them both, admitted, and they never let anyone forget it; now, as Rennie caught Loya's eye, the little she-weasel simpered patronizingly in acknowledgment. Ted, steadily plowing his way through a plank-sized slab of sirloin almost as slab-like and plank-like as himself, never even raised his head.

Rennie smiled evilly back, putting on a mocking high-pitched voice that she knew Loya could not hear; if the bitch read lips, so much the better. "Ooo-oooh, look who it is! Loya Tessman, the Queen Teen Angel herself. Fallen angel. No, not even that interesting. Septic cow. And her little dog Ted too."

"She hates you," said Prax, absently studying the menu.

"Why, yes, she does, my pearl, and likewise she detests you and Turk and Ares. My best friend and my consort and my best friend's consort. And for the life of me I can't figure out why. We none of us ever did anything to her. Well, except mock her on suitable occasions. Every occasion."

"Maybe that's why," said Keitha Clay vaguely, from down the table's other side. "You lot ignore her and make fun of her. We talk to her all the time, Niles and me, and she likes *us* absolute *tons*."

They let that pass, in a kind of chilly perfection of negative silence that could have re-crisped wilted lettuce; then Rennie remarked, with a definite air of changing the subject, "Has anyone seen Belinda here? Because I need to ask her something."

But no one had, and so instead Rennie merely gazed smugly across the room at the paired portraits that hung on the wall above Loya and her clique. Both were of the same slender, generously endowed, fair-skinned girl with long, long, gold-brown hair: in one, the girl wore an elegant lace pantsuit, in the other she was totally naked—the poses

being a hippie homage to Goya's Clothed and Nude Majas.
And both of the girls were Rennie, who, in oils, looked like a
rock infanta, reclining on Prax's heavily carved Indonesian
chaise longue. The portraits had been painted four years
ago in Sausalito by an impoverished artist friend of Praxie's;
he had gone on to great fame and note in the New York
art scene, and Mickey Ruskin had accepted the paintings
for the restaurant, as he often did, in settlement of a rather
impressive bar bill. Maybe that was what Loya was pissed
off about: her own tits were pretty much concave-minus
and *la bella Ravenna*'s lovely, all-of-a-color, ivory 34D's
were here on display for all to view—and envy Turk his
possession of.

It pleased Rennie no end that such gossipy bitches of
all genders and persuasions as Valmai LeVanda, kabuki-
makeup'd magazine empress, and Zsa Zsa Briscoe, fashion
editor and arbiter, and pretentious experimental filmmaker
Frink (just Frink), and Camden Ransoff, puce-haired painter
of trashcans and city buses and strutting New York pigeons,
not to mention their little pal Loya, were obliged to sit
beneath her own glowingly painted likenesses, at the round
table that was reputedly the coolest in the room. Yeah, only
in their own minds: Rennie wouldn't have sat there herself
if it had been the only table left on earth, and anyway, those
were not the kind of people with whom she cared to sit. She
preferred to think that it was what you did and what you
were, not where you sat and who you thought you were,
that made you cool; besides, wherever Turk Wayland was
sitting was by definition the head of the coolest table in any
room, and Turk, of course, invariably preferred to sit where

he could see a painting of Rennie bare.

They ordered, or rather, they told the bored black-clad aspiring actress who condescended to wait upon them to just bring them their usual, and she rolled her eyes, much put-upon, and vanished without a word. The Wayland-Strides came here often enough, and ordered the same thing every time — prime rib medium rare for Turk, off-the-menu crabmeat-stuffed lobster for Rennie — so the serving staff knew their preferences, and the two were free to helpfully guide the choices of the others at the table. When her customary dry sherry was set before her, Rennie took a sip and gazed around again. Yeah, in spite of all the affected pompous posers that infested the place, Max's was okay, and sometimes even phantasmagorical. For that, she could put up with the fish-faced Loya and her clusterfuckery of prizewinning pseuds. Also she and Turk were generally left alone here — always a plus.

Oh, his legend could not be entirely escaped: occasionally, when on quiet nights they sat in a booth out front, next door to Cary Grant or Michael Caine or other such riffraff, Turk would be the subject of mute awestruck gogglement from popeyed college kids at Rennie's old table near the bar. Remembering her very own pop-eyed college-kid days here, mutely goggling awestruck at famous folksingers, she gazed benevolently upon the children and did not scowl. But for the most part nobody bugged them. Tourists were sent scurrying upstairs before they could profane the hipper precincts, and even though the back room was sometimes unbearable with self-congratulatory preening, at least it was safe. Which was just fine with the prow house crowd.

Over their meal—decent and even tasty, though people didn't really go to Max's for the grub—Rennie saw Belinda Melbourne stroll in arm-in-arm with Diego Hidalgo, and she smiled proudly to see them. As well she might: what a talented matchmaker she had been there. To look at those two, you wouldn't have thought they'd hit it off in a million years; yet there they were, joined at the hip, or more accurately the crotch, and had been ever since Rennie had introduced them in New York the week after Woodstock. She had happily sat back to watch as lust at first sight felled them both like toppling redwoods; Diego had been so smitten that he'd dumped L.A. for the nonce and moved in with Belinda around the corner from Turk and Rennie. Not a bad day's work: Belinda had needed someone to make her feel sexy and special after finally dumping that lunatic Hacker Bennett, and Diego had needed to finally meet a woman who had great brains as well as great breasts. *Seems as if my recipe came together, so to speak...* Odds were it wouldn't last to Easter, but it would end amicably and affectionately; no worries there.

They saw Rennie's beckoning wave and detoured to the table, dragging over two chairs and happily squeezing in, deliberately ignoring Loya's hopeful little moues and abortive tiny handwaves and the only too obvious mental script she was running, Oh noooo, Diego, come sit over *here* with the cool kids not with that loser Rennie Stride and her misguided allies, you can even bring your annoying girlfriend if you must. Yeah, right. Clearly the two new arrivals knew who the *real* cool kids in school were. Belinda gave Ares and Turk the usual fond peck on the cheek, blew a kiss to Gray Sonnet, whom she couldn't reach to kiss across the table, civilly acknowledged Keitha and Niles, and warmly hugged Rennie and Prax and Prue; Diego gallantly kissed the ladies' hands and nodded to the gentlemen.

Sitting down next to Turk, Diego began eagerly discussing Lionheart's Garden show, as Cold Fire was scheduled for one of its own in March and he wanted to find out all he could to avoid problems beforehand. For his part, Turk was happy to answer a fellow artist's professional concerns and share the strategies with which he and Lionheart had coped with the Garden's notorious vibe, while Niles contributed advice of his own and Gray tossed in suggestions from his vast Budgies experience.

By now their table had gravitationally tipped over to being the hippest one by *far* in the restaurant that night, by the sheer magnitude of rock starpower that had casually accumulated there—two rock goddesses, two Lionhearts, a Budgie and a Cold Fire. Plus the junior varsity: a pair of front-page scribblers, a supermodel and the chief protector of pretty much every famous body that needed bodyguarding. The table was like a neutron star of celebritude, dense and solid with superstarriness right straight through. Rennie could see the annoyance on Loya Tessman's pouty, pointy little face exponentially increasing by the second, her lipless little mouth puckered like a hen's bum, and secretly smiled to see it. Because really, who would pay attention to superannuated fashion icons or hack daubers from Iowa or, indeed, editors of teenybopper fan rags, when there was a tableful of rock legends of the first rank to be admired? Couldn't have worked out better if she'd planned it herself.

Too bad Leonardo wasn't around to paint it, the Next-to-the-Last Supper. He'd have been sitting at their table in any case.

"Soooo," began Belinda, all bright-eyed and rosy-cheeked from the cold weather and regarding Rennie meaningfully, "how's it going, princess?" Without waiting for an answer she signaled the still-bored waitress and rattled off a complicated food and drinks order for her and Diego both, unaware of the challenge she'd just given the actress manqué, then turned back to her friends. "What's new in Murderville? Any new clues?"

Rennie laughed. "As if I'd tell *you*! You'd go running off like Jack with his magic beans and write your own story. Leaving me empty-handed in front of our mutual employer and you with a big fat beanstalk and the goose that laid several golden front-page eggs."

"Oh, like that would ever happen!" protested Belinda. "You know you're Fitzie's forever favorite. I'm just the redheaded stepchild, content to take what crumbs spill from the never-ending feast that is Rennie Stride's table of journalistic delights."

Prue scoffed disbelief. "More like the Sorcerer's Apprentice. We'll be seeing dancing brooms around the Sun-Trib offices before much longer."

"A very apt 'prentice too, if I do say so myself," Rennie remarked. She lowered her voice. "How are you and Don Diego doing these days?"

Belinda smiled languidly and let her eyes rest on her darkly brooding boyfriend. "He really is a Spanish grandee, isn't he... And, thanks to me, much improved from the nitwit you first introduced me to. Well, we're coming to the end of the idyll, I think. Not in a bad way — we're both just getting a bit antsy. He keeps bugging me about moving back to L.A. with him, and I keep telling him I don't want to do that."

"Whyever not? You like it there. Oooh, Turk and I could rent you two our place in Nichols Canyon. It comes equipped with Ares as resident caretaker and guard, you know. If I recall correctly, Diego doesn't own a house there, he *likes* to rent, so this would be perfect. We'd charge a mere pittance to friends, if anything at all. It's a very nice house."

"I'm sure it is. But if he goes, he goes alone. And rents alone," said Belinda with finality. "I'm not living anywhere west of Lafayette Street. And if that means we go our separate ways and it's happy trails to us, so be it. It was never meant to be long-term. It's been a *lot* of fun, though," she added. "All hail Strider for setting us up."

"Well then, my work here is done," intoned Rennie. "Happy I could help out."

Prue gave a delicate snort. "And what have you been doing lately to help *Niles* out? You, my friend," she continued, "should be unleashing the Furies, not futzing around with the NYPD and one of Fitz's hacks. Not meaning you, Miss Belinda; I refer to that crime reporter bloke who's the other half of Strider's Baker Street act, the Watson to her Holmes. Come on, where's that avenging investigative spirit we all know and love and are just a little bit afraid of?"

Rennie narrowed her eyes, just the tiniest bit. "I think it's in the shop just now for its twenty-thousand-mile tune-up."

"Not acceptable."

"Be that as it may. And don't sneer at Ken Karper, either; he's no hack. He's a good reporter and I'm very fond of him. As a matter of fact, though, Linny, I did want to ask you something," began Rennie, and her friend raised elegantly interrogative brows. "I need to find out about a particular drug. I don't know its name or even if it exists, just what it does, or might do. Do you think you know anyone who could help me?"

Belinda grinned. "Well, *that* really narrows it down! But sure. Hacker, of course. Not only is he a walking drug encyclopedia all by his little old self, he is a valued patron of every dealer in town, and if he himself does not know, he will know exactly who you need to ask to find out."

Having advanced by now to the dessert stage, Rennie was appreciatively dealing with a slab of cheesecake, trying to defend it from Turk's insistent and acquisitive fork and also pay attention to Belinda at the same time.

"Could you mention it to him, please, as soon as you get a chance? Just tell him that I need some information and the name of a dealer I can ask for specifics."

"Easy peasy. But remind me. I'll probably forget."

Rennie gave up and let Turk triumphantly claim the rest of the cheesecake. "Let's hope not."

After they finished dinner, the group split up. Niles, Keitha, Ares and Prax headed back to the prow house, Belinda and Diego decided to hang around Max's for a bit longer and mock the hipper-than-thou set, while the Sonnets and the Waylands polled the table to see if someone knew someplace they could go. As it turned out, Jimi Hendrix was playing at a tiny West Village club, as a warm-up to his New Year's Eve concert with his new band at the Fillmore East, and they traipsed across town to say hi and catch the last set. Toward the end, Jimi smilingly pointed to their booth in a dark corner by the back wall, elevated with others on a low dais above the tables; Rennie shrank back, knowing what was coming, and Prue patted her arm reassuringly.

"There's a couple of cats here tonight I think you might know," he said in his soft voice. "Old friends of mine, chaps from London. What do you say we get them up here and make them play for us?"

To a tsunami of cheers and whistles, and it must be said hardly reluctantly, Turk and Gray joined Jimi on the small stage, slinging on spare guitars propped up against the wall. Jimi threw affectionate arms around their necks; they conferred briefly and then effortlessly launched into an old Robert Johnson blues. The audience collectively swooned and then paid close attention, not wanting to miss a note.

When a rather flushed and elated Turk and Gray returned to the booth several numbers later, Rennie smiled at them. "You'd better go back up, rocklords. They're banging on their shields."

As well they might be, the audience. They could never have expected a surprise treat like that in a million years, something that would be talked about forever and go down in rock annals, and they were practically drunk on actually being there for it. The principals obeyed the encore call, a little more shyly than their initial acquiescence, and the room noise redoubled as Gray beckoned his spouse to join them.

"There's also a beautiful English lady sitting over there you might like to hear from. What do you say, darling?" As the crowd began stomping, Prue looked helplessly at Rennie, who just shooed her away with a big grin, and then ran up to take the mike her husband was holding out. As the augmented group kicked off Lionheart's "Sleeping Dogs Lie" with an absolutely astounding guitar run — Jimi telling the audience he'd really like to cover it on his next LP, and the audience expressing mad keen approval — Rennie wasn't surprised when someone got up from a table on the other side of the room, walked over and slid into the booth beside her. Turning her head, she saw it was Nick Sattlin, which did surprise her. Into instant suspicion.

"Fancy seeing you here, Detective. I didn't know you were a fan."

"Does that seem so strange, Miss Stride?"

"Well, on further consideration, perhaps not so strange as I first thought. After all, who am I to say where you should spend your free time? It *is* free time, I assume, and not business? You're not just keeping tabs on us?"

"Not at the moment." He glanced toward the stage, his face full of wonder, and shook his head. "I wouldn't have missed this for anything. What an amazing thing to get to hear — Wayland, Sonnet and Hendrix playing together in a club, twenty feet away from me, and Prue Vye singing in."

Rennie felt her heart inexplicably incline kindly toward him, though she was still suspicious. "Turk and Gray and Prue have been friends for years. I first saw Jimi and Turk play together at Monterey, back in '67. But they knew each other from London before that, as Jimi said, when he — "

" —had gone over there to get some musical respect because he sure wasn't getting any here. Oh yeah, I know all about it."

They happily discussed music until the sounds from the stage indicated that the gods were ready to resume play, and then they maintained a respectful silence, even between songs. After a while, though, Rennie decided she needed to address a few things.

"How *is* it all going, then? The murder investigations?"

He turned to her, almost relieved that she'd brought it up before he'd had to. "You know, that is something we need to talk about."

"You and Turk? You and me? You and Niles? You and me and Turk and Niles?"

"For now? Just you and me and my partner. Tomorrow at the stationhouse? Three? Three-thirty?"

"Either one."

When the four of them left the club in the exceedingly small hours of the morning—Nick Sattlin having reluctantly departed a long while before, he had to get up early for work—it was to the unpleasant realization that a tabloid reporter and accompanying photographer were lurking about in the dark street. Rennie was displeased, to say the least. *Uh-oh. Somebody let off their mouth...*

"Turk, Turk, what can you tell us about Niles Clay and the murder charge? Is it true he—"

Not even letting him finish, Turk snarled a swart oath recommending an anatomical impossibility and swung at the reporter, who, with long-practiced ease, ducked just in time for the photographer to get the shot. Which of course made for a spectacular picture in the New York Pillar the next day. But at least it hadn't been one of Fitz's rags.

"Goodness!" said Ares, spreading the tabloid over the dining-room table, where most of the house's inhabitants were winding up breakfast with crumbcake and coffee. "Nice right cross you've got there, your lordship. Nothing *I* ever taught you… You learn that one on the mean streets of Oxford?"

"Eton, actually." Turk looked rueful, though actually he was regretting only that he hadn't gone for one of Ares' bladechops across the guy's larynx.

Gray laughed. "Oh, *that* den of roughnecks. Good thing you didn't connect. That would have hurt your pick hand something fierce."

"Equally good thing Detective Sattlin had already left our company," remarked Prue, peering at the paper. "Has he commented yet?"

Rennie shook her head. "No." She stared bleakly at the photograph of Turk. "But he will."

And—with Detective Casazza joining in—he wasted no time doing so, when she strolled into the stationhouse at three-fifteen precisely.

"Well," she said, when they were finished with what they had to suggest to her and had leaned back waiting for a reaction, "you boys certainly ask a hell of a lot of one little writer girl. Turk won't be happy as a lark about it, either, I can promise you, when he finds out. I'm not exactly thrilled myself."

"He should be used by now to your extracurricular activities, no?" murmured Sattlin.

"Should be, but isn't. And this cuts rather closer to home than anything we've engaged in so far."

"I know, and I'm sorry." Sattlin looked it, too. "But I wouldn't be asking if I didn't think it was important. Especially now that you've finally told me about Miss Cairns' guitar episode."

Rennie herself looked as if she were at the end of her patience, or theirs. "You think it all ties in, then? You really do?"

Casazza chimed in from his seat across the room. "That's what we need to find out, Miss Stride. This is the only way we can think of to do it. And we need help."

She straightened and stood up. "That's what you people always say."

CHAPTER FOURTEEN

LIONHEART HAD BEEN SUMMONED to the weekly singles meeting at Centaur's New York offices, on a high floor of a handsome black basalt Art Deco building across from Bryant Park and the big library. Such meetings, usually held once a week, were ordinarily attended by the a&r guys, promotion personnel, product managers, p.r. and advertising people and assorted other label brass, to discuss the upcoming singles and decide how and where to promote them, and to listen to the radio spots the ad department had recorded.

Even at holiday time, the music biz never sleeps, and Lionheart's wasn't the only Centaur single recently released. Timing was critical: sometimes it worked out, sometimes it didn't. This time, the label was gambling on the positive momentum generated by Lionheart's Garden show; it had been reviewed everywhere as the most miraculous performance since the loaves and the fishes, apparently. The forward propulsion had been impressive—even the backlist catalogue had been given an impressive jolt, and the greatest-hits album was surging up the charts. So a good, solid single like this one, pre-scheduled as it was, was only gravy. It worked both ways, though: if the concert had stiffed, the single still might have carried the album over, and even though the show had been astounding, the single itself still might not go anywhere. It was complicated, and you just never knew.

The bands who actually *made* the singles, though, were seldom invited to these purely in-house nuts-and-bolts occasions, being deemed largely unnecessary and indeed inconvenient to the label's purposes. But Freddy Bellasca figured that since Lionheart was in town, they should be the featured polestars of the week's meeting, and, further, should come and hang out and make nice with the people who worked for them.

Or for whom they worked — Freddy was never really clear on which way that went. But such command appearances were infrequent, so Lionheart didn't mind. They had had the mandatory Centaur dinner after the Garden show, and now this, but that was it. They'd been hanging around in New York because Turk had asked them to stay on a bit; now they all planned to be on their way home tomorrow or the next day, for Christmas in England or Switzerland or L.A.; Gray and Prue had left that morning after breakfast. Of all the Lionhearts, only Turk would be remaining in New York over the end of the year. And Niles, of course. And Niles.

As Turk entered the handsome, airy room with Rardi, he saw a&r chief Gerry Langhans sitting in a power position at the glossy mahogany conference table, and as Turk took the seat to which Freddy grandly gestured him, he and Langhans exchanged warm greetings. Gerry, arbiter of these meetings under Freddy's gimlet eye, was a childhood friend of Rennie's, and he and Turk had become friends themselves last year, in the wake of Tansy Belladonna's murder. With his wife JoAnn, Gerry had been invited to the post-Garden dinner and party, and they'd also been asked to the upcoming Wayland-Stride Christmas dinner — Freddy's presence had not been requested at either prow house festivity, of course. Turk was more than glad to have Gerry here. At least he'd have one ally at his back. If he needed one. Which, from the looks of things, he just might.

The other Lionhearts were scattered around the table, and they and Turk and the rest of the room exchanged hellos and casual chat, while a breakfast buffet was set up by minions along the window wall. Once everyone was well carbed and caffeinated and seated round the table, Gerry nodded to a corner of the room. Yet another minion put the new single, "Walking With Tigers", on the overhead speaker system, and they all listened intently as it was played three times through.

Turk found himself, as he always did when he listened to Lionheart's recorded output, second-guessing himself about how they might have done it differently, maybe better: his guitar riff was good, but it might have been even more killer if Rardi had taken it on piano the way they had originally thought; kind of muddy there in the bridge, too much multitracking, must watch that; Jay-Jay had some nice drum stuff coming out; that lead-in accordion was startling but really good, not a boring old sitar like everybody and their granny threw in these days; maybe they should have gone with that other vocal take... Which was why he so seldom listened to his own music once recorded: he heard only seams, not grooves.

They discussed the single for a while, then put on the

B side and went through the process all over again. The promo guys outlined their plans for getting airplay; the ad people showed off the spec trade and consumer campaigns and laid out ideas and hooks for radio and even TV spots, which no rock band had as yet gone in for; and everybody discussed the pros and cons of everything.

"Turk. I've been thinking," said Freddy Bellasca, after everyone had had at least their initial say. He drank off his orange juice, and then stared up at the ceiling until he was sure everyone was properly attentive. "Creatively thinking."

Uh-oh. Freddy thinking about creative stuff almost never ended well; he lacked the required equipment. Turk looked around for another cup of tea, and one of the product managers leaped up to fetch him one, which he gratefully accepted. Going to be a looooong morning.

"Oh yes?"

"Yes, about the producer you boys need for the new album. Now I know you have someone you're considering, and you can certainly do it well enough yourselves, as always, but why don't you consider this instead?" He paused dramatically, and around the conference table everybody prepared to cover up the expressions of retching they fully expected to be wearing as soon as Freddy pronounced his choice. "Andy Starlorn."

Hmm. Turk leaned back in his chair, more pleasantly surprised than he cared to let on, and took a sip of tea before he spoke.

"He's more of a Phil Spector type than I had in mind," he said at last. "I had been thinking of Britt Halsey, he's done such a great job for Cold Fire, or maybe Eddie Kramer, the guy who produces Hendrix."

"But he might be really good for us, you know — Starlorn," offered Rardi. "The new songs could use that kind of big dramatic production. And he's got that great new studio open now, Vinylization."

They tossed it back and forth for another hour: not just the producer but the studio, the engineers, the songs themselves — and, not least among the discussed items, the fact that Turk wanted to pull Lionheart off the road for a year. With no tour, they would need a more aggressive recorded presence out there than usual, to ensure themselves *some* publicity and keep themselves alive in the fickle fan memory. Perhaps the coming summer was the time for that double-disc live LP they'd been wanting to release for a while — there was certainly enough good material, especially now, with the Garden stuff. And of course Turk's long-planned solo album, which would serve to keep not just him on view but also, indirectly, the band itself — though there was some feeling in the room that three albums in one year, unless very well spaced and maybe not even then, might be a bit too much.

When Shane finally called for a band-only vote on Andy Starlorn, Lionheart hands were raised around the table in support of the hire, and Turk could see he was outnumbered. As legal proprietor of the band's corporate entity, he had the power to set their opinions aside and do whatever the hell he wanted, of course, but that wasn't his way. At least, it hadn't been so far. *And not about to change now, even if it means a victory for Freddy...* He straightened in his chair.

"Well, he's not whom I'd have first thought of, out of the gate, but if that's who you want, then that's who we'll go with."

Niles narrowed his eyes, but given his current personal situation, he didn't dare make any difficulties for Turk, especially in public, because Rennie would undoubtedly hear it happening from miles away, like Odin, and hurl a thunderbolt, like Zeus. Her superpowers were invincible and her spies were everywhere, so he contented himself with a question only.

"But you're not happy about it. May we hear why?"

"Not entirely happy, no. Starlorn's a fantastic producer, no question. But we've all heard the stories: what an obstinate bugger he can be for insisting on his own way to the artists' detriment, his fondness for imprinting his own musical mark to overshadow the band's, his tendencies to massively overproduce and spend a bloody fortune of the band's money doing it. His studio costs, in his own place, are higher than we usually budget for, let alone like, and he takes a much bigger cut of the advance than we're used to giving producers, so don't forget that. We've been doing just fine producing and engineering ourselves, with Thom and Rafferty; I'm not sure we even need a formal producer at this late date. What can he add, really, that we can't do ourselves? We can certainly talk about it, but if we're going to pay out a ton of money on him, we'll need to save as much as we can elsewhere."

"How?" demanded Freddy, alarmed.

Turk noted the alarm for future reference. "Well, for instance, we could contain studio costs by recording at my place whenever possible and feasible — I'd charge only what it runs me for electricity and supplies, not hourly board time or equipment rental, I have everything we'd need — and not using outside venues except when we absolutely must, like for overdubbing and mixing. It would be fun to mess around at Starlorn's place, though: I've heard some great things about all their new gear. Still, his rates, though they are indeed high, are really almost reasonable by comparison to some other places we've used."

That was a shot fired right across Freddy Bellasca's bows, a flaming arrow of warning, and no one there missed it, not even Freddy himself. It was common knowledge that Centaur overcharged their acts extortionately for recording time in the label's fancy new L.A. and New York studios, and also that Centaur had built said studios almost entirely thanks to their profits off Lionheart's staggering success — Lionheart to whom Centaur never gave a cent's discount on recording costs.

Turk's implication was clear to everybody there: if the band was going to use an outside facility at all, and pay out from their advance the usual fortune in studio time, or an even bigger one, the money might be better spent buying hours at Vinylization with its state-of-the-art equipment, not Centaur's in-house place with its rather less splendid and already outdated facilities. Or else save as much as they could by recording entirely at Turk's, and just mixing elsewhere. If they did that, they could even save on catering costs, if Rennie was amenable and Galina or Hudson felt like cooking: people would be surprised how food bills for delivery suppers or midnight lunches at outside studios added up, and the artists always picked up the tab, written into the general expenses—at least at the prow house they could get away cheaply, with urns of coffee and pans of lasagna and simple sandwiches and trays of homemade cookies. Not to mention daily teatime.

The shot had hit the mark, as they all saw: Freddy looked as annoyed with Turk as he felt he could afford to look, but he kept his mouth shut.

"We could do that," said Shane, nodding in answer to Turk's suggestion. "That's quite the set-up you've got at the house. Not much we couldn't do except major multitracking and mixing."

"Still, I'd have to personally let Andy Starlorn across the threshold of my dwelling place. Don't vampires have to be invited in?"

Down the table, Mick Rouse laughed; ever since Turk had offered him the key-man clause he'd been hoping for, which offer had been instantly accepted, he'd been in an ebullient frame of mind, happy, reassured and relieved.

"Oh, you can control his excesses. With a pointy stake if nothing else. But really, Turk, I think he could be quite good for us. You said yourself we need a new perspective on where we're going, that's what taking a year off the road is all about. Why not *his* perspective? Let's give him an audition."

"Audition?"

"Sure. Have him produce one cut with us at Vinylization. If we like it and get on with him, we hire him. If we don't like what he does, and it turns out he's an impossible little prick and we hate him, we'll just have to scrap one track, not half an album. Would he go for it, do you think?"

Turk showed his pleasure that Mick, always a steady band wheelhorse, had produced such a solidly workable and creative suggestion, validating his new status, while Francher shrugged hopefully.

"We can only ask. He can only say no. What do *you* say, Turk?"

Freddy Bellasca added, "It would mean a lot to me, Turk."

Meaning that Freddy owed Starlorn, in some obscure music-biz way. And not forgetting the flicker of alarm when Turk had suggested not using the Centaur studios. And his lordship hadn't kept Lionheart on top of the mountain for almost eight years by ignoring the broken leaves and twigs and bent grass stems that marked the trail...

He pretended to consult his handsome brown leather pocket diary, a recent gift from Rennie; it was more than his life was worth if she caught him not carrying it, but he'd never scribbled anything more in it than guitar model numbers or odd bits of lyrics and music notation or ideas for her birthday.

"Can we set this audition up right away, then? Get it over with before Christmas? Rennie and I have plans, and I know everybody else wants to go home to be with their own families." Turk gestured around the table, addressed himself to Freddy. "In fact, they were all leaving within the next day or so—is it okay with you guys, staying on a bit? Week at most?"

He quite deliberately did not suggest that the other Lionhearts should move into the prow house for the extended stay, joining the guests already there. He knew that Rennie, if he asked her, would undoubtedly acquiesce, however reluctantly, even to her own detriment, just because the request had come from him; but he also knew that they didn't have enough bedrooms prepared for more company and that having three couples already in residence was pushing her limits as a hostess. She wasn't used to that sort of thing; hell, he wasn't fond of it himself, and they had both gotten a bit snappish on occasion over the past couple of weeks. And though in their distant ducal future they would have to deal with a *lot* more than six guests at a time and some of them royalty, better to start out small and unthreatening and ease themselves into it. In any case, no band member was suggesting that they vacate their current hotels, so that seemed okay…

Though Freddy seemed far too pleased with himself, which was maybe not so okay. "Great, great. Thanks so much, Turk, knew you'd see it. I'll try to get hold of Starlorn right now; you could record maybe even tonight, no, no, not tonight, tomorrow then, if he's got the main room free, though he'd probably clear it out for you guys, we're done here, aren't we?" He jumped up and left the table, appearing much too excited for anyone to feel entirely comfortable.

Turk pushed back his chair and stood up, preparatory to leaving, and everyone rushed to follow his lead; clearly the meeting was over. Something had happened, and he couldn't figure out what it was. But he would.

"Well. Right, then. Later." He thanked all the label personnel by name as they left, but didn't make any moves in that direction himself.

As everyone filed out of the conference room, Gerry

Langhans noticed Turk's disinclination to leave, and when his lordship bent a significant glance in Gerry's direction, he too lingered, until the two of them were the only ones left.

"Did you want to talk about something more, Turk?" asked Gerry curiously, and Turk nodded.

"I do, actually. We didn't really get a chance to discuss things at the party after the Garden show."

Gerry's puzzlement grew. "No, we didn't... Well, how are you and Herself handling the Niles-as-houseguest situation? All going smoothly? Nobody putting ground glass in the coffee? Nobody drinking it out of pure spite?"

Turk laughed. "No, nothing like that. Not yet, anyway. Surprisingly, they're both on their best behavior, and that's saying quite a lot."

"I'm hip," murmured Gerry, courteously ushering Turk down the hall to his rather grand corner office, with a spectacular view over the park and the library. "Has our girl been poking around? I had a feeling she might find herself a little circumscribed by the NYPD."

"No doubt about that," said Turk with a scoff, smiling at a picture of Gerry's wife JoAnn that sat on the desk. "But she's been using rather creative diversionary tactics to get around the restrictions imposed by the cops, who have, I must say, really been quite patient with her. More than I would have thought. Firm, but patient."

"How is she diversioning—oh, you mean the Sledger stuff?"

"She's mentioned it?"

"Well, we *have* known each other from birth, as you're aware, so she does tell me some things she keeps from even Prax. Though I'm guessing not from you."

"You might be surprised," said Turk dryly. "But yes, Sledger."

He filled Gerry in on the adventures of Nefer Almond at the Chelsea, and when Gerry had finally stopped howling with laughter, Turk gave him a rueful glance.

"So you see how it is. But you knew that. And the amazing thing is, she finds stuff out."

"Such as?"

"Well, she seems to have figured out that something was going on with the two victims, Biff and Scarlett, and that it somehow connects with Sledger—the guitar theft and ransom. I'm not sure quite *how* she's figuring it, but she is. And now"—Turk became visibly reluctant as he neared the subject he'd wanted to broach—"she also seems to think that it might tie in with, well, us. Which is why I wanted to talk to you, as it might involve—indirectly—Centaur."

Gerry grew still and attentive. "Let's hear it, then."

When he told Rennie about the Centaur meeting—though not about his discussion with Gerry, that could keep for a bit—at dinner in Chinatown that night, at their favorite Mott Street basement hole-in-the-wall, Wo Hop, he was surprised to hear her agree with Freddy, for whose artistic opinions she generally had only the deepest contempt. Except for Lionheart, Plato Lars, Prisca Quarters and Tenwynter, she didn't think that Centaur, under Freddy's direction, had signed anybody over the last couple of years who justified the few cents' worth of plastic they were pressed on, and she didn't exactly make a secret of how she felt.

"You got it right, what you said to the boys," she

remarked, loading duck lo mein and shrimp lobster sauce onto Turk's plate. "Starlorn can be amazing. He can also be a colossal pain in the behind. You'll have to keep him on a tight rein, and who better than your lordship to do it? Judging by what I've heard around the house lately, I think he could do a lot for the way you want to take this album. And you must admit, he's got a fantastic facility. Quite the super sonic playground. I've been to some sessions there— you guys will love it."

She'd get no argument from him; the whole industry would have agreed. Vinylization, on the ground floor of a beautiful old nineteenth-century former printing plant and then speakeasy over on Washington Street, on the edge of the Hudson River in the far West Village, had been built with the vast proceeds of Andy Starlorn's legendary Fifties and early-Sixties girl-group and doo-wop recordings; completed only a few months ago, it was absolute state of the art. Unlike the big-label in-house studios, it was geared not to the needs of symphonic orchestras or aging crooners but to those of rock musicians, pure and simple. It had the finest equipment, purpose-built rooms, the best session players in New York on call; and its hip young engineers, like Hollis Flynn and Rosie Landers—one of the very, very few chicks working at a studio in a non-receptionist capacity—were already making a name for themselves.

Turk chopsticked a mouthful of duck. "That's all very well, but I'm not sure yet that I even want us to work there." He glanced up at her. "We're going over there later tonight; the guys want to see it so we can make our final decision. We could be recording our little audition tomorrow, or the day after, depending on Starlorn's availability. Want to come with and check it out?"

"I do not. There's nothing I hate more than the rocklord's consort tagging around after him when he's out and about on music-business business. Don't like to see it, don't like to do it. You'll get more accomplished on your own anyway. I'll drop by once you have the actual sessions going, if that's where you decide on. Besides, I've already seen the place, remember? When I did that piece on hip studios for Mod magazine: Abbey Road, Wally Heider's, Sunset Sound, the Record Plant."

"But you're not *any* rocklord's consort, you're *my* consort. And you haven't really listened to the place with us in mind, and I need your ear."

"And you shall have it. Both of them. I will lend them happily." Rennie poured them both more tea. "Just not tonight."

"Fair enough. But just so you know, come January we may end up doing a lot of the recording at home after all. I don't want you being surprised and cross when the lads are tromping through the house and messing up your kitchen and raiding the fridge."

"The kitchen's more your turf than mine, Chef Boy R.T. But why would you be doing this?"

"Oh, just to bash a little on Freddy. Which I like to do whenever I can. He seems to have something going with Andy Starlorn, and I want to do my heroic best to thwart his evil scheme, or at least subvert it to my own ends."

"Plus you can save money by recording in our cellar," said Rennie shrewdly, "since, as you quite correctly pointed out, Starlorn and his studio would run up a much bigger tab than Rafferty and Thom at the board and loving hands at home fixing soup and sarnies. All of a piece with how you stuck it to Freddy in L.A. last year—which was very well done, I might add. But what about Janson?"

Thom Courtenay and Leo Rafferty, aided sometimes by Janson Bridges, were Lionheart's longtime engineer/ producers. Though in actual practice it was Turk and Rardi who wielded the true scepter of sound and had the last word on every track, that was not to say they didn't depend on their producers of record. Rafferty was an old friend and former sound guy/equipment manager, a lean, dark Irishman from Finchley in north London, who had fallen into the producing gig because in the early days the band had had no money to spend on a real producer, and by the time they did, they were too used to Rafferty's ways, and he to theirs, to split up.

But if Leo was the ears of Lionheart, Thom was the hands—a master splicer and a genius on the mixing board. They'd found him in London working at the BBC: he now resided here in New York, but he was as English as they come—a hippie John Bull, complete with magnificent muttonchop whiskers. He'd been at Cambridge with Turk's lookalike cousin and sometime stand-in, Oliver Buckle, and he'd come to America right after university to set up shop. With great success: he now had his own studio, over on Seventh Avenue, in a rickety old building with lots of music-biz tenants and history, and a client list of stunning distinction. But he always came through for Lionheart when the band needed him.

It was a partnership made in vinyl heaven: Turk and Rardi created the vision, and Lionheart as a unit made it all happen. Rafferty heard the balance and Thom mixed the creation to perfection, with Janson as a kind of overall clean-up editor. It wasn't a formula to be tinkered with lightly, and Rennie, who was very fond of all three guys, pointed this out now to her mate.

Turk had begun working on a big bowl of roast pork congee. "There'll be no tinkering. Nobody's cutting Thom and Leo loose. And Janson's busy with Stoneburner in L.A., so we can't have him for this album anyway. It's just that we want to get back to our old sound, only different, and we need a different — sensibility this time."

"Sensibility sounds fine," said Rennie, and reached across to squeeze his hand. "But just please be sure there's some sense in there as well."

After their tour of inspection at Vinylization, which was well reported on by Turk to a curious Rennie, the Lionheart boys spent all the next day in the prow house cellar, working on vocal tracks to have something to show Andy Starlorn, while Rennie, desperate to get out of the house, took Prax and Ares out for some touristy travels, hitting the Cloisters, the Cathedral of St. John the Divine and the campus of Columbia University, her own old grad-school stomping grounds.

They ended up back in the East Village at around four in the afternoon; after dropping in at the prow house to see what, if anything, was going on — the band was still immersed in the new songs — they skipped out again and walked down a few blocks to Ratner's, the famous Jewish dairy restaurant next door to the Fillmore East.

They were all very familiar with the place and its fabulous food and irascible waiters, and loved it, and they immediately realized how lucky they were to be seated almost without a wait at a table against the wall. The place was strict dairy kosher, no meat; so, exhausted from their hard day's sightseeing, and with supper still many hours away, they decided they needed to restore themselves with specialties of the house.

After a very happy and heavily carbohydrated hour, Rennie suddenly saw Nick Sattlin across the restaurant aisle, sitting in front of an empty plate that had held kasha varnishkes, at present tucking into a mile-high slab of strawberry shortcake. Not surprising that he should choose to dine there, as the stationhouse was only a block away and he was probably just getting off his shift, but it did rather seem like fate. On an impulse, she got up and went over to his table to loom imposingly over him, and he glanced up as if he was not in the least surprised to see her there.

Uninvited, she sat down across from him. "I see you're making great progress on the case, Detective Sattlin. Spending time in clubs, eating lavish lunches, asking humble ink-stained wretches to do favors for you. Must be nice. Maybe we can actually get our life back shortly. If that's not too much to ask."

"Nobody asked you to give your life up in the first place, as I recall." He dug into the shortcake. "And I'm certainly entitled to a good lunch without being badgered by persons of interest, or persons interested in their own interests. I've told you once, Miss Stride, now I'm telling you again. In the nicest possible way: Back. Off. This is why you pay the exorbitant city taxes that you and Mr. Wayland pay; let us do what you pay us to do. This is New York, not San Francisco, not London, not Los Angeles, certainly not the Sullivan County boondocks. We can figure it out without your help. Stop trying to do the cops' job and just do what we asked. That's more than helpful right there."

Rennie picked up a spare fork and deliberately helped herself to a load of whipped cream off the back of Sattlin's slice of cake.

"Yes, well, as for figuring it out without my help, we'll just see about that. And if I had backed off in L.A., Turk would be on death row right now for the murders of our good friend Tansy Belladonna and her manager and several groupies, and I'd be dead myself, killed by the same lunatic who did the other killings. And if I had backed off in San Francisco, Prax McKenna would be in the cell next door to Turk's, for killing Jasper Goring and Fortinbras De Angelis, and possibly even Tam Linn."

"That's not quite the way I heard it," he told her, and Rennie laughed shortly.

"No, I'll bet it's not. Who did you talk to, my ex-cousin-in-law ex-detective Super Secret Agent Marcus Lacing Dorner? No, no, you don't have to admit it, I can see that you did."

Sattlin smiled in spite of himself. "Well, he certainly had some interesting things to say. But he did tell me you had been very helpful. He also said you were smart and observant and brave. And that I shouldn't give you an inch because you'd push it to a mile. Several miles."

"What a prince."

"Does a prince outrank a future duke?"

Oh nooooo, this surely cannot be...what gods have I offended to merit such a terrible punishment? Not to mention the perfectly horrendous timing. How does this always happen to me, and why *does it happen...*

She turned and looked up, dreading what she knew she was going to see. Super Secret Agent Marcus Lacing Dorner his very own self stood beside the table, thwacking his leather gloves into the palm of one hand like a gangster, and smiling like a polar bear. Well, wasn't he just too spiffy for words today, in a beautifully tailored gray cashmere overcoat. Much nicer than his grubby Woodstock threads, what he'd been wearing when she'd seen him last. Now he was gazing down at her as though he'd done something exceptionally clever and wanted to make damn sure she knew it.

"He does not," she said coolly. "At least not this particular prince." She drew her left hand under her chin, pointedly angling it so her engagement ring lay face up and obvious. "Nor this particular future duke."

Marcus noticed the ring—hard not to—but chose to ignore it.

"So are you here as an official agent, Agent? Again agent?"

"As a matter of fact, I am."

"And why, pray, is the FBI called in on this? If you indeed even officially *are* FBI, which question I don't think we ever settled to my satisfaction. And you really do need to stop popping up like a pantomime villain. It's getting very old very quickly."

"There's some evidence that's given rise to concern about interstate trade issues," said Marcus coolly, ignoring everything else she had said and nodding to Sattlin, who seemed even less surprised to see him than he had been to see Rennie. "So we were invited to come help. And me specifically because, well, you know why. Same reason as always."

"What reason would that be? And you still haven't said definitively if you're FBI or not. Jesus, Mary and Joseph, are we *never* to be rid of you? Or get a straight answer out of you?"

Marcus sat down beside Sattlin, folding his overcoat neatly and placing it on the back of an empty chair, then raising his eyebrows at a passing waiter, who, unheard-of for Ratner's, actually stopped in mid-flight and scurried straight over to take his order, which Rennie watched with disbelief. *Huh. Pays to be a ruler of the universe, apparently; at least it empowers you to snag a Jewish waiter's instant attention by vibes alone. Which is no inconsiderable thing...*

"Not as long as there is something big and nasty and illegal going on in the rockerverse, as you like to call it. So, given my experience in such matters —"

"Thanks entirely to me, sir!"

He made her a little bow from where he sat. "Be that as it may, they sent me along to check things out."

"You think the murders are tied into other stuff. Which is what some other people think." She gave Sattlin a pointed stare, but he ignored her gaze and just kept shoveling shortcake. Clearly he was sitting this one out.

"I do think that. Tied in with big old knots." Marcus looked her straight in the eyes. "Turk's-head knots."

Aware of Prax and Ares at their table across the aisle, listening hard though trying to seem as if they weren't, and attempting vainly to lip-read at the same time, Rennie froze at the word "Turk" and shot him a sharply attentive glance.

"Which means precisely what? More than what Detective Sattlin here had to tell me? Do you think Lionheart is involved? *Turk*?"

"Turk? Not actively, probably, no. At least for now," he added as by duty bound. "No, though I'm sure Detective Sattlin set it out admirably, we think the, ah, problem is on a rather humbler but also a rather more serious level. I think he may have already discussed it with you."

"Well, why don't *you* discuss it with me, then?"

So he told her.

"Marcus thinks *we're* involved with this? Lionheart, I mean. How? *Who*?"

Turk stared at Rennie, who as soon as she had arrived home had gone straight down to the studio to report to him about her meeting. As a rule, she never interrupted him when he was working, so since she'd broken into his session, he knew it was important.

She nodded miserably. "He didn't give me a *whole* lot of details. Not a lot more than Sattlin did. Just that there's some big bad stuff going on and there are apparently connections to Sledger and the deaths of the sound guy and the groupie. And to Lionheart." She pulled over a chair and sat next to him, putting a hand on his knee. "Maybe even to Niles."

Turk slid the faders up and down, listening to the playback but not really hearing it. "What do they plan on doing about it?"

"Finding out, I guess."

"Marcus… He does seem to be the bane of our existence, doesn't he." He ran the piano track back again, looking savage, though Rennie couldn't tell if his wrath was with Marcus or with the track. "I thought once we'd left L.A. we were thoroughly shot of him. Yet there he was at Woodstock, and now here he is again, like a really bad sixpence. Like Banquo's ghost."

"At least you didn't have to deal with him personally at Woodstock," said Rennie crossly. "Unlike myself. No, you had been ever so conveniently poisoned and were tucked up all comfy and nice at home by the time he crossed my path. He's not going to tell me any more than that, and neither is Sattlin, not just yet anyway. But I have an idea of my own, something along the lines of the Barney Levine caper we pulled off at Abbey Road—"

He rewound the tape for another go at a better rough mix. "I'm sure I shall regret asking this until my dying day, but what do you want me to do?"

So she told him.

CHAPTER FIFTEEN

AFTER MUCH DISCUSSION WITH HIS BANDMATES, Turk had decided to sacrifice not one but two really good songs on the audition altar of Andy Starlorn, a heavy rocker and a ballad. It would be defeating their own purpose to give him something that wouldn't reflect the band at its strongest, and besides, as Mick had said, they could always junk the tapes and re-record if it didn't work out. They were all wildly curious to see how it would go, so Turk and Rardi had picked a lovely ballad they'd just finished writing, "Is It Raining Where You Live?", and another new song called "Steel Roses", a bluesy pounder with long, intricate lyrics and some typical Lionheart musical twists, which if it worked out would be the album's title track, and handed them over.

As recording began the next night, at Vinylization — might as well audition the studio as well as the producer, Rardi had pointed out, and, very conveniently, the big main room, Studio A, was available — Turk's misgivings receded further the longer the sessions went on. His chief fear had been that Starlorn was going to put his big old muddy pawprints all over Lionheart's complex balance, with its clear, almost Bach-like separation — whatever went on in a Lionheart song, you could always hear each instrument with perfect clarity, even the rhythm guitar chords, and he didn't want to lose that. Typically, in a Starlorn mix little stood above the bed track, and certainly nothing stood *much* above it, not even the lead vocal—hence the "sonic flood" descriptor the press had attached to him. *More like sonic sludge...*

But Andy was already surprising him: he was keeping the overall cleanness Turk preferred, while at the same time tightening the rocker, dirtying it up with distortion and bottom, and treating the ballad with gentleness and an underlying tension. Both songs turned out absolute gems. When Starlorn gave the band his notes for the rest of the album, especially the two prospective singles, they were all knocked out, and even Turk had to agree that, at least for this album, Andy was the man for them.

In fact, the whole band was so jazzed that they had immediately decided to stay on in New York working until the last possible minute before Christmas, and blocked out major time right there on the spot for serious recording, in both the prow house studio and Vinylization. Turk invited some in-town friends to sit in whenever they felt like it—Hendrix, Diego, Sledger, Jimmy Page who was in from London with the Zep, among others—and figured he'd sort out the label legalities later.

Tonight Dylan had dropped by: Rennie sat on the control-room couch with Sara Dylan and exchanged rockwife war stories—Sara recounting how her notoriously privacy-obsessed husband had once ordered her to hide in a closet to avoid a reporter, Rennie raising it with the tale of Turk's hidden blue-bloodedness and the ghastly way she'd found out about it. They both agreed their men were a bit crazy, then broke off to listen as Bob blew harp and Turk bluesed it up on his early-Christmas-present Gibson—a not-yet-finished song called "Wide Open Faces."

"Those boys can *play*," said Rennie when the track was done. Above her head behind her at the desk, Andy Starlorn was muttering to Thom Courtenay about multitracking and fuzzing and reverbing, and Thom was diplomatically but desperately attempting to dissuade and looking to Turk for backup. By now, in the course of her years in rock, she had sat in on enough recording sessions to be well aware of what was going on. And what was going on here was power trip, big-time. Which was only to be expected, and both she and Turk *had* expected it.

The Dylans departed, and Rennie half-turned her head to bring Starlorn into her field of vision and continued to listen to the conversation, which had now moved on to Starlorn ranting about how he should just throw out all the tapes and replace them with alternate tracks. *Yeah, you could do that, but if you screw this up for Lionheart, maybe I will just throw out all the tapes and replace them with your shredded tendons...*

She reached a lazy arm for the wine bottle going around, and watched Turk through the glass of the big picture window as he and Rardi worked out some temporary musical logjam. He was wearing that new dark-red shirt she'd bought for him the other day and a pair of black corduroy pants, and he had his reading glasses on as he studied the chart and she studied him.

Objectively studied him, not as her mate but as the superstar he was. The consummate rock god, really: just nuts enough, in the best way, to make gorgeously innovative and creative music but not nuts enough to buy into either the hype, the hysteria or the hate. He was super-intelligent. He was insanely beautiful. He was witty and well-spoken and English to the core. He gave great interviews, not to mention giving great—other things. By no means was he perfect: at times he could be moody and unaccountable, arrogant and withdrawn, even snarlingly angry or coldly furious, but he was never petty or cruel. Failing a total and unlikely meltdown, he was grounded enough not to go off the rails with tantrums and groupies and drink and drugs the way so many already had, and he'd never end up dead of an o.d. In short, he was a man, not a boy, and it was reflected in everything he did.

It was the way he was by nature, mostly, she considered, but also because he had that lordship thing going for him. He dismissed it most of the time, but it was always there for him and he was always aware of it—a sort of day job, rock-solid, as it were, so that his music, though it was his life, wasn't his only life.

They were now into the last few days of recording before the band dispersed and went home for Christmas and New Year's, though Niles of course, being constrained by polite but insistent police request, would be staying on. Turk had wanted to get as much done in both studios as he could, and they had all moved over to Vinylization two nights before. Now Rennie leaned back and just listened: there was superb sound flooding in now over the huge speakers hanging above the big picture window, but she put on headphones so she could listen to the mix just as the musicians were hearing it, and the band's and Andy's and Thom's and

Rafferty's comments as well when they cut in.

She really liked this new song, and they already had a solid bed down for it: drums, bass and rhythm guitar. For the next few nights they would be laying in lead guitar, second lead and keyboards, then it would be time for vocals. It was an intricate arrangement with a lot of double-tracking that required a lot of work, and the song wouldn't be finished right away, maybe not even before everybody split the city. But she would definitely *not* be coming here every single night to sit on the couch and listen, which was fine with Turk. She had work of her own to do: things to write, crimes to solve…and at the front of her awareness, and at the back of Turk's, there lurked the little rattlesnake that Marcus and Sattlin had put there, coiling and uncoiling and ready to strike—the one with Niles's name on.

Staring into the darkness of the studio behind the window, she could see Andy Starlorn's ghostly image reflected floating in the glass. Now there was a man who could find his way around a recording studio in the dark. He wasn't tall, maybe five-seven, more wiry than strongly built—probably with quite good tendons, too. Mussy, mousy long hair mostly graying by now, pale, protuberant eyes framed by Buddy Holly glasses, about twenty years older than the oldest person in the room. She could see him counting, as indeed he did, as one of the great young-genius producers of the previous rock and roll age. All those amazing hits he'd brought off in the Fifties and pre-Beatle early Sixties: countless rockabilly and doo-wop and girl groups, not to mention his work with a shoal of music idols.

No surprise there, really: Andy was a member of the

famous Starlorn family of Appalachian musical geniuses, third child of the legendary Clary Starlorn, country guitar king, and country-song queen Clovia Jackson Starlorn. His name wasn't short for anything as far as she knew, just Andy, though perhaps he merely hadn't allowed it to become public knowledge. Or maybe Clary and Clovia could not have been bothered thinking up a decent fantastical name for him, as they had for all their other children. But chiefly he was the younger brother and sole producer of Fifties icon the late and indeed legendarily great Jordemain Starlorn, he of the platinum pompadour and swiveling hips and incredible voice; and if Andy didn't share Jordy's amazing vocal talents, or their other brothers' instrumental gifts, he certainly did share the Starlorn musical DNA in a different and effective permutation.

Not to mention sharing the Starlorn family's unapologetic and, regrettably, rather entertaining trashiness. They were real mountain monsters: their roots went back centuries, to the first Scots-Irish settlers. They had been, basically, dirt-poor white trash for all those generations, living a hardscrabble life way back in the hills and hollows, or "hollers" as those who lived there would say, home-taught out of the family Bible and dining off whatever they could shoot or trap or fish or grow for the table, until Clary Starlorn came along. Clary, as he had quickly shown just about the whole world, had been handed down from his mother a wondrous maverick gene for musical brilliance, which he had prospered from himself and duly passed along to his eight sons and daughters.

So now they were rich and famous white trash, Rennie

reflected; they wore shoes and everything these days, and hadn't eaten a possum in years, not unless they wanted to, and they had certified their trashiness by building themselves a palace of staggering ostentation and bad taste, back there in those same hollers and hills. And they had also kept alight their end of a spectacular feud of many generations' standing, with the equally rich and famous and musical Harkinger family, definitely *not* white trash, who came of considerably more refined bloodlines and better dietary habits. It wasn't a traditional shooting feud; well, not anymore, at least. Though it could be again with very little provocation: there had been a recent bit of hotly protested intermarriage between the two clans, real Montagues and Capulets stuff, and when the patriarchs, Dannah Harkinger and Clary himself, had found out about *that*, well, shooting hadn't been far off the table, and it sure wouldn't have been squirrels for the pot.

Rennie shook herself free from the tangled, though diverting, affairs of the Starlorns and Harkingers, and returned to consideration of Andy himself. She hadn't been terribly impressed when Turk had introduced them, especially when she recalled the gossip that Andy'd shacked up with his brother Jordy's blonde and blowsy teenage ex-wife, Tula, though at least Jordy had been decently divorced from her first. Which was just, well, ick. But Rennie wasn't the one who needed to be impressed with him, as long as the band was.

On balance, it was probably a good thing Lionheart had decided to go with him and Vinylization, at least for the mixing. Lately groups were taking longer and longer to record; drugs, fame, new studio tricks and out-of-control egos were chiefly responsible for that. It had been easier in the early days: when groups had just been starting out, they had had little money available and limited access to studio time, and they'd had to make the most album they could with the few resources they could muster—in, play, mix, master, out. With small advances that not only had to pay for recording costs but for trivialities like food and rent, they hadn't been able to wallow about in musical self-indulgence. As a result, those early albums, though they were often raw and could have used a bit more polish, had a lovely, uncontrived appeal about them, immediate and strong.

Now, though. Very different. Just about every group had pretty much endless amounts of money and time, and few people were in a position to rein them in—Starlorn not being one of them, being excessively indulgent himself. Though, to be fair, Lionheart had never been one of the blatant offenders in that quarter. Looking at *you*, Airplane, Tenwynter, Stones, Dead, Fairfighter, Janis, Beatles, Beach Boys: they and others had shifted studio-time expectations from weeks to months, years in some cases. Geologic epochs, even. New coral atolls formed faster than some of these bands pushed out promised albums: two LPs a year had been an early industry norm—now, it was more like one every eighteen months. Or even longer. Which was more realistic, and undoubtedly more humane, but also was more conducive to excess. An album a year was the aimed-at ideal, for bands and fans alike; it was just that, between touring and songwriting and the need to actually have a bit of a life, so few of the bands could manage to achieve it.

Still, knowing that every lick cost them money, Lionheart wouldn't be any more self-indulgent here at Vinylization than they were in Turk's basement. He'd make sure of that, and Starlorn's high prices would help him do so—nobody liked to waste studio time when they were the ones who had to pay it out of pocket, either up front from an advance, as was usual, or deducted from royalties later on, as Lionheart had the clout to arrange things these days.

As a rule, Rennie avoided recording sessions like the plague, figuring Turk didn't need the distraction, and herself not enjoying the endless takes and retakes and stops and starts and creative hissyfits, and the fact that the engineers and producers all too often cut their glances over to her, to see how the in-house critic was reacting to what was going on. Not to mention the annoyance of being surrounded by other Lionheart ladies, none of whom she had ever really become friends with, except for Christabel Green, and most of whom she found as dumb as paint, again with Christabel being the exception. But every now and then she showed up for a session, and Turk was always happy to have her there.

Or just always happy to have her… I got your symbolism right here, mister. In case you were wanting some…

Turk had called for a break and was standing in the middle of the studio, hands in pockets, looking at Rennie through the glass. Holding his gaze, she casually undid the top few buttons of her panne-velvet shirt, letting a generous curve of breast appear in the opening. After all, there was a perfectly good vocal booth going unused at the moment, and it had a nice thick rug…

"Take an hour, people," said Thom diplomatically, over

the speaker. And they did.

"Have you fixed up what we talked about yet?" she asked, reassembling her clothes.

"I have," said Turk grimly. "And let me tell you, I am not happy about it. Do you really think Sattlin and Marcus are on the right track?"

"Well, they think so. I'm so sorry," she said then, with sudden sympathy.

He waved it off. "I don't want to talk about it. What you asked me to do, I'll let it happen, because *you* asked me. But I just want you to know it's worse than what we had to do to Barney Levine at Abbey Road."

"Hey, you enjoyed that… Oh, honey, I know this is different. But it has to be done."

"Yes. Probably. Be very sure I'm going to take it out of your hide, madam."

"Promises, promises…" Rennie grinned and reached for the vocal mike, switching it on to purr into it, startling everyone at their lunch. "Good evening, Mr. and Mrs. Rock and Roll and all the ships at sea."

Turk grabbed it away from her, spoke into it himself. "Pay no attention to that woman behind the curtain…"

"Oh, you're no fun," she said with mock annoyance as they exited the booth, unobtrusively scanning each other to make sure they were all buttoned and zipped again. "I think maybe I'll head home, if you're going to be here for a while?"

"No, don't do that. We shouldn't be more than another hour, we're just wrapping this one up. Do you think you can stick it out that long?"

"Sure. I'll just wander around a bit. This place was supposed to have been a speakeasy at one time, you know," she added. "Maybe I can find some secret passages and stuff—Thom told me there was a hidden staircase somewhere. Like Nancy Drew."

"Right up your street, then."

Turk went back into the live room to consult some more with Rardi and Starlorn, and Rennie started her wandering around, as she had said. This was really quite an impressive place, the décor being as beautiful as the sound. Studios, by virtue of their need to be functional, were all furnished pretty much alike; the only variations you ever got were stylistic. And Vinylization was nothing if not stylish, in the usual hippie studio way: teak paneling and paisley baffles and stained-glass lamps; pillowy leather sofas; Spanish-tiled main desk; several original, and gorgeous, bronze Art-Deco wall panels; even, out in the well-landscaped backyard, a glassed-in meditation-tripping-toking sun lounge complete with koi pool and tropical plantings and burbling fountain and giant statue of Kuan Yin.

Seeing as no one was about to stop her, Rennie swung open the thick, heavy soundproof double doors, like a bank vault's or a submarine airlock, that sealed the studio off from the corridor outside—God, she hated those things, essential as they were, she had to use her whole small body to push them wide—then began prowling the halls. Offices, storage rooms, a small kitchen, other studios smaller than the big main room Lionheart was using, more lounges, even a couple of "on-call" rooms complete with bunk beds and showers for those very special all-night sessions, recording or not.

The building itself was a beautiful old structure, taking up most of a city block and full of music-business tenants; the ground floor and second floor were all Vinylization, hallways and public areas awash with gorgeous coffered ceilings inlaid with maroon and gold; the floors and walls were polished marble, the fixtures old patina'd brass. The windowed interior corridors formed cloister-like areas, the windows framed in beautiful oiled dark wood, original to the building and open to skylights six stories above.

It wouldn't be at all surprising if there really *was* a hidden staircase somewhere, she mused, the two ground floors having once been a famous speakeasy and all. There was a semi-secret entrance opening onto a narrow little alley that ran down to the river, conducive for clandestine sneakings about and convenient for exciting escapes when the Prohibition cops showed up, and the fabled secret staircase would have led to upstairs boudoirs for clandestine booze-fueled trysts and political deal-making; but the second floor had been lost or demolished decades ago, or so people thought.

According to music-biz legend, there was supposed to be a concealed door leading to that floor, a door and stairs which had been located somewhere in the main speakeasy premises, perhaps behind the bar, or in the office of the boss. That would put it in one of what were now the four studios on the first floor; but in all the decades since those merry years, no one had ever found it, and if it still existed, it had no doubt been sealed over when Andy Starlorn had done his renovations and restorations. Still, it was fun to think about.

She sat for a while on the broad windowsill overlooking one of the little cloisters, eating from the small container of beef fried rice she'd grabbed from the kitchen, where a Chinese-food buffet had been laid out in case anyone got hungry; then she drifted down a few dim, promising side corridors, tapping occasionally on likely walls. But nothing gave off a hollow resonance bespeaking surreptitious flights of mysterious, twisty steps, so she got bored after a while and went back to the studio.

The guys were wrapping up the session, just as Turk had promised. He gave her a wave connoting Done, get your coat, we'll be out of here in five, and she waved back, communicating No problem, take your time. The guests and guest stars had all gone home long ago, and it was down to just Lionheart and its assorted belongings. Pudge and Thom were packing away equipment and tapes, and Andy Starlorn had already grandly departed the premises, leaving his own minions to tidy up for tomorrow's sessions.

Emerging into the biting, diamond-clear wind of three in the morning on the West Side Highway, Rennie clung to Turk's arm while he raised the other one to flag down a passing cab. He held the door for her and she scrambled inside, huddling her fox coat around her and snuggling up against him. For his part, Turk leaned against the corner of the back seat, eyes closed, seeming really beat and not saying anything more than giving their address to the driver.

Which was fine, his silence: he'd worked hard tonight, and if he didn't feel like talking, that was okay with her.

She'd never be a fan of sessions; it really wasn't much fun if you weren't the one doing the recording yourself—and sometimes even if you were. Certainly a lot less fun than people outside the business thought—though that little interlude in the isolation booth had been excellent. But there had been an air in the room tonight, some complex interaction of vibes amongst the participants and observers. Someone had been up to something; perhaps several someones, and she didn't like the feeling.

As the cab bore them away home, she cuddled closer to Turk, and he put both his arms around her. Whatever it was, she'd find out. She just hoped it would be soon.

CHAPTER SIXTEEN

"IXEN."

"Prat."

"Virago."

"Ratbag."

"Termagant."

"Tosser."

"Bossy cow."

"Dozy swine."

"Bourgeois bint."

"Overbred ponce."

"Vindictive shrew."

"Effete limey."

"Meddlesome hag."

"Overrated tunesmith."

"I could keep this up all day."

"I'd rather you kept other things up all day."

"That too can be arranged."

"So you say, gasbagging blowhard…"

"Blow *something*…"

Rennie and Turk were having breakfast by themselves at the, in their book, ungodly hour of ten a.m. As a rule, they acknowledged only one ten o'clock per day, and this was most definitely not it. It had been a little dicey for the past thirty-some hours: after their arrival home from the studio, by the time they'd gotten up the steps and into the house

Turk had been in the clutches of one of his periodic moody silences—the mood where he didn't want to speak or be spoken to or see anybody or hear any sounds but natural ones, and he had spent all the intervening time immured in his top-floor stronghold, portcullis down, drawbridge up, moat full of piranha, approach at your peril.

The other prow house residents were well aware of his lordship's state of mind, and had prudently found other things to do elsewhere on Manhattan Island. Rennie had remained mostly at home just in case he needed anything, though she didn't ply him with sympathy or fuss over him, or do anything but quietly leave trays of food outside the door, and take away the cleared plates—at least he was eating, and if he wanted anything else or more, he could damn well fend for himself. She'd learned early in their association that when he retreated into the dark and twisty region that she called Turkshire, even she wasn't welcome across the borders. Not until he chose to come back to the rest of humanity.

So she had amused herself with the dog and the kitten, and read, and worked on her book and columns and articles, and took a little nap or two, and made a quick trip down to Chinatown and returned laden with sackfuls of dim sum for the house to enjoy, and presently the bedroom door had quietly opened at about six this morning and Turkshire's Lord Mayor and sole inhabitant sidled in, slipping into bed with her and offering her the most very heartfelt and acceptable of apologies. Afterward, when he had fallen asleep beside her, she had lain awake, one arm flung across his bare back, her hand idly stroking where it rested, thinking.

It was good that he had won out over his black mood and his little jaunt to Waylandia, as he himself called it; good too that such visits were getting briefer and more infrequent the longer they were together. He was learning how to manage them better, and she flattered herself that she might have a small hand in that; the moods would never go away, nor should they, as they seemed deeply linked to his creativity as an artist. But at least they didn't seem to hurt him quite so much as they once did, and that could only be a good thing.

Now, trying to keep straight faces, they were taunt-dueling over the breakfast table. No one else in the house was awake yet, and the two of them wouldn't have been either if Turk's father hadn't called from England, forgetting the time difference, and gotten his son and heir all worked up as well as woken up, as soon as he and Rennie had finally, exhaustedly fallen asleep.

When Rennie had rather cautiously asked about it, after he'd put down the phone and slammed a few things around the bedroom, he'd said it was just stupid social dukely stuff. When she hadn't let it go, he'd finally confessed that there was some big huge formal ball coming up, where major royals would be present, at which his parents were requiring his attendance, and, surprise, surprise, Rennie's too. Beyond that, he hadn't wanted to discuss it, and she was mildly hurt at his refusal—thus the litany of invective that had ensued down in the kitchen. But they had been laughing throughout.

She felt it safe to return to the topic now, pushing another poached egg onto her toast raft. "I thought you were glad they were including me in stuff, now that we've all met and are civil and you and I are lawfully engaged with Great-Great-Granny's ring and everything."

"I am," he said, sighing pathetically. "It's just that this particular ball is going to be infested with former suitors — suitresses? suitrixes? — for my hand, and I don't want you, as the victorious claimant, exposed to that sort of riffraff. Upper-class county Englishwomen can be as vicious as a pack of East End whores fighting over a client."

"On-the-make limey trash with titles? Please! Piece of cake. May I remind you of the charming Lady Bum-in-a-Sling, no lady she, who we encountered in that restaurant in London back last January? I thought I wrapped her up and tossed her out pretty efficiently, and so did you think at the time. But if little trampy peerage rejects start coming on to you in front of me, I may have to punch somebody."

Turk's mouth twitched. "It's quite bad form to hit a woman."

"I didn't say I'd punch *them*."

The twitch redoubled to a grin. "I'll keep it in mind. And I do indeed remember your encounter with dear Lady Pandora, or hers with you — a lovely moment, yes. But this will be different. More like the dancehall scene in *West Side Story*, only with posh accents and tiaras. Or maybe more like the rumble scene."

"I get to wear a *TIARA*? That settles it. We are definitely going. Even if I have to bring a switchblade to fend off the riffraff."

"Traditionally, only married ladies wear tiaras to such

events. And not even American beauties get to attend armed. Sorry to break the news on both scores. But I can see that archaic social conventions aren't going to cut much ice with you."

"Well, not when I can be actually *wearing* the ice, no." Rennie gave him her best puppy-dog eyes, and he snorted. "Technically, I have *been* a married woman, so wouldn't that count?"

"It may have done, but you have also been annulled, so I think that wipes away your status pretty effectively. For which I am most grateful, as I've said many times."

"Well, I don't care how many disappointed contenders for the position of your future Duchess show up and stomp their hoofs and try to scratch my eyes out. If they even *attempt* to mess with me, there will be broken bones littering the ballroom floor like the bottom of Death Valley, and I assure you they won't be mine. *I'm* the one with the ring, *I'm* the one going home with the handsome studly nobleman, and *I'm* the one wearing the tiara. Correct procedure or not. I *can* borrow one, can't I?" she added anxiously. "I do have that emerald one you gave me last year, but it might not match my dress and your family does seem to have an awful lot of them lying around."

"Bushels. Literally. Grandmother will be delighted to root you out one to suit not only the occasion but your gown, whatever color it will be. She too likes breaking social conventions." He looked at her with a kind of bleak tenderness. "I would desperately love to have you with me at the ball—it really is rather a big deal, and I am certainly not going alone, so it's both of us or neither. I just don't want you to be thrown in at the deep end of the shark pool for your first formal appearance as the future Marchioness. Yes, I know, you were by my side for my grandfather's funeral and people found out about us then, thanks to the tabloids, but this is a whole other level of stress and operatic-type drama."

"Oh, piffle. We managed just fine at that little drinks rodeo you threw at Tarrant House, when I actually had to play hostess."

"Would that be the one where you almost got taken hostage at gunpoint? Oh wait, no, you *did* get taken hostage at gunpoint."

She beamed. "Yes, that's the one! So you do remember! Well, this ball thing won't be for a while yet, plenty of time to plan, hopefully no guns need make an appearance. In the meantime—"

"There's nothing we can do about it now," said Turk with an air of finality. "Let's just pretend that the resultant adventure will help us grow as people and leave it at that."

"And hope that hijinks will ensue," she said. "For now, though, it's Niles who- must remain at the forefront of our attention. And, yeah, I guess Sledger too. And whoever else is creeping around this situation. Murders to solve, perps to catch. If we were in England, it would be my belief that the butler did it. Perhaps it would be your belief as well."

"Oho, not *our* butlers! Though, now that I think of it, it could be. I've always had a sneaking suspicion that they're all a pack of street brawlers underneath their impeccable tailoring and manners, so they would have to come top of your suspect list. Do you even *have* a suspect list?" he added, curious. "It's been an active case long enough for you to have worked up some idea of who's to blame. So does anyone have form, as the coppers say in my homeland?"

She twirled her teaspoon for a moment or two. "Yes," she said finally. "But I don't like it. And neither will you."

Rennie was still sitting at the kitchen table when Prax descended for breakfast, long after Turk had cheerfully vanished into the cellar for the day's session. The new arrival raised her brows to see Rennie moodily slouched there, but merely nodded a greeting and poured herself some coffee. After a long-drawn-out silence:

"So, Nancy Drew, how are you doing with your Niles project? We haven't really talked about him lately, have we. And I wonder why that should be."

"No..." Rennie brooded a while longer. "Well, he's pretty much gotten on my last remaining nerve, so I like to stay away. It's a rather crowded nerve, what with Sledger and Marcus hanging out there too."

"Marcus!" said Prax, startled. "Marcus *Dorner*? I know we encountered him in Ratner's the other day, spoiling my enjoyment of all those pierogis, and I was going to ask about him then but you seemed in no answering mood. I was wondering what he was doing in New York. So I'll ask now: what does he have to do with Niles?"

"Yeah, no, I didn't tell you. Turk's not happy about it, so don't mention it to him, if you think you can remember not to. Our Marcus was there having a meeting with Detective Sattlin, so it's sort of relevant—he's been called in, the way he was at Woodstock, as a consultant with arresting powers, apparently. But he annoys me something chronic, and so I'd not mention him in any case." She paused a moment. "He's gone freelance, as you may remember, does special-agent work now."

"Like Bond James Bond? Well, *that* could be trouble!"

"It could. And it probably will. But hopefully not today."

Prax finished her coffee and roll and headed back upstairs again; the rest of the house gradually woke up around noon and came shuffling down like rock undead, intent on scrounging late breakfast before it was actually lunchtime. Safely ensconced in the morning room by now, Rennie, alerted by Macduff's suddenly directionally pointed ears, nipped up the back stairs to her writing room before any of them could come in and bother her. It seemed to be her turn to withdraw, as Turk had done previously. She felt like such a bad hostess, but she *so* did not feel like sitting around with her guests today. She was bored with it all, so desperately bored that she could scream her boredom as long and loud as a freight train hauling hard across the wide Missouri. But she still had some major work to do on her column quota this week for Fitz, so she took advantage of the situation and wrote her brains out for several hours, uninterrupted, pleased with the flow and speed.

Then, judging that the coast might be clear again, she ventured back down to the kitchen and peered down the cellar stairs. A faint and melodic glaze of music floated up to her ears: Turk must have left the studio door open, as he had habitually done in L.A. She could hear him talking to whomever was down there with him—sounded like Rardi and Shane, they were clearly just mixing, not recording.

Good; that would keep them busy for a while. She scribbled a note and magneted it to the fridge; then, grabbing the coat and bag she'd brought down with her, and a few har gow for the road, she snuck out the back door and galloped away to the west.

She caught the crosstown bus at Third Avenue and rode it over to the Sixth Avenue subway, whence she headed uptown to Ken Karper's office, wanting to be sure they were on the same page regarding what both of them, at least, were convinced were murders, even if the cops were still being coy about it. Ken thought they were similarly located, page-wise, although the page seemed one they had read many times before and they had nothing new to show, and to improve Rennie's mood, he suggested she go drop in on Fitz. But Rennie didn't feel strong enough for that today, and bidding farewell to her collaborator after an hour's earnest discussion, she went downstairs again to the downtown train.

An uneventful express ride later, she got out at West Fourth and walked east along Bleecker. Her destination was the Village Gate, the renowned musical venue that took up most of the ground floor of the imposing brick building at Bleecker and Thompson Streets. Waving as she went in to proprietor Art D'Lugoff, whom she'd known since her college days, she went up the stairs to the Top of the Gate, the intimate performance space and bar, where Bosom Serpent, who were among her favorite bands and favorite people alike, were booked in for an extended engagement, while the musical revue/cabaret *Jacques Brel Is Alive and*

Well and Living in Paris continued its wildly successful run in the theater downstairs.

Seeing the revue's posters, Rennie could not forbear a grimace. Prax was crazy about the damn thing, and had been playing the cast album of rather lugubrious *chansons* constantly, ever since she arrived at the prow house, not to mention having seen the show every free night she'd had and singing some of the numbers at every opportunity, thinking to include a couple on Evenor's next LP. Over her bandmates' dead bodies, every single one of them had told her, separately and collectively, with point and bitterness; so probably it wasn't going to happen. Rennie liked two or three songs, sure, and they sounded really good when Praxie sang them; but mournful 1930s Montmartre all day, every day, in hack Tin Pan Alley-English translations, was too much. Or perhaps she should say *de trop*. In any case, bor-ing.

As she crossed the bar area filled with empty tables, chairs upturned on top of them for cleaning, Serpent's twin leads Lindon and Lucian Dolabella glanced up from where they were fiddling with their guitars for a cursory sound check, their identical faces warming with identical grins to see her. The three had first met on the Sunset Strip club circuit, during Rennie's early days in L.A.; they had been friends of Owl Tuesday in Venice and the Byrds in Laurel Canyon and Powderhouse Road here in New York, and they had become friends with Rennie as well, and later with Prax and Turk and the Sonnets. They all encountered one another at fairly infrequent intervals, due to tours and gigs, and now they set the guitars aside and settled down to do some serious catching up.

It was Lindon who mentioned it first. "I hear you're up to your usual tricks, Strider. Up to your ears, in fact. How's it going with Niles?"

"Oh, you've heard? Well, cutie, how do you *think* it's going?"

Lucian—Lucky to his nearest and dearest—chuckled darkly. "As well as that, then."

Rennie sighed. "Got that right... He's such a *pest*. He wants me to clear his name of suspicion of killing those two people in the cemetery; you've read about that, I'm sure. When it suits him, I'm Murder Chick the Magnificent, capable of seeing into the souls of murderers and magically drawing forth the truth, like Excalibur. But more often he's this petulant little brat who seems bent on thwarting everybody at every turn, Turk and me most of all. And I'm getting sick of it. If I hadn't promised..." She stopped abruptly. That was private, that was Lionheart business; she wasn't about to spill it to outsiders, even ones she knew as well as these two.

But the twins didn't seem to notice. She gave them the rocknroll onceover: they looked better than ever, having matured nicely from their Strip days. Attractive shoulder-length brunettes, whom the casual glance couldn't tell apart; both tall, though well short of Turk's altitude; both possessed of engaging smiles. The only differentiation came in their eyes: Lucky's were hazel, while Lindon's were almost gold. They had come to New York from L.A. not long after Rennie had arrived there from Cornell, before she'd married Stephen and left for the Coast, and they had shared a rattletrap Avenue B tenement flat with half of Powderhouse for a while. The filthiest apartment in creation, Rennie had dubbed it, flatly refusing to clean it up for them or even sit on a chair there—it really had been a pigsty. But they were delighted to be back in the city again, happily now able to afford a nice two-bedroom furnished sublet in Chelsea—complete with cleaning woman—while they played the Gate, and Rennie had been thinking to meet up with them for several days now.

"Well, if Murder Chick can't figure it out, then no one can," offered Lucian. "But it's always hooked up in rock, right? Even us—that cat Biff, who died in the cemetery? He did some work for us in L.A., before Sledger's tour started up and he left with her."

"Oh yes? Turk said Biff did freelance with quite a few bands. Kind of like Pudge Vetrini, though Pudge is more on staff with Lionheart these days. Biff has been working with Sledger pretty steadily for a while now. Had been."

Lucian nodded, his face clouded. "That's true, what Turk said. But Biff had been a little bit, what's a good word I can use, *persona non grata*, among certain bands lately. There was never any proof, but the word was that he was known for fiddling more on the sound board than just levels. And he wasn't the only one."

Rennie felt her slaydar, so christened by Prax back in their Haight days, suddenly switch on. "Tell me more."

Lindon moved a little closer, glancing around to make sure no one overheard. But the nearest person was D'Lugoff himself, who was all the way downstairs talking to some of the Jacques Brel people, and Lindon turned back to her.

"As Lucky said, there's no proof, but we've had problems with bootleggers lately, and we're not the only ones. The talk was that Biff had hooked up with some big-time, well-financed dude to bootleg live shows straight off the sound boards, and then clean up selling the really good-quality resultant tapes. Always decent, in-demand acts: Jimi at Mile High in Denver, us at the Cow Palace and the L.A. Forum, Sunny Silver at Cobo in Detroit, Externity in Philly at the Spectrum..."

Her slaydar had its high beams on now. "Hmm. All big gigs, stadium shows."

"You noticed. Yes, which makes it a little easier to get away with. Small venue like this, for instance" — he waved his arm at the extent of the Top of the Gate, with its bar and tables and mini-stage — "it would be difficult to manage a ripoff. No place to hide, board right over there, everything out in the open — everyone would know what you were up to. Everyone who knew what was what, anyway."

"No, yeah, I see that... Okay, Biff had been semi-suspect and notorious for recording off the board for bootleg purposes; so why didn't Sledger see fit to mention it to me?" asked Rennie. "He was her minion, after all, and that's a damn good motive. I will officially slaughter her, the wretched little toad. She is such a selfish old thing. All she cared about was getting her damn guitar back, and she didn't want to upset the applecart. And she did get it back, though I didn't really have anything to do with it."

"What's this about, then?"

She filled them in on the tale of Veronica Lee Cairns and her kidnapped axe, and they were suitably dismayed. "It's

starting to not seem all that unconnected, isn't it, though...
Biff is bootlegging, say, and turns up dead, Sledger's axe
goes missing and isn't returned for days. And why, maybe?
Because maybe the person who pinched it is dead, and so is
a girl who looked a lot like Sledge."

Lucian shifted uneasily. "That does sound a bit too
hooked-up for *my* peace of mind, Strider. We've also
used Turk's guy Pudge, you know, and Dandiprat's guy
Shiva Dass and Cold Fire's guy Bill Waxman, besides Biff
Nydborg. I'm not saying any of them was on the take or
making bootlegs, you understand. Lots of people had
access to lots of sound boards right around the time when
the boots started turning up like magic mushrooms, and
still do. But it wasn't just us, and it did seem a little, well, a
little too convenient."

"Big gigs for sure," said his twin, seeming just as
unhappy. "And seeing as Lionheart just came off a tour with
a *lot* of major venues, you might want to tell Turk and Rardi
to keep an eye out for things popping up that shouldn't be
popping. From the Garden in particular."

"It being yet another big gig on a tour that had a lot of major
venues," agreed Rennie lightly, but her heart was far from
light within her. A Lionheart double album with the super-
excellent Garden live material was going to be an enormous
seller, and a good-quality bootleg, released a lot sooner than
the lawful album could be, would cut significantly into their
sales, especially in Asia and South America, where genuine
label albums were often very expensive and hard to come
by. But she couldn't, and wouldn't, believe for a heartbeat
that Lionheart producer-engineers Thom Courtenay, Leo

Hafferty and Janson Bridges had ever dabbled so much as a pinky toe in such piracy. As for the other techs and roadies — well, Biff wasn't in Lionheart's employ, but someone else the twins had mentioned sure was...

She hung around for a while as the rest of Bosom Serpent arrived, full of cheerful greetings, and allowed herself to be persuaded to stay for drinks and the first set. Usually the Top of the Gate was a snazzy, jazzy venue — Nina Simone, Albert Ayler, Pharoah Sanders — but like Bill Graham a mile across town adding in jazz to his shows, Art D'Lugoff was expanding the boundaries a bit, and Bosom Serpent was among the first of his midweek extended-run rock slates.

So, sipping a very nice gin and tonic, Rennie perched on a high-backed barstool a dozen feet from the stage and put her suspicions aside, listening with pleasure as the Serpents worked through a very representative set for a very enthusiastic audience. It was fun to watch the Dolabella boys at work, she thought, as they began to wind the set down. They switched off effortlessly on both guitar and vocals, and were backed up by bass and drums, played by bandmates original to the configuration — nobody'd changed over the years — and there seemed to be an almost telepathic vibe going on.

A very different dynamic to Lionheart, though the Lions have that telepathy thing too; but all bands are different, really. I so hope that they're wrong about what they suggested; but when I put that together with what Sattlin and Marcus had to tell me...

It needed two more gin and tonics and a plate of bar food, chicken wings and pigs-in-blankets and a small burger, to get her through the rest of the set. Thinking required a lot of fuel, and sometimes drink as well.

When she finally came through the front door at almost midnight, Turk was right there to grab her by the arm and pull her to him, almost angrily.

"Where have you *been*? I was getting ready to send out search parties."

"I left a note on the fridge that I was going up to Fitz's to talk to Ken Karper. Didn't you get it?" She stood there wrapped in his arms and let him support her, she was so tired and it felt so good…

"Yes, but that was ten hours ago. I called around trying to find you, but nobody had seen you. I even rang up Fitz; we had a nice chat, but he said you hadn't been to visit him, only Ken. Do you have any idea how worried I was?"

"I'm sorry," she said, letting him slide off her coat and draw her into the living room. "I went to the Gate to talk to Lucky and Lindon, and they coaxed me into staying to catch Bosom Serpent's early set. They all say hi," she added vaguely, looking around at the others sitting there by the fireplace. Just Prax and Ares; well, she could deal with that. She gazed longingly toward the kitchen; she was so hungry, maybe she could get something to eat before Turk started in on her for her irresponsible absence…just some soup, or a sandwich? Even cold pizza, if they had any in the fridge?

"How very kind of them, I'm sure." Turk had gone a little frosty. "I think maybe it's about time we discussed this plan you have put together. The one you've darkly hinted at but so far haven't really come across with any specifics."

No sandwich for her; how sad. She was sleepy, too. Bed

would be nice... Rennie regarded him as she flopped into one of the big overstuffed leather armchairs, and sighed. "You're probably right. Especially on account of what Lindon and Lucky had to tell me... But you first. Ares and Prax can hear," she added, and smothered a laugh as those two immediately perked up like puppies invited for a romp and sat up eagerly on the sofa.

Turk ran a hand over his beard in his usual gesture and sat down across from his mate. "Well, as you know, since you're the one who told me so, with information from Detectives Sattlin and Casazza, and your egregious ex-cousin-in-law Agent Marcus" —a pause for pained groans and accompanying eye-rollings from the other two, who knew Marcus well, to all their detriments—"it has been determined that a number of criminal actions have been revolving around the Fillmore East, and to the best of such determinations, all said actions seem to be connected. And you claim to have a plan to sort it out. So. Over to you, sweetheart."

"Okay, then." She covered a yawn with the back of her hand. "The plan I have in mind sort of borrows a little from what we did with Barney Levine at Abbey Road, which you three will all doubtless recall. Since people we know have been suspected by others of snorking stuff off sound boards to put out as bootlegs, I thought we'd leave a fake master or two lying around for these people to snitch with little apparent risk to themselves. Especially since the Dolabellas had some things to tell me."

She went over what the twins had in fact told her, and jaws dropped around the room. "Of course, the persons or persons in question may already have glommed the Madison Square Garden concert, or chunks of it—easy there, my lord," she added, as Turk scowled and shifted in his seat. "Very unlikely, though. Thom and Rafferty were doing the actual recording in the sound truck, and you were sitting on the masters afterward like a cranky goose on her golden eggs, so it would have been hard to get at the tapes unless they were physically grabbed out of your possession. So the bait I think we should be leaving for the possible rat is just that: masters from the concert, heedlessly unguarded, waiting to be nicked. Or so it would appear—they won't be real, of course, just totally useless outtakes. Should be tempting enough, though, don't you think? And before you say it's entrapment, you're perfectly right. And your point would be?"

Quicker at leaping to conclusions than the guys, Prax's eyebrows had hit her hairline. "Oh my God. It's *Pudge.* You're talking about Pudge. You really suspect him."

"Well, nobody *wants* to, no," said Turk, as if he'd known all along, though he concealed the fact that Pudge's name had staggered him like a kick to the ribs. "But given what Rennie's heard from Bosom Serpent, and what other people he's worked with had to say, and given how many bootlegs are currently out there from those actual people he's worked with—"

"And given that I found him oozing around the downstairs studio, with plausible yet ambiguous excuses for being there—I mean, how many times can he come over to fetch away guitars in need of repair?" Rennie sighed and glanced at Turk, judging her audience. "I didn't tell you, but I even found him upstairs one afternoon. He claimed he was just trying to find a bathroom, but he knows damn well where the studio loo is."

"So, snooping," said Turk flatly.

"Yeah. I'd say. So the other thing: we've set up a little Q&A with Detectives Sattlin and Casazza, with him specifically. We'll see if he goes for the bait, and then the tecs can whale on him." She let her head rest on Turk's shoulder. "It's sad. I really don't want to have to do this. My spirit, she is broken."

"Rubbish. You are the cause of broken spirits in others, and don't you forget it."

"Oh well, I didn't think you'd buy it. So let's go whack a few spirits into submission, then, shall we?" She drew in a deep breath, let it slowly out. "Right. Moving on from the possibly suspect Pudge to the egregious Niles—it may come to where we have to set a not dissimilar rat-trap for him too. I'm sorry, honey. I know you and he are working on establishing some sort of contractual accord, and this could smash it all to bits. But we do need to know. For the record, I don't think it's him. I think it's more likely that he's being worked on, or is about to be. Just because he was in the cemetery with the two victims is not enough proof of anything."

Turk waved a regally dismissive hand, though his face showed great unhappiness. "I understand."

"Yes, you say that, Turk, but in a way that makes me wonder if you really do." She considered for a few moments, spoke hopefully. "Is it possible, do you think, that Niles was maybe tripping when he fed us that story about the cemetery and the mysterious visitor in the snow with the snow?"

"Anything's possible, of course. But he's never been a great one for the psychedelics. Well, none of us is. It's just not our sort of thing. If he'd dropped enough acid to make him say the stuff he said to us, he'd have been flat on the floor when he said it."

"Curled up like a hedgehog and falling through his hands," Prax suggested.

"Like that," agreed Rennie doubtfully. "But he was obviously on something that made him forget where he was and what he'd done, or not done—and who he was with."

"There's a lot of stuff could do that, if you took enough of it," said Ares. "But it most likely was brown sugar."

"Excuse me?"

Ares grinned. "Not what you're thinking. No, it's this new street thing, I only just heard about it the other day: it looks just like, well, brown sugar—hence the name. On the high side, it gets you off on the order of coke; on the down side it dozes you out more like smack, though a little rougher. And on the really fun side, it works like liquid Valium, producing amnesia if you take enough—when you come off it, you remember pretty much nothing of what went down when you were high. It varies, but as a rule it kind of hoovers up your immediate memory."

"Now that's interesting." Rennie thought about it for a while. "In fact, that's exactly what I've been trying to find. No, no, idiots, not for me! But the night we all had dinner at Max's, I asked Belinda Melbourne about a drug that could do something like that, and who could supply some. And she said she'd ask around for me. You could have told me yourself, Sakura," she added reproachfully.

"Hey! What part of 'I only just heard about it the other day' eludes you? Of *course* I'd have told you sooner, if I had known, and if I'd known you needed to know."

Rennie handwaved it away. "Yes, yes, whatever. So whoever killed Biff and Scarlett and took Niles in from the cold, whom I am presuming to be one and the same person—"

"—could have given him some of this brown sugar stuff so he wouldn't remember anything about anything," finished Turk. "How very convenient. And how very premeditated."

"Well, yeah. But why kill them when Niles was around to see in the first place?" objected Prax.

Rennie sat up, eyes bright again. "Oh, but they weren't killed then, were they, and the sugar wasn't necessarily premeditated. Niles said that when he left the cemetery, Peggy and Biff were still alive. Presuming he's telling the truth about that, or at least the truth as he remembers it, then the killer was watching, saw Niles leave, and passed them the doctored coke. Then he went after our lad to take him wherever, make sure he didn't remember anything, then kept him safe overnight and dumped him on the park bench next day."

"That would be pretty quick work for one person," said Turk doubtfully. "Maybe there were two people: one who gave the coke to Biff and the girl and the other to go after Niles and give him the brown sugar, as you said, to make him look guilty, as if he'd run away. Though Niles is pretty solid on how it was just one guy plus the other two. But what could he possibly have remembered? He hasn't said anything to me about anything he hasn't told everybody else."

"Something the victims said? Something he saw? Maybe who the killer actually was?" Ares shrugged. "Or maybe the killer was just worried, and he was only making sure."

"Why not go all-in and kill Niles too, then?" returned Prax reasonably. "Since he was already involved."

"Maybe he had other plans for Niles," said Ares. "If he was using Biff and/or Scarlett, maybe he thought he could use Niles as well. Or maybe he thought it was unnecessary."

Turk's turn to frown. "But how could he get them to take something that would kill them? Most people wouldn't just blindly snort or drop anything a stranger gave them. Most intelligent people. Most non-members of the Grateful Dead, at least."

"Then he wasn't a stranger and they obviously knew him and they didn't know the stuff was fatal," said Rennie, thinking hard, and playing idly with a hairclip. "Since there were no signs of struggle, according to what Ken Karper told me. My guess is they all knew one another. So. Niles does coke with Biff and the groupie. Mystery guy comes into the cemetery as Niles is leaving, maybe says hi to him, then raps with the other two a bit, they all snort up a bit. Niles heads out into the snowstorm, accompanied or un-, at least at first. Mystery guy goes after Niles. He takes him home, gives him the sugar, and Niles doesn't turn up again until the next day on that bench and then on our stoop. Whatever was in the stuff either killed the two victims right there or put them out so deep they froze to death without waking up again."

"No, no, won't wash," said Turk. "I remind you that Niles, according to our and the fuzz's best guesses and his own admission, was snorting from the same original stash as they were, nothing about the mystery guy or his personal stash. And Niles is not dead. So nothing in the coke. Well, nothing in *that* coke."

"Damn." Rennie threw her head back in exasperation. "Okay, okay, Niles does the non-killer coke with Biff and Scarlett only, before Mystery Dude gets there, and Dude gives them the bad stuff after Niles leaves. So then if Niles does do this brown sugar, he would have done it later, and with someone we don't know. Mystery Dude seems likeliest. Or maybe we do know who it was, in the sense that we are acquainted with them, but we just don't *know* yet. We're hunting for something that involved not only Biff and Scarlett — Peggy, her real name's Peggy, I must stop calling her that stupid groupie name — but Sledger too. Don't forget, she got death threats and her guitar was kidnapped and the original coke was originally in the possession of her sound guy and a groupie who looks like her. Those are all commonalities that might give us a lead to someone who would have benefited by having them dead. Somebody tell me some more about this sugar stuff. Who deals it? Why would people do it?"

"I don't know who deals it around here," admitted Ares. "Maybe somebody who's lived here longer than you two could help you out. Somebody who actually does it, or at least sells it; it seems to be more of a West Coast thing, but that's where everything starts out. As to why people do it: well, like anything else, because it's fun, at least at first. It's a drug, why *else* would people do it? Chris Sakerhawk was heavy into it for a while; you could always ask him or Nancy about it." At Rennie's glance: "Maybe not. But it's supposed to be fairly hard to score, as it's new, and hard to get off once you're on it."

"Probably any of the New York writers would know, if it's new and big here," said Rennie with conviction. "They won't do it themselves, maybe, but they'll know about it, maybe even know where to score some. Belinda's ex, Hacker Bennett, works for the East Village Khaos; they're all stoned out of their gourds over there, all the time. She said she'd ask him for me, if she remembers I asked her the other night at Max's, only I didn't have a name for it then. I'll phone her, or run around the corner to her place next time I'm outside. Or that kid Hipshot, he's always high on something, I could ask him."

Turk looked annoyed. "Oh no you won't. I don't want you giving that urchin any encouragement."

"What's this?" said Prax, with interest.

Rennie laughed, embarrassed. "Hipshot McGowan. He's this sixteen-year-old fanboy who writes for the bitch Tessman's rag. He's harmless."

"He's got a pash for Rennie," said Turk grimly. "He follows her around like a lovesick puppy. And I'm tired of seeing his swoonful little babyface mooning over you from across a crowded club, Ravenna Catherine, so no to the smitten child. But ask Belinda again, by all means, now that you know what to ask about. Or just go straight to

Hacker. Or your pal Gerry Langhans. Hell, there are masses of people who do masses of drugs around here, *some*body must know *some*thing."

"I'm quite sure somebody does," said Rennie in her most soothing tones, though whether she was soothing Turk or herself no one could tell. "Perhaps rather a lot of somebodies." Her voice turned surprisingly menacing surprisingly swiftly. "And by all that's holy I swear I'll make them give it up."

"I hadn't forgotten!" protested Belinda, when inquired of the next day, when they were having brunch at Veselka, their favorite Ukrainian coffee shop, around the corner on Second Avenue and a block away from where they both lived. "As it turns out, I've already got a name for you from Hacker. Wings Walker. He hangs around the neighborhood a lot, mostly on the far side of the park, way east, where such ladies as you and I decline to tread."

Rennie was enthusiastically dealing with a plate of Ukrainian meatballs with gravy and noodles. "Do you know how to get in touch with him?"

"Sure. I told you Hacker would find somebody, and he can set up a meeting as well. This Wings cat comes up to the offices of the Khaos every Wednesday to make deliveries, and Hacker's a very loyal customer. It's their press day, and they always need chemical assistance to get through it. I can ask him if you want. Hacker, I mean."

"Would you? I mean, it won't be awkward or anything? Hacker has no personal issues with helping you out, because of Diego?"

"None whatsoever. Or vice versa, for that matter." Belinda fork-cut into her blueberry pancakes. "No more than there are issues with Turk when you talk to, say, Ned Raven or Marcus Dorner."

Rennie snorted. "By God, there had better not be! I didn't have ex post facto issues with Tansy, after all, for having slept with Turk, and she was one of my closest friends. It just never came up. But then she was dead by the time Turk and I got together, of course., so maybe that changed things."

"Yes."

"Yes. Because it's really stupid to obsess about previous amours. Also because he and I do not have noodles in our heads. Well, he doesn't. I might have a few. Noodles of the first rank, naturally. Not unlike these. But mostly not."

"You really don't think like everybody else, do you."

"No. I'm different."

Belinda raised her egg cream in smiling salute. "Well, fab-dabby-dozy to that!"

Rennie finished off the last meatball. "Or words to that effect."

CHAPTER SEVENTEEN

ONCE WORD HAD GOTTEN AROUND the music biz that Lionheart—with or without Niles Clay—re-upping with Centaur after the next album was far from a sure thing, and that it was all Freddy Bellasca's fault that Turk Wayland was considering jumping ship, the long knives had been unsheathed in the rockerverse. Turk had been asked out all over town with the express purpose of seduction, label bigwigs competing against one another with sales pitches and lunches and dinners and even bribes of varying degrees of lavishness: Clive Davis at Columbia, Leeds Sheffield of Sovereign, Jerry Moss of A&M, guitar legend turned RCA Records exec Chet Atkins. Which last, needless to say, had thrilled Turk right out of his boots, and all they'd talked about had been, of course, guitars and the playing of them—nary a mention of contracts or signings all the livelong day, and a spectacular gift pair of cowboy boots from Nashville arriving in the next day's post for Turk.

He and Rennie had even been invited as guests of honor to a very select black-tie society dinner up at Mica and Ahmet Ertegun's East Eighties townhouse, a major pitching of formal woo that the urbane Omelet—who pointed out that he too was a Turk, at least by nationality— clearly hoped would prompt a label switch from Centaur to Atlantic. Rennie, wearing Gina Fratini ombré chiffon and the sapphire necklace Turk had given her for his birthday back in September, as was becoming their custom, had duly admired the Erteguns' Magritte, and Turk, resplendent in a knee-length black frock coat, his idea of evening clothes, had told the table an amusing story of a murky canvas that his grandfather had sold for a pittance because he'd been too damn cheap to have it cleaned first and didn't realize it was really a pretty decent Caravaggio—though, laughing at the late Duke's short-sightedness, he'd assured them that the Tarrants still had plenty of very nice pictures left.

But despite all the courting, Rennie knew that Turk was hoping to work things out with Centaur. He was a very loyal person, and for all the myriad disadvantages of continuing to belong to Freddy Bellasca and his minions and corporate overlords, he very much wanted to stay on the label, or at least continue to be associated with it. She mostly avoided indiscreet or prying questions with him, but at home after the Omelet dinner she casually inquired as to what his intentions might be.

"Is it the guys who're keeping you from deciding?"

But he was in a cranky mood, and did not welcome the query.

"What do they have to do with it? I'm the lawful proprietor of Lionheart; all their deals are with me. It's *my* band. I did the hiring and if it comes to it, I will do the firing. Of course we're all equals as band members, but…"

"But Turk Wayland is a little more equal than the others?"

"In a word? Yes, I am. Three words. Contractually, what I say goes and if they don't like it they can leave. It might not be a hippie ethic, but then I'm not a hippie."

"Quite," said Rennie. "I see where a thousand years of

breeding for command will out. Is that how the de Tarentes treated their serfs?"

"Don't start with me, Rennie, I'm very much not in the mood."

"It's just that Marcus told me the cops were asking about the key-member provision of the Lionheart contracts. They seemed pretty interested in who has one. He said."

That caught his attention, diverting him right off the crabbiness. "I wonder why they would be."

"So?"

"Well, it's complicated. As I said, I own the name, so wherever I go Lionheart goes with me. In fact, not to sound too grandiose about it, Lionheart *is* me. At least in the eyes of corporate law. Thank God for the clever Locksley solicitors my grandfather sic'ed on Freddy Bellasca. Without once using my real name, too; it was all done as a blind corporate entity with Turk as the controlling partner. Anyway, they got me a deal with Centaur that even if I fired everybody, which legally I could do, and hired five smackheads off the street to replace them, again which legally I could do, as long as it's still me it's still Lionheart and Centaur would just have to suck it up. Nobody else can use the group name, not even if it comes down to all five of them against me. Apart from that, to answer your question, Rardi, Shane and Jay-Jay were the only ones who had key-man clauses written into their contracts from the start; but with me, not with the label."

"Because of the songwriting."

"Exactly. And because of the sound, and because they were with me from the start and should share in the rewards accordingly. They're partners now. The other two were on contracts — extremely well-remunerated contracts, I might add. Which I have since reconsidered over the past months on tour."

Rennie let her surprise show. "You did? You mean all of them are now on an even footing? This key-man thing?"

He nodded, watching her. "Not on a *perfectly* even footing, no. There are still a few gradations, but I would have to say as even a footing as makes no matter. And I still haven't managed to tempt Niles into making his scribbled mark on the treaty. The first-comers have a slightly sweeter deal than the latecomers do, which seems fair to me, since they were there from the beginning and helped me create the band, in a very real way. But I doubt any of them will be up and quitting in a fit of high dudgeon. I say in all modesty that I've been more than generous. And even if every single one of them did quit, which is of course their right since I'm told your Mr. Lincoln freed the slaves, or if I fired every single one of them in a fit of pique, which of course is *my* right and not even your Mr. Lincoln can tell me I can't, it's still Lionheart if I say it is."

"But none of that would ever happen."

"No. I would never sack any of them. No, madam, not even Niles, so you can lose that charmingly derisive expression right now. They're *all* responsible for the sound. I wouldn't want to lose any of them."

"Since the sound is what you exist to serve."

He grinned, restored to good humor. "Correct. It wouldn't be Lionheart without them, not now. And if I could have tied Niles up with a key-member clause, believe me, I would have done, long ago. But he prefers to be an independent contractor. Just to annoy me, I'm sure. Though I'm still working on it, and he did say a few days ago that he's considering accepting."

"Maybe we can make that happen for real," mused Rennie. "But could it be that someone is trying to frame Niles specifically to *get* him to leave the band? One way or another."

Turk shrugged. "Could be. But it seems like a waste of effort. He's quite that way inclined all off his own bat."

"Right, right—and how would Niles leaving Lionheart benefit this unknown murderous person anyway?"

"Maybe someone's angling to get Niles' job himself."

"How could this hypothetical cleverdick control whom you pick to replace your lead singer?" she scoffed. "You're as stubborn as a mule army, even Freddy Bellasca can't make you do anything you don't want to do. Well then, maybe it's to get Niles to do something instead—against you, against the band…"

"What something?"

"I don't know! I can't see any plan like that. And *why* would he do it, anyway?"

"Out of pure bloody-minded pique?"

"Yes, well, there's that… How about starting your own label?" she asked out of the blue, and saw his surprise. "The Beatles have Apple, the Stones and the Airplane are each talking about setting one up for themselves…surely you must have thought of it."

"Oh, I've thought of it," he said after a while. "It would even make a lot of sense to start it up right now, since after this next new LP we'll be contractually free and unencumbered. The Centaur deal was for five records: the double album will take us off. But we've already started laying new stuff down here and there for the one after that, and for my solo album as well."

Rennie pfffed dismissively. "Nothing is settled or signed yet. You've been recording at home, mostly, except for the work with Starlorn, so not a huge loss there if you decide to chuck it all and not a problem of contractual obligation if you decide to hang on to it. I bet that you and Francher and your sharkish ducal solicitors could have the legal framework for a Lionheart label built within a month. You could even have Centaur distribute and promote for you, for a reasonable fee of course, none of these extortionate rip-off rates we've been seeing since they signed you. We all know that Freddy would sell his own mother to keep you guys, even if it's on an artist-owned label. It would be more prestige for him, like being a commodore instead of just a captain. I like it. It could solve a lot of problems. Maybe you could even buy or negotiate the Glisten catalogue back from Freddy's clutches to reissue on your spiffy new label. And of course that first solo album of yours, the unlawful and illegitimate accursed bastard one born of outtakes and club bootlegs, whose name we do not speak. What was it again?" she inquired with a touch of malice.

"*Young Turk*," he replied after a moment, in a savage voice, and she laughed.

"Yes, that was it... But what would you call an independent label, if you had it?"

Turk smiled at her with equal malice. "Ravenna Records. What else?"

"Oh. Oh, that's…well."

"Bit lost for words there, duckie?"

Rennie had regained her composure. "Very flattering, my lord. But perhaps not very politic."

"You think? Well, we'll see. Names are the least of it."

"Maybe. Maybe."

He made an effort to turn the subject. "Speaking of names… Guess who I had lunch with today up in the private Centaur dining room. Come on, guess."

"Won't."

"Well, *you're* no fun. Alvy Larrable."

"What, him? The Beast That Walks Like A Man? Know then that I would not share a bowl of grits on the moon with him."

"You've never eaten grits in your life!"

"That's all *you* know, Britboy. I've eaten grits in Nashville and poi on Kauai, black pudding in Lancashire and haggis in Skye. Hey, that sort of rhymes. Maybe you can get a song out of it."

"Goodness, the things you tell me."

"So how *did* lunch go? Man, I'd have been put seriously off my feed, having to sit across the table from that pig."

"And yet he spoke so highly of you… Well, it was interesting, in a creepy, pathological sort of way. But you're quite right: Larrable is indeed a pig. Started sniffing around our private lives right out of the gate for something nasty to put in his Pillar column. I was sorely tempted to brag to him about how I made you come six times in one fuck the other night, which of course makes us both look so good. Not that I was counting. But in the end I didn't tell him. Though I bet they heard you in Hoboken."

"I'm disappointed. I love having people know about our fabulous sexual compatibility and prowess and stamina. I like making them sick with envy. And it was seven, actually. *I* was counting."

Turk laughed. "Slipped one by, did you? Well done us. But it's an educated pig, for all that. Once I made it clear that our sex life wasn't up for discussion, and neither was Niles and his current difficulties—which Larrable seemed to know rather a lot about, actually, more than I was happy with him knowing—we energetically disputed straight through the entrée as to whether Shakespeare *really* was Shakespeare and not Francis Bacon or Christopher Marlowe or Queen Elizabeth I. Freddy was quite cross, as he couldn't join in and it wasn't anything useful for publicity anyway. Larrable's doing another one of his quickie books, this one on the Budgies; that was his main purpose in wanting to chat, unless Freddy had some evil plot of his own that we never got round to broaching."

"You never know."

"No, you never do. At any rate, Larrable wanted to glean material from us for the book, about Gray and Prue, but I said not in a million years. Not after those vile, sensationalistic pieces of slime he did on Tam Linn and Baz Potter and Tansy. All dead people who can't fight back, and friends of ours too, and now he's moved on to live prey. Besides, he trashed us pretty nastily in those ones anyway, you and Prax and I. He didn't seem especially heartbroken by my categorical refusal, so he'll probably just make things up the way he always does. We should be prepared."

"You look wiped out," said Rennie with sudden concern, instead of what she had been going to say, and not caring a damn about the loathsome Alvy, one of her least favorite pop journalists and human beings alike, detested on a par with Loya Tessman. "Go upstairs and cop some z's, your lordship, will you? You have a late session scheduled tonight and I don't want a sleepwalking zombie for an old man."

He shook his head. "I'm just hungry. Blood sugar's low, and that always makes me cross and tired. I talked too much at lunch and I didn't get enough to eat. I'll go rustle up something in the kitchen."

"There's shrimp in the fridge. Wouldn't take any time at all to rustle it up. Shall I?"

"Sounds good, but no, I'll do it myself. After that, I'll crash for a bit. I promise."

Having eaten quite a lot of shrimp sautéed with leftover pasta alfredo, Turk went up to their bedroom and obediently sacked out for a couple of hours, while Rennie took advantage of his naptime to dash over to the Ninth Precinct stationhouse on Fifth Street, where, alerted by her phone call, Detective Sattlin and Marcus Dorner were expecting her.

"So." Marcus leaned back in his chair. "Based on what the Dolabellas had to say, and your own observations, you think Pudge Vetrini is the catspaw of an unknown bootlegger king, who ordered him to go after Sledger and Lionheart. And you think you now know who this person is."

Rennie nodded. "I think you do too... He's had all the

opportunity he could want to pull off his little capers. But he needed help; hence Pudge. He had been trying to pinch Lionheart masters whenever he could, until Turk started keeping them in a safer place. It doesn't surprise me that Pudge was hooked up with Biff Nydborg, who had been doing it more and longer. So maybe Nydborg was killed by the bootlegger king, for reasons unknown but which were probably about money. I think," she added uncertainly, watching Marcus's impassive expression.

She hadn't had that much contact with Marcus this time round, she realized; now that he was a secret super-Fed, or whatever the hell he was, perhaps he was above fraternizing with the little people like her. Or was it something less professional still: that he was feeling weird about the annulment? That made no sense whatsoever. He had had no qualms about sleeping with her a few times two years ago, long before Turk entered her personal picture, when she and Stephen were merely separated. And now of course it was Turk forever, and Marcus knew that perfectly well. Still...

Detective Sattlin, who'd just been listening up to now, picked up the ball in play. "And the groupie girl Scarlett? Peggy Scoca?"

"Collateral damage. Maybe the fact that she got herself up like Sledger just pissed someone off."

"Or maybe that resemblance was part of the diabolical plan."

"Could be. In any case I don't think the resemblance was part of the randomness. In fact, I don't think there was any randomness there at all. I think they're all in it up to their eyeballs. Or were."

"Hmm." That was apparently all the commentary Marcus was going to make, at least just now. Silence in the office; outside in the main stationhouse area, perps and police milled about like minnows in a sluice. At last he stretched his legs out and shifted in his chair again, ignoring Sattlin, who wore a vaguely perturbed expression but was apparently not perturbed enough to say anything about it. "And if form prevails with you, you want to do something about it; but, something new and different, you want us to sign off on it first."

She smiled at him with unexpected sweetness, relieved that he seemed to be going along for the ride. "But of course. For insurance, if nothing else. I love it when I'm the sole voice of reason in the room. It makes the universe feel all fizzy and askew. It doesn't happen all that often, so you see why I like it so much when it does. But let me tell you about it. It can be your Christmas present to me, or an annulment parting gift from the Lacing family." She was even more relieved to see the reluctant grin split his face as he shook his head, resigned. "And then, of course, what I find out could be yours."

CHAPTER EIGHTEEN

UNDAUNTED BY THE HEADLINES—even *bad* publicity is really never bad *publicity*—Wyvern Records, Sledger Cairns' label, was throwing a press party for her and Externity at Maxwell's Plum, in celebration of their successful Fillmore East gig, and naturally Rennie had been invited in both her capacities, rock critic and girl detective. Otherwise she wouldn't have been within a mile of the place: she hated press parties and though she always dutifully promised publicists she'd be there, she often didn't bother to turn up. The flacks never seemed to hold it against her, or to stop inviting her; they just assumed they'd missed her somehow in the crush or they'd been too stoned to remember talking to her, and she did nothing to disabuse them of that thinking. Though she'd been glad enough to scarf free food at press parties back when she was a literally starving freelance. So she was really a terrible ingrate for not showing up when she said.

But she changed her tune once she got inside Maxwell's Plum, surely one of the most gorgeously over-the-top, massively superdecorated eateries of all time and space, with its acres of Tiffany glass and gold-veined mirrors and Art Nouveau décor, and scanned the room like a whaler looking for a spout. Well, even if she didn't get any information out of it, it'd be good for a couple of drinks and some nice nosh and hopefully a few cheap laughs…

Oh, oh, Eric Clapton over by the bar, under the stained-glass skylight—thank God the silly boy wasn't wearing that stupid Afro anymore. He'd only done it to try to copy Hendrix, and he'd need more than frizz to bring *that* off, poor lamb; but why bother, he was so *cute* with long straight hair, and he'd grown an excellent 'stache. But the perm was now as vanished as the whammy bar on his Gibson. Well, who knows why he got rid of the trem, but some chick probably told him lose that goofy 'fro or you won't be using that slow hand on *me*. He was kind of like Eeyore, really, Eric was—adorable but, well, *grim*.

And then there was that very troubling story about him being madly in love with Pattie Boyd, George Harrison's wife, and he and George were best friends so how complicated was *that*. There was a much nastier rumor Rennie'd heard about how the desperately besotted Eric had allegedly given the lovely Pattie an ultimatum: leave George and run away with me or I'll do this whole bag of heroin. She very much hoped it wasn't true, and Turk, a friend of both guys from everyone's early struggling days, had loyally refused to comment.

Right now Eeyore was deep in shoptalk with Juha Vasso and Sledger herself—a guitar mini-Olympus. And Turk was on his way over; she'd seen him come in, and her heart had slammed into her ribs and she'd gone all weak in the loins, the way it always was whenever she saw him. *Fuck me sideways, but he's gorgeous…oh wait, he already did that…*

Three of the best guitar players in rock, a fourth en route, and not one of them had ever gotten off a single lick that could be mistaken for anyone else's. Rennie sipped her

Pimm's and considered. Technique and talent aside, it was emotion at the bottom of it, of course, just as it underpinned most everything else in life. *I wonder if there's a nice little thinkpiece in that for Fitzie…maybe when all this mystery is done with, I'll plan it out…*

But it was already writing itself. Some lead guitarists played menacing guitars, axes in more ways than one. Eric played angry, though that might change once he had a band that was really his, not to mention a decent personal life to go with it, while Sledger played total terror guitar because nobody had ever given her an inch that she hadn't had to fight for tooth and nail, and as a woman she was rightly pissed off about it. Other musicians played more amiable instruments, like Jerry Garcia, happy and *so* not sappy. Juha was Bach-clean and intricate, while Gray Sonnet was built more along lush, melodic Mozartian lines and Jimi was a rock Stravinsky. Turk played an exalting axe, a symphonic axe, a Beethoven axe, though not to roll over — that was the only way she could put it. It lifted up her spirit like a bugle in the clouds. But perhaps she was a tad bit biased.

He came into view again just then, taller than everyone there, moving leisurely through the crowd like a full-masted ship coming up the river on the morning tide. *Oh man, why even* look *at anybody else, they're all nothing but leftovers next to him…* Like a good guest, he went to greet his hosts, said hi to the band and the record company people, then worked the room a little, talking to reporters both trade and consumer; he'd been doing this sort of thing for years, and he and Rennie had exchanged amused glances as he crossed the floor.

Rennie went back to watching Sledger as she talked animatedly with Eric and Juha as a pro among pros, and grinned to herself. Sledger should really be equipped with flashing yellow warning lights, like a road hazard. Which, come to think of it, she was: not only could she outplay almost any guitar stud going when she was really on, she could also outdrink, outdrug and outfuck any guy in rock, or out of it. That was no overhype, either. Her appetites were notorious, like her father's before her: country guitar legend Galt Cairns, who was as it happened one of Turk's longtime musical idols, wasn't known as the Tennessee Tomcat for nothing, and his daughter was following in all his footsteps.

It had even been tested. There had been a wild and infamous contest one night at the Chateau Marmont, where Sledger had taken on a team of three supergroupies — San Francisco groupie queen Kaleidah Scopes, the coffee-skinned, six-foot-tall Mink, a Sunset Strip favorite, and Diego Hidalgo's dizzy ex, Portia Paradise, now rolling with a couple of Stones — to compete for the glory of who could last the longest and do the mostest: who could consume the most cocaine, the most liquor and the most sexual partners, male and/or female. People, talking about it afterwards in tones both awed and appalled, said there had been coke like flour heaps for a bakeoff, enough vodka to float the Sixth Fleet, a fuck line that would have foundered the Empress Messalina. But after everyone else, including her competitors, lay gasping on the floor like gaffed salmon, Sledger had been sitting up naked as a jaybird and fresh as a daisy and perky as a bushy-tailed squirrel, looking around for the next fun something, or someone, to do.

"Ever get it on with Sledger?" she asked Turk innocently when he came over to join her at last, and was charmed to see him blush.

"*NO*," he said with some heat, and she laughed. "I swear to you on a stack of Marshalls, never *ever*."

Rennie raised teasing brows. "Not even tempted? She's a total fox. If I were a man, or even if I were bi, I'd sure want to do her. In fact, I believe Janis and Praxie both have. On separate occasions, of course."

"Well, thank God for that, at least, though I don't think my cortex will ever be free of the searing image you just planted there. Tempted, you ask? Certainly I was tempted; every guy who sees her is tempted. Don't give me that look, it was long before I met you! But then I heard her play. And then I talked to her. You can be bloody scary when you want to be, but Sledger is downright terrifying without even trying. On just about every front, especially the front front. So not so much the making it with her, no. Ever."

"And yet you guys treat her as the ace guitarist that she, you know, is."

"Well, she being her father's daughter and all, it seems easiest to deal with her as an honorary man, the way Arab princes handle it when Her Majesty the Queen pops over to Saudi for a state visit."

Rennie laughed even harder. "Men! I don't *believe* it!"

"She's—distracting if you don't think of her just as a musician."

"Oh, and you boys *aren't* distracting? Go bend somebody else's strings, Flash! You your own adorable self distracted Tansy plenty at Monterey, or have you forgotten? Eric and

Jimi and Gray and Keith aren't distracting? That's *so* bogus. Sledger plays the way her daddy taught her, which is too knockout and macho for your idea of a chick guitarist, so instead of just thinking 'Okay, wow, strong powerful guitarist who oh by the way also happens to be a woman', you solve your self-created problem by thinking of her as a man. Les Paul in a barn! So why don't your male colleagues, or mine for that matter, treat *me* as an honorary man? Do I write like a chick? No. Do I talk like a chick? Nuh-uh. Do I think like a chick? Very much doubt it. And yet I *am* a chick, so the way I write and talk and think *is* the way a chick writes and talks and thinks. The way *this* chick writes and talks and thinks. The way a *writer* writes and talks and thinks, the way a *person* writes and talks and thinks...or the way a guitarist plays. Not the way a man or a woman plays. The way a *player* plays. That's all."

Turk was wise enough, and knew his woman well enough, not to pursue it. He'd never win anyway. Besides, he agreed with her. Mostly.

"What's the latest police line on that sound guy and groupie?" he asked instead.

Rennie groaned, instantly sidetracked. "It just keeps getting more and more convoluted... Jason—oh, you do too know him, Jason Kim, Externity's manager!—told Sledger the cops think Biff and Scarlett's deaths were just an ordinary overdose, and Sledger told me. Still, that's not what we've been hearing, is it."

"It certainly is not."

"No," she agreed with a sigh. After a pause: "Actually, the newest thing is someone sent death threats to Sledger."

Turk flung back his head, roaring with laughter. "To *Sledger*? Do they *know* her? Death threats, my sainted aunt! Death *wish* is more like it...don't they realize what a purely suicidal proposition grabbing her would actually be?"

"You'd think, but apparently not. She told me not to say anything even to you until it was back, so I haven't mentioned it before, but they abducted her favorite guitar, as a shot across the bows, and the note said it was their promised prelude to committing mayhem on her own personal self if she didn't do what they told her. Which they *never* told her, or so she claims. So who knows really."

He sobered at once. "Oh. Now that's very different. Which guitar did they take? Is it okay, is it back?"

God, he's such a musician... Threaten a friend, yeah right yawn. Threaten a guitar, send in the Royal Marines! Yet he'd be totally bewildered if I called him on it...

"How the hell do *I* know which guitar? You people have more axes than Paul Bunyan. She said it's the one she uses to compose on, her father gave it to her. Yes, it's back. Yes, it's fine. She called it Duchess."

"I know it. Beautiful old Guild, great tone. Believe me, I'd sooner a kidnapper snaffled all four of my sisters than my work Martin. Though I don't anthropomorphize my own instruments. And before you protest 'What about Sparky?', it was the fans, not I, who christened it that. As you very well know." He took a hit off Rennie's Pimm's. "Well, whoever they are, I'd not give much for their chances if Sledger ever finds out who was responsible. She's not exactly a non-confrontational sort of person, is our Veronica."

Rennie grinned. "She'll give 'gut-string guitar' a whole

new meaning. Now that's something I'd pay to see." After a moment, she nudged Turk with her hip, jerking her chin at where Eric Clapton was being backed into a corner by Sledger, who was fiercely arguing with him about something or other. "Go over and help Clappers out. He's looking trapped — I think he could use another Brit for reinforcement. Go, go on, save him. He'll spontaneously combust if she really gets going on him, and we can't be having with that. Besides, Sledger needs to be freed up to circulate, it's *her* party. She can't just be hanging out in a corner talking guitars, however enjoyable she might personally find it. And I want to talk to some people while they're still capable of human speech and thought patterns."

She suited action to word as Turk obediently set off to rescue Eric, then she saw Jim Morrison in a corner, canoodling with his editor honey, and detoured over to join them. Nobody was supposed to know about them, though ever since gossip queen Lillian Roxon had cattily written in Rock magazine about politely stepping over their nakedly entangled bodies asleep on his publicist's living-room floor, one memorable West Hollywood morning, that horse was out of the barn and accelerating down the road. But of course it was adorable watching them pretend it wasn't, even as they were making out in the middle of a press party.

But they were quite happy to be interrupted by Rennie, and they greeted her warmly. Rennie and the editor, who lived two blocks away from the prow house, in an old brownstone on the north side of Tompkins Square Park, had gotten to be friends since the move of the Wayland-Stride household to New York, and now Jim, in town to visit his girl for one of their secret long weekends, was seriously thinking about following Turk's lead and ending the bicoastalism. L.A. was no place for rock stars with brains, or the brainy women who loved them.

After they'd all agreed on that, they chatted lightly for a few more minutes and then Rennie disengaged, heading back across the crowded floor to Turk. Rock relationships were inevitably a lot trickier than they looked. Or probably needed to be. Look at those two. Look at Gray and Prue Sonnet, or Ned and Melza Raven. Look at almost any of their friends. Look at themselves, even: though they were of course idyllically happy, there were still any number of complications flying at them like sleet from all directions. Only Prax and Ares seemed to be enjoying an unstrained association; so was that because they weren't officially committed to one another, and hadn't ever been? Rennie hadn't given it much thought before, but the odds that Prax and Ares would permanently end up together were probably fairly small, unless it was a completely open relationship on both sides.

She considered her own situation. She and Turk had gone public pretty much by force; they'd had no choice in the matter, what with a dead groupie turning up in their bed in L.A. and all the rest of the horrific and subsequent developments, in California, England and here. They'd found themselves on the front pages with a certain degree of regularity, whether they will or nill. Most definitely they'd nilled. But it had happened anyway. It would have sooner or later, in any case.

She smiled and set the scowly thinking aside as Turk

loomed up on her right and dropped a kiss on the top of her head. "Mission accomplished?"

"You mean rescuing Eric from Sledger, I take it. Oh, yes. It wasn't too difficult to divert her onto the horrors of recording with Andy Starlorn. Which, quite honestly, I was all ears to hear."

"Really? She had problems with Starlorn? That surprises me not at all, actually."

Turk signaled the barman for more drinks. When they arrived, he handed one to Rennie and studied her. "Is anything wrong? You seemed rather pensive sitting here alone as I came over. What's on your mind, sweetheart?"

"Oh — I was just considering the various rock couples we know and how our relationship stacks up by comparison. People like Gray and Prue. Paul and Linda. John and Yoko. Those two." She jerked her chin at the table in the corner where the Morrisons were deeply involved in celebrating Jim's twenty-sixth birthday two weeks late, or perhaps still; for all the attention they were paying to their surroundings, they wouldn't have noticed if the continental shelf had collapsed. "It all seems so difficult, in so many different ways...I was thinking I was kind of grateful, actually, that all we have to deal with is your ultimate dukeliness."

She absently touched the necklace she was wearing: the smoky-blue-and-deep-red jade dragon pendant that so perfectly complemented Turk's smoky-red-and-deep-blue phoenix one. He still wore his on its usual leather cord, as always, but he'd recently surprised her by having hers strung on a strand of black pearls. *I remember Ling giving me this...I remember when I first really noticed Turk's...well, hard not to notice it, me being underneath him at the time and the pendant being the only thing he had on besides me. God, he was so beautiful that night…God, he still is…*

He gazed down at her quizzically. "Anything in particular bringing on this unwonted state of contemplation?"

She shook herself, and put on an air of mock dudgeon. "Hey! I contemplate all the damn time, mister, as you should perfectly well know by now, so don't be so dismissive of my contemplative capabilities… But since you ask, no, not really. Just maybe a premonition, I would say. But it hasn't been particularly helpful. Maybe I could exchange it for something really useful, like a headache or a goldfish."

"Hang onto it," he advised, nuzzling her bare shoulder. "You never know when it might be just the thing we need."

"Hmm. I think I see where this conversation is headed."

"The land where sarcasm is king?"

"That's the place! But you still haven't told me what Sledger just now told you about her problems recording with Starlorn."

"Oh, didn't I?" he asked, with an aura of faux-innocence that earned him a narrow-eyed glare. *Bugger, she never misses anything…* "Well, it wasn't much. She just said she had perhaps not the best damn time on the planet working with him on her last album."

"Nothing specific? Nothing you could hope to benefit from?"

"I wouldn't say so, no. She did mention what a paranoid little control freak he was about keeping his hands on all the tapes at all times, but a lot of producers are like that. They just want to be sure nobody messes with the goods and that the tapes are always accessible when needed. I'm a fairly paranoid little control freak myself, as you know. I don't exactly sleep with the masters under my pillow, I know how you'd object to that, but I do prefer to have them nearby. As you may have noticed."

"Can't say as I have, actually. I don't hang around much in your subterranean studio realm, Orpheus, so I couldn't really tell. Well, now you've interested me strangely: so, if not there, where *do* you keep the masters? There must be boxes and boxes of them...oh wait, is *that* what you have stashed in your dressing room, then? All those cardboard boxes I've been thinking were full of shirts just back from the Chinese laundry? I was wondering why you seem to have so many clean and pressed shirts tucked away and yet all you ever wear is those ratty old sweaters."

Turk looked pleased and proud. "See? The perfect hiding place. And if we ever need to flee the house in a hurry, I can just toss them in a handy laundry bag and we can both jump out the window two steps ahead of the revolutionaries. I know you have exactly the same plan in place for your jewelry, so don't start with me."

"Priorities," she said vaguely. "Well, if you and Starlorn both like to hug the masters close to your paranoid little hearts, whose will is going to prevail here as to where the Lionheart ones reside? Pot, meet kettle. You're both black."

"Polestar of my life, in the all too few years that you have known me, have you ever so far seen a major professional point of contention where my will did *not* prevail? Right. And you're not going to see it now, either. Lionheart is paying for all this, and those tapes are going to be where

Lionheart wants them to be."

"And by 'Lionheart' you mean, of course, you... Well, whatever you say, Dimples, I'm the last person on the planet to try to buck your control freakitude. As for Starlorn's, perhaps it's something he got into the habit of as a child, growing up with all his musical sibs, especially big brother Jordy. The family was very poor, as you know, and maybe such a luxury as recording tape was very scarce in the backwoods, at least until Jordy started bringing in the big bucks, so they all had to compete like hungry hound puppies for whatever scraps of Ampex they could get their paws on. And now he can't break the hoarding habit."

Turk grinned and drained the last of her second Pimm's. "You could be right... Have we had enough of this drinkfest, do you think, charming though it has been?"

"Yes, I think we have. I'll call Sledger tomorrow and thank her for both of us, and likewise her publicist." She fitted herself against his side as they headed for the door, waving to Sledger as she went. "So you've decided to commit to Starlorn and his fancy little bordello of a studio, then?"

"Well, you heard how the tracks have been sounding. What would you do?"

"You're inviting my professional opinion?" She looked delighted, but there was a shadow of something in her eyes, something she wasn't telling him. "Well, well, let's just see now. If I had to decide—yes, I think I'd do just what you plan on doing."

"And what's that, then?" He dropped a kiss on the top of her head as they stepped out into the uptown night.

"Though of course I didn't expect you to say anything else."

"Nice. Exactly what you said you were going to do right from the start. Recording as much as you can at home and then taking the stuff over to Vinylization for the overdubbing and final mixing. Which is why it does make a certain degree of sense for you to keep the masters in your dressing-room. I wonder now if that wasn't what Pudge was prowling around hoping to find," she added darkly, "that afternoon I found him upstairs."

"You may have something there, about Pudge, much as I hate to think it… You realize that if anything happens to the tapes now, I'll have to smother you with a pillow? Because you're the only one besides Rardi who knows where they are. I thought you always did, actually."

"Curses, foiled again! And here I was going to sell them back to Freddy Bellasca so he could put out a secret bootleg and split the take with me. It's a plan."

"No one ever said it wasn't a *good* plan…"

"Ah well," said Rennie as they flagged down a speeding cab. "You can't forsake the mob for a more rewarding career as a federal prosecutor, you can't take it back after you scream your ex's name in the throes of ecstasy with your new squeeze, and you can't let even your nearest and dearest in on your criminal agenda because they'll smother you like Desdemona."

"And so we see, yet again, that crime really doesn't pay."

"Or else it's its own reward in more ways than one."

CHAPTER NINETEEN

"I WOULDN'T HAVE CARED if they'd stolen one of the fancy stage axes," Sledger was saying, carefully rolling another thin, firm, elegant joint to add to the stack that lay before her on the coffee table, like a pile of pretzel sticks. "Sure, I would have been *pissed*, but I wouldn't have minded as much. But they knew exactly which guitar to take to really hurt me. Duchess...my daddy gave her to me when I first started playing. I have much more expensive axes now, but Duch is the one I'd rassle into the lifeboat after the ship hit the iceberg. Turk knows her."

They were in Sledger's bedroom at the Chelsea the next day, sitting on pillows on the floor in the late afternoon sun, rolling joints out of the contents of their combined stashes. Earlier, Turk had dropped Rennie off and gone over to the Centaur offices to do some interviews, planning to swing by again when he was done and the three of them would go out for dinner somewhere that had yet to be determined, possibly just to the old-school Spanish restaurant downstairs.

Rennie lit up, took a judicious drag, passed the joint over, spoke around the held-in toke. "Yes, so he said. Where's the ransom note, Veronica Lee?"

Sledger produced it out of a pocket, passed it over. "I saved it—I thought you'd want to see it."

"But you've already paid the money."

"A thousand bucks? Damn straight I did, just like I

promised. It was a bargain; and Duchie was back in her case as if she'd never even been away. Just like *they* promised."

So, someone on the inside then. On the inside of Externity or the inside of the Fillmore East, that is. It seemed unlikely, on the face of it, that a stranger could have snuck anything the size of a guitar past Fillmore security without questions being asked, even someone who'd seemed as if he — or she — belonged there. But a roadie, a house crewman, a sound guy, a member of Sledger's band, a member of *any* band really, most importantly someone known to the Fillmore staff — any of those could have strolled out of the stage entrance with a guitar case, unchallenged and unnoticed. If of course the guitar had ever even left the building at all.

She said as much to Sledger, who had moved on from rolling joints to chopping coke into lines on top of the nearest flat surface, which happened to be one of her own album jackets, and who nodded absently at Rennie's observations.

"Could have been, for sure. I guess we'll never know, will we."

"What is *wrong* with you, you don't seem to even care about this…you're the one who asked me to help in the first place! Never mind. Who else was on the bill with you? Lord, it was hardly two weeks ago and I was there, and I can't even remember —"

"Well, as headliners we were the last on, of course. That new funk-jazz band, what's their name, Cattywampus, no, Corybungus, opened, and Iron Butterfly was in the pocket. Bold programming. Well, that's what Wolfgang does. Bill. I like to call him Wolfgang; he doesn't seem to mind. Man, if I had a name as cool as his real one, which is Wulf Wolodia

Grajonca, I'd never call myself Bill Graham…though I have heard people call him Bobo. Or *Mr.* Bobo, I guess when they're being formal."

"Really? My God, the nerve of some people. I wouldn't dream of it, myself. But getting back on topic: it seems unlikely that anybody connected to those bands would have pinched your axe and then had the balls to shake you down for money. Much less your own band. But it also seems pretty pointless, to steal the guitar and then give it back a few days later, even for a grand," mused Rennie, thoughtfully tapping an unlit joint on the table top. "If it wasn't just somebody who needed quick drug money? Otherwise, it seems like they were only messing with your head—proving they could get at you whenever and wherever they wanted."

Sledger's dark eyes were round as blueberries. "But why would they want to?"

"I have no *idea*! Power? Control? Blackmail? Ooh, now there's a thought. You have, let us say, to put it kindly, a colorfully checkered past, one that would seem rife with opportunities to shame you with disclosures of an embarrassing nature; what do you reckon?"

Sledger took a delicate sniff through a silver straw. "When I was living in Nashville," she said precisely, "I let myself be staked as collateral in a poker game. My then-boyfriend bet the use of someone's car for a weekend against the use of me for a weekend—with my enthusiastic approval, I might add, since we had no money and we desperately needed a car to get us to a couple of gigs so we could make some, and also we were all very, very drunk. We ended up making a

straight trade, and I ended up gangbanged by five guys."
Seeing Rennie's face: "Oh, no, babe, don't, don't, that's
not even the worst thing about it. The worst thing is that I
completely enjoyed it and I've never been so turned on in
my life. So it wasn't worst at all really, was it." She beamed
and bent her head for another snort.

"But it was—"

"It was nothing of the sort. You can't rape the willing,
peaches. And I was about as willing as willing can be. I
must have come fifty times."

Ohhhhkay, REALLY don't want to be hearing this, way *too
much information...* "And why do you tell this story now, to
me?" asked Rennie carefully, after a long pause.

Sledger attended to the other nostril. "Just to let you
know that nobody can tell any big bad stories about me that
I myself can't, and won't, top with even bigger and badder
ones. I'm blackmail-proof, babe."

"Good point," Rennie conceded. "So then why—"

"Well, that's what I was hoping you'd find out."

"*Sledger.* Where's the other note, the death threat one?"

"Oh, right." She scrabbled in the big tapestry bag that
was on the floor by her feet. "Here. There were two, actually,
but the other one I think got used to snort coke through the
other night when I couldn't find my straw."

Rennie sighed with exasperation, but read the surviving
note attentively. "Can I keep this? I want to show someone."

"Not if it's the fuzz." Sledger made a grab for it, but,
stoned, misjudged the distance, and she fumed as Rennie
pocketed it.

"Really you should have shown it to the cops yourself,

missy. This is a murder investigation, if you recall — your own sound guy being one of the murderees — and anything could be relevant. Besides, the cop I'm going to show it to, I think we can trust him." She looked at her friend, who smiled angelically back at her, and tried again, knowing it was all in vain. "Sledger. *Listen* to me. If they can get at your guitar, they can also get at *you*. What part of that don't you understand?"

Coming out of Sledger's bedroom ten minutes later — the volatile Veronica Lee had decided to pass on going out to eat, in favor of more joints and a really cute blond male reporter from Creem who'd just shown up, yeah, right, we all know how *that's* going to play out, see you all tomorrow morning — Rennie headed down the hall to the suite's living room, where Turk, who had just arrived to collect her for dinner, was talking to Externity manager Jason Kee. On her way to join him, she was intercepted by a very short, very young, very stoned guy with a huge joint in one hand, who appeared absolutely delighted to see her and who promptly backed her up against the wall.

"Oh — hi. And I see you *so* are... You're Sledger's new guitarist, aren't you? Nigel, is it?"

" 'S right." He beamed and pressed closer. "And *you're* just the thing I was looking for. Come on, let's go to my room, it's that one over there."

She glanced down at what he was waving around with the other hand, in what he obviously and yet so very mistakenly thought to be an enticing fashion. *Huh. Not quite so huge a joint as the other one, is it...well, compensation is everything…*

"And what were you thinking to do with that?" she asked politely.

"Come on, cutie, it's what you're here for, all you little groupie chicks. You know you want it."

"*That*? No, Nige. No, I really don't think I do. It's not quite up to my usual standard, if you'll forgive my saying so."

"Hey, it ain't the meat, baby, it's the motion."

"Well, you can keep both to yourself, thanks very much. I'm already being very well taken care of in both departments."

She had to struggle to keep from laughing at his expression when Turk, who'd been watching out of the corner of one eye, got up and came casually but purposefully strolling over to put his arm around her, in that possessively manly mode guys get into when other guys try to hit on their women. Geese and ducks and horny teenage hounds better scurry, when the alpha male shows up to chase them away from sniffing around his mate…

"That was very, very stupid," said Turk to that mate, after Nigel had first blustered a bit, Hey asshole I saw her first so I get to fuck her, go find your own damn groupie, then when realization dawned, had fled with many and flustered apologies, sorry, man, *so* sorry, ohmygod didn't know it was *you*, didn't recognize you, didn't know she was your old lady, never EVER hit on her again, sorrysorrySORRY, oh hey, man, by the way, can you tell me how you pull that riff out on "Svaha" with nothing but a wah…

He bent his head closer. "Yes? Quite a lot of noise in here, I don't think I heard you. How stupid was that, again?"

"Very, very—well, you weren't exactly Captain Subtle yourself, you know."

Turk grinned. "He didn't want subtle. He saw a desirable female and wanted to paw the ground and clash antlers."

"And we all know you have the biggest pair in the forest…for which I am duly grateful," she added, chastened but damned if she'd let him see. "Even if I do feel like a tree you just peed on to mark your territory. I hope you realize that you just blew my cover completely? The little buggers really had no idea who I was, or that I was with you and you with me in a non-groupie manner. Now I'll never find out anything from anyone in Externity."

"Never mind," he said consolingly, putting his arm around her again. "You do well enough as yourself, any day. I now declare your undercover groupie career officially over; come on, let's go eat, I'm hungry."

Rennie cheered up as they left the suite, headed for the downstairs Spanish restaurant, El Quijote, and its fantastic paella. "Well, at least little groupie me bagged a lead guitarist."

"And there's that silver lining!"

Nick Sattlin carefully placed the note in a flat plastic bag. "Well, the damage is done, but it's not your fault; thanks for bringing us this, at least, however belatedly. Miss Cairns should have handed it over to us at once."

"Yes, I told her that. Then you think it's related to the murders?"

"No idea, but I can see where it might be."

"Well, could you *be* any more cryptic? No, I don't think

you could."

He smiled unwillingly. "I hear that you've been hanging around the Chelsea Hotel playing detective in groupie disguise. Didn't I tell you to leave that to the professionals? The detective part, not the groupie part. Haven't you been told that very thing on any number of occasions?"

"Yes, you did, and yes, I have. But was it a professional who got that note away from Sledger? Was it a professional who found out about the bootlegs from the guys in Bosom Serpent?"

"You have a point there. Two of them. Good ones. But all the same, I'm going to have to ask you yet again to back off and just let us do our jobs. You're not helping."

"I'm not trying to. At least not to help *you*, necessarily."

"Oh? Then who, pray?"

"Me, of course." She grinned at his exasperated expression. "And Turk. If I figure out who did it, and it gets Niles Clay off the hook, that benefits Turk, and what benefits Turk benefits me. And, all police-ish matters aside, he's the only one I care about helping. Of course, you guys would be the indirect beneficiaries of my skilled endeavors. And also me again, because if I figure out who did it and it gets Niles Clay off the hook, I have another nice fat scoop to present to my employer Fitzie, like a cat putting a mouse on its owner's pillow, thus earning me a pat on the journalistic head, a pleasant and not insignificant raise and a lovely piece of jewelry, as is our devil's bargain. I think I'll ask for a nice opal bracelet this time."

"Lord Holywoode…" Sattlin sighed. "He does seem at times to be a co-conspirator right along with you."

"Of course he is. Or perhaps more of a sleeping partner. Though no, that would really actually be Turk… But then, Special Agent Marcus Dorner is Fitz's opposite number on *your* side of the chessboard, not so? The one *you* want to be the mighty hunter bringing dead mice to? Yes, I do believe he is." She sat back in the rickety chair and contemplated Sattlin, who was glaring at her. "But Fitz and Marcus don't really figure in this, not as first-string, not the way I see it, anyway. And you, Detective Nick, are a perfectly horrid liar."

"I don't have much cause to practice the art," he said frankly. "Unlike some people I could name who aren't a million miles away at present…"

Ouch. Well, if he wanted to fence a bit… "I don't lie, *really*, so much as hide the truth, or perhaps dole it out in dribs and drabs as necessary. Like Halloween candy to the trick-or-treating little brats. Not everyone deserves the truth, you know. And some even prefer not to be offered it."

"I've noticed that myself. But do you think this is one of those occasions?"

Rennie's face had gone very still. "Could be. I also wanted to let you know that I have finally brought your scheme to his lordship for approval, and Turk and I have cleared the way for your little heffalump trap. And may God have mercy on your soul, for surely I will not, if doing your bidding messes anything up for Lionheart or for Turk personally. I think we understand each other? No, don't even. Turk is risking a lot to let your little scheme play out, and my Spidey-sense tells me that something big and bad is about to happen all over the place."

"Okay then, you might be interested to hear that the trap's been primed but not yet sprung. We just need to clear a few things up first. And I don't think I'm giving any trade secrets away when I say we might not have caught the big bad heffalump just yet, but we may well have caught the woozle. Or at least a jagular. Let me explain."

"By all means, Piglet, do."

When he was finished explaining, Rennie was silent for several long moments, and Sattlin watched her under his eyelids.

"So, you'll still do it?"

"I said I would," she said after a long moment.

He regarded her regretfully. "I'm only telling you the whole thing so that you know we have very good reasons for what we're doing, and I know you'll keep quiet about it. Tell Mr. Wayland, by all means, but only in the most... general sense."

In spite of herself, Rennie managed a smile as she stood up to leave. "I would never have figured you for a Winnie the Pooh fan, Detective Tigger... Well, if all that's true, then I have to think very seriously about the Four Horsemen and the moon turning to blood and the End of Days."

Sattlin smiled again, a real smile. "Apocalypse can be *such* a bitch."

CHAPTER TWENTY

"JUST FILL US IN," said Nick Sattlin comfortably. "What's a typical day like as Mr. Wayland's guitar tech? We don't really know how it works—take us through your routine."

Pudge Vetrini looked terrified, his gaze darting all around the living room of the prow house, as if seeking some sort of help. Finding none—Turk was upstairs in his Fortress of Solitude, Rennie had withdrawn to her morning room and only lawyer Shea Laakonen and her assistant were there to support him—he returned his attention to the two detectives, and Shea nodded at him encouragingly. This wasn't an official suspect/lawyers/cops jamfest, but as there was indeed a possible legal subtext to it that could affect Lionheart, Turk had thought it best to have Shea there, and Rennie had concurred. Seeing as this was the scenario that Rennie had pushed Turk into arranging, though he had been kept ignorant of whom it was aimed at, she figured on-the-spot legal counsel was the least they could do.

Pudge seemed to have gotten himself under control. "Oh— well, it varies. Some days I walk in and it's a piece of cake, everything under control, no snags. Other days, I'm freaking because everything that *can* go wrong *has* gone wrong and is *still* going wrong and Turk is on his way to the gig."

"What do you actually *do*, though? You personally."

"I work for Turk, of course," said Pudge nervously. "I'm his tech, like you said. I get to the venue, I get out the guitars he wants for that night, and I start setting them up. That means restringing them, stretching out the strings, tuning them the way he likes, getting everything ready for him."

"And you're there through the whole performance."

Pudge nodded. "I keep backups handy in case he blows a string, and I don't leave until everything's back in its case after the show's over."

"And when the tour's over?"

"Turk doesn't keep a lot of guitars out. Just his major working axes — a Strat and a Gibson to try new material on, for the different sounds, and his favorite Martin, which he does his actual composing on when he's not composing on the piano. He has about a hundred — half here, the other half in the L.A. house."

"And you're responsible for them all."

Pudge nodded proudly. "Plus I check out anything new he buys. It drives Rennie crazy. She can't understand how any human being could possibly need a hundred guitars. But he does. They're all different, they all do different things for him. They're the tools of his trade. He'll probably own a thousand at least by the time he unplugs for good. If he ever does."

"And in between tours and album sessions? What do you do then?"

"He keeps me on the band payroll full-time, if that's what you're wondering. There's not as much down time as you'd think. When the tour or the record is done, I go over all the guitars he's used: clean them up, repair or rebuild them if they need it, arrange repairs or rebuilds if I can't do them myself, then put them away till he needs them again, and make sure all the other ones are ready in case he wants one of them. Sometimes I work a few gigs for other bands if I really have nothing to do for Turk. He doesn't mind. Plus when the band is recording, or Turk is, on his own, I work as the resident studio tech, oddjob man, whatever. In L.A., and now here."

"What about concerts themselves?" asked Sattlin.

"I set up Turk's part of them, as I said. The roadies and the house crews do the rest. On this tour just past, Turk and Rardi were introducing a lot of new songs they'd never played before, that they were writing on the road. That's not typical. But the tour hadn't been going well, they weren't selling out the venues. Which is also not typical. So Turk thought new material would maybe change the vibe and change the luck."

"Was he right?"

"He's always right about that kind of thing. The new songs charged them up: they got interested and excited again, and then the fans got interested and excited, and the critics picked up on it, and the rest of the tour was a sellout. It was hard for him and Rardi to write on the road, they're not used to it."

"How does that work?" asked Casazza, shifting in his chair, absorbed — more fanboy than detective at the moment. "I mean, do they just hand the other guys the songs and say here, do it? What if nobody else likes the songs, or someone else has a song they'd rather do instead?"

"Before every tour or new album, they all get together

and play new stuff for each other, and then they hammer out the set list for the tour or what's going on the record. It's pretty democratic within certain parameters, like how much new material there is and how many album slots they need to fill and where each song best fits for the flow. If someone *really* hates a song and has good enough reasons, it won't get used, but they've been together long enough that they all know pretty much what everybody else likes. In the end, it's Turk who calls it."

"And money?"

"I couldn't say about that," admitted Pudge. "The band makes a *lot* of money, everybody knows that. Turk and Rardi get more off the record sales because they write most of the songs. That's how it works for most bands, unless they've agreed to go equal shares on the publishing royalties, which some do."

"Sounds like Wayland's a pretty demanding guy to work for," said Sattlin. "Do you find that annoying?"

"That's what he pays me for," said Pudge, startled. "I love it. I'd do it even if he didn't pay me. Why would I be annoyed?"

"He must pay you fairly well, I would think. Or not, and that's why you do outside work?" Pudge made no reply, and Casazza continued, "Still, it's a very special job, isn't it?" Correctly interpreting a tiny nod from Sattlin: *Now that we've got him going nicely, get the guy talking more about himself.* "I mean, there can't be too many other people around who do what you do for someone like Wayland. He must trust you a lot, to take care of the guitars for him. If you mess up, then he messes up."

Pudge relaxed again, though he really shouldn't have. "Every player has a roadie or a quippie to change a broken string. Lately a few of the really top guys—Keith Richards, Eric Clapton, Jimi Hendrix, Gray Sonnet—have started to hire people like me as private help. But no, there's not a lot of jobs like it, not on that level. I'm very lucky. I joined Lionheart's crew as a roadie, three tours ago now. Turk heard I had a lot of guitar, well, expertise, and he asked me if I'd like to take over as his assistant when the incumbent left."

"Who did you work for before you got the job with Lionheart?"

"Oh, all sorts. Hendrix, Chris Sakerhawk, Sunny Silver, the folksinger Ania, Bosom Serpent, Jerry Garcia, Sledger Cairns, bunch more. They were all kind enough to recommend me to Turk. I do some work for Jethro Tull and the Airplane, freelance at the Fillmore East and some of the clubs. Before that, I was part of the local crews when the Stones and the Beatles came to town, things like that. I started out in the Village guitar shop where Dylan and Peter, Paul and Mary bought their axes. Just journeyman stuff until Lionheart came along."

Sattlin jotted down a note or two. "Why did your predecessor leave?"

"He was fed up with the road. He wasn't a guitarist himself, just a sound man who got into helping Turk out on a regular basis. He helped *me* out a lot, when I was first easing into the job. I can do the sound stuff he did too, even though Lionheart has a regular sound man, Boanerges Rivera."

"Name? Of your predecessor, I mean."

"Don. Donnie Waters. He runs a small studio now, outside London. You can call him."

"We might do that." *And check out the regular sound guy too...* "So, Wayland offers you the job and you're pleased to accept."

"Sure. Who wouldn't be?"

"So, what's he *really* like?" asked Casazza, deadpan.

"Easiest rock star to work for in the business and one of the nicest people I've ever met," said Pudge without a second's hesitation. "Never any ego attitude like some of the other big guns. He's generous, he's considerate, he's just a really, really nice guy. Well, he's an English lord, you know, went to Oxford – I guess it comes with the turf."

"Fights?"

"Within the band? Like any other, but no more than the usual. They yell and scream and get it over with, then they all settle down and do what needs doing. Turk would be the first one to tell you that, though he does very little of the screaming and yelling himself. That's not his style, and he really doesn't have to. He's almost never in a bad mood when he knows he has to work – though when he does throw a fit it's a bitch and a half. Since he hooked up with Rennie he doesn't sleep around *ever*, not even on the road, but he never did before he met her anyway – he was always a real one-woman-at-a-time guy. No groupies; his girlfriends were all classy ladies. He hardly ever drinks, and the drugs he does, it's very occasional and light and never while he's working." He looked dismayed. "Oh – I shouldn't have said that, about the drugs...or the no groupies..."

Casazza's mouth twitched, and Sattlin laughed out loud. "Don't worry, his dreadful secrets are safe with us. We're not some Mickey Mouse English bobbies out to bust him for a couple of joints, like Lennon or Jagger."

Pudge laughed too, a little uncertainly. "Well, I guess I've just made him sound like Shirley Temple or something. He's not, you know. He can be as moody and cranky as the next guy, and when he's really pissed off he can be terrifying. He's just not mean or full of himself, and no repercussions or grudges. That's not a terrible thing."

"Refreshing, actually. And in spite of him being arrested for murder last year, too," drawled Sattlin, and Pudge recoiled as if Sattlin had slapped him. "Yes, we know, he was cut loose. With Miss Stride's help, of course; she does seem to always be there to save the day for her nearest and dearest: Wayland, Miss McKenna, Mr. Ned Raven... So, do you ever do things for the other musicians in Lionheart, or maybe the producers or engineers, say?"

"No," said Pudge, still a little shocked at the murder mention. "I'm Turk's guy—they all know that. I have enough to do for him. It's a nice little family: we all get along really well. Yes, we do," he added, flushing, as the quality of the police silence registered.

"Don't most bands?" asked Casazza mildly. "I thought all you people were into that peace and love thing."

"Not really. But Lionheart's special. Some bands on their level, they treat the crew like dirt. Not our boys. Well, not most of them."

"Would one of the boys who do happen to be Mr. Niles Clay?" Now they were finally getting into it; it had taken long enough.

"Niles is hard to figure out," said Pudge at length. "He was the last band member to join—there was a guy before him who left after one album, Fids Porter—and I've always thought Niles was a little oversensitive and more than a little jealous of Turk."

Sattlin leaned back. "In what way?"

Pudge shrugged. "Well, being the lead singer, Niles sees himself as the superstud sex symbol; that's the way it is in most bands. But that's not how it is in Lionheart. Turk and Rardi create the Lionheart sound between them, as songwriters, and Turk puts it out there as lead guitarist, so Niles feels he comes in a distant third. But it really is Turk's band. He owns the name, he hired the band members, technically everyone works for him. It's a partnership, but it's not a democracy."

"But that's not how he actually runs things."

"God, no! He'd hate that... No, everybody has a vote, not just band members; the manager and the producers and the engineers all have input, and just because he's the main man that doesn't mean he always gets his way. Strider—Rennie—gets consulted, too. Unofficially, of course."

"How do the other musicians feel about that?"

"It's been—an issue from time to time, at least that's what I've heard," said Pudge, after another pause. "It's not the usual rock hookup, that's for sure: most old ladies stay strictly out of band business. Frankly, most of them aren't bright enough anyway, and that's how the cats like it. Not Turk. I give him major credit for that. And I'll give *her* credit, the way she bends over backward to keep her opinions to herself. But of course he's gonna ask her. She's a pro, she knows her stuff."

"Plus she sleeps with him."

"That too. You saying you don't pillow-talk about work with *your* old lady?"

Sattlin laughed. "No, I guess I wouldn't say that."

"Still, she knows how the guys might feel about her whispering things into Turk's ear, so she's really careful not to step on anyone's toes. She's not a member of the band, so she stays away. But if he asks, she's *absolutely* gonna let him know what she thinks; she doesn't hold anything back from him, even if she knows he won't like it. That's their deal. I don't know how it is for them in their private life, behind closed doors—you can see it's obviously good between them, and they're getting married in England next fall, which is great. But band-wise, no matter what Rennie or anybody else says, it's whatever Turk says that goes."

"If someone wanted to leave the band? It seems to be common knowledge that all is not well between Clay and Wayland, that Clay maybe wants out."

Pudge muttered something that sounded surprisingly like "Good riddance to bad rubbish", then, louder: "Nothing to stop him. Well, that's not entirely true. There's something called a key-man clause, which prevents band personnel from just up and quitting whenever they feel like it. So, like, they couldn't just walk off a tour or a record."

Nick Sattlin felt the little spark as he met his partner's sudden and equally sparked glance. "Who has that kind of clause in Lionheart?"

"You'd have to ask the lawyers, or Francher Green, the

manager," said Pudge guilelessly. "I would guess Turk has one with the record company, with Centaur. Though maybe he doesn't; he wouldn't really need it. I mean, he *is* Lionheart. As for who has one with Turk: probably Rardi, on account of the songwriting; maybe Shane and Jay-Jay as founding members. I don't know if Mick and Niles do. Turk keeps that kind of information very private; I'm not on that level of need-to-know." Pudge leaned back in his chair, frowning a little. "You seem to be very interested in Turk."

"Frankly, we're more concerned with Clay just now, as the one who was present at the murder scene, but we're just trying to get an idea of how it all works," said Sattlin smoothly, which was not exactly the purest of truths. "We don't know a whole lot about the inside rock scene, how bands do things. If we can get a clear picture from what you say about Lionheart, it may help us with Miss Cairns' situation as well. You worked for her too, you said."

Pudge looked surprised. "Sledger? She's not a suspect, is she?"

"Nobody's been ruled in or out just yet. Well, except for the people here in the house after the concert, for the party; it's pretty definitely not one of them, the timeframe won't allow it. They were here until dawn. It would have taken a while for the victims to have died after they got drugged up—they were discovered as soon as it was light out and the snow stopped. When people came out on the street and saw them through the cemetery fence. The coroner said they'd been dead for several hours. So the people at the party are off the hook."

That wasn't strictly true either, but Nick Sattlin wanted

it out there. He was working two distinct angles here, and maybe someone would get careless or overconfident, and let something slip. Or maybe someone's memory would be jogged, though with that crowd, and with all the drugs that undoubtedly had been passed around, that was a long shot.

Still, Sattlin wasn't planning any drug busts at the prow house. Miss Stride had quite forthrightly told him that apart from stuff legally prescribed for stress or plane flights—she had taken great care to emphasize the "legally", and she'd promptly supplied their totally respectable physician's name, no Dr. Feelgood he—she and Wayland never did anything stronger than some occasional pot and a little cocaine every now and then, and yes, both drugs had been going around at the party and if he wanted to bust them for it he was welcome to knock himself out. No acid, certainly no heroin, no peyote or anything more exotic—or lethal. He didn't know why he believed her, but he did.

Casazza, seeing that his lead was processing the information they'd received, stepped in to pick up the questioning. "I understand that Lionheart is doing some serious recording at the moment."

Pudge nodded. "They weren't going to start until the end of January, but the record label got them together with this famous producer, Andy Starlorn, you know, Jordy Starlorn's brother, and everything clicked. So they decided to take advantage of it. It's just for another few days, in Turk's home studio downstairs and also at Starlorn's place over on the West Side, Vinylization. Then they're all going home for Christmas and New Year's; they'll be back in January to start up again on the original schedule."

"What's your job when they're recording?"

"Me? Oh, the same really. Just taking care of Turk's axes. Helping set up in the studio and break down when they're done for the day."

"And you keep track of the—masters, I think they're called?" Sattlin carefully didn't have his eyes on Pudge, but he knew his partner did, and from the corner of his eye he observed the sudden nervousness he had been hoping, or not hoping depending on how you looked at it, to see. *Damn. But also hooray...* "And as you said earlier, you have access to the sound board during concerts."

But those questions had been like the extra grain in the supersaturated solution: suddenly it all came precipitating out, to lie at the bottom of the beaker. Pudge stood up, clearly alarmed, as he saw himself being driven into the tiger trap, just as Shea Laakonen put out a hand.

"I don't see what that has to do with anything about me and Lionheart. And I think I'm tired of answering your questions. And since I happen to have a lawyer right here, if you'll just—"

Sattlin threw a quick and significant glance at his partner, who unobtrusively stood up and moved nearer to the door.

"Charles Vetrini, otherwise known as Pudge, you're under arrest."

And Shea Laakonen and her assistant sighed, and stood up with them.

In her morning room, Rennie had been listening unseen over the intercom—well, okay, spying—and as soon as she heard the front door close behind the cops and the lawyers and Pudge, she ran up to the top floor. Knocking, she waited to hear Turk bidding her come in—even she didn't go in without permission—and then she quietly entered the bright, skylighted sanctuary. As soon as Turk saw the look on her face, he laid down his guitar and went very still, waiting for her to speak. Which she did, carefully, hesitantly.

"Honey, I'm so sorry...the trap worked. And Pudge was the rat. Just as we thought. Well, as I thought."

"Pudge."

"Yes."

"—*Pudge*?"

"There's no doubt."

"And nobody else?"

"I don't know for sure about that yet, maybe the cops do, but I bet you anything that Biff Nydborg was in on it. And now he's dead. Little groupie girl Scarlett was too, and dead likewise. And don't forget what Lindon and Lucky told me. About stealing Sledger's stuff, and the Dolabellas', and apparently quite a few more bands'. And—well, yours."

Turk was silent for a long moment. "How?"

"You remember how I said Pudge kept coming over here to check on your guitars? Well, I didn't tell you because I didn't want to upset you until I knew, but I thought it was a little suspicious, so I started checking up. Counting tape boxes. Counting counters on the machines, how much was on the dials. And it turned out that every time he came to pick up or drop off a guitar, he'd run off a dub of whatever was there and take it away with him. Not to mention that time I found him upstairs: he was heading toward our room when I caught him. I have no doubt that he was really hunting for the masters and thought he could find them there, since they weren't downstairs."

She dared a glance at his face, but he was turned away from her. "There's no doubt about it, I'm afraid. He was building a Lionheart album of his own off the rough mixes."

"To be released as a bootleg before our actual album comes out in the spring."

"And from which you and the rest of the band wouldn't get a penny. Also," she continued doggedly, "I think he's the one who stole Sledger's guitar and held it for ransom, just to put pressure on her." *There, that's it, that's the worst of it out in the open...at least the worst for now...*

Turk ran a hand over his beard, stood up and stared out the window, over the churchyard across the street. "Marcus?" he asked after a while.

Rennie nodded, then realized he wasn't looking at her and spoke aloud. "Yes, that was why he was called in. Marcus has evidence that an organized crime ring, operating across state lines, hence FBI, was stealing tapes from a lot of bands, not just you guys: he said the Sonnets hadn't been hit, among all our friends, because they record at Pacings, which is of course a castle and apparently too hard to get into."

Turk gave a short laugh. "Maybe we should record at Locksley from now on, ourselves. That's an even more secure castle. Kept out Henry VII and Cromwell. Should be able to keep out a few tape thieves." He turned to her, and the pain on his face meshed with the bitterness in his voice. "I can't believe Pudge would do that to us. *Why* would he do that to us? Just money?"

"I don't know. I suppose we should have considered the possibility. But I think, I mean I know, he had a record."

"Well—"

Rennie shook her head. "Not that kind of record. A *police* record."

"So do most of the people in rock. It's a badge of honor: Janis, Jagger, Ned Raven, Lennon, half the Grateful Dead, even Gray…"

"Yes, but Pudge was in for grand larceny and some other stuff. Violent stuff. He did a year in the slammer up in Massachusetts."

Turk went very still. "Oh. That's…different. You knew?"

"I did. But only because Sattlin told me the other day." Rennie's mind was flashing, inescapably, on a snowy graveyard, and two huddled bodies lying in the snow. *Please, no, not that, anything but that…* "At least he didn't kill anyone."

He had seen the flicker of doubt. "Well, we trust not. But if he offended once on that level, then… As for me hiring him, what can I say? He's good. Even though I didn't know about it, I can honestly say I don't regret giving him the gig; he deserved that second chance." Turk was silent for a long moment. "But perhaps not a third."

After the revelation of Pudge's perfidy, the mood in the house was distinctly funereal. Turk went down into the studio and locked the door behind him and wouldn't open to even Rennie, and supper was a silent and strained affair. By the time the rest of the house was finished with the meal,

Prax glanced around the table, and, as usual when she felt situational ice needed to be broken, she just walked on it.

"So. Pudge really was the one doing the stealing. Just like you said. Of masters, of guitars…"

Rennie gave her a look. "Sledger's guitar…yeah. But he told the cops that he didn't know who the mastermind behind the bootlegging operation was, only that he'd been threatened with exposure if he talked, that Turk and everybody else would be made aware of his criminal past if he didn't cooperate. He swore it was a oncer and would never happen again."

"That we know of."

"That we know of."

Prax hesitated. "You don't think he could have been —"

Across the table, Ares shrugged. "Involved with the deaths? No. No, I don't think that at all. Do you?"

"Not sure, frankly. But probably not. Anyway, it doesn't matter what I think. It's what the cops think that carries the weight on this one."

Niles looked up from the plate he'd been staring into. "So does this mean I'm no longer the prime suspect?"

"Most likely," said Rennie, after a fraught little pause, and made an unnecessary clatter with her flatware as she rose from the table. "Perhaps we can consider that *your* Christmas present."

When Rennie heard the buzzer next morning, after a solitary, troubled breakfast, knowing no one else was up yet, she went to check out the closed-circuit camera vantage; when she saw who it was, she called Macduff the Thane of

Gondor to her side and flung the front door wide open.

Standing on the steps, a somber-faced Pudge Vetrini gave her a small nod.

"So they let you go."

"Own recognizance. I didn't commit murder, you know. Or at least I hope you know that. Can I come in, Rennie?"

She still kept the door half-closed against him, and her hand in Macduff's collar. "You think you deserve to? After what you did?"

" —Probably not, no. But I just want to explain to Turk—"

"No. Turk can wait. First you're going to explain to *me*."

Commanding the collie to the kitchen, she pulled Pudge inside and down the hall to her morning room, carefully sliding the pocket doors shut behind her. "And you can start explaining right *now*. You want to tell me what the hell that was all about? The whole story, Pudge. It was you who stole Sledger's axe, wasn't it?"

"That was a joke! Nobody was meant to get hurt. I was to hide the guitar, then bring it back after the show. It was just a goof. Nobody was supposed to—"

"And yet two people did. Plus Sledger got really upset. And the death threats on her, those were a goof too?"

He was silent for a long moment. "I know. I'm really sorry. I wouldn't have hurt her. But I had my reasons."

"Reasons? Turk put plenty of noses out of joint to give you the gig as his personal tech," snapped Rennie. "He went miles out of his way for you, and *this* is how you repay him?"

"You're right, there were at least three other cats who should have had the job before me. But he picked me. No way I'd screw that up…"

"And yet you did," said Rennie. She was so furious with him she was actually shaking, and now she carefully laced her fingers together so that he wouldn't see, or so that she wouldn't punch him. "You were less than honest with him on so many levels. And, that little matter of concealed noble identity aside, he has never in his life been anything less than purely honest with anyone. Did you really think he would hold it against you? That he wouldn't understand?"

"I didn't want to take that chance."

"Then you don't really know him at all, do you! Do you have any idea how upset he is by this? By you stealing his work? Do you know how much you hurt him?"

"Rennie—"

"No. The words you're looking for here are: 'Shut'. 'The'. 'Fuck'. And 'Up'. I mean it. Turk won't fire you. He likes you and he needs you. And in spite of this, he still trusts you, though I think he's insane to do so. You don't have to worry about your job from his side of things. But you sure do from mine, and if you quit now, you'll be hurting him more than you'll be hurting yourself. And then I'll be doing the hurting. *On* you." Her eyes went glacial. "And I *swear* to you, if you do anything else to mess him up or let him down or screw him over, I will personally see to it that you not only won't be working for him anymore, you won't be working for anyone else I know either. And I know a *lot* of people." She sat back. "So, do you still want to quit?"

"I don't. I won't."

"Then we understand each other." She smiled at last, though it was not a very nice smile nor yet a very big one.

"So, what do you know, and what did you do? All of it."

Pudge heaved a titanic sigh of relief. He'd known that facing Rennie would be a zillion times more rugged than facing the cops, or even Turk. He figured he'd be lucky if she didn't beat the living crap out of him, literally, and now it appeared as if he was being given a big giant get out of jail free card, much against the giver's will. Well, he wasn't proud, he'd take it and run.

"Just what I told the cops when they took me to the precinct. It doesn't matter now. I had gotten a call awhile back from this guy—I swear I never knew who he was, never met him—who said that he'd tell everybody about my past conviction if I didn't agree to cooperate in bootlegging new albums. Either copying the tapes off the sound board or from the studio or outright physically stealing them, though that was only when I couldn't get them any other way. When I got my hands on them, I was to give them to that sound guy, the one who died, Biff Nydborg. Starting with Sledger, expanding out to other artists I worked with: Bosom Serpent, Ania, the Airplane, bunch more." He spread his hands helplessly, and apologetically. "Lionheart. He said I'd be well paid and he'd keep my name out of it."

Rennie snorted. "And you believed him? Pudge, he was setting you up! If anything had gone wrong, I promise you, you'd have been the one to take the fall. And Turk would have understood about the bust, he wouldn't have cared. He would have even helped you out of the situation with this creep." *Oh God, at least I hope he would, I have no freakin' idea of what he would have done. Or of what he'll do now...*

"Yes. I see that."

"You'd better talk to him," she said at last. "He's in the studio. And if it comes to where you need a lawyer for real, I'll send Shea Laakonen again."

"That scary lawyer chick? Would you really do that for me — after what I did?"

"I just said so, didn't I?" She softened the sharpness of her tone. "Go. Go talk to Turk. He's downstairs. He needs to hear."

After Pudge went down to the studio to face the very literal music, resigned to his fate but also deeply relieved that the scam and the charade were finally over, Rennie went upstairs to the bedroom, flung herself down on top of the coverlet and curled up under Turk's shearling coat, nuzzling the thick soft fur, breathing in his scent, feeling herself calm down. The winter sunlight was streaming in through the high arched south-facing windows, onto the bed, and the strong warmth through the glass was making her drowsy, so she slipped her uppermost arm through the coat's right sleeve to hold it in place and began to consciously turn off her mind, relax and float downstream.

But it was no good. Little bits of information went skittering along her neural pathways hunting for homes, and mostly ended up living in the streets. It was all too much: Niles, and the two murder victims, and Pudge... Suppose Niles really had been involved. She'd been trying not to think that, but maybe it was an idea whose time had come. How horrible it would be, though: it would tear Lionheart apart,

She struggled to focus meditatively on the large white dragon she could see out the window, flying over the neighborhood in lazy circles. She thought, vaguely, that she would like to meet that dragon sometime, yes she would. When it dawned on her that it was not a dragon in the distance but a mourning dove close at hand, she laughed at herself, then pulled the coat collar up to her nose and took deep and resolute yoga breaths, the way Praxie had taught her, drifting off.

It was very pleasant under the coat, the warm weight and softness, it was just like Turk holding her, enfolding her...then she woke up and realized it really *was* Turk holding her.

She smiled and turned in his arms, a little groggy and headachey from what had turned out to be, to her surprise, a two-hour nap. "When did you come in?"

"Just now. Out of curiosity, do you often sleep under my coat? We have perfectly good blankets, you know, right over there in the blanket chest."

"Well, since you ask, yes, I'm afraid I do. At least when you're not around and you're not wearing it. It smells like you. It makes me feel, I don't know, secure. Safe."

"Can I say how incredibly touching and strangely arousing I find that? Weird, but arousing."

"So I see."

When they began to think about getting up for dinner, Rennie put her arms around him and summoned her courage and asked about Pudge.

"Are you okay?" she asked, after his silence had grown a little scary.

"No," he said after more silence. "No, I can't say that I am."

"If it helps, he's desperately sorry. As I'm sure he told you."

"Not as sorry as I am." He lay back on the pillows and stared up at the underside of the bed canopy.

When the silence had grown from scary to unbearable: "So, are you going to fire him, then? Pudge?"

"Do you think I should?"

"That's not my decision to make. I've told him you don't want to. And in fact, since you ask, I don't think you should. You've said yourself he's the best guitar tech around. Speaking purely in a practical way, if you did let him go, he'd probably only get hired by Jimi or Eric or someone else like that, and you'd hate it."

He managed a smile. "I *would* hate it, yes. But he really did what they say he did. After doing more hedging than my grandmother's topiary gardener, he finally broke down and told me."

"He confessed to Sattlin and Casazza, too. And to stealing Sledger's guitar."

Turk started to run a hand over his beard in his usual gesture, realized it, irritably snapped the hand away and ran it over Rennie instead. "He admitted to bootlegging the masters," he repeated, as if he could change things if only he said them enough times. "Or, well, planning on it."

"He did. It was only because you don't keep the masters down in the studio that he couldn't swipe more than a couple. Clever old you, paranoia actually paying off for once. So he just made copies of whatever he could get his hands on, whenever he came over and was alone downstairs. You remember, I caught him down there that one night, when he claimed he was just picking up one of your axes for repair. I should have insisted on checking inside the guitar case."

"I remember that… I could press charges, I suppose, have him busted."

"You could."

"I could." He drew a deep breath. "But I won't."

She kissed his bare chest. "Good, because however bad he was, he's not the real bad guy here. And we still have another plan. And when I say 'we'…"

"Oh Christ…"

"He has nothing to do with this."

"Turk, aren't you taking the masters home with you tonight?" asked Thom Courtenay curiously, watching Turk stack the dub boxes on a shelf in the control room at Vinylization at about four in the morning. "You always do…"

Turk shook his head, not looking at his longtime friend and engineer, hoping not to be rumbled. "Too much else to carry. They'll be perfectly safe here over the holidays. Who's going to pinch them? Father Christmas? You?"

Thom laughed. "Oh yes, because my secret plan is to rip them off and put out bootlegs and make a small fortune and retire to a bijou cottage in Torquay." At the suddenly uncomfortable expression on Turk's face: "Joke."

Turk resumed stacking. "Oh, I know. Who'd want to retire to Torquay?"

CHAPTER TWENTY-ONE

RENNIE DRAPED THE antique Egyptian silver shawl over an indulgent Turk's bare chest and back and shoulders, crossing it and arranging it until he seemed to be clad in a coat of gleaming mail. The shawl—the correct name was *tulle bi-telli*, but nobody she knew called it that—was a long rectangle of black gauze netting; each and every fine-threaded net intersection was folded with four-way pieces of silver, so that the gauze was invisible and the whole shimmering thing looked as if it had been woven out of solid metal. It weighed a ton. It was an idea she'd had for a photo shoot Turk was doing, and he was patiently obliging her. When she finished her styling, they both stared at the rather startlingly medieval image in the mirror: the beard, the long hair, the softly glowing silver folds.

"Nice look for an album cover. Yes. Richard-in-Iron…"

"*What?*" he asked, laughing.

"Richard-in-Iron. Richard, Lord Burke. He was the English husband of Graínne O'Malley, an Irish sea-queen, well, pirate, of the first Queen Elizabeth's time. I bet some of your ancestors met her at Liz's court; there was a famous and not altogether successful visit, though pretty hilarious. Anyway, her hubby went around in armor all the time, probably a wise idea, so they called him Richard-in-Iron. Not so wisely, he'd given her his strongest castle as a wedding gift, and one afternoon when he was riding home after a hard day of oppressing the peasantry, she barred the gates against him and shouted out three times before witnesses that she divorced him. And by Irish marriage law, that was enough. So she had *his* castle and *her* freedom."

"Clever girl. And not a bad album title, either — Richard-in-Iron, I mean."

"For the solo album, of course."

"How did you know I was thinking about solo record titles?"

Rennie laughed. "Sweetie, I'm a critic, remember? I know how rock stars' simple, adorable minds work."

"Don't you mean 'simply adorable'?"

"No...no, I don't think I do. We've been talking for at least the past year about you doing a solo album. You've even mentioned it to the label. Doesn't take much to figure out you've gotten to the title and album art stage, even if just in your head."

"Do you think it's a good idea, the album?"

"No, I think it's a *great* idea, as I've said many times before. You can do all the stuff you can't do with Lionheart. Who would you have behind you?"

"Rardi, obviously. Shane, maybe. The others not. It'll be great fun playing as many instruments as I can myself; that's what overdubbing's for, after all. For guest shots, I was thinking Eric and George and Gray. Prax and Prue, if I need backup vocals. All our friends. It all depends on what I end up writing, and what arrangements I can make with their record companies. And who's in town, of course."

"And lead vocals? You know whose voice *I* want to hear."

"And perhaps you shall. But I'm not sure yet how many vocals it's going to have. If any. It might be all or mostly instrumental. I have a lot to work out yet."

Rennie tugged on the silver shawl and it slithered off Turk, leaving him bare-chested and barefoot in black jeans. The scarf had belonged to Tansy Belladonna, and singer Tokalah Broken Bow of Turnstone had passed it on to Rennie at the Chateau Marmont wake, along with a bunch of other things Tansy had owned. But Turk didn't know that, and she wasn't sure he needed to.

She remembered Tanze buying it in Nancy Sakerhawk's boutique on Sunset, right after they'd all moved down from San Francisco. That was the new big L.A. thing: flaky rock-star girlfriends opening clothes shacks all over Hollywood—at least half a dozen by now, all of them more like toking hangouts for the hangers-on than proper shops that actually sold stuff to actual customers. Rennie avoided them like the plague, an easy thing to do considering they were hardly ever open for business, dependent on the whim and drugged-out status of their proprietresses, and she mostly stuck to Holly Harp when she bought clothes in L.A., though the decidedly non-flaky Nancy's designing genius had lured her into a bit of a spree.

Rennie herself had been one of the first-ever rock designer-seamstresses, in her San Francisco Haight days. When she'd moved out on Stephen, she'd had a hard time supporting herself on her writing work at first, so she'd gone into making clothes to earn some extra bread. She'd done very well, selling pieces out of little boutiques to people like Janis Joplin and Grace Slick and visiting Brits like Brian Jones; and as her journalism career picked up, she gradually didn't have to depend on the clothes sideline to put food on the table and pot in the little Chinese jar. These days, the demands of her job and her life with Turk had made her cut way down on the sewing—and the pot too. Once they'd decided on living in New York, she had even considered opening a shop of her own: rent a nice little Victorian storefront over on Ninth Street, lots of pier mirrors and polished old oak, sew a bunch of one-offs from her funky patterns to sell in it, maybe jewelry, some curtains and bedspreads and pillows too, or antique furniture—but in the end she had reluctantly decided against it.

Too much to do already, what with Turk and writing and the house and the upcoming wedding, and she wasn't about to come late to what was already a cliché. Plus she wouldn't be able to control who shopped there, and she refused to put up with stoned idiots or clueless suburban straights or supergroupies or rockwives, however much they spent. Her own *book*shop, now—*that* would be new, perhaps fantasy books, all the stuff she loved, King Arthur and Tolkien and Narnia. For her, clothes designing and sewing were pretty much a thing of the past. Though— maybe a combination boutique *and* bookstore…

Clothes for Turk—both stage and civilian—were the one exception she'd put aside other duties to find time for: she still custom-made him as many things as he'd consent to wear, and he was delighted to wear whatever she made. She felt that they were weapons and armor and magic charms as well as simple adornment, that somehow when he wore them she was there with him, protecting him, as if the clothes were her arms around him and her shield in front of him and nothing bad could happen to him as long as he wore what she had made. He felt that way too.

"It's an interesting look," he said now, weighing the surprisingly heavy scarf in his hands, "but the little metal bits pull on my chest hair. And they scratch, too. Like wearing a shirt made out of mosquitoes."

"Well, we'll figure out something else, then. It was just a thought. I don't want anything scratching your chest or pulling on your chest hair. Except me, of course." *Whatever it takes to keep his mind off things...*

"What are you doing this afternoon?" he asked, as he tugged his old Fair Isle sweater on again.

Clearly that keeping his mind off stuff is going to take more than a rehearsal for a photo shoot — I was hoping he wouldn't ask me that... "Oh, just skipping across the park to the East Village Khaos, to talk to Hacker Bennett, and that Wings Walker cat Belinda told me about."

He scowled at her airy tone, and she noticed. "Oh, what! I have to do these things, you know. It's my job. What about when you posed for that snooty fashion rag last week wearing nothing but those python pants I made you? With a cheetah on one side of you and that gorgeous model Artemisia clinging *naked* to the other side of you wrapped in a *real* python? I think I'm going to feed that editorial excrescence Valmai LeVanda *to* that snake, next time I see her. Because she *is* a snake for planning a shot like that. Anyway, did I complain? Well, okay, I complained a little. A lot. But still I let it happen. Because that's *your* job. And I know you didn't enjoy it, yeah right of course you didn't.

Because rock stars *never* enjoy stuff like that, do they. Any more than I'm going to enjoy this. Which I really will not."

Turk gave up, though he also gave her a warning glare. "I'll expect you back in two hours, no more. I don't like that side of the park, and I really don't like the offices of that demented paper. If you're not home by then, or at least before dark, I'll come after you. With Macduff. And possibly Ares. Armed."

Over on the corner of Avenue B and Twelfth Street, Rennie stood outside a cavernous ground-floor antique warehouse, cautiously peering up a dim, psychedelically explosive staircase that vanished upwards into Day-Glo-punctuated regions unknown. *Ooh, maybe I can go shopping for a couple of pieces after I get done with the druggie stuff, we could use some extra dining-room chairs for Christmas dinner. Nice ones...*

But yeah, this was the place, all right. And Khaos was obviously the right name for it. She began to climb the rattletrap steps, emerging on the second floor into a vast, fluorescently lit loft space crammed with desks and posters and rickety cubbyholes full of newspapers. There seemed to be people about, but it was hard to make out what they might be doing.

As she reached the top of the stairs and stood there uncertainly, someone yelled something across the room, and Hacker Bennett emerged from a little side area and beckoned.

"Rennie, over here!"

Rennie and Hacker—real name Max—had met three years ago at Monterey, when he was living in San Francisco doing freelance for the Oracle and the Berkeley Barb, before she'd moved down to L.A. with Prax and he'd moved to New York and gotten the managing editor's gig with the Khaos. And moved in with Belinda Melbourne for the first time. There had been, to date, four occurrences of Hacker and Belinda moving in together, since one or the other of them was always moving out in a huff. Often with good cause, like Hacker nailing all Belinda's shoes to the floor so she couldn't leave. She had just bought all new ones and left anyway. Until she came back again.

Of course, now that Belinda was publicly with Diego Hidalgo, and had been since right after Woodstock, she and Hacker were definitely over. But though the relationship had been an explosive one, and a strange, almost mutually using one, especially sexually, it had never been a committed or a passionate one. They'd never been in love, and as a result they were still friends. When they weren't pissed off at each other, of course.

Between Hacker and Rennie, on the other hand, there had never been anything but amused friendship—he was too intense in a way that didn't jibe with her own intensity. But he was cute as a button: poli-sci degree from Princeton, light-brown Jewish Afro, blue eyes like fried marbles behind steelrims, trademark fringed buckskin jacket and leather clogs. He had a reputation for always being stoned out of his mind, and very often he was, but usually he was just registering his considerable personal and political outrage through his equally considerable intelligence, and if it looked like being stoned, well, he couldn't really help that.

"Seen Linny lately, kiddo?" he asked, after a hug and

kiss on the cheek.

"She went up to Woodstock yesterday to start her story on Ushuaia for the New Yorker."

"Yeah, she mentioned. She's got a great hook there: Ushuaia, majestic black former First Lady of Folk Music, trying to find herself a place in the new rock world. After Pierce Hill cut her loose from Rainshadow — you remember, before he was murdered at Monterey — Elk Bannerman wanted to keep her on, and at first she stayed, but the more she thought about it the more offended she got, and finally stomped off. Now she can't find a label to take her. Then two months ago Shai gets attacked while she's staying at Big Pink, and, guess what, Rennie Stride and Prax McKenna are in a house right next door, just hanging around admiring the autumn foliage."

"The merest coincidence." But Rennie looked distinctly uncomfortable.

Hacker grinned. "Uh-huh... So naturally, being only half-past dead, her wounds attested to and even first-aided by Murder Chick herself — I guess that's useful to know, seeing you're so frequently around gore — Shai's gotten tidal waves of sympathy and media attention. Record offers are not exactly what you'd call flooding in, but there's been a very respectable trickle. All she needs is one good one. You know Dylan himself is putting the screws on Columbia to sign her? Linny's story could really help."

"Could help Belinda too," said Rennie. "She deserves that kind of major shot. Even Fitz was chuffed that the New Yorker asked her to do the piece."

"And speaking of shots..."

They had arrived in what it pleased Hacker to call his office, a former closet cubbyhole down a few steps and around a corner from the main chaos of Khaos, with boxes of papers and records and crammed bookshelves making walls and mazes to screen the occupant even further. It was an unholy mess, but it was very private from the rest of the ramshackle loft space: no one could see or hear. Not that anyone would want to, but you couldn't be too careful.

She ran her gaze around the room, uneasily remembering. The Khaos had been the chief outlet for the astrology column written by the criminally bonkers Kaiser Frizelle—another reason for Turk's reluctance to let her go alone. True, Kaiser was locked up for murder in an upstate maximum-security prison; he'd copped a plea, so it hadn't come to trial, and he was away for a long, long time. He wasn't lurking around these premises; but still she felt a trace of his psychic presence, like walking through a nasty sticky cobweb. She wanted to scrub it off her face and hands, but with an effort she controlled herself and continued her scan of Hacker's little lair.

Over in the dimmest corner, what had seemed to be a pile of colorful rags in a broken-down armchair suddenly stirred and sat up, and Rennie saw that it was a person wearing an indescribable assortment of clothing—tie-dye, denim *and* fringe—and showing long stringy hair under his hat. This, then, must be the elusive Wings Walker she'd heard so much of. The source of, or at least the guide to, the equally elusive brown sugar.

"Don't tell him your name," Hacker muttered to her, his back turned to Wings, and she nodded imperceptibly—

standard drug-deal etiquette—as she perched gingerly on the seat of the equally decrepit sofa facing the chair, brushing away piled newspapers and other detritus as she did so, not daring to let her back touch the back of the couch. *God knows what's living in it…or who's done what on it…*

Wings peered out at her from under the matted hair and hat brim, like a bright-eyed prairie dog. His voice when he spoke was surprisingly high and light for a man, almost countertenor range, and he both looked and sounded most definitely unstoned.

"So you're the chick who wants to know about brown sugar."

"That would be me." She held his gaze. "Are you the one who can tell me?"

He nodded. "Not too many people in New York who can. You're a lucky little lady."

"So I've been told. But why does no one else know about it?"

"I didn't say *no* one else knew. Just not that many. And that's basically because it's such a new thing. Why are you asking?"

Rennie shifted her weight on the edge of the sofa. "My old man and I are bored with the usual stuff, and we want to try something new. Lash out a bit, if you know what I mean."

He laughed, a high-pitched cackle. "Oh, I do, I think I do. Well, what do you want to know about it?"

"What kind of high is it?"

"Feels great while you're on it. Coke-ish going up, needs something to smooth it out coming down."

So far, so good. "Anything weird about it that I should know?"

He studied her for a moment before answering the question. "You forget things. It's kind of like Chinese food, where you're hungry an hour later? With this, you don't remember an hour later that you even had it."

Bingo! "Could be—inconvenient."

"Could be. Could be. But when I say you don't remember—you also don't remember what you were doing *before* you took it. Not even that you took it at all."

She let surprise show on her face. "Suppose you want to?"

"Too bad. It's gone. Oh, you'd remember you did something and you felt good, you might get flashes of what you did, little quick pictures, or dream about it, even, but basically that's about it."

"It seems kind of—scary."

"Nah." There was suddenly a gleam of intelligence in his eyes, and she was unsettled. "It's a perfectly safe side-engineered derivative of midazolam. Of the benzodiazepine family—like Valium—with anterograde amnesic properties. The side engineering makes the amnesia a little more extended into what happened before you dropped it. That was deliberate, so patients wouldn't remember being afraid beforehand of a procedure they were undergoing, like an endoscopy, as well as the actual procedure itself. Not necessarily limited to medical use, but if there's something you don't particularly want someone to remember happened to them—maybe someone who needed a bit of not so gentle persuading, let's say. Not dangerous in itself, if that's what's freaking you."

"I see." And she really did, not liking all the ramifications and undertones she'd heard in what he'd said. She also remembered where she'd seen that eye gleam before, both brilliant and nutso: Clovis Franjo. *Oh great, another mad biochemist using freak coloration for a cover...*

He smiled slyly and relapsed into his previous persona. "So if you want to use it for when you and your old man are seriously getting it on, say" — his eyes ran over her body, lingering on her breasts and legs, and she felt his gaze like horrid crawly little spiders — "you better take pictures, because you won't remember a thing about it after, no matter how good it was. And it will be, because the sugar helps that along like you wouldn't *believe*. Relief of inhibitions, and all that. You'll both be coming like an earthquake for hours. Though I'm guessing inhibitions aren't really a problem for a chick that looks like you."

Eeewww. "But if we just want to hang around the house and feel trippy?"

"Waste of money. Waste of the sugar. You'd do better snorting mesc. I can get you that too, can get you pretty much anything you want. Except smack. I won't do that myself and I won't sell it."

Well, good to know he has some principles; most dealers do, of course. At least the better sort.

She shook her head with a fine show of regret. "I think I'll pass on the sugar, then...if I'm going to ball my incredibly gorgeous and sexy boyfriend's brains out, I at least want him to remember I did."

Wings nodded understandingly. "I can dig it." Again he gave her the roving-eye once-over; again Rennie felt besmirched, suddenly wondering uncomfortably how he himself had maybe employed the brown sugar, and on whom.

His gaze still lingered. "I can really dig it," he repeated, almost regretfully. "Well, keep me in mind if you need anything. Old Max here can always reach me."

Almost as an afterthought, she artlessly tossed out a question, though she didn't expect to get an answer. "Just out of curiosity, you sell a lot of that stuff, do you? The sugar?"

He paused, considering, but seemed to find nothing incriminating in answering her query. "Enough. People in music really seem to like it: I sold a bag a couple of weeks ago to two record-biz dudes. But I do that all the time, and they never know if they're coming or going anyway, so I guess it doesn't really matter."

After Rennie had purchased some beautiful green-gold pot, perfectly cleaned, as a polite reward of sorts, a quid pro quo for the information, Wings shambled off, presumably to supply the rest of the Khaos staff with their usual Wednesday drug supplements, and Rennie allowed herself to look triumphant.

"I want someone to give me a job as a Delphic oracle! I seem to have all the answers these days. Failing that, I'll accept the crown of philosopher-queen. Hacker, you are a thing of beauty and a joy forever. Thank you, thank you, thank you. I shall sing your praises to Belinda. As a kind and caring friend only, of course."

Having checked out the antique warehouse for chairs—
it was as vast and dusty and crammed and creaky as the
Khaos offices above—Rennie found none suitable, so she
bought a handsome old oak icebox instead and arranged its
delivery to the prow house; another Christmas gift for Turk,
should look good in his lair after Hudson's husband Daniel
had converted it to a file cabinet or something.

Out on the street again and heading west across Tompkins
Square Park long before her mate's threatened deadline,
she stood a few moments to admire the peach-and-pewter
winter sunset going down in the west beyond the bare trees,
drawing a deep breath of the cold frost-sparkled air. *God, I
feel icky…what a piece of work that guy is. Still, I've danced with
the devil before to get information, so this wasn't really so bad, I
guess. And that grass does look good…*

Arriving home, she went upstairs to toss her things and
shower, to get the Khaos cooties off her and change into at-
home comfortable clothes, then went bouncing down to the
kitchen. No Turk, though Macduff, who'd been sleeping in
his nice comfy dog bed near the ever-warm Aga with the
kitten curled up beside him, woke up, stretched lazily and
came over to her, putting his cold collie nose into her face
as she bent to ruffle his thick mane. As she straightened,
Hudson came down the back stairs from her house office,
and smiled to see them kissing each other, gazing soulfully
into each other's eyes.

"A girl and her dog," she remarked fondly, and Rennie
laughed. "I was to tell you Turk's down in the studio and
asked not to be disturbed unless you were late getting back
from, as he put it, 'that radical cesspit across the park', so he

could go and fetch you home, probably armed to the teeth. But here you are, so I guess we can just leave him down there."

"It's usually best." She went across to the fridge and poured herself a glass of chocolate milk. "Are they really working or just messing about?"

"From what he said when he surfaced to fetch the tea-tray about an hour ago, really working."

"Good, good. I can wait until he comes up for air again. Where's everybody else?"

Hudson filled her in on the locations of the houseguests, as far as she knew, and Rennie nodded. "My night to cook, I do believe. Well, they'll have to have Grandma Vinnie's lasagna. I don't have either the time or the energy to do the spaghetti and meatballs; much too big a production. The lasagna I can just slap together, stick in the oven and forget about it till it's done. They can like it or lump it. But I'm betting they'll like it."

She didn't tell Turk the results of her little talk with Wings Walker until much later, when they were alone in their rooms and getting ready for bed. As she had expected, she saw the instant comprehension leap into his face as he reached the same conclusion she had.

"So if Niles had been given this brown sugar stuff in the cemetery—"

"—he wouldn't have remembered a thing about it, or those two people. So he didn't do it until later, after he'd left, and he didn't remember he'd been there, not until he saw it on the TV news," she finished. "He didn't even remember who gave him the sugar in the first place. Presumably the same person who dumped him on that bench in the park. Presumably the person who murdered Biff and Scarlett. Presumably the mystery guy in the graveyard."

Turk gave her a long, impressed, measuring gaze. "Well, this is a very big thing, then. But you need to tell our friends the 'tecs about it. Or at least Marcus."

"In good time. Mine, not theirs. This isn't exactly classified top-secret; they are all perfectly capable of finding out the same information and reaching the same conclusion. And I need to find out a bit more first."

"Like who were the two music types Walker sold the brown sugar to."

She looked at him somberly. "Exactly."

He flopped on the bed. "And just how do you plan on doing that, if I may ask? Because know this, madam: I will not hesitate to shut you down like a slammed portcullis, or throw you in the oubliest oubliette I can find, if I think you're endangering yourself, or even merely getting in a bit over your head. Did no one ever tell you that messing around with dealers is not the best nor the safest thing to do? I'm sure you didn't miss those drug rape-ish implications of his any more than I did."

"I do love your medieval similes…comes of growing up with such features around the house, I guess. Well, not to worry. I have sources and forces and resources to do that sort of work for me."

"Ken Karper, you mean," he said, not much reassured. "He's just as bad as you, taking risks to get information. Probably worse. But on the whole I'd much prefer for him to be the one digging around in Dealerworld."

"Ken, mostly," she agreed. "But he's not the only one."

CHAPTER TWENTY-TWO

CHRISTMAS DAY AT the prow house. Turk and Rennie were afoot bleary-eyed and early to start cooking; the houseguests, who'd been up late with said host and hostess for midnight services at St. Mark's Church across the street and present-giving after, trickled downstairs around noon to forage for coffee and challah rolls and wakeup pills. Toward two, guests began arriving, and promptly at three o'clock sixteen people sat down to Christmas dinner.

And it was a white Christmas! How much more perfect could it *get*! Rennie had been thrilled beyond all measure when she'd come out of church with Turk and the others at one in the morning, feeling all virtuous and Dickensian, and had seen the inch of snow that already dusted the ground; it had kept on falling all day, and by dinnertime almost four inches carpeted the entire city. *What a great omen for our first Christmas together in our new house…*

Presiding over their festal board for the first official time, the host and hostess had decreed that everybody must dress for the occasion, and the resultant formal turnout was impressive — everything from Prax's tea-dyed lace-tablecloth gown, a Rennie Stride original, to Chris Sakerhawk's show-stopping kilt. Well, he had the legs for it, no question.

Rennie, curvy in the floor-length gold velour Biba dress she'd bought in London last year and the necklace of grape-sized ruby beads that was this year's main Christmas present from the Marquess of Raxton, beheld it all and saw that it was good: the table gleaming with bone china and cut crystal, the antique linen, the heavy vermeil place settings. This was even more fun than Christmas at Pacings, last year...too bad Gray and Prue had gone home, it would have been nice to have them here for a reciprocal Yuletide. But they had the kiddies waiting for them back at the castle, so she could understand their wish to make it back to Blighty.

Over the dining-room mantelpiece, hung there only days ago right where no one could possibly miss it, was a big eighteenth-century-style oil painting in a massive carved gold frame: the lady of the house, with no clothes on. Rennie had commissioned the picture from her friend and former Haight-Ashbury landlady, the renowned portraitist Sharon Pollan, as her main Christmas gift to the Marquess of Raxton — which had made the Marquess very smug, their guests very amused, and Rennie very proud.

It was starting to become a habit, posing nude for her portrait. She'd spent three days sitting for this one, the second Sharon had done of her, when she'd gone to San Francisco in April to clear out her stuff from the Haight flat to ship to New York, and she'd collected it when she'd flown back there before Thanksgiving with Eric and Petra to sign off on the annulment — the portrait being the other big secret of the trip, stretched, framed and dry enough to travel. Seeing it, some of their friends had been a little — nonplused. But if Max's Kansas City could own two paintings of Rennie, and one of them nekkid, it seemed only right that Turk should own one himself. Even though he already owned the model.

And maybe this wasn't the way most rocknrollers lived, but it was the way *they* lived.

Looking handsome and masterful in a dark-brown velvet pirate coat, Turk sat at the window end of the table in a high-backed, leather-cushioned throne, and smiled first at the portrait and then at its original, who was seated in queenly fashion in a matching chair at the table's other end. At least the original had her clothes on today… They really must do this as often as possible, though: it was rather grown-up fun having guests and dressing up for dinner — the lord of the manor with his lovely chatelaine — and since he'd be off the road for the next year if his plan went through as scheduled, they'd actually have the chance.

As dinner progressed, proudly served out with surprising professionalism by the housekeeper's teenage niece and nephew, Rennie kept a weather eye on all her guests — Diego Hidalgo had been given the guest of honor place on her right with Ned Raven, staying at the Pierre with his wife in transit to London the next day, on her left, while Melza Raven and Belinda Melbourne held down the same spots at Turk's end, everyone else sitting wherever they liked — but especially on Niles. He seemed fine, enjoying the company and the dinner alike, but you never knew with him.

The menu was superb, and would have done credit to the house's original Victorian owners: clear consommé, a huge, sizzling platter of lobster and sole and oysters and shrimp and scallops all swimming in a delicate cream sauce, two roast turkeys the size of Volkswagens, assorted veg. His lordship had cooked everything but the birds and stuffing and gravy — that was Rennie's province — including a veggie terrine for the couple of non-carnivores and three different desserts.

Sipping a very nice light Meursault as Turk did the carving honors and plates began to fill, Rennie continued to study the Clays. Niles and Keitha, often billed in gushy fan rags as twin souls, seemed more like half a soul apiece sharing a single brain between them. Or single brain *cell*, she thought uncharitably, listening to Keitha prattle on in her East London accent about a simply soo-pah Paris hotel she and Niles had stayed at, called, apparently, George's Sink.

Oooh, maybe *Keitha* was the killer? She let the delicious thought melt in her mind like a tiny meringue: the beautiful, insipid, ebon-haired half-Persian half-Cockney model Keitha Shiraz Clay, pissed off at her husband for running around with the beautiful, insipid, tangerine-haired all-American groupie Scarlett, so she killed her, then had to murder the sound guy to keep him quiet—a tempting thought, but no. Keitha was too stupid to live, much less smart enough to kill. Anyway, Niles had no fuck history with Scarlett. Though he certainly had some with the beautiful, utterly *un*insipid, tangerine-haired good ol' girl Sledger, of course, as pretty much everybody knew — and as pretty much everybody else also had.

The meal progressed, until everyone was so stuffed they were falling into food comas. After Turk's signature dark-chocolate soufflé with raspberry sauce had closed it down, Rennie rose, telling the kids to feed themselves in the kitchen before they cleared away and they didn't have to do anything else but wash the crystal, and her guests rose with her. Inspired by living in this place, and by Prue Sonnet's example at her London house, Rennie was determined to single-handedly revive this ancient custom in New York, if only in rock circles: the ladies therefore withdrew to her morning room, to lounge on the brocade sofas and the new swan-backed fainting couch, for sherry and joints and ribald discussion, while the gentlemen retired to the library for the same, though probably not quite so ribald, oiled with some vintage port the Duke of Locksley had sent his son to lay down in the cellar.

Half an hour later, everybody reassembled in the rehearsal room of the basement studio. There had been a lightning raid on the guitar vault, and now the players took their places at the setup that was always left standing and began casually tuning up, while the others disposed themselves on the couches and pillows and overstuffed chairs. *The entertainment portion of the evening will now commence…*

It was nice to live with a musician, Rennie reflected as the wine and Wings Walker's excellent pot started going around, nice to have musician friends… This was what it must have been like being a member of the family who had lived in this house when it was new, back in the days when you and your guests made your own amusement on social occasions. Well, sort of. No pot then, probably. Maybe hash and hookahs, still a popular diversion. Cocaine, like Sherlock Holmes, another modern favorite. Or laudanum for the hard-core. True, a mere writer couldn't exactly hope to compete—she really didn't think anyone would want to hear her read a chapter from her new book, or even recite a John Lennon poem—but it made her feel very Victorian all the same.

Turk played a quick rippling fugue to get his fingers warmed up, then pushed up the gain on his amp and blasted out the bubbling intro from the old Ventures hit "Pipeline" on his newly acquired Gibson—the vintage one he had coveted and that Rennie, true to her word, had given him as one of his Christmas presents. He'd been as happy as a kid with a new train set. As he got down into the singing lead riff, Shane Sheehan picked up second lead on a favorite-model Guild, and Niles and Prax and Diego sat on bar stools before open vocal mikes, waiting for something they could sing. Chris Sakerhawk was at work on the galloping cymbal/drum line, while Rardi was doing shimmering runs on the Hammond and Ned kicked out on bass. What a pickup group.

Rennie had a small, contemplative smile on her face as she watched Turk dig into the descanting bridge and stretch the song out for twice its length in stunning variations, then seamlessly segué into "Walk Don't Run" by the same band, who were high among Turk's personal favorites and chief influences. God, lead guitarists were so studly. Even more so than lead singers. Maybe because they actually *did* something: that easy, deceptively casual command over the axe. Technical mastery—of anything—was always sexy. You knew you were in good hands. You figured if he could handle a guitar like that, he could certainly handle *you* with equal authority.

Glancing out the open door from where she sat beside Melza Raven on one of the big squashy sofas, Rennie noticed the niece and nephew shyly loitering on the stairs beyond the open door, chores done, longing to be close to the music of the gods yet not wanting to annoy and get banished from Valhalla. She smiled and beckoned, and they crept in like thrilled little mice to sit entranced on the huge soft floor pillows, while the vocalists sang anything anyone could think to play, and everyone joined in on Christmas carols, which always made Rennie cry.

"And the nicest thing," Ares was saying, as Diego and Niles finished off a "Wake Up Little Susie" duet that had it been conducted onstage would have had people standing on the seats, "the nicest thing is that bed is right upstairs. I tell you, I could get used to this communal living trip. Sometimes hippies have the right idea. Though otherwise we scorn them, of course."

"Of course."

"Anything new in the Niles department?" asked Melza quietly, so that Keitha did not hear.

Rennie shook her head and passed the current joint. "Not really. Though moodwise he's been up and down like a tart's knickers, as your bloke would say."

Melza smiled. "What does *your* bloke say?"

She glanced at Turk, who, riffing idly now, had smilingly engaged the two awed teenagers in conversation, drawing them out expertly until they were happily prattling about their favorite rockers — present company chief among them, of course. *He never lets people feel uncomfortable around him, he always makes sure attention gets paid...*

"He doesn't say much," she said at last. "Well — not about that, anyway."

Giddily clutching autographed albums and guitar picks

and well-stuffed pay envelopes, the niece and nephew had long since been safely dispatched home in one of Ride On!'s psychedelically painted limos, with Lionheart's favorite driver Tough Tony at the wheel; the visitors had gone and the houseguests had retired upstairs. Even the dog and kitten were asleep. Outside, it was bitterly cold: the temperature was down in the teens now, and the snow lay for the most part undisturbed, all down the street, only a few half-filled footprints and flattened tire tracks marring its smooth white perfection. Inside and out now, a silent night indeed.

Rennie wandered barefoot through the fir-fragrant living room, blearily admiring the towering and well-bedecked Christmas tree, doing some vague tidying, until Turk came up from behind and wrapped his arms around her.

"Bed," he said authoritatively.

"Dishes," she said tragically.

"Nope." He slung her over his shoulder and carried her through the hall to the birdcage lift; she thought this was an excellent idea, and lightly drummed on his rear as they went. "That's what we have a dishwasher for. I just turned it on. So now you can turn *me* on. Let's have you, baggage. I want to have my way with you."

"And I so want you to have it." She rattled her gold charm bracelet at him as the lift decanted them out on the bedroom floor. "I love the new charms, did I tell you?"

"I think you may have mentioned it once or twice."

When they had first begun living together, Turk had noticed the charm bracelet that Rennie had owned from childhood, and had noted too that it was pretty well filled up, with the blamelessly adolescent birthstone calendar and Sweet 16 and diploma and ballet and sports and travel charms contributed by parents and grandparents and aunts. So with a sweet sentimentality that among all rock stars ever born only a British one could have pulled off without terminally embarrassing himself, he had bought her another—heavy, antique English gold, with a heart-shaped and quite functional padlock and key, which symbolism appealed to them both—and established a tradition of gifting her with charms to commemorate days of significance.

She'd been delighted, and had immediately decreed the new bracelet to be all about them: its links now dangled a lion, a heart, a star, their initials and birthstones, a British passport, a coronet, the college seals of their respective alma maters, a miniature Royal Albert Hall with a guy at the piano inside, a typewriter, a record player and a teensy gold Strat. Back last February, shopping with Prue Sonnet in Bath while their spouses messed about with cars back at the castle, Rennie, in a fit of stupendous serendipity, had even found a tiny gold replica of Turk's vintage Bentley, with yellow diamonds for headlights and rubies for taillights. She'd had the jeweler solder it immediately onto an empty bracelet link, and happily jangled it all the way home.

Not to mention X-rated items like the naked couple artfully entwined in *soixante-neuf* configuration or the fourposter bed with two occupied occupants or the set of handcuffs that commemorated his murder bust last year as much as their fondness for light bondage. Oh, and not forgetting the cute little tarantula she'd put on there herself just to twit him, "Tarantula" having been his unlovely nickname at Eton. Well, a major title, a surname like Tarrant, upper-class British schoolboys being what they are—it was inevitable.

Whenever Turk added a new charm, he'd leave the augmented bracelet on Rennie's pillow for her to find before she went to bed. She'd discovered the newest ones the night before: a beautifully enameled Christmas tree, with tiny jewels for ornaments, to commemorate their first holiday in their new home, and a miniature gold record, engraved "Svaha" on one side and "Love at First Light" on the other—the two most beautiful songs he'd so far written for her, the latter about their first night together and the former about their spectacular breakup a year ago, both of which songs had played no small part in getting them back together and had been Number One and Two with a bullet for weeks on the singles charts.

"Well, anyway," she said as he swung her off his shoulder in their bedroom and she began unbuttoning her dress all the way down to the floor, "thank you again, my lord."

"For the charms? You're most welcome, my lady." He had his back to her, banking the embers in the fireplace and making sure the brass screen was safely positioned; in winter, they liked to fall asleep with the logs glowing in the hearth across the room, visible from their bed, and having taken careful precautions against sparks. She approved of that, and approved even more of the view she now had of him—he'd discarded the velvet pirate coat long ago, downstairs in the studio, and was at the moment stripping off the pirate shirt he'd worn beneath it.

"Those, but I meant for the songs themselves. Even though it was hardly fair of you to use them on me like that."

Turk smiled the smile of a man who, contemplating his prize, knew that he'd damn well won. He was still nervous about his victory, though, even after ten months' unofficial engagement and a couple of weeks' official, which was ridiculous. It wasn't Rennie he doubted, and certainly it wasn't himself—it was circumstances. He wouldn't feel completely safe until they were married in the sight of God and man and Queen and he had her safe in his castle, and that was still another ten months away. But it was hugely better than it had been, and he kept his insecurity hidden from her as much as possible.

"You think? In a fight for your life, you use whatever weapons you've got. I'd have written a hundred songs if that's what it took to get you back. Oh, and leave the jewelry on. It looks best when it's the only thing you're wearing besides your tattoos."

"When do you plan on getting back in the studio? And what are you going to be doing there when you do?"

Rennie was lying back languorously on the pillows on her side of the bed. She was playing with Turk's hair as he sprawled across the width of the fourposter, his head resting on her bare belly and strands of her own long hair trailing across his face. Both of them were contentedly exhausted by their exertions of the past couple of hours—completely unassisted by brown sugar or anything else, Rennie thought smugly—but though they were tired they were not in the least bit sleepy, and they'd been idly chatting for a while now.

"I thought maybe tomorrow? Take Boxing Day—today, now—off to eat leftovers and play with our presents and mess around. Or there's that concert up at the Cloisters we could go to."

Rennie seemed oddly evasive, but he was too tired to notice. "We could do that. The Cloisters in the snow with Renaissance music is amazing—I did that once when I was still in college, with some friends. You can't hear any traffic noises, or even see the city except for the river and the Palisades. The snow cuts you off completely, and you really feel as if you're back in the Middle Ages. Though that's nothing new for you, of course. You've got all that at home anytime you want." She yelped as he pinched her thigh and ran a finger down the inside to her knee.

"We haven't even been to my own personal castle yet. Torc Castle, seat of the Marquess of Raxton. Away the hell up in the Highlands. Small, but quite good. Fifteenth-century, haunted, and cold enough even for us. We could spend part of our honeymoon there."

"I wouldn't mind going right now—it might do us both good to get away from Niles and the whole thing."

Turk brooded for a while, watching the fire. "That brown sugar—do you really think that's what it was that made Niles forget?"

"Circumstantially? Yeah, I do. That dealer said he'd sold some to a couple of music-biz types, and though that's no proof and plenty of other people use the stuff, I bet anything that it was Starlorn and Nydborg; it feels right to me. I'll tell Sattlin and Marcus about it. Speaking of the long blue arm of the law — "

"Yes?"

She quickly outlined her last conversation with the detective and Special Agent Dorner, and Turk nodded, fitting it in with his own guesses. "That's fine," he said at last. "Are you going to tell Sledger about Pudge being the guitarnapper?"

"I'm going to have to. She'll find out eventually, and she'll kill me several times over if I hadn't. Besides, she's part of the plan."

"Yes — the plan." He turned his head to nuzzle her bare tummy. "Are you going to tell me what it is, at some point?"

"At some point." Rennie let her hand wander down Turk's front, and smiled as he sharply inhaled. *Men are so easily distracted. But then again, so are women...* "Besides, what could possibly go wrong?"

CHAPTER TWENTY-THREE

THINGS WERE FINALLY BEGINNING to move. No further developments had, well, developed after Pudge Vetrini had been sprung by the cops. No doubt there would be consequences that even Turk's forgiveness could not shield him from, that remained to be seen; but according to Marcus, probably no jail time would be involved, given that Pudge's information was helping to track down some of the bootleg distributors—just probation and perhaps a fine, which Turk had graciously agreed to pay.

But the chief operator still remained a mystery; and since whoever it was doing the operating was also likely to be the person who had murdered Biff and Scarlett and fed Niles the brown sugar, tracking him down was top priority. If the cops and Marcus's furry little friends had any leads, they had not communicated them to Rennie. Though they *had* grudgingly allowed that Niles was probably off the hook for murder, which was a huge relief all around. Rennie had already jumped the gun by communicating this last to Niles and Keitha and everybody else in the prow house, but she didn't feel the need to confess her impetuosity to the law, and trusted that by the time they caught up to her, the whole case would be neatly solved.

It was the third day of Christmas, and music-making hadn't stopped for the holiday, though since the band had gone home, nothing new was happening, just Turk and Niles messing around with mixing. Turk and Rennie had reluctantly put off leaving town at least until after New Year's, and she had been filling the time perusing travel brochures of snowy places they'd never been to, with excellent food and skiing and old-fashioned hotels with nice big old-fashioned beds.

But there was business to be attended to, serious business, and that afternoon Rennie put away the brochures. Time to push matters to a conclusion, some conclusion. It couldn't be left any longer, really: Turk had done his bit, leaving the bait trail, and now it was time for her to do her own. So she was going over to Vinylization, and Sledger was going with her. Lionheart wasn't recording there at the moment, but Rennie had given it out that she was doing a story on one of the engineers. There would be a tour of the facilities and then Rennie was to interview said engineer, with Sledger to add in questions only a pro musician would think to ask. But really she had something very different in mind.

In the spirit of being ready for possible action, Rennie was wearing a skintight Mrs. Peel-style jersey jumpsuit tucked into high suede boots, an ensemble that allowed for efficiency of movement, topped off with the fluffy-lamb-trimmed maxicoat she'd bought in London last year and, for luck, the ruby beads Turk had given her for Christmas. Your basic all-purpose rock chick ninja apparel, as she explained to Sledger.

Who was highly amused. "Sure, except that most rock chicks make do with humble strands of little Indian seed beads they buy on St. Mark's Place for a buck, not hunks of quality Burmese corundum big enough to use in a trebuchet."

"Not my fault my old man's into jewelry. And how comes it you know such a word as 'trebuchet', my poppet?"

Sledger scoffed. "If you'd spent as much time as I did in my younger days minstrel-strolling at Midwest RenFaires dressed as a busty tavern wench, you'd have learned words like that too. And a lot worse. But mostly because I wanted to load up the nearest such device with annoying drunk gropy tourists and fire away. Such a *useful* appliance."

"I can see where it would be, yes. I wonder how far Niles would travel if we bunged him into one and let fly."

"Oooh! Can we, can we?" She glanced at Rennie. "Are you still having probs with that little putz? I thought you had sorted him out."

"Well, we have a sort of truce, I guess you could call it. But it's not a very easy or a very pleasant one. Bottom line, I told him that I'd only help him with his murder difficulties if he behaved himself to Turk."

"Good motivation. And has he? And have you?"

"Sort of and sort of. He hasn't been as assholic as he usually is, so I guess that's progress of a sort, and he's coming close to agreeing to the deal Turk wants him to sign. And I did manage to call off the NYPD bloodhounds, at least for now. Our pet detectives Sattler and Casazza claim to have their noses officially lifted from the Niles trail."

Sledger gave her friend a hard look. "You're sure that he really isn't guilty, are you?"

"As sure as I can be," said Rennie after a long beat.

"Much as I'd like to think he is guiltier even than Cain. But not really, because if he were, it would be the end of Lionheart. And I'm willing to do quite a lot to make that not happen. For Turk's sake, but also for my totally selfish own: the prospect of living without any more Lionheart music is just not on. Even if it meant that Turk would have to do vocals again, which I personally would just love to bits."

Sledger nodded. "I'd like that too. But speaking of vocals...shall we get down to business? Where's our hostess?"

They had taken off their coats and were standing in the familiar Studio A, where they were waiting for engineer Rosie Landers, a young, cheerful and competent redhead who was one of the very, very few women behind the board in rock. In fact, the only one in New York. Rennie had met her on several occasions, and Sledger had been working with her on the album that Externity was currently recording in one of Starlorn's other studios. Hence the bogus cover story. But even Sledger had not yet been made privy to the entire reason that they were there today. Nobody knew just yet. Except Rennie, of course. But it was time at last to 'fess up.

She drew in a long deep breath. "Sledger. I've got something to tell you..."

"Okay, let me get this straight. We're here because you suspect certain people of running a bootlegging operation, stealing tapes from a bunch of us, and also of being the ones who murdered Biff and Scarlett."

"Yes."

Sledger was staring at Rennie with a face granitic enough

to look right at home on Easter Island. "Then we are not here because you're writing a story about chick engineers featuring Rosie Landers."

"No. Well, I *am* writing one, but—no."

"Are you going to tell me who it is you're suspecting?"

A pause. Then: "Also no. Because it's not a hundred percent certain, and I don't want to say so until it is."

"I see."

"No, you don't. Not yet. But you will. I hope." Rennie put out a hand. "It's all tied into everything else, as I said. Your death threats, and Duchess going missing, and Biff and Scarlett, and the bootleg scam...it was need to know, and I guess now you need to know."

In a few brief, clear and very pointed sentences, she explained the situation, but long before that, Sledger had begun to rumble dangerously, like a very small volcano about to blow up big.

"You *see?*" said Rennie. "That's why I didn't want to tell you right off the bat. Because I knew you'd flip out."

"Because I have good fucking reason to!"

"Yes, you do. But the thing is, we have to get proof that's going to stand up in court. That's why we're here. We're going to make sure that what we need is here and that the cops get it."

"Why didn't you just tell me straight out, Strider? You may like mysteries, but I most definitely do not."

"Understandable. And I don't like mysteries per se, but I certainly do like resolving them when I get forced into it. Okay..."

She outlined the further situation as she saw it, and

Sledger, instead of exploding all over creation, grew quieter and quieter — for her, an unusual and dangerous sign. Much like, again, a volcano. And equally not to be trusted.

"You're saying that he killed Biff and Scarlett on purpose, to keep his dirty little doings from going public."

"Yes. That's what I'm saying. On the other hand, Pudge, thankfully, doesn't seem to have been involved in the murder aspect. Even though he did steal your guitar. And pass along threatening notes. He's not the one to blame."

"I'm going to fillet him like a catfish and hang him on a cactus to dry, so the spines nail him there. Not Pudge. The other one." Sledger snarled a few more delightfully home-grown Texas invocations, and Rennie just let her roll.

Finally, when the spate of fury seemed to have run its course: "Quite finished, Veronica Lee? All good? Can we get on with things?"

Sledger opened her mouth, but a sound came from outside. "That doesn't sound right."

"On the contrary, it sounds like just what I expected. Someone's coming, and it's not Rosie…"

They moved to the side of the live room, where they could observe the dark figure that entered the control booth and started rummaging through the tape boxes.

"Trying to find the masters Lionheart did the other night," whispered Rennie. "Turk left a box labeled that. But it isn't. It's bait. Now please God just don't let him play it and actually find out that it isn't…"

They huddled together against the wall, and Rennie most unfortunately knocked gently against a piece of the drum kit, so that the cymbals shivered, a misty silver sound. The invader seemed to freeze momentarily, though he didn't turn his head; then he left the tape boxes lying there and turned to go.

Out past the studio airlock, the soundproof door opened on the long corridor leading to the front entrance and the way out to the street. Almost two feet thick, like a bank vault or submarine door, as Rennie had noted a few days ago, it weighed a freaking ton, probably literally, and you really needed help to pull it open, or at least two strong hands. Standard equipment in all serious studios, of course, especially for ones where rock or symphonic music was recorded, and very much necessary to keep the sound where it belonged, either in or out. Or other things besides sound in or out.

If Rennie had been a split-second slower, she would have missed it. But just out of the corner of her eye, she saw the outer door swinging shut, and someone was pushing it closed from the outside.

Guess he heard us, all right... She dashed for the door, and Sledger was right with her. Though the door was all but closed, the two of them clung onto the inside handle with all their might, trying to keep it open, but after a few struggling seconds, the person on the other side was victorious, though they never got a glimpse of who it was. The door slammed home in its frame with a booming thud; Rennie flipped the bolt, because she couldn't think of anything else to do, and then they stared at each other, breathing hard from their effort.

"What now, Batgirl?" asked Sledger, after their heart rates had slowed a bit.

Rennie was bent over, hands on her knees, still breathing in deep intakes. "At least—at least we got it locked on our side. So whoever it is, and now I know who, can't get in here. On the other hand, it might not have been the smartest move to lock ourselves in. Even though it also means he's locked out."

"But is he, though? Locked out, I mean. Is there another way in—or out, for that matter?"

Rennie shook her head. "That's the whole point of soundproof, as you should know. One door in, no other ways for sound to sneak through, so no one can hear us even if we shout right vigorously for help. We'll just have to stay here until someone comes. Hopefully, Rosie will wonder why the door's locked and why we're nowhere to be found; hopefully, she'll call Turk. And hopefully, he'll call the cops."

"Yeah, but no, that's not true. There *is* another door. There's even a secret staircase."

"That's just a story, Sledge."

"No, it really is true. In fact, it's right here in this studio. This funky old building, it used to be a speakeasy, and there's secret hidden stuff like that all over. Thom Courtenay told me about it one night, and Froggy damn near had a cow thinking that the place probably wasn't soundproof enough to suit him, not if there were secret doors strewn all over the place like empty Coke bottles."

"God, he's such a purist," said Rennie fondly. "Now that you mention it, Turk told me about that door too. I even wandered around during a session last week, trying to find it, to no avail. And now I know why: because I was looking for it outside, not actually in the studio itself. It sounded like some kind of urban myth. So did Thom tell you where it is, or do we have to tear the room apart to find it?"

Strangely, or perhaps suspiciously, they found it right away. In fact, the secret door was actually standing ajar, as if it were waiting for them. It was hidden away back in a corner behind the vocal booth, behind one of the heavy, ornate bronze screens left over from the original speakeasy; a screen that was apparently not quite as innocently ornamental as it appeared. The door itself was almost invisible under the bronze scrollwork patterns and between the heavy paneling on either side, and the only reason they found it so readily was that it had been left wide open.

Rennie rolled her eyes. "Oh, rrrrilly! This is just too stupidly predictable, right? We come to the studio, lock ourselves in for safety against a mysterious thief and probable murder, and suddenly, as if by magic, the legendary secret bordello door nobody could ever find since the freaking nineteen-twenties is right here and waiting for us. Please."

"He knew we'd be here."

"Uh, *yeah*, that was the whole *point*? But if he wanted to shove our noses in it, he couldn't have been more obvious. So either he was going to use it as an escape route himself — it's probably how he comes and goes when he doesn't want people knowing he's been here, if it worked for the speakeasy patrons it'd work for him too — or else he wants to herd us into it, like the Sioux stampeding buffalo into a ravine for the hunt, and pick us off as we get trapped. Not exactly the high road to safety."

"But you are going to go in, right?"

"What am I, an idiot? Of *course* I am. Or rather, we are."

The door behind the bronze screen was almost as heavy and thick as the main airlock one, making Froggy's soundproofing worries irrelevant. Probably for safety concerns, Rennie mused: such a door could have held up against raiding cops long enough for anyone on the floor above to flee out the back exit. It was obviously much, much older than anything in the studio itself, and on first inspection it appeared as if it hadn't been opened in years. Which was clearly not the case. Beyond it could be seen only old worn steps rising up into dusty darkness. And, faint but clear, footprints in the dust.

Rennie and Sledger met each other's gaze. "If we go up —" began Sledger.

" — and if he's waiting for us there. I know. He *wants* us to. And it would probably be smart not to say anything aloud from here on in — this is a sound studio, after all, and I bet he's got every mike live and open. Wait here for a second, just let me go check out what he was doing in the booth."

She went over to the door into the control booth, running a quick glance over the scattered tape boxes. They were all marked as Lionheart master tapes, and they were all the dummy boxes that Turk had left there. *Yeah, that just about seals it…* She knew for sure now who it was, who she was dealing with, and she knew she had to be extremely careful if she was going to get herself and Sledger out of this alive and hopefully intact.

It was an assessment she'd made a week ago: "a man who knew his way around a studio, even in the dark"… Stepping out again into the main room, she felt a tiny current of air out of nowhere; and before she could think what to do about it, she found herself face to face with Andy Starlorn.

CHAPTER TWENTY-FOUR

"Y OU," SAID RENNIE with no particular inflection and no surprise whatsoever, noting that the producer had managed to get Sledger in a chokehold in front of him, one wiry arm bent across her throat and the other twisting her arms behind her back, her wrists bound in yards of silky, shiny recording tape. *Hopefully blank.* "All the time."

Starlorn nodded. "Me. All the time. But you knew that. Concealment is at an end."

"So it appears. And yes, I did. Well, sort of. I got the idea from various sources that you might be involved, but— Hey there, Veronica Lee. You doing okay?" She grinned at Sledger, who was pretty much incandescent with fury at all three of them: Starlorn for getting the drop on her, herself for being gotten the drop on, and Rennie for the nonchalant attitude. "Don't worry, we'll get you out of there."

"She's all wrapped up, I'm afraid, " said Starlorn, smirking. "Can't stop to talk."

"Yes, I can see that. Well, you and I can still have a conversation… Did you have to kill Biff and Scarlett?" Rennie burst out. "They hadn't hurt anyone."

"On the contrary," said Starlorn, readjusting his hold on Sledger. "Biff was about to blow the whistle on me because I wouldn't cut him in for more money. And sweet little Scarlett was losing her effectiveness."

Rennie looked surprised, as indeed she was. "Meaning?"

"Meaning I'd been using Scarlett to our mutual benefit. Well, mostly my benefit—she was pretty useful to me making profitable little pornos pretending to be this little wildcat here." He felt Sledger trying to work an arm free for a crotch-slam, and tightened his grip again. "Ah ah ah, little darlin', you don't want to damage the goods..."

His voice took on a fakey saccharine quality. "Oh, you didn't know about that, did you, rock detective? Pretty Peggy-o was getting bored of copying our dear little Ronnie Lee and she wanted to go back to her natural blonde self. What use would she have been to me if she did? My customers were paying to see somebody, or some body, they thought was the wild and lascivious Sledger Cairns—and you did help me out *so* much with your well-publicized escapades, Veronica, there's no denying that. I had the pornos in reserve, for blackmail use in case I never needed it."

"Mm. Pity Sledge is pretty much blackmail-proof, as she pointed out to me a few days back. Aren't you, Sledger dear?" Rennie grinned at the savage look on her friend's face. "But do go on. I'm interested to hear where you take this."

"Enjoying this, are you? Well, you won't be for too much longer. Scarlett would have backed up Nydborg if he went to the cops about my extremely profitable bootleg operation, which has been making all of us so much delightful bread. I'd been balling her, of course—though not for filmic purposes—and the little bitch just knew too much."

"And Niles...you were going to try the same trick with

Lionheart. You were going to make him look guilty of the murders so you could blackmail him, and by extension Turk. That's why you started in on Pudge Vetrini and began gaslighting Sledger with notes and a stolen guitar. You were out to steal Lionheart master tapes and sell them as part of your little sideline. But you were foiled there too, because Turk keeps those master tapes almost as close to him as he keeps me. Then you sent Pudge to the prow house to lift them. I caught him snooping around the guitar vault and even sneaking upstairs. Except since the tapes are kept safe nowhere near Turk's studio, he couldn't find any."

Rennie assumed a relaxed pose, as Emma Peel-ish as she could get it, trying to remember Ares' so-useful combat instruction from two years ago, hoping for a change in Starlorn's posture that would allow her the opportunity to employ it.

"Maybe you've been doing that for years, with other acts. I wonder just what kind of unreleased recorded legacy your dear late brother Jordy left, and what you've been helping yourself to there. I doubt he'd be best pleased to find out. Though I'm sure you waited till he was decently dead to start the grave-robbing."

She was gratified to see Starlorn's face tighten. *Ah, hit a nerve there, I think. When this is all over, I'd be interested to see what the accountants for Jordy's estate and label will have to say...*

Starlorn was studying her with anger, but also with grudging respect. "How the hell does Wayland stand having you around? You knowing everything and being right all the time, I mean."

"I guess he's more of a real man than you are," said Rennie sweetly. "He doesn't think he needs to compete with his woman to prove his manhood. Which is, I might add, considerable."

He laughed shortly. "I'm sure. You must be a really great lay, otherwise why would he bother, with all the trouble you are. I don't suppose I can persuade *you* to join forces with me? You've got all-access all over the place: Lionheart, Thistlefit, Evenor, Bluesnroyals..."

Rennie pretended to consider. "Oh, I really don't think so. And if you're thinking to get rid of Sledger and me right here, I wouldn't advise it. Funny how everybody who ever sang that song to me is either dead or in jail. I'd be happy whichever way it goes with you, actually."

She leaned her backside against the wall of the isolation booth. "So why don't you tell me a little bit more? Just to pass the time. Like what happened in that cemetery, and how Niles walked out alive and Biff and Scarlett didn't."

Starlorn made a face of purest exasperation. "I never wanted *Niles* dead. He was crucial to my plan. So I followed him, after I gave the other two idiots the coke—laced with epinephrine, as you no doubt figured out."

"I hadn't, actually." Rennie showed her surprise. "But that was very efficient of you. Epi leaves no trace for pesky coroners to find, I hear."

"Right about that. Anyway, I left them to basically snort themselves to death. Then I took Niles to my place, where he wrapped himself around some nice fresh brown sugar and promptly crashed. Which was why he didn't remember a thing next day."

"Ah. And I bet I know who you bought the brown sugar from, too. That utter sleazeball Wings Walker. He told me two music types had scored from him: you and Biff, right? But the whole thing was so ad hoc: Scarlett and Biff frolicking down Second Avenue to the cemetery, Niles joining them. You couldn't have planned it all."

He viciously jerked Sledger's arms up behind her, and she yelped in uncontrollable pain; Rennie's fists closed. "Not all of it, no. I had arranged for Biff to be there for a tape handoff as usual. That groupie slag came with him. I tell you now, I thought it was this one here. I couldn't see clearly in the snow without my glasses. But I figured I'd take advantage of the opportunity and get rid of her at the same time. I had the tapes I needed, so I didn't need her anymore." He tightened the arm across Sledger's throat, forcing her head back.

Oh. "You really *did* mean to kill Sledger. Then or later. Because if she was dead, your holdings of her unreleased tapes would go through the roof in value. Scarlett was just a bonus because she could assist you with other stuff, like those pornos."

"And the penny drops!" He grinned at her, having moved between her and the door, dragging Sledger with him while Rennie pondered and Sledger, who had finally come to grips with the facts, was swearing like a river, swartly informing Starlorn what she was going to do to him as soon as she could get her hands on him, for daring to sub Scarlett for her in cheap porn flicks. To Rennie's amusement, her friend seemed more insulted by that than anything else.

That's fine, Sledge, try to distract him as much as you can…

"So, what came next?" asked Rennie bluntly. "You were going to systematically slaughter half the bands around? All the ones you'd stolen tapes from, with Pudge's help?"

He shook his head irritably. "No…that would be stupid and obvious, wouldn't it. I was just going to blackmail them, as you said. Starting with Lionheart."

"Through Niles."

"Through Niles. And then you decided to help him out." The raspy voice became a snarl. "I'd really counted on you standing away and letting him hang, because you hated him. Do you know how many plans you fucked up, being so noble for your boyfriend's sake?"

"No, but I can guess. It wasn't just for Turk's sake, though. It was for the band."

"Oh, of *course*, I forgot. Rennie Stride, loyal servant of rock and roll."

"That's right." Rennie smiled briefly, the kind of smile that sends a real smile running for its life in the opposite direction. "And don't ever forget it again."

What she was smiling about became immediately apparent, as Starlorn tripped over a mike boom someone had left lying on the floor and lost his grip on Sledger. Rennie took equally immediate advantage, pushing off the wall in a sudden flurry of energy.

"Sledger! Run!"

But Starlorn recovered at once, and dragged Sledger across the studio floor and up the secret staircase, slamming the heavy door behind them. Rennie tore after them, but by the time she got the door open again they were gone. Though they had not gone in silence: she heard Sledger unleashing a perfect storm of hate and loathing at her captor, somewhere up ahead. *Maybe I should go out the main door, look for help, call the cops? At least unlock the door, they won't be able to get in that way if I leave it...* Torn, she hesitated, then swore quietly though sincerely, and went up the ancient stairs like a hungry cat up an alley wall, though she would not go at a speed to endanger her footing or blunder onto an ambush, which was all too likely. *Okay, it's going to be a game of dodge 'em in the dark, then...*

At the top she found a warren of dim passages that led away in all directions, with peeling wallpaper and thin ragged carpeting, and for all her urgency, she stopped and stared, utterly astonished. What the hell *was* this place? And how to go? *Where* to go? Most importantly, how to make sure someone knew she'd been there? Well, she'd figure it out as she went along. She hoped.

She ventured forward into the dilapidated corridor, still hearing Sledger up ahead, now to the left. Looking back down the stairs, Rennie realized with wonder that they were in between floors, and it came to her that this must be the old secret bordello, upstairs from where the speakeasy had been, back in Prohibition times. Once, maybe fifty years ago, someone had walled off this entire floor, for reasons of their own, and for all those decades it had been left just the way it was, until Andy Starlorn had come along a few years back and bought the place and discovered its secrets. There was no electricity, of course, but shafts of far-off daylight pierced the blackness, and the passages seemed endless, interconnected like a honeycomb.

The light was coming down from the roof through the

interior cloister shafts that Rennie'd noted on the ground floor, and it revealed strange lumpy sheeted objects that might once have been divans or couches, in rooms where powerful men had once sealed political deals or been entertained by beautiful women, or both together. Cobwebs wafting from discolored crystal chandeliers brushed her face as she moved cautiously down the corridor, trailing her fingers along the tattered velvety paper upon the walls. It was as if nothing had been changed from the days of the speakeasy bordello: the rooms she glanced into as she passed by, former boudoirs, all had antique beds in tarnished brass or warped oak, ornate draperies silk-rotted with sheer age, mattresses reduced to mere rusted springs with a few wispy mats of horsehair here and there. It was really cool to see, and also spooky in the extreme. She just prayed there were no rats.

What the hell had been in Andy Starlorn's mind, to keep the floor like this? In its dusty, creepy, ruinous state, it didn't look as if he'd ever used it at all. Perhaps he had plans for it? Now wasn't the time to be a tourist, though. When all this was over, and Starlorn no longer owned the studio—because he would be in jail for all the rest of his born and livelong days—maybe Turk could buy it, and then she could come back here and explore at her leisure. But not now.

She hadn't gone far when suddenly the lights in the studio behind her went out, and the air conditioning outlet gave out with a dying fall. Oh, that was smart—if they went back now they wouldn't be able to see or breathe, and eventually air hunger and claustrophobia would do

Starlorn's work for him, forcing them back up the stairs...
Ahead, she heard a sudden tussle and Sledger's renewed
swearing.

"Rennie! Go back! Get help!"

Yeah, easy for her to say. But how was help going to *find*
them? Her hand strayed to her throat as she considered
her pitifully few options. Then it was all an Aha! moment.
Hansel and Gretel time! She didn't even bother unclasping
the ruby necklace, just wrenched the strand off her neck,
carefully catching the beads before they spilled off the
string. *Good thing those beads weren't knotted; easier to liberate
them when you need them to be bread crumbs...I'll have to ration
them, though; there's only thirty-six here...*

Twisting a bead off the string, she dropped it, not without
a pang at its going. Farther down the corridor, another; as
she turned at a junction with a new corridor, two more.
Only this was no fairytale, and the person she was trying
to follow was as big and bad as any monster the Grimm
Brothers ever came up with.

She could hear the beads clatter as they hit the wall one
by one, and then the silence as they fell onto the moldering
carpet. When help arrived — and it would, oh God, it
would — they could tell, hopefully, where she had gone, and
follow. And also hopefully, she was still behind Starlorn
and not ahead of him. Because the beads could tell him too.

Far away, suddenly she heard Sledger again, shouting
more imprecations, using every ounce of the very
considerable power of which her famous voice was capable.
She sounded as if she were back in the studio; apparently
their attacker had doubled back through the honeycomb of

hallways to familiar territory. Rennie wondered briefly why Sledger's voice came so clear, then realized that the mikes were on; she grinned in spite of herself. Judging by what the alleged hostage was snarling, it sounded as if their attacker was getting very much the worst of the situation.

She had come to the end of the bread crumbs. Maybe she could manage to sneak back herself, if the killer had managed it, even dragging Sledger as he'd been. If she did, she could maybe open the airlock door for the cops. If she could remember the way. *Oh, duh, Gretel...*

She tossed the last ruby bead and worked her way back through the maze. It wasn't difficult to see the beads in the filtered light from the cloister windows. Good; if she could follow the trail, so could the cops. *If Rosie Landers called them...if they ever show up...if they find their way into this quite literal Twilight Zone...* Coming to the stairs again, she went down the creaky steps as quietly as she could; at least the Emma Peel suit was easy to move in, and she'd left her coat and bag behind in the studio, so there was nothing to impede her.

Edging cautiously around the corner of the secret door in the increasingly airless dimness, only the control room lights on across the floor, she found herself behind the vocal booth, which gave her a little time to consider her position. *Sledger, where the hell are you? More to the point, where are you, Starlorn, you weasely backwoods bastard?*

"Come on out, Rennie! I know you're there. I've got our little orange-haired friend and I'm going to do something very painful to her if you don't. Wayland too, when he shows up, as I'm sure he will, being such a white knight and all. I can always get away out the secret door, shut it down and leave you two ladies choking here. So be a good girl and come over to me."

Oh, not good, not good at all. There was no way he was going to let them go, and equally no way Rennie was letting him hurt either Turk or Sledger. And she was certainly not sacrificing Sledger for Turk, either, that was *so* not going to happen. If she killed the little creep? Well, she'd try not to, and if she did, she'd live with it later.

She put her mouth close to the nearest mike, and the sound came from the overhead speakers, so that her opponent couldn't triangulate on her voice. "If you touch either one of them, Starlorn, I swear to God I will fucking *end* you."

"No need for that. I'm not going to hurt either of you. Not much, anyway. But I'm also not going to kill you, not unless you do something stupid to make me. No, I'm just going to lock you in here with the a/c and the lights off, and do a runner to the hills of home. A man who knows how to live off the land can hide for years back in the hollers, and I know that country from childhood like the back of my hand. I've got kinfolk to help me who have no love for the law, and places to go to earth where not even God could track me down. When the heat's off, I'll slip out of the country and find me a nice comfortable place to live, somewhere oceanfront and warm and non-extraditable. After all, I can afford it: I have a pile salted away, legitimately, but a bigger pile ill-gotten, thanks to my little sideline and what I could steal from my late dear brother Jordy. Don't worry about me. Just you hope your beau gets here with the cops before you both run out of air."

"Rennie, he's full of it, don't listen to him!"

Rennie had no intention of doing so — *Why prolong the painful narrative?* — but instead she circled soundlessly across the studio floor, along the walls in the shadows, heading for the mike stand that stood about five feet behind Starlorn. He'd let go of Sledger, having cut her wrists free of the binding tape, though she still wore the ragged loops of it like a pair of bracelets, and now he was holding her immobile with a gun; she was facing him, and facing Rennie too as she crept up behind him. Clearly the mad producer was expecting her to come from somewhere in front of him, from where she'd been in the vocal booth, not sneak up, as she was doing, on his unwary rear flank.

On the other hand, Sledger could see Rennie perfectly well, and like the trouper she was, kept her totally blank gaze fixed on Starlorn's face, never glancing at Rennie at all. Right up until the moment when the mike stand came scything down in a glittering steel sweep. It connected hard with the side of his head, and he went over like a poleaxed steer. The gun flew out of his hand as, grabbing the nearest instrument, which turned out to be Froggy Livingston's second-best Fender bass, Sledger whacked him edgewise in the groin as he pancaked to the floor, a swing worthy of her name.

As Starlorn folded from both directions and lay unmoving, Sledger caught the gun as it skittered across the floor; then she looked at Rennie, who had ended up on her knees behind the producer's fallen form, so hard had she swung the metal stand. Leveling the gun at Starlorn, with an ease born of long practice — well, she was a West Texas girl, after all, and she was also Galt Cairns' daughter — Veronica Lee managed a smile.

"Hail Dorothy," she offered.

Rennie smiled back, a little shakily. "Nice shootin', Tex."

The cops came rushing down the secret stairs a few minutes later. They'd been called by Rosie Landers, who had gotten worried and angry when she'd found herself locked out of the studio and had come across a strange new door standing open, a door that led to rickety stairs and a kind of Miss Havisham mystery ruin. The police were only half a step ahead of Turk, who had also been called by Rosie, and who didn't let any foolish concern for the integrity of the crime scene stop him running straight to Rennie and catching her up in his arms. Ares, who'd accompanied him, did the same for Sledger, who was just as unsteady as her friend. Neither wanted the two girls to look at the mangled heap on the floor that was Andy Starlorn, but Rennie pulled free of Turk's immobilizing hold; stepping quite deliberately to Starlorn's side, she resolutely stared down.

He was probably breathing, but it was hard to tell — it was all very messy and there was a fair amount of blood. Well, it was what it was. She had done it, and she would do it again if she had to, and it was only right that she should behold her own work.

"What the perishing hell am I going to do with you?" Turk muttered savagely into her hair, pulling her away again as the EMTs started their work on Starlorn. To his great gratification, she suddenly clung to him like a limpet and burrowed into his chest like a quahog into wet sand. "And no, spare me the obvious. But are we never to be free of this sort of thing?"

"I'm hardly a damsel in distress, you know," she muttered almost inaudibly. *Though I'm certainly hanging onto him like one...*

His voice came from above her head, now filled with exasperated amusement. "Perhaps not, but you are far and away the most distressing damsel I have ever met."

She laughed, though she knew very well she shouldn't, and kept right on leaning into him; she'd started shivering, and his arms around her felt so very very nice. Freeing himself a little from her convulsive grasp, but only a little, Turk held out his upturned leather hat, which he had been carrying pinched together in one hand as carefully as if it contained eggs, or grenades. Something less lethal and fragile, though far more precious—Rennie glanced down to see the ruby beads she'd used to mark the trail.

"You'll be glad to have these back, I'm sure," he said. "I'll have them restrung as soon as my guy in the diamond district opens up in the morning. Rather expensive breadcrumbs, Gretel."

Thirty-four, thirty-five, thirty-six...yes! Rennie was counting them to make sure he'd found every single one, and then, relieved that they were all there, tilted the hat to spill the beads into her shoulderbag, which she'd retrieved from the studio floor. "Well, they worked, didn't they?"

"I'd say so." His voice altered just a little. "The mike stand is your handiwork, then, I take it. And Sledger?"

"Lived up to her name. It was a thing of beauty, and I'm

very glad I got to watch, as one doesn't often get to see a man gelded with a musical instrument. Her aim was true, as one would expect, and at least it wasn't *her* Fender she whacked him with. Froggy won't be pleased when he hears. Or maybe he will." Rennie nodded expressionlessly at the figure of Starlorn, as he was being loaded onto a stretcher for removal. "Is he dead?"

He felt her tighten up as she said it, the bleached colorlessness of her words, and pulled her close again. "No, love. No, he is not, which is probably just as well. Big old concussion, though, I'll bet, at the very least. Maybe worse. I can't feel sorry for him, and neither should you."

"Ah. Well, I've heard that prison doctors are pretty good."

She tried to conceal her great relief that Starlorn wasn't killed after all, but she suddenly began to shake again, this time so intensely that she needed Turk's arms around her to continue to stand up. Over the course of her career as Murder Chick, she had of course given sober consideration to the fact that possibly, at some point, though please God don't ever let it happen, she might have to kill someone. She had thought about it long and hard, and had come to the conclusion that she probably could do it, but only to save Turk or Prax or herself, or perhaps a bus full of nuns, orphans and puppies. Or orphaned puppy nuns. And she honestly had thought she *had* killed Andy Starlorn, and she had honestly thought she could live with that for the rest of her life. How very wrong she had been.

The cops let them all go after some minimal questioning: everything seemed to be already known and what wasn't could apparently wait till later. There are good things about having a cop on your side, if it is the right kind of cop, and for all that Rennie got her usual scolding from Marcus Dorner, and Nick Sattlin tore off a strip or two as well, she felt that on the whole she had gotten off lightly, and had expected no less. In fact, she had expected quite a lot more, like being arrested and charged on assault with a deadly weapon, or a weapon she had so creatively made deadly. But once Starlorn's gun had been handed over by Sledger, and explanations had been made, all that the police were saying was perfectly justifiable self-defense, and not to worry, and they could both make statements at their leisure.

Somehow word of the escapade had gotten out almost immediately, though none of them had said a syllable, making it into all the eleven p.m. TV news shows and morning papers. The media seemed to think that ten Christmases had arrived at once. Also a Cubs World Series victory, a couple of coronations, and all the ponies they had been denied in their sad little childhoods. From the instant she had grabbed that mike stand and swung, Rennie had known that it would be so, and had resigned herself to whatever the outcome would be.

Fitz, not surprisingly, was deeply thrilled with his pet reporter, but, also not surprisingly, deeply protective of his young friend, and he offered luxurious sanctuary in his twentieth-floor Fifth Avenue triplex to her and Turk, and to Sledger as well. But they politely declined, preferring to all huddle together in the prow house—along with Niles and Keitha and Prax and Ares, and Lionheart's publicist Pie Castro in case statements needed making, and Francher Green who had jumped on the first redeye back from L.A. as soon as he'd heard and arrived at the prow house in time for breakfast. It was a bit like a siege, and a bit like house arrest, and a bit like a pajama party, but at least they were all together, and Detective Sattlin had thoughtfully put a uniformed officer on both prow house doors, just in case.

From the other direction, Turk's father had instantly dispatched to the aid of the future Lady Raxton the very bulldoggiest of the Tarrant family solicitor bulldogs, one Sir Adrian Whitby, even though that fearsome individual couldn't lawfully practice in New York and was there purely for the intimidation factor, much enhanced by the power of the double-starched accent. At his son's suggestion, the Duke had additionally hired King Bryant in his own formidable person, who could indeed practice in New York and who had fortuitously been in town at the time. The two legal Godzillas had instantly male-bonded over cognac and cigars, much to Rennie's amusement, though they had both politely declined her offer of guest-room space, and were currently crashing in more suitable style at the Pierre and the St. Regis respectively.

Rennie herself was still badly shaken: by now she was beginning to verge simultaneously on the philosophical and the hysterical. Well, he'd asked for it, hadn't he, Starlorn. Was she supposed to just stand there and let him kill her and Sledger both, and Turk when he turned up? Because that just hadn't been on. Besides the crippling blow to the crotch, Sledge had, she'd admitted cheerfully, been fully

prepared to shoot as soon as she got hold of the gun, so one
way or another, Starlorn was going down. Neither girl was
sorry in the slightest, but Rennie, at least, did wish it could
have fallen out otherwise.

"Really, it's just too good to miss, right?" she asked
rhetorically. " 'Murder Chick Commits Almost-Murder',
'Maxwell's Silver Mike Stand Came Down On His Head',
'Producer's Final Take'...man, the headlines just write
themselves, don't they."

"Not murder," protested Ares. "Self-defense. Anyway,
Maxwell, he's not dead. Not even critical."

Rennie laughed shortly. "Just almost dead. Half past
dead. What would *you* call it, then?"

Ares' expression was sympathetic. "Taking out the trash.
Literally taking out. Literally trash."

Rennie nodded and turned her eyes elsewhere. To be
honest with herself, and she usually was, she had to admit
she wasn't too troubled by the whole thing, or at least
nowhere near as troubled as she'd always thought she'd be.
Maybe that would come later — bad dreams or something —
and if it so fell out then at least she had Turk to comfort her.
For the moment, yeah, it was horrible and upsetting that
she had almost killed somebody. Almost. She clung to that
word as hard as she'd clung to Turk. Oh, she'd blustered
quite a bit over the past few years about how she'd like to
launch certain offenders into eternity with casual aplomb,
but deep down she'd known she probably never could.
Even Jacinta O'Malley and Kaiser Frizelle, because of what
they'd done to Turk, had been spared by her hand to live
to see the inside of a jail cell, though not after that hand,

both hands, had achieved a respectable, and painful, bit of punitively cathartic damage.

At bottom, hers was a proud and self-restraining nature, and quite honestly, she'd have been more upset if she'd killed or hurt an animal. Vengefulness didn't really count as a mitigating factor here; she had thought long and hard about that part of it, and had decided that no, it hadn't been some kind of misguided and misapplied revenge, unholy vindication for everybody she'd lost and everything she'd endured over the years. No. It had simply been — as Marcus and even Detectives Nick and Bob had gently told her when she'd burst out to them in all her shock and distress and desperation — a case of deadly force being needed to stop deadlier force. Regrettable, but there it was. Cops had to think that way all the time.

But she wasn't a cop, and she hadn't killed him. Had. Not. She kept coming back to that. *Would* she have? *Could* she have? Well — if he'd hurt Turk, no question about it. None. She'd have knelt on his arms and dug into his windpipe with her bare hands and held on until he'd stopped flopping, and that she knew for immutable fact. And he *had* killed two people, Starlorn, so it would have been totally deserved. But she wasn't going to tell anyone that but Turk himself, and maybe not even him.

As far as her ongoing career as Murder Chick went, almost-murder wasn't going to slow her down. Oh, she might consider distancing herself from any future scenes where death might play a part, but that seemed more a matter of luck and good taste rather than any kind of control she exercised over the situation. But maybe it was now time to do just that. For self-protection too: eyes would be watching more closely now, to see how she did, if perhaps she was going to make a habit of this, had developed some kind of weird bloodlust craving for physical violence, as lesser women might develop a jones for caviar or sable coats or deliberately mismatched socks.

But by the same token, she certainly wasn't going to stand away, either, just because she was afraid of people maybe thinking that. Hopefully this phase of her life was now rapidly drawing to a close, and she would be able to retire Murder Chick, with full military honors and a thirteen-gun salute, when she married Turk. "Murder Chick" was bad enough, but "Murder Marchioness" was not to be even *thought* of.

She knew too that she wouldn't be doubting herself anywhere *near* this much if it had in fact been Turk who'd been in danger instead of Sledger and herself. There would not have been a heartbeat of hesitation there, not so much as a scintilla of second-guessing. And maybe that was wrong too: shouldn't one human life imperiled be of equal value with another? Theoretically, yeah. Where Turk was concerned, for her part, no. Oh, sure, she would have done whatever she had to do, to save Sledger—she had lost enough people she cared about, and frankly, it had felt *great* to hit back. But that was a slippery slope, and she was hanging on by her fingernails as it was.

At least it was finished now, and it had ended about as happily as it could have. Hopefully, she would never have to do anything like that again. But she knew, and Turk knew, and undoubtedly Agent Dorner and Detectives Sattlin and

Casazza knew, that if she had to, she absolutely would. If she had to. And that was something that all of them could live with. Because they had to.

CHAPTER TWENTY-FIVE

"**I** THINK YOU SHOULD SACRIFICE LIVESTOCK to the glory of my name," said Rennie, with a certain amount of perhaps forgivable preening. "Maybe not so much for figuring it all out," she added honestly, "as this time I really didn't quite, but for being the clear star of reason and taking the necessary heroic action. And by 'heroic action' I mean sacrificing my ruby necklace so that we could be tracked to the scene of the crime. You have no idea how it tore at my vitals to scatter those beads to the four winds."

Turk grinned. "A very temporary sacrifice, madam, as the necklace was restrung mere hours later under your anxiously hovering supervision. But a very real one, I'm sure. Will flowers, chocolates, more jewelry and a nice dinner at Lutèce suffice as an offering? I don't think we can actually *get* a fatted calf without special advance notice to the butchers."

She waved her fingers in good-humored dismissal. "You know my methods, Watson. You should really be better prepared for these moments by now. Since you know another one is almost certainly coming along sooner or later. Nice line in ass-kissing, though, your lordship," she added.

"Wait till I get you upstairs."

It was two days after the scene at Vinylization and two days before New Year's Eve. They were in their living room for the usual post-case deconstruct: Prax, Ares, Sledger, Ken Karper, Shea Laakonen, Belinda, Francher and Pie Castro, with special guest stars King Bryant and his English counterpart, Sir Adrian Whitby. Even Niles, who with hitherto unsuspected delicacy of feeling had previously barricaded himself upstairs in his rooms with Keitha, had come down for the great unraveling, though the NYPD detectives had absented themselves, politely declining on the flimsy grounds of having too many loose ends to tie off, but really making excuses because they didn't want to set a precedent here with regard to Rennie Stride. *Too late for that, boys...*

Neither was Marcus Dorner present, for that matter: he'd moved through this whole tangle with uncharacteristic self-effacement, as behind the scenes as he could possibly get without being in another time zone. Which was just fine with Rennie. She didn't foresee any cozy ongoing future relationship with either Marcus or the NYPD, which probably suited them even better than it did her. Anyway, it wasn't that complicated a dénouement this time: Rennie could handle it herself, with a little help from the supporting cast. So they'd all assembled, lounging round the fireplace on the big soft leather chairs and sofas, and Hudson had brought in trays of tea and fresh babka from the Ninth Street Bakery, and now everyone was comfortably sitting back and rehashing the case.

Rennie stretched out a little more on the sofa nearest the hearth, hooking her legs over Turk's lap. She and Turk and the others had of course discussed the case over the few days since its short sharp climax, but only to Turk had she unpacked her inmost feelings. Right now she was feeling almost her usual chipper self again, now that everything was all copacetic, and there had been no nightmares. At least none that she was going to admit to in public: there had been one or two occasions when his lordship had been pressed into nocturnal shrink duty, waking her up from whimpering tussles with her pillows and holding her gently, murmuring consoling words and singing softly to her until she fell asleep again. Much as had been the case back in L.A. after the run-in with Malachite and two bullets. But it was better now, and only going to get better still.

She had of course obliged Fitz with the usual first-person story, as well as being interviewed for the straight-news front-page piece, reported again as usual by Ken Karper and, again again as usual, exclusive to the Fitzrovian press empire. It was getting to be almost comic, their little double act — the George Burns and Gracie Allen of crime reporting, snotty or jealous journo colleagues sniffed — having been performed as often as it had, but they all knew there was nothing in the least bit amusing about it. Indeed, Rennie had come to regard it almost as a psychological purge of sorts, both necessary and helpful.

"I do love these fun little get-togethers," confided Rennie then, shaking herself and gazing round the room. "Perhaps we can think of a suitable band name for ourselves, since we seem to do this sort of thing so often. Murder Ink? The Deathwatch Beatles? The Rolling Bones? Death's Doors? Ungrateful Dead? We could have some little pins or badges made up, secret handshake, t-shirts, password, the whole exclusive thing? No? Okay, whatever. Well, well, where to begin..."

She paused a moment, musingly, and they all sat obediently awaiting her account, like travelers in a medieval inn, junketing to Canterbury and waiting for that cleverclogs Chaucer to tell them one of his rollicking tales.

"Right, then. It started with Biff Nydborg, who as you all know by now had been ripping bands off from the first. He was Sledger's sound man, so he had access to anything Externity that he wanted. He started in small, just stealing to make amateur bootlegs for himself — and not just from Externity, but from other groups he worked for free-lance. Sometimes he copied right off the sound board at concerts, sometimes he thieved from studio sessions. He had a thriving little business going; then Andy Starlorn took notice when material from Vinylization sessions started appearing on boots. He got hold of Biff, I don't know how he figured out who was responsible, and proposed they start working together, ripping off Externity and any other group they could get access to, for the Far East and South American markets."

"And the Sledger clone? Scarlett?" asked Francher.

Ken Karper's face hardened as he took up the story. "He employed Scarlett to help pull off some of his scams against Externity and of course against Sledger herself, in his little porn sideline, using the resemblance to Sledger that Scarlett capitalized on. So at first it seemed logical that Peggy Scoca — Scarlett — must have been the target. She looked like Sledger, she was there where she shouldn't have been, in the cemetery with Nydborg and Niles."

Turk shook his head. "We only thought it was because

she *did* look like you, Sledge. We're so used to people looking like other people, by design and intent, that we never stopped to consider anything else."

"She just happened to be with Biff. She was along for the ride. And she died." Ken was silent a moment. "But soon it began to seem instead that you, Miss Cairns, *were* the real target. Or maybe even a suspect: the letters containing death threats, the theft of your guitar, all that could have worked to either divert suspicion from you or to focus it on you if he needed an out. It could have been slanted either way, as needed. When Starlorn came into the cemetery to meet up with Nydborg and get the latest tapes and hand off the drugs, he saw Scarlett there and thought she was you, and took his chance. When he found out he'd been mistaken and it hadn't been you but your groupie double, he figured he could make that work for him too. For his purposes, Scarlett *would* be better off dead. And now she was. He could always get you another time. And then he took aim at Turk."

That gentleman stirred in protest. "But—"

"Starlorn didn't go after you directly, Turk," said King Bryant, "because he knew that, one, you're too smart and too wary, and two, if he even tried, Rennie would be on his trail like the She-wolf of the Fillmore. But if they could get their hooks into someone Rennie didn't like and wouldn't care about defending or helping to prove innocent—sorry, Niles—well, they'd be good to go. Starlorn knew all about the bad blood between Niles and Rennie, and Niles certainly fit their bill. What Starlorn didn't foresee was Rennie and Niles trying to make it up between them, and her deciding to help him out for Turk's sake and the band's sake."

Pie Castro looked confused. "So where *does* Lionheart come into it, then?"

"The bands Pudge and Biff were ripping off were beginning to get suspicious," said Karper. "Rennie, you said that the Dolabellas and Bosom Serpent were starting to feel leery about Pudge, and I bet if we polled some of the other groups Pudge was working for they'd say the same thing. So, the scam with Pudge as an active player was beginning to run its course. Now Starlorn had to find a new group to feed on, a bigger group, and when he heard Lionheart was searching for a new producer for the upcoming album, he lobbied Freddy Bellasca into pushing him for the job."

"Do you think Freddy was—" Turk began.

King shook his head. "No. At least not what you're thinking, anyway. There *was* some mutual backscratching going on, sure. Bellasca owed Starlorn, as you suspected; nothing serious, just enough to force the band's decision for Starlorn to be your producer. And Starlorn really is a great producer, so it wouldn't seem suspicious for Bellasca to puff him up to you guys."

"Well, it seemed quite suspicious enough to me," said Turk. "If only I had decided against giving him the gig in the first place—"

"Caligula's horse," murmured Rennie absently. When they all stared at her: "What? Carry on."

"Not just you, Turk; we all fell for it," said Francher with some bitterness, "and we all agreed to give Starlorn the gig."

Ken nodded. "Setting up Niles as a suspect for the murders was a pre-emptive strike, to get Niles to cooperate with the Lionheart bootleg operation he'd planned for down the road." Over in his chair by the window, Niles looked a little uncomfortable, but said nothing.

"Plus the murders cleared away the two people who were getting to be thorns in his side, who were starting to get out of his control and losing their usefulness," said Belinda. "Biff and Scarlett. He kept Pudge around, though, since Pudge was already in with Lionheart and hence still of service, at least for a while."

"Clever girl!" said Rennie, winking at her friend. "You must be a journalist or something."

"He couldn't run the same scam exactly, though, with Lionheart," remarked Shea. "At least not for the porn flicks. For one thing, nobody else looks like Turk the way Scarlett looked like Sledger."

"Well, my cousin Oliver Buckle comes pretty close," said Turk, grinning. "We posed as each other a lot at university, when I was still running my dual identities. But I don't think Ollie'd have agreed to a scam like this one. As the son of a marquess himself, he doesn't need the money, and he certainly wouldn't want the headaches. Though quite possibly he'd do it simply to give me one. Still, I can't see him impersonating me in an Andy Starlorn porno. He just doesn't have the requisite — requisites."

Rennie grinned back at him as they all laughed. "No doubt. But be that as it may, Starlorn modified the overall plan to cover the new circumstances. Pudge was still helpful, which he'd proved by stealing masters, but Niles would be Starlorn's real way into Lionheart. He'd frame Niles for the murders he'd committed himself, then offer to keep quiet if Niles went to work for him, stealing and copying the masters, and Turk would be none the wiser. Alternatively, he could always tell Turk that Niles was guilty of the murders, that there was proof, and work the blackmail that way. Turk would want to protect Niles and the band, so he'd presumably agree to anything. Starlorn would force Niles to sign the key-man clause that Turk wanted, and maybe get a key-man clause of his own with the label or with Turk. Either way, he'd be sitting pretty, able to bootleg away to his heart's content. He'd have Niles in his pocket, and he'd still have Vetrini there to help with the dirty work."

"Or be the fall guy if necessary," observed Ares.

"But Niles ended up agreeing to the key-man clause of his own free will," said Turk, smiling encouragingly at his lead singer, who had been growing paler and smaller as the discussion continued, shrinking into the depths of his armchair. "No blackmail necessary."

"And then it got nasty anyway," said Belinda somberly. "And that's when people started dying."

"The cops found the brown sugar stash in Starlorn's freezer, in a bag of frozen corn," said Karper, rolling his eyes. "Creative, but *so* stupid — they all think they're being so clever, and they never realize it's been done a thousand times before. But that wasn't all they found."

"Coke? Like you thought?" asked Prax.

"Coke, yeah," said Rennie. "But not the stash Scarlett and Biff had been snorting from with Niles. Starlorn gave them this other stuff before he left the cemetery; you never had the tiniest sniff of it, Niles, so count your blessings and thank your guardian angel. It had been heavily cut with epinephrine. When they snorted it, it just ripped their hearts up like a knife. Their pulses got sent into orbit and they died, and then they froze. They never knew what hit them. It wouldn't have hurt, so that's—that's something. But yeah. He gave it to them on purpose. He arranged to meet them, he followed them from the Fillmore East, and then he killed them."

They all sat in a little silence for a moment, thinking of people they knew, laughing and frolicking in the snowy churchyard; the dark figure approaching, smiling at them; words exchanged; then the hospitable offer of coke, no hard feelings, here, have the whole bag. And then the terrible stillness after. Right.

"There was no trace of it in the autopsies?" asked Niles quietly, speaking for the first time. "The autopsy found coke in their bodies, you said. But the other?"

Rennie shook her head. "There wouldn't have been. Epinephrine leaves the system within minutes, and no one found the bodies till hours later. No test could have shown it had been there. I'd say it was merciful, but it wasn't."

"But why did he kill them in the first place?" burst out Sledger, who had been gradually getting angrier and angrier the more she thought about it.

"What he told Rennie: Nydborg had had enough, and was going to rat him out," said King Bryant. "Biff thought Starlorn was getting too greedy and was endangering the scheme, and also he started remembering—too late—that he owed Sledger a lot. As for Scarlett, she was out of her mind and out of control, and Starlorn was afraid she'd spill the beans about the porn, if nothing else."

Sledger growled so malevolently that Macduff, lying at his master's feet, raised a startled head. "So unflattering. The least that slimy bastard could have done was ask me first if I wanted to do it myself. For a decent cut of the profits, of course," she added, and again the room exploded with laughter.

"Yes, well," said Ares. "I would think he just didn't want news of his agenda getting out to someone who could put it all together. Someone like you," he added, with a nod to Rennie.

Rennie smiled. "Why, sir, y'all are such a sweet-talker!"

"And the brown sugar?" asked Pie.

"Starlorn gave it to Niles when he took him home that night," said Rennie. "That's why you couldn't remember, Niles. You had been doing the coke from the stash the two victims had, not Starlorn's stash cut with ep. When he followed you out of the cemetery and took you home to chat and get warm and crash overnight, he stuffed your nose with brown sugar so you didn't remember a thing. That's why you weren't left frozen dead like the other two, just dumped on the park bench the next day. Starlorn didn't want to harm you, just control you, because blackmailing you was instrumental to the new bootlegging plan Starlorn had for Lionheart's tapes."

Turk added, noting that Niles had turned a distinct shade of eau-de-Nil, "And of course you thought exactly what he wanted you to think: that you'd killed Biff and the groupie in a drugged-out haze."

"If Mr. Clay was suspected of the murders," said Sir

Adrian, speaking up for the first time, in an Oxbridge voice you could have bent horseshoes around, "Mr. Starlorn could hold an alibi over his head for him to jump through hoops for, and that would work out just fine. He'd be able to control Lord Raxton as well, perhaps, ultimately. I have no doubt whatsoever that Starlorn would have killed you too, Miss Cairns, sooner or later. As it was, he just put the frighteners on to discourage you poking about, by having your guitar stolen and kidnap threats made."

Turk grinned at the pure fury that instantly leaped back into Sledger's face. "Yes, we know, tigerlily, it takes more than that to scare *you* off. And Duchess is back safe in her case. But by then it was all coming apart anyway: the scam had started to go off the rails once it had expanded to involve Niles and the rest of us."

"Rennie especially," put in Prax.

"That alone should have been the clear indicator for him to back off," said Whitby gallantly, and Rennie smiled a modest little smile. "Is no criminal capable of joined-up thinking these days?"

Ken nodded. "It would seem not. But wait, there's more! Starlorn not only thought he'd blackmail Niles with the murders, or rather the implication that Niles had committed them, but he thought he could reverse-blackmail Turk as well: offer him a key-member clause on Niles in return for a free hand with the bootlegging, say, or at least a blind eye turned to it."

"And he really thought that would work?" asked Rennie indignantly. "Who did he think he was dealing with? Turk would never— You wouldn't have, would you?"

Turk feigned serious consideration, to much amusement. "No, of course I wouldn't. But that was smart thinking on his part; that clause is the one thing I *might* have considered doing it for."

"Just about the only smart thinking he did," said Prax.

The other Murder Ink members had gradually dispersed, leaving Rennie, Turk, Prax and Ares sitting in silence for a while, contemplating. Finally Rennie stirred where she lounged in Turk's arms on the leather sofa and looked up at him.

"Well, wrangling the studio is going to be a piece of cake after this. But you're not really thinking of going back to Vinylization, are you?"

"Entirely your call," said Turk. "Do you think you can bear the idea of hanging out there while we finish the mixing, even with a new producer whom we do not as yet have? Vibes won't freak you out too badly? At all?"

Rennie snorted. "If I could go back to sleeping with you in a room where a groupie turned up dead in our own bed, or a beach house where I was shot, *twice*, I very much think I can manage to continue to join you for a few odd sessions at Vinylization. But that has nothing to do with Starlorn; just with me being bored to tears in the studio."

"Heart of a lion," said Turk proudly.

"Lady Lionheart," said Prax with equal pride.

"Yeah, yeah," said Rennie uncomfortably. "Don't let's dwell on the cleverness of me, shall we? If I'd been a bit cleverer to begin with, so much of this could have been avoided."

Turk shrugged. "Maybe. But don't let's forget how much worse it could so easily have gone, either. If Rosie Landers hadn't found the door open that Starlorn used to come and go by, leading to the secret stairs, it would have taken us hours to break down that airlock door, since you had so cleverly bolted it from inside. What the hell were you *thinking*, may I ask?"

"I have no idea."

"So what now?" asked Ares. "About Pudge, I mean."

"Didn't want to go along with it, from what I've heard here," observed Prax. "He obviously hated hurting Sledger and Turk."

"And yet he did," said Rennie coldly.

"And we've discussed it, Pudge and I," said Turk, in a tone that precluded further discussion. "And he stays. No arguments. I'm not losing the best guitar tech in the business. He was scared and weak and they capitalized on it, and now they've paid for it, or they soon will. Just a lapse of judgment. It won't happen again."

"What are you going to do about replacing Starlorn?" asked Ares, changing tack. "He's not exactly going to be allowed out of the slammer every weekend just so he can join you in the studio."

Turk laughed shortly. "No, I suppose not. Pity, really. He may be a murderer and a thief and a ripoff artist, but he's still a damn brilliant producer. Lots of bands would, uh, *kill* to work with him."

"Not to sound like a publicist, and thankfully Pie didn't, but that could have made for a quirky little selling point," remarked Prax after everyone had dutifully groaned.

"That it could," agreed Rennie. "But not to sound like a critic, it would have made a pretty lousy musical point. You guys are better off with somebody new."

"We'd better find him soon," said Turk gloomily.

CHAPTER TWENTY-SIX

BEFORE FINALLY HEADING HOME to London with Keitha, Niles came to Turk of his own accord and solemnly reiterated that he was ready to agree to do whatever it took to stay with the group: long-term contract, key-member clause, whatever Turk wanted. As long as Turk still wanted him? Which Turk most assuredly did, and said so; and producing the contract again, he went over it with his lead singer preparatory to signing it later that afternoon up at Centaur, in the presence of Freddy Bellasca, the label lawyer Harvey Levitt and Sir Adrian Whitby, whom Turk had ordered to stay in New York for a day or two, hoping for the very outcome that had just transpired.

When he and Turk finished with the contract review, besides unalloyed pleasure at the extreme generosity of the terms, Niles' face showed relief, and a certain reassured peace as the pens were put away.

"I don't want to sound soppy, God forbid, but Lionheart really is a family, and I finally realized it's *my* family too, not just you other blokes'. It's where I want to be, and I want to be a real part of the band. I thought I was, and I guess I was, but not the way I thought… And even though it took a couple of murders and Rennie's help to get me there — well, I'm here now. And I'm so bloody sorry to have been such a total git."

"You've always been a real part of the band, Niles," said

Turk, moved. "*I'm* only sorry you could never believe it until now."

Niles raised his head, eyes suspiciously bright, and smiled at his friend. "Right. I'll drink to that. And sign to it, too, just as soon as we get uptown. But tell Rennie — tell her —"

"Why don't you tell her yourself?"

Next day, New Year's Eve eve, the prow house was warm and quiet, smelling of pine from the four lavishly decorated Christmas trees — the huge one in the living room, smaller specimens in the dining room, library and rear parlor, just as a good Victorian family would have had. At the kitchen table, Rennie, in sweatpants, shearling slippers and one of Turk's sweaters, was happily addressing a hot turkey sandwich dripping with gravy and butter and salt, with a huge wodge of her trademark thyme-and-onion stuffing on the side. In her opinion, the best thing about holiday dinners was the leftovers, and she always made sure there were plenty from Thanksgiving through New Year's. Even if she had to roast a couple of extra birds to bridge the gap.

Taking a big contented bite, and dribbling gravy and melted butter down her chin and over her fingers, she glanced up as Niles came down the stairs from the dining room, dressed for the plane ride home. Her expression quickly hardened to wariness, and his was no better, as they regarded each other like two begrudging volcanoes, ready to lob lava bombs over the distance between them.

WhywhyWHY does he always have to interrupt me having a peaceful stodge? First it was tea, then it was ice cream, now it's a nice hot sandwich. And then we always fight, and then I'm just not hungry anymore, which is such a freakin' waste... Still, the little dishfaced divot's on his way out the door and home free to London, and not to jail, and he owes that to nobody else but clever little mememe...

"Niles." She nodded, but didn't remove her attention from the sandwich. "Ready to leave? Keitha's all packed? You should have a nice smooth flight, according to the weather report."

A small, electric pause; and then Niles opened his mouth and started talking, and as he spoke on and on, her own mouth opened, and not for a bite of sandwich either, and her jaw dropped until it practically hit her lap. All about how he'd finally cleared the air with Turk, and how he'd signed Turk's key-man deal which of course she already knew about, and how much he owed her and was thankful to her for.

Sink me and stap me vitals! I did know about the contract, Turk told me last night, but I was not expecting the rest of that...

"Well—thank you, Niles," said Rennie at last, having listened with a fair degree of mute astonishment to Niles' awkward little speech. "I'm only glad I could help out."

The Lionheart world was poised on the brink of lasting peace for just an instant, teetering and balancing. Then Niles blew it all to hell. Again.

"I owe you, as I said, Keitha and I both do, and I really am grateful, but that doesn't mean anything's fundamentally changed between us, you know."

Rennie inwardly rejoiced. *Hooray, he cracked first! I don't have to be nice to him now, how excellent... Mr. Clay, I was willing to let you walk out of here, like the person of honor I am and you're so clearly not, but now you get the full-on both-barrels smackdown…*

She set her sandwich half carefully aside, put her feet up on the neighboring chair, and smiled pleasantly at her nemesis, her voice dropping a whole register and purring with satisfaction, like Bagheera the black panther's before he bit into the throat of a hapless antelope.

"Oh, Niles, Niles, Niles, you *know* that's not true! Things *have* changed, and they're never going to be the same again. The way I see it is this." She settled more comfortably in the chair. *Oh, I'm going to enjoy this, and I so deserve it…* "You came to me begging for my help, and I agreed to do what I could, and I did. You wanted me to get you off the hook for the murders. Right. I was happy to render assistance. For Turk's sake, not for yours, just so we're both very clear on that. So I duly off-hooked you and now you owe me, as you just admitted, and you're going to have to play my game. The day of reckoning is at hand. So we're going to make a little deal, you and I."

He sent a narrow gaze her way. "Which means?"

"Which means I don't give a rat's how you behave to me, you wanking little tripehound, though simple courtesy from a guest under my own roof would be nice. But you will fucking well stop passive-aggressively hassling Turk. You will stop sniping at him and undercutting and second-guessing and badmouthing him. You will stop muttering nasty things behind his back and then pulling that so unattractive British 'You heard' crap when he asks what you said. You will support him unconditionally in whatever creative direction he wants to take the band. You will perform to the best of your staggeringly considerable ability. You will give him total respect and total loyalty in public and you will conduct yourself courteously to him in private. And by God you will mean it; or at least you will convincingly make it *look* as if you mean it. And you will never, *EVER*, forget that Lionheart is *his* band, not yours, and that you are now contractually bound to it, and that you owe him forever and ever, amen."

She paused to take a breath and a bite of stuffing. "Oh, and Turk is not to know anything about this little arrangement. I'm not telling him, and if he finds out from you, or if you tell anyone else and Turk finds out about it that way, our deal is off. I swear I'll somehow come up with new evidence against you, or invent it myself if I have to, and I'll virtuously pop it round to the police like a good citizen, and then I'll let the NYPD nail you to the wall and I won't lift a finger to stop it. Do I make myself clear, or is this too complicated for you?"

Niles looked as if he were about to explode, then visibly calmed himself, almost by physical effort. "You're a hard chick, Rennie Stride."

"Where Turk is concerned, yes, you bet I am. He can take care of himself, of course. But my job is to make sure he doesn't have to. That's part of *our* deal, and it works the same the other way round." She stretched elaborately and reached for her glass of milk, and smiled again. "And in return, I will continue to do my absolute best to assure absolutely anyone who asks that you had absolutely nothing to do with the murders *or* the bootleg scam. Absolutely."

"Murder Chick Rides Again?"

"If you like." Rennie leaned forward. "Let's face it, Niles. We've discussed this before, sort of, but clearly we need to lay it all out here and now… We're each jealous of each other's place in Turk's life. I'm jealous of all those years you had with him when I hadn't even met him yet—years I can never have, years of him I missed out on. I'm jealous because I can never know the Turk that you know, because I can't say I knew him when, the way you can, before he was who he is now. You're jealous because I have something with him you can never have. You're jealous because you feel you're not as important to him as you were now that I've come along, that I have his attention and consideration and love in a way you never can or will. And you're quite right to feel that way. But so am I. We're each envious of how he needs each of us, how much he needs each of us. But he really does need us both. So we had both better just suck it up and learn to live with it. Because we're both going to be in his life for a long, long time. Forever, for my part."

Much to her surprise, Niles didn't immediately fire back, but instead looked surprisingly thoughtful. After a while, he shifted in his chair. "You're right. You're right. I *have* been jealous. But not only in the way you think. I don't expect you to understand, but in Britain we have this class thing—"

"And he's on the top of it and you're on the bottom," she interrupted. "Yeah, I know all about it, believe me, and I *do* understand, because I've been learning the hard way. Nobody ever considers how Cinderella felt once she married her Prince and had King and Queen Charming for in-laws.

But I also know Turk's never let you feel that disparity, any more than he lets me feel it. He treats you, and the rest of the guys, and everyone in the world, as a total equal. Because that's just the way he is, that's the way he does things. He doesn't condescend across the vast social gulf that you perceive to uncrossably lie between you and him, which, let me tell you, exists *way* more gulfishly in your mind than it does in his. Less of a gulf between him and Shane and Rardi, them all being fellow Oxonians, though of course nobody else is a lord. Jay-Jay was studying there when they all got together, but he's an American so he doesn't buy into this class crap anyway, but because he too is an Oxford man, he sort of does. Even Rouser went to public school, if not perhaps a top-drawer one."

Her voice gentled. "So it's just you sitting all alone below the salt, and it bugs you, and maybe it should, at least a little. Maybe it's because you were never loved enough as a child. Or as a grown-up either. Or some damn thing. Anyway, despite all your success and deserved acclaim—yes, I said deserved, I've always given you the props your talent merits, and you know it—you've never felt yourself to be the equal of the other guys, and I'm far from the only person who's noticed. Which is just silly. Art has no class distinctions. Talent like yours lifts all boats, from liners to dinghies, and you're no rowboat. You're every bit as welcome as Turk is in any social circles you care to move in. Perhaps you'll be *Sir* Niles one day, for services to the arts."

He was silent again for a bit, not wanting her to see that he had been at all affected by her words, which he had been, deeply and unwillingly—she had hit the gold on every shot. "It's not as simple as you make it out. There's more complications going on than that, you know."

"I do know. But you're a scrapper and so am I, probably the only thing we have in common, so I swear to God we're going to scrap our way through this together, and not, I repeat *not*, at each other's throats. I know you love Lionheart. Well, I do too. And I love Turk. It doesn't take much to make him happy, it really doesn't, but it does take very specific things. And we're both going to do our best to make sure he gets them. I'm glad you decided to sign his damn key-man clause of your own free will, because if you hadn't, I would have twisted your arm and every other appendage you have, yes that one especially, until you did sign it, screaming. So that's the first part of our deal, the signing; that's your thank-you to Turk. For the rest of it, you will unbegrudgingly do whatever he says and whatever he wants. That's your heartfelt thank-you to *me*, for keeping you out of the slammer, the quid for my pro quo. In your professional capacity as lead singer, you can creatively disagree with Turk all you want; I'm not unreasonable. But if you ever, *ever*, do anything to hurt him or embarrass him or cross him again, I will make a change-purse out of your scrotum."

She got up from the table and cleared away her sandwich rubble, putting the plate and glass and cutlery in the sink. "Not that it could fit more than a farthing or two, but still. Have a nice flight home, Niles. I'm glad we're finally on the same page. Or at least in the same book."

"Ladies first," said Niles, with a mocking bow, standing aside to let her pass to the stairs.

"After you, then," said Rennie, bowing back.

Now that their wayward offspring were out of the headlines, at least for the moment, two very exasperated mothers had grimly teamed up and set about transatlantically accomplishing some world-class maternal guilting. The result was that Turk and Rennie instantly announced their formal engagement: the stunning official photo, by their friend Francie Nolting, appeared three weeks later in Country Life — bumping that of a newly affianced bishop's daughter, who once the rock couple had sent her something nice from her registry list at Harrods by way of apology hadn't minded at all — Turk in his blue leather stage outfit, predictably, and Rennie in a new Gina Fratini gown, artfully displaying her ring. Though as a good reporter and loyal employee she gave Fitz's rags the full scoop first. It seemed only fair, not to mention politic; and the engagement news made all the other papers anyway. Even Rolling Stone reported it, much to Turk's disgust. Well, they would *not* be inviting any of the Stoners to the wedding, that was for damn sure...

New Year's Eve morning, to her vast surprise, a large packing case arrived at the prow house, shipped special-delivery from San Francisco, with the Lacing name and address boldly stenciled on it along with her own. Agog with curiosity — *what fresh hell could* this *be? Did Motherdear find some of my old knickers locked away in an armoire? If she did, has she been wearing them? And eeewww, would I even* want *them back?* — Rennie asked Daniel, Hudson's husband, to help her lug it into the dining room, and they set it on the floor, where there was plenty of space around for the uncrating.

Just as curious as she was, Daniel went to fetch a crowbar and clawhammer from his cellar workshop, and they eagerly went at it. Between them they managed to get the board strips off and the lid unwedged, without puncturing themselves with nails or splinters, and they carefully removed the seeming metric ton of wood shavings and excelsior and padding from around the three well-wrapped objects the crate contained.

"It's like Goldilocks," Rennie puffed, winded from her exertions. "A big one, a medium one and a little one. Too big, too small, just right."

"Hmm. I have a feeling that everything here is just right." They had lifted out the largest item, unwrapped it, then stared and stared and turned to stare at each other and stared some more.

"Well," said Rennie at last. "*This* is a surprise."

Daniel smiled. "Yes, and it seems like something you and Turk should be dealing with alone, so I'll leave you to it."

Rennie distractedly thanked him as he left to return to his flat, but she couldn't stop staring at the painting that the coverings and packing material had protected. *Oh my God... it's her. It's really her...* What lay before her on the dining-room table was an oil portrait of Charlotte Vidler Lacing, done around the time of the big official one that was kept at Hall Place, which Rennie well remembered. But she'd never seen this one before. Not a stiff full-dress formal pose, but an intimate half-nude one, it showed Princess Charlie wearing only gauzy drapings, with her long auburn hair tousled, half up and half down, squared bare shoulders and the white-pearl flash of one roundly ample breast.

She plucked the small ivory card from where it had been tucked into the ornate gold and velvet frame, read the brief words, and smiled. Then she unwrapped the other two items. Then she ran to the living room phone to call Stephen.

"No, no, we want you to have them all," said Stephen, when she had finished breathlessly protesting the gifts' extravagance. "The painting of Charlie is only a little one, and we have at least half a dozen more. "

"So you're sure it's not a painting of one jumped-up Lacing whore being sent to another Lacing whore making a similarly jumped-up marriage?"

Stephen laughed. "Hardly! It's a remembrance. You *got* Charlie, the way nobody else in the family ever did. They all laughed at her, or sneered at her, or were mortally embarrassed by her. No one else ever saw what you saw. You deserve a picture of her as I like to think she really was. It was the General's idea and the painting is from him, but Eric and I totally agree."

Rennie was finding it a little difficult to speak. In fact, she was trying to keep herself from bursting into tears, though she knew Stephen knew exactly what she was doing.

"Yes, okay, sure," she finally managed, "but a *tiara?*"

"From Eric and me. That particular tiara was Charlie's too; again, we have others, and as you will doubtless recall, this is the one you wore to the General's party. Nobody wore it since she did, until *you* did," he said fondly. "Maybe it was just a bit of nastiness from my mother, insisting you wear it for all their friends to see—two Lacing whores, as you put it—but you made something else out of it. Everybody else had only contempt for Charlie, including my mother, but you didn't. You thought she was cool and brave. Like you. And my mother had contempt for you too. But you outclassed her, my dear. You earned it."

His voice took on a teasing tone. "Besides, you'll be needing a tiara of your very own to go up against all the Tarrant ones, of which I'm sure there are heaps. I understand they usually have names: you can call this one the Lacing-Stride. Or the Vidler."

Rennie laughed. "Oooh, good name for it. Turk said they have fifteen, I think, so I'll be spoilt for choice... As for the last thing: I gave *you* that little oil sketch Sharon did of me. You should keep it."

"Again, you should have it. It's you as you were before Turk knew you, and he deserves it. And no, Ling isn't making me return it or anything all soap-opera like that—I just feel that you need to have it back. I had it when I needed it, and now Turk needs it instead—it can hang on the walls of his ancestral palace next to the Gainsboroughs, as Sharon and you both deserve. You're his future Duchess, and he needs to see you like this more than I do. Because he didn't know you then, and I did."

A long, somehow full silence. "Stephen"—her voice faltered—"thank you. Thank you For everything. And Eric and the General too."

"You're welcome. Always. You know that. Mother had a fit when she found out what we were sending you, but she didn't dare go against all three of us. All five of us, really, counting Ling and Petra."

"Oh, I bet Motherdear just *loved* that... But—yes."

A chuckle came down the phone. "Yes, well, you might not lawfully be a Lacing anymore, but we never did play by the rules."

"A remembrance, as you said. And an inspiration. I have a feeling I'm going to need it."

"That too."

After they hung up, after many expressions of affection and understanding and thanks on both sides, love to Turk, love to Ling, Rennie returned to the dining room. Where she peered again at the vivid face glowing among the layers of brown paper and protective padding, and smiled. Princess Charlie gazed at her, with a lively expression of wicked amusement and mocking perception, looking about to smile right back at her. Very much as she must have been in life.

Sharon would have painted her just like this. I would have loved to hang out with her, she must have been such a trip... Well, she'll have a good home with us for the next few centuries at least. We can hang her in Turk's sitting room at Cleargrove...

"Who's that?" Turk inquired, coming in and bending over her and dropping a kiss on her head. "Lovely woman. Nice little picture."

Rennie reached up to hug him with one arm. "You think?"

"Yes, I do. Good painter." He looked more closely. "*Very* good painter. She reminds me of you, somehow. Any relation?"

She smiled. "Not exactly."

"That was quite decent of the General," said Turk, when

he had been filled in on the backstory of the engagement present. "I can see it means a lot to you."

"It does...he's pretty smart, the General. Shame we didn't get to be friends sooner. It wouldn't ever have kept me married to Stephen, of course, but it might have made my life a bit easier if I'd felt I had him on my side." She picked up the domed leather case that was sitting on the table and handed it to Turk. "This is what Eric and Stephen sent me, as the Lacing sons and heirs. It too belonged to Charlotte."

Turk opened it and whistled appreciatively. "Oh, very nice. Let me guess: he gave you this because he knew you'd have more use for it than anyone else. Well, he'd be right. I'd say English Georgian, probably Huguenot work. You see a lot of this style dating from back then, when Huguenots persecuted in France came over to us. Many really skilled goldsmiths among them."

"So speaks the expert." Rennie lifted the sparkling diamond tiara from its nest of mushroom-colored velvet. "I won't keep it forever, of course. I'll pass it on to young Miss Charlotte Rennie Lacing, ultimately, like a good godmother, back into the family when she turns eighteen. In the meantime, I'll be proud to wear it. But see what else Stephen sent. He said this one is for you."

She cleared the padded coverings from the portrait of herself, giving a quick history of it, and Turk put his hands on her shoulders and leaned over to see. When he said no word for a long minute, she twisted to gaze up at him. Astonishingly, he had tears in his eyes, and she turned fully to him in a swift consoling rush.

"Oh, sweetheart, don't...don't. It's not all that."

"It is, you know."

He brushed his fingertips gently over the light-filled oil sketch: a Rennie four years younger, long hair tumbling, unbuttoned dress leaving her almost uncovered, posed on a pile of velvet cushions in Sharon Pollan's studio, looking blazing and vulnerable, unfinished and powerful, soft and strong.

"I see this girl now and again. I see her writing in her study, I see her watching me from the wings when I'm onstage, I see her sleeping next to me. I wish I'd known her back then—I never met her, for which I will be eternally regretful. But I do meet her every so often even now, and I intend to keep on meeting her for the rest of my life. As long as she intends to keep on meeting me... And to have a painting of her is just—it's more than I ever imagined I could have, or would have. Sharon is a great artist, but she's an even greater friend. And so is Stephen. Makes me glad the band committed to play at his wedding."

Rennie hugged him hard, for a long time. "Me too."

EPILOGUE

BREAKFAST AT THE FILLMORE EAST after Jimi Hendrix's New Year's Eve show with his new group Band of Gypsys, which had lasted until daybreak. After scarfing the scrambled eggs and orange juice and bagels provided by Bill Graham for the revelers, and hanging out a while in the dressing room with Jimi and the band, Rennie and Turk walked home in the cold brilliant dawn of a new year, happily banging on toy tambourines — there had been one on every seat, so that the audience could help out with creative percussion — and went up to bed and slept till three in the afternoon.

It was strange to have an almost-empty house again: only Ares and Prax were still in residence. They had a quiet New Year's Day supper that night, just the four of them. Belinda, Diego and Sledger came over for dessert, Sledger solo for a change and uncharacteristically subdued, as she had been ever since the events at Vinylization. Which was only to be expected. Nobody stayed long; the combination of New Year's and the sharp, dramatic resolution of the case had wearied them all, though no one mentioned it. By tacit consent, nobody mentioned Andy Starlorn, either, and Rennie, who was hypersensitive to studied gazes of concern and all other things along that line, and pretty much sick and tired of everyone tiptoeing around her, was very glad of it.

"Alone at last... Nice way to start 1970," said Rennie presently. She was reclining on the sofa under the new red, green and white Christmas affagan her grandma had crocheted for her, watching the logs smoldering in the fireplace; the dog and the kitten were curled up asleep, as close to the hearth as they could comfortably get. Ares and Prax were up in their bedroom, desultorily packing: they'd be heading back to Los Angeles sometime in the next few days, but nobody was rushing it.

Over on the facing sofa, Turk was playing banjo, which he loved and which Rennie loved to listen to — a beautiful, intricate new composition that had somehow segued into "We Three Kings," Rennie's favorite carol. There was the usual Nagra on the floor beside him; he didn't like to let even the play-around-the-house music go unrecorded, just in case. He had another in the bedroom, and one of his practice guitars, on the off chance that a riff of unparalleled splendor might come to him in the night, and if it did at least he would have the means to get it down on tape before it disappeared forever. Rennie, when she discovered this charming quirk of his on first moving into the Hollywood Hills house, had just rolled her eyes, but everybody in the rockerverse knew that the Stones' "Satisfaction" riff, possibly the most famous rock riff of all time, to date anyway, had been captured by Keith Richards in just such serendipitous fashion, so who was she to argue? As long as Turk didn't jump off her while they were making love in order to get down with a bit of music instead, she was cool with it.

Anyway, the faithful, unwieldy tape recorder had

followed them from L.A. to London to New York. Rennie sometimes thought it was like having a child tag along, though at least it didn't cry and get cranky and need to be fed and changed—still, good practice for the future. Lionheart had, as Rennie'd predicted, happily gone along with his plan for a year's sabbatical, once the reasoning behind it was explained. So with no tours ahead and only the gigs in Asia and Hawaii on Lionheart's plate, Turk was scheduling his long-delayed solo album among his projects, before putting a well-rested, creatively re-energized band back on the road a year from now, and if this was any example of how the solo album would sound, she was all for it.

She watched the firelight on his face and beard, the fall of his hair, the movement of his fingers on the strings and neck. His picking was amazing; he sounded like at least three players, not just one—the silvery banjo notes cackling and clanging, clean and crisp, somehow conveying joy and an aching minor-key yearning all at once.

He didn't look at her, but nodded agreement. "Jimi? Or this?"

"Well, all of it, but I meant having the murders solved and Niles out from underfoot and from under a cloud of suspicion and you boys set up to really move ahead on the new album. Set up with everything except a producer, actually."

He laughed, muting the sound but continuing to play, following yonder star into some baroque variations that took her breath away.

"Yes, well, there's that. We could always continue to do it ourselves, of course, us and Thom and Rafferty, the way we've always done. But I got a message yesterday from Andy Starlorn through his lawyer, saying sorry, can you believe it, and recommending Hut-Sut Rawlson for the producer's job."

"I know him," said Rennie, surprised and interested. "I interviewed him once, anyway, for a piece for one of Fitz's rags. He's done some amazing stuff. Gray and the Budgies used him on their last album before they broke up; he produced one of Prue's solo albums, also Mary Kingdom, my old pals Powderhouse Road, Peach Clymer, Bosom Serpent's last but one, bunch more I can't think of just now. He put together that Potter & Hazlitt retrospective last summer, too. All over the map — rock, country, folk. But I never would have thought of him for you boys."

She reached for the Waterford pitcher that stood on the coffee table beside her, offered Turk some of its Evian contents, which he declined, poured a glass for herself.

"What the hell kind of a name is Hut-Sut, anyway?" she inquired. "Sounds like a professional wrestler. More to the point, would you even *want* to work with anyone Starlorn recommended?"

"Oh, sure. Just because Starlorn's a thief and a fraud and a murderer doesn't mean his musical judgment can't be trusted. Why are you laughing? Besides, as you say, this bloke Rawlson's got a great track record, and very good word of mouth. I talked to Gray about him today, and I think he'll work really well with Leo and Thom. So we're probably going to go with him. At least for this album; we'll see how it turns out, and then after that we can decide if it's a long-playing marriage or just a one-album stand. I might ask you to ask your Powderhouse friends for a reference, some advice on how to deal with him."

"They'd be happy to help you out. Oh, and speaking of names, I found out Andy Starlorn's real name. Ken Karper got it from the police record. It's Adonijah. Seriously biblical-hillbilly. That would explain a lot, don't you think?"

He chorded off and put the banjo aside; leaning back on the pillows, he closed his eyes. The kitten, waking up, staggered across the carpet, determinedly scaled Turk's leg and lurched like a tiny, fuzzy drunk onto his chest, where it fell asleep again as he absently stroked it.

"It would. And does. But as for Rawlson, I absolutely refuse to call him Hut-Sut; that's a deal-breaker."

"You make everybody call you Turk. I don't see how that's different."

"Well, it is. His real name is Stuart, and that's what I intend to call him."

And so he did. Record producer Hut-Sut né Stuart Rawlson became Lionheart's producer of record, producing their record in record time. Whether the cause was a new producer or getting back to their roots or a reaction to the murders being solved, the band was revved up and ready to rumble. They reassembled in New York the second-last week of January, staying at the prow house and recording downstairs or at Vinylization, and Rennie was delighted to play hostess to them all, even Niles, though at times it seemed that she was housemother to a den of frat rats, or Wendy Darling herding the Lost Boys and Peter Pan and Captain Hook all together.

Maybe it was the relief of Niles being off the other sort of hook, or merely Turk's iron control over the sessions, or over Hut-Sut, but *Steel Roses* was recorded and mixed in a miraculous eleven days. It was almost as if it had been pre-existent in their heads: it was tight, it was together, it was seamless and incredible. Centaur rush-released it with a media blitz and it rolled up the charts like a blues-rock tsunami, carrying all before it, two top-ten and two number-one singles popping out within the first two months.

That still left space for the double live record's summer release date, and also freed Turk up to work on his now very definite solo LP for release after the honeymoon, in time for Christmas. Which was, as everyone from Freddy Bellasca to the promo guys to Turk himself pointed out, a *lot* of Lionheart product for one calendar year, but they all agreed that as the band was off the road, a heavier than usual chart and store presence would be all to the good, and Turk's album was a solo one, anyway, not a group effort. Besides, the records would all be well-spaced and different enough so as not to really compete with themselves. At least that way the fans would be hopefully consoled for not getting to see their favorites in person through all of 1970. As if anyone would forget Lionheart anyway.

Even Fastbuck Freddy was not entirely unhappy. Deeply relieved that all that distasteful, inconvenient murder stuff had been sorted out with minimal impact on him, he didn't mind as much as he might otherwise have done that his handpicked producer Andy Starlorn had been summarily removed under a rather thick and ominous cloud. At least it meant that Freddy's little obligation, nothing serious, just a favor or two, was gone also. Yeah, there was to be only a severely abbreviated Lionheart tour this year, but he was secretly grateful to have gotten even that much, as Turk's original plan had severely included no road trips at all.

But circumstances had altered a bit. There would still be no domestic gigs, except those two in Hawaii, where the band hadn't played since 1968, and there would be six carefully scheduled overseas dates in Asia, timed so that Lionheart would be in Hong Kong to play at the July reception following the formal and hugely splendid Buddhist wedding of Stephen and Ling Lacing. That ceremony would itself follow the couple's hastily planned and executed San Francisco wedding in January and the birth of their first child in February—who had been a son, to the joy and relief of everyone concerned, especially Marjorie.

So Turk and Rennie felt they deserved time off for good behavior, and they went to the Dolomites after all.

Outside, a March blizzard was smothering Cortina d'Ampezzo in tiny swirling flakes, so that the knife-edged, towering mountains outside were totally invisible. In the enormous bed in the old hotel's best suite, as the wind rattled the wood-framed casements and snow seethed on the panes, Rennie snuggled blissfully on and in and under and among a foot-thick featherbed, an even thicker king-size down comforter, two cashmere blankets, a set of crisp lavender-scented linen sheets and eight huge puffy down pillows. She was wearing nothing but her engagement ring, the gold and diamond and pearl adornments Turk had given her for Christmas a year ago, and a leather body harness that left nothing, or perhaps everything, to the imagination; and after their first full day of holiday, which had been spent skiing, eating, shopping and lovemaking in roughly equal proportions, she was very happy indeed.

Shivering a little, being likewise bare save for his jade phoenix medallion, Turk set a few more logs on the bedroom hearth and gave a jab to the fire with a poker, then shut the doors and pulled the heavy velvet curtains across to keep out stray drafts. Spreading Rennie's chinchilla cloak over the top of everything, he thankfully joined her in the warm hollow underneath, while the firelight flickered in the big marble hearth and the air grew imperceptibly warmer.

She smiled and handed him a filled wine glass from the nightstand and said, "[*There's a lagoon in the kitchen!*]"

"What's this you tell me?"

"That guidebook I bought for the Hong Kong trip? I'm trying to learn a bit of Cantonese before we leave."

"Is that so?"

"Yes. I tried out some phrases on the girl at the dim sum place."

"How did that go, then?"

"Well, when she stopped giggling, she wondered why I was asking if the dumplings were swimming to China."

"Ah. [*Surely this will anger the lobsters' uncles!*]"

"I see you've been dipping into it too. [*Does the rain forest have noodles?*]"

"Of course I have. [*Here are the queen's pork mittens!*]"

Rennie laughed and moved closer, brushing back the long blond hair from his face. "Best to rely on translators, then... God, it's cold outside this bed, and that's the way we like it! Fireplaces are great. Furs too. You're not so shabby yourself. Heat-wise, I mean."

"Why, thank you. Speaking of heat, have I told you how nice that harness looks on you? Especially with the jewelry. It was so thoughtful of you to get me such a thing for a Christmas present. Most women wouldn't have. Though I suppose the complete present is you *in* it."

"My pleasure, my lord. Literally. You really do know how to dress me. Even in undress. But as far as Hong Kong goes, Stephen and Ling won't let us run around over there without a translator, a chauffeur and a bodyguard, bare minimum—for prestige's sake as well as security—so it won't matter that we can't speak anything but food. Food is what's really important. Food and jewelry. Food and jewelry and some of that gorgeous silk, oh yes... I could really fancy a nice Imperial jade necklace, which I bet Ling knows exactly where to get, being a gem dealer and all, though moss-in-snow jade is nice too, and one of those padded silk jackets, and oh my *God* just think how good the dim sum must be..."

"We're there for a gig, a wedding and a christening, sweetheart. Not a shopping spree and an endless buffet. Do try to keep that in mind, even a little." Turk refilled their wine glasses and bit gently on one of the nipple rings. "What did you say they've called the infant?"

"Tyler. Actually, he's called Tyler Hua-Chen Robert Pierre Lacing." Seeing Turk raise his brows: "I know! But as Stephen said when he phoned, even though nobody's entirely happy with it, especially Marjorie, neither is anyone entirely insulted or offended, and they did manage to work in both grandfathers' names, which I thought was very diplomatic. He's a cutie — you saw the picture they sent."

"He looks like Winston Churchill."

"All babies look like Winston Churchill. Well, ours won't, of course. But all the other ones do."

"I wonder what Winnie looked like as a sprog, then."

"Cigar-shaped teething ring, little tiny bowler hat…"

"I trust we sent them appropriate wedding and christening gifts? The Lacings, I mean, not the Churchills. Though in centuries past the Tarrants and the Churchills have indeed exchanged prezzies on suitable, usually highly political, occasions. And this is a pretty highly political occasion too, come to think of it."

"Never fear. I know my social duties as upcoming marchioness. We sent a lovely little gold Cartier christening cup for the young dauphin. Engraved in English, French, Cantonese *and* Mandarin. And a huge and quite frightful solid-silver Georgian épergne for a wedding present for his parents. Found it in that snobby place on Fifty-seventh Street. Even Marjorie will be impressed."

"Well done you, then."

She reached up and tugged his beard. "No, well done *you*… It was terrific of you to volunteer the band to play at the reception. Way beyond the call of duty. Stephen and Ling are thrilled, and the people who need to be impressed, like the parents both sides, are. So thank you, my lord."

"Not a bit."

Turk lazily stretched his toes down toward the bottom of the vast expanse of bed, and still couldn't reach it — unusual for someone who stood over six foot three in his bare feet, and very pleasing, as most mattresses caught him around the ankles and he hated to have said bare feet dangling over the end of the bed.

"We love Hong Kong; we've played there three times and always done very nicely, and Francher was able to set up the tour to everyone's satisfaction. Well, everyone's except Freddy's; he's still moaning about why couldn't we at *least* go out on a big European swing if we're not going to play the States this year, but that was never the idea. We can all write off our personal expenses—everybody's bringing their wives and kids—and it'll be short, easy and fun."

"A pleasant change from your usual tour insanity, then."

"Isn't it… We insisted on a humane travel schedule with enough downtime between dates so we can actually do some sightseeing and relax a bit. As much equipment as possible rented locally, though not of course our instruments, and I'm allowed only three axes plus spares. Dead simple, like the old days. And more than worth our financial while, especially the Hong Kong and Tokyo dates, keeping us very comfortably in the black. So we can well afford to play a little charity gig on the side."

"The Lacing family. Some charity." Rennie shook her head. "But not *really* like the old days, though."

Turk kissed her bare shoulder and tightened one of the harness straps, making her gasp and him smile. "No, not really. Anyway, as I said, everybody's happy. Plus you and I get to see Japan, Australia and New Zealand as well as Hong Kong. The two Honolulu gigs on the way back, and after that we're free. We might stay on for a bit in Hawaii—I could get in some surfing on the North Shore, or we could spend time on Maui."

He looked at her and saw no objection on her face. Because, really, who would object to spending time on Maui? "Then I was thinking we could go to L.A., stay for a while, make sure the house is okay, see Prax and Ares and our other friends—"

"—play a hit-and-run solo gig at the Whisky or the Aquarius to try out the stuff for the solo album—"

"Can't slip anything past *you*, can I, Miss Music Biz... Well, I know it's not quite what you and I had planned, I know I promised the band weren't going out on the road at all this year. But we're not, not really. This won't be a real tour. More like a holiday with occasional gigs. And it'll be nice having you along long-distance."

"I've never really traveled with you and the band before; just the odd weekend here and there. It *will* be nice. Not to mention it'll bestow some major face on Mr. and Mrs. Stephen Lacing in the eyes of their kin, both sides. Lionheart playing at their reception—not many people ever get a wedding present like that. In fact, none ever. You don't fool *this* girl, Ampman."

"Ah well," he said, slipping his fingers under her collar and pulling her closer. "I've had a soft spot for Ling ever since she gave you that fateful chunk of jade. You could almost say she got us together. Besides, I feel that I owe Stephen *something* for his forbearance, me living with his wife, or not-wife, for two years. Annulment notwithstanding, we're really just husbands-in-law."

Rennie smiled, and poured more wine.

STEEL ROSES

Stems of green in thawing ground
Flowers pushing toward the sun
Once a love we thought we'd found
Time to stay was time it's done
Bud and bloom and leaf and root
were a marvel in our eyes
Every tender vine and shoot
reaching toward the summer skies

Garden of our love and lives
We had planned to tend and weed
Now it's brown and no more thrives
All our flowers gone to seed
Roses that were red and bright
all have turned to killing steel
Slice my fingers like a knife
Stabbing thorns that never heal

Steel roses in the garden of the heart
Steel roses that don't wither and don't fade
Steel roses that must bloom and grow apart
Steel roses only blossom in the shade
Long lost what we once had found
Steel roses
Not real roses
Steel roses in the cold and stony ground

Cherish gardens while you may
Season's short and gone too soon
Killing wind can rue the day
Frost can come in smiling June
Shattered petals cold and dead
on the stem and in my hands
Cold hard rain bleeds out their red
The flower in season understands

Steel roses in the dark and in the light
Steel roses need no watering to grow
They bloom in sad despair and love's despite
Steel roses saw us come and saw you go

[bridge]

When you shut the gate behind you
you left the garden green
and you left the roses blooming
But I missed you
Couldn't kiss you
I looked but couldn't find you
The flowers stopped perfuming
Their joyfulness consuming
Velvet petal turned to metal
and the change went all unseen

Steel roses in the garden of the past
Steel roses that don't wither and don't fade
They flourish in the fierce and bitter blast

Steel roses only blossom in the shade
Long lost what we once had found
Steel roses
Not real roses
Steel roses in the barren stony ground

Summer come again may bring
roses in a new love's arms
Not for us the flower ring
or the fragrance rich and warm
Maybe someday these may once again abound
But begging your mortal pardon
and remembering that garden
Plant real roses in the heart's hard stony ground

Steel roses in the garden of the heart
Steel roses that don't wither and don't fade
Steel roses that must bloom and grow apart
Steel roses only blossom in the shade

So I beg your loving pardon
Please remember well that garden
Feel roses
Not steel roses
Plant real roses in the heart's hard stony ground

~Turk Wayland

From Daydream Bereaver: Murder on the Good Ship Rocknroll, *the seventh Rennie Stride Mystery...*

Prologue

*T*HE OCEAN LINER SAT AT A MIDTOWN DOCK *on the Hudson River, as it did every Saturday before it made its weekly shuttle voyage down to the northern Caribbean and back again. On the small side, not big like the Atlantic-crossing ones that were still left — and fewer and fewer of those every year — but an exceptionally beautiful vessel, a "lady" of her type, as sailors said, dainty and graceful.*

Carrying at capacity some six hundred souls, as the lexicon had it, two thirds passengers, the other third crew, the ship was called the Excalibur, and the line was Sword Lines, sailing out of Liverpool; her five sisters were also named after historic famous blades — Curtana, Clarent, Durendal, Tizona, Joyeuse.

But workers had just lashed canvas-strip masks to bows and stern, a temporary and humiliating renaming for a week's hired sail; and now the lovely Excalibur, affectionately known to her crew as Callie, was forced to take to the seas as the Good Ship Rocknroll.

In an hour, the tide would start ebbing down the broad, shining Hudson estuary, the North River as watermen called it, and when it did the ship would go with it. Of course, the tugs and its own great engines could take her out of harbor whenever the captain pleased; such vessels were no longer dependent on wind and tide. But the owners of the line were sticklers for tradition: their vessels sailed on the ebb and docked on the flood, and not a moment sooner.

This trip, the Excalibur had been bought out privately, for a press junket cruise to the Grand Palm Islands and back again. She was carrying two hundred of rock's most powerful movers and shakers and shapers: critics, editors, photographers, trade writers, record company people, a luminous slate of musicians. All to hear the new music of one of the most popular and famous groups in the world, who were also aboard, and who were, in fact, the hosts of this little nautical adventure.

But though the group may have been popular and famous to a ridiculous extent, as all of them knew well, it was perhaps not one of the best and most artistic groups in the world. And that was both the reason for the cruise and the problem with it. And also it was what, directly or indirectly, would lead to murder on the high seas…

Chapter One

"*T*HIS IS *SOOOO* STUPID."

Belinda Melbourne, writer on rock matters for such varied journals as the New York Sun-Tribune and the Village Voice and Life magazine, leaned on the rail next to her good friend and colleague, fellow journalist Rennie Stride, both young women watching with interest as the controlled confusion of imminent departure spread like an oil slick over the pier. She looked wickedly bright-eyed and bushy-tailed, like a clever, pretty squirrel on speed.

Rennie, herself looking sleek and vaguely dangerous, like a bored panther who might do anything for a laugh, raised delicate eyebrows.

"And yet I notice we're both here."

"I said *this* is stupid, not *we're* stupid. Who would be stupid enough to turn down an all-expenses-paid week's cruise to the Caribbean and back?"

"Turk. Turk turned it down," said Rennie, smiling. "And we all know how unstupid *he* is. Furthermore, he said—let me make sure I get this right, he hates it when anyone misquotes him—he said that he'd sooner eat his own toes with a nice hollandaise than let himself be trapped at sea aboard a floating tub of hell with critics and label scum and, God save him for his sins, the Weezles."

"Gosh. That boy of yours has such a turn of phrase."

"Doesn't he though. Even for an Oxford-graduate superstud guitar god. But I remind you that you and I and the hundred and ninety-eight others like us are not only trapped aboard this floating tub of hell but we have to kind of, well, not *sing* for our supper, that's the Weezles' job, but at least *listen* for it. Work for our room and board. For *our* sins, we have to listen to our hosts trying to persuade us that they're a real live creative cutting-edge rock and roll band. And not just a tricked-out, made-up, total and hugely successful fabrication."

Belinda grinned. "Talk about ship of fools... I ask you! Is it too late to shout 'Away all boats and abandon ship!'?"

Rennie rather thought it was, and as if to punctuate her opinion the ship shuddered under them, like a horse vexed by a fly, and began to back out slowly and throbbingly into the Hudson, shoved by feisty little tugboats into a giant aquatic three-point turn.

Belinda glanced behind them at the pier, and ahead down the river. "Can't escape now, Strider."

"No... Well, maybe it won't be as bad as we think."

Maybe, she privately considered, it might even not be bad at all, and that wasn't false hope talking. Though it could be worse. It was just—oh man, it was the freakin' *Weezles*, for God's sake! They were a sort of third-generation print-off, the illegitimate lovechild of the Beatles and the Monkees, with the Stones as godfathers. If the Beatles were the Fab Four, and the Monkees were the Pre-fab Four, then the Weezles were the Post-fab Four. And their success level was beyond all levels of fab together. Four cute boys with terrific hair. Irresistibly catchy tunes. Millions upon millions of records sold.

Trouble was, it was all bogus, in a very seriously non-bogus sort of way. The Weezles had been cold-bloodedly assembled from a talent hunt five years before, like an Erector set, or erection set, a sort of hybrid trans-Atlantic response to the British rock invasion and the American counter-reaction to that: lead guitarist/vocalist Luke Woods, drummer Matt Cutler, bass player/vocalist Brian Moretti and lead vocalist/rhythm guitarist—and designated heartthrob—Hoden. No last name, please; just Hoden. Then their evil overlord manager, Jo Fleet, had sprung them on an unsuspecting world, and the rest was pop history.

They'd all been picked strictly for their cuteness and biddability, not for their musicianship. Which was, at least when they began and except for their uniformly excellent singing voices, insufficient by most genuine rock standards. Oh, they were quite pleasant to listen to, but save for the singularly cognomened Hoden, who was truly talented—though not allowed to use his talent in any real way, and for five years he'd had to pretend he didn't possess it—none of them could play an instrument on a level anywhere *near* matching their almost instantaneous and pretty darn near global fame.

Of course, that hadn't stopped the public from instantly taking them to its heart, if not its actual mind. Such nice clean-cut boys, those Weezles! No swearing or drinking or wenching or drugging, like, oooh, those awful Rolling Stones! Well, at least none that anyone knew about, anyway. Who cared that they couldn't play! That's why God made overdubs! And session guys! And lip-synching! They were adorable! They had great hair! They sang simple catchy songs by great pop composers with simple slick lyrics that any simpleton could understand! They made tons of money! All the teenies lovedlovedlooooved them! And so did their mothers!

What more could you ask for? What else mattered? And for five years, and many millions of people — and many, many gold records, and many more millions of dollars — nothing did.

But a year ago the worms had turned and shown their fangs. And it was Hoden who had rallied the charge. The Weezles were done with the fraud, done with being biddable and nice: they were fed up to here with bullies — whether those bullies were the label, the audience, the critics or their own management — and they were going to take charge of their own image and their own souls. They were going to play their own music, the way they wanted to, the way they'd always known they could, the way they'd secretly worked their asses off for the past five years to perfect. The way every other band in rock and roll did.

So, between one album and the next, they'd *Sgt. Pepper*-ized themselves. Luke grew a beard, Matt and Brian began sporting droopy mustaches, Hoden let his hair get *really* long, and they'd all begun writing songs like madmen: intricate music with dense, brilliant lyrics. They'd proudly put the new stuff on their last album, released a month ago to instant gold; to keep their public and their label's promotion department happy, they'd sprinkled in among the hard stuff a few poppy little bouncetunes coldly calculated to be chart-toppers—a sop to the Philistines—then sat back and eagerly awaited feedback, knowing they'd done a bang-up job, rightly expectant of being praised by critics and populace alike.

"And you know what happened as well as I do," said Rennie. "Nothing changed. Not a goddamn thing. Because nobody cared but the band. And a few people like, in all modesty, you and me, who gave them full marks for the breakout. Credit for trying, and credit for what was good."

"Some of it was really good."

"Some of it was *great*. Oh, and we did administer nice sharp smacks upside their head for still pushing the crap, for trying to have it both ways and not cutting loose completely from their bogusness. That's fair, surely."

"They deserved what we said about them," agreed Belinda. "All of it. But they've been desperate to prove their cred for at least a couple of albums now. You remember, it started right after they had that humongous hit with 'All Four Won'. Then they talked Dylan into writing something for them, and it turned out to be 'Double Barreled', which just blew everybody's mind, and they saw they could be a serious band after all. And then they started writing their own stuff. And then we saw they could be a serious band after all. Maybe they always knew that, you know—that they could be serious. Even if most of us didn't. Even if their fans didn't give a rat's. Maybe that's why they're so extra-hot to prove themselves now."

"They're not exactly innocent little music-biz virgins, may I remind you," said Rennie with a knowing glance. "They've been bending over for Jo Fleet, Manager from

Hell, for five years now. And by all accounts, both parties have been satisfied with the transaction."

Belinda was laughing. "See, that's where a classical-humanist education comes in so darn handy. It teaches even rocknrollers not to make bargains with Satan."

Her friend nodded. Joslin Fleet, known as Jo to all but his parents, was notorious even in a cutthroat business. He was a rock hyena, no, a whole hyena *pack*, all on his own, and he had never troubled to hide his scent upwind as he closed in on his prey, out there on the vast open savannas of rock and roll. Because he knew he was an unstoppable predator and it didn't matter if his prey knew he was coming; they couldn't escape. Sure, he did well for his many big-name clients, very well indeed, but they all knew the devil's bargain and the final tab they had no choice but to sign for: he'd get them what they wanted, and in return they couldn't complain when the hyena jaws clamped down on their own vitals, as sooner or later the jaws always would.

"Can you say 'Faust', boys and girls? Yes, I think you can," opined Rennie dryly. "Really though, they should have known Manager Mephistoph-fleet-les and the label would never let them get away with anything like a higher order of musicmaking. Frankly, I'm amazed they even got to do the Dylan song at all. Fabulously popular and staggeringly commercial was all they were ever supposed to be. And so they have been. And now they're trapped in it."

"And popular and commercial isn't enough for them anymore. Which is why we're all here."

"Uh-*huh*. We the so-called movers and shakers of rock and roll, forced to spend seven nights listening to the

Weezles' new music, down to, among, and back from the Grand Palm Islands. And one of those nights to be devoted to witnessing and attesting to the world premiere performance of their new rock opera. With a reprise on the way back. Have mercy."

Belinda chortled. "Yes, yes, comes now 'Paize Lee: The Story of A Little Hippie Girl'! Uninterrupted setting, no distractions. Angels and ministers of grace defend us! They actually plan to use this to get us to rate them right up there with the Airplane and Hendrix and Lionheart and the Dead. Riiiight..."

"It's that uninterrupted no distractions part that's freaking me out," said Rennie darkly. "Do you realize we can't escape, not unless we call for a Coast Guard helicopter to lift us off? But it's still not too late, maybe. If we jump overboard right now, into the river, we can get away before anyone knows we're gone. Look, there's the West Side Highway, not far at all, you can see cars and people. Come on, hold my hand, you won't even feel it when we hit the water. I promise. We could swim to shore, grab a cab and be home in ten minutes. Dripping, but home."

"Oh, I don't think so. If the fall doesn't kill us, then the pollution will. Cheer up—'Paize Lee' isn't until our second night out."

"True." Rennie brightened a bit. "Maybe we'll all be too seasick by then to even leave our cabins. But marooned in oceanic isolation with fellow rock hacks isn't my idea of perfect bliss either, even with a gorgeous Caribbean island-nation and my handsome sexy English boyfriend waiting for me at the end of the voyage."

"It's not just hacks like us." Belinda paused to admire the double-lattice steel framework of the World Trade Center, just beginning to fling itself into the sky above the Battery. "Weezies also wanted the company of peers. So they invited some. There's a bunch of artists on board you wouldn't think would be along for the ride in a million years. I am expecting *serious* jamming. Plato Lars, Judy Collins, Mary Kingdom, some of the Yardbirds and the Dead and Canned Heat, John Sebastian, Prisca Quarters, David Crosby, he's always up for a boat trip, even Hendrix is here — must just be that 'free Caribbean cruise' thing."

Rennie nodded sagely. "Not to mention the artistic legitimacy that their presence confers on our hosts. But that's nothing new. They've all been friends for ages, oddly enough. You'll remember Jimi actually opened for the Weezles on that summer tour three years back, and they've been best buds ever since. Same with Crosby and the Dead. Luke dated Judy before Stephen Stills did and Mary before Hendrix, and Hoden knows the Yardbirds from his Lunnon days."

She whipped out a small camera and snapped a picture of Belinda with the Statue of Liberty behind her. "I must try to talk to Crosby and Mary and Plato — they've all been promising me an interview for months, and now I have them cornered. As for the gratis nature of the voyage, it's not as if any of that lot can't afford to pay for a cruise on their own."

"Well, sure," said Belinda. "But free is always nice. Especially record-company graft. Or rock-star graft. In fact, the Weezles' management said so many big names called up wanting in on the trip, for whatever reasons, that they had to bring in Pig Blue's outfit to do security. Though why security would be needed on a floating lockbox like this...I mean, it's not as if we're expecting to be boarded by pirates or anything, right? They tried to get Ares Sakura first, of course, to handle things, but he was unavailable, as you undoubtedly know. And lest you think it went unnoticed, which it most certainly did *not*, just what was that ever so casual mention of your handsome sexy English boyfriend awaiting you at journey's end all about?"

Rennie's mouth quirked at the lower right corner. "Yes, well, I did know about Ares, and what's more, I know *exactly* where he's being unavailable just now. He and Prax went to stay with Turk at his house in the Grand Palms. The little pieces of garbage. You'd think my superstar fiancé and my superstar best friend and her super-rock-bodyguard boyfriend would be a bit more diplomatic and caring of my feelings, but no. Both Lionheart and Evenor are off the road and not recording just now, so the lead guitarist of Lionheart and the lead singer of Evenor and the head of Argus Guardians have been sunning and surfing and sailing and swimming and eating like kings for the past week, the bastards, while I was stuck in New York and now while I'm stuck on this damn dinghy. But when we get to Palmtown I'm jumping ship to join them."

"Ares has a house in the Grand Palms?"

"No, Turk does."

"Ah. Your pronouns were a little fuzzy. But I didn't know Turk had a place in the Caribbean."

"His family does, yeah. As seems to be ever the case with

them, they've owned it for like a thousand years. Though in this case, only a measly three hundred."

"The house?" asked Belinda, impressed.

"The *island*. It's called Lion Island. Tropical, quite sizable, they own the whole freakin' thing. I don't know much else about it, except there's a mansion, well isn't there always with them, and great surf breaks and some famous kind of local *ham*, if I heard Turk correctly. Oh, and it had real pirates, too, back in the day. One of them was even a distant ducal ancestor. And the Tarrants own it all, and Turk Wayland, or rather Richard Tarrant, Marquess of Raxton, is its crown prince."

She stretched, luxuriating in the cool breeze. "Anyway, here we are, and so is everyone else, and it is after all a free junket to the latitudes of palm trees and blue waters, and there are shipboard buffets, mmm, yes, and the Weezles aren't at all bad for, what, one little mini-gig a day, and some mandatory one-on-one interviews? They're always a lot of fun to talk to. How hard can it be?"

Belinda nodded wisely. "Ah, but you're forgetting 'Paize Lee: The Story of A Little Hippie Girl'. Two performances. We may have to mutiny. Where's Fletcher Christian when you really need him?"

As the ship passed under the Verrazano Bridge and began the great sweeping turn for gray open Atlantic waters, Rennie took a deep breath of salt air, and suddenly, causelessly cheerful, she looked back at the towers of New York rapidly receding astern.

"Oh, I expect we'll survive. Somehow."

They would, too. Well, most of them.

CPSIA information can be obtained
at www.ICGtesting.com
Printed in the USA
LVHW080441230821
695856LV00021B/781

9 780692 322611